THEY DON'T ADVERTISE FOR KILLERS

THEY DON'T ADVERTISE FOR KILLERS

KAIS ALKURAISHI

ALEX KRIEG

overthrow press

Published by Overthrow Press, South Los Angeles
www.overthrowpress.com

Edited and Designed by Girl Friday Productions
www.girlfridayproductions.com

Editorial: Clete Smith, Jessica Gardner, Erica Avedikian
Interior Design: Paul Barrett
Cover Design: David Drummond
Cover Image Credits: © Shutterstock/Bardocz Peter; © Shutterstock/IfH

ISBN (Paperback): 9781732164109
e-ISBN: 9781732164116

First Edition

Printed in the United States of America

All characters appearing in this work are fictitious. Any resemblance to real persons, living or dead, is purely coincidental. Los Angeles does not exist.

For the first time, a benevolent psychopathology beckoned towards us, enshrined in the tens of thousands of vehicles moving down the highways.

J. G. Ballard

All I wanted in the world was to push my Buick Roadmaster over some peckerwood's face.

Chester Himes

INTRODUCTION

All pathological environments must metamorphose the creatures in it.

Jules Henry, *Culture Against Man*

Los Angeles is a city built for murder.

This, according to the Tocqueville Institute of Paris, whose multivolume follow-up, or "sequel," to Alexis de Tocqueville's seminal *Democracy in America* (1835), playfully (or erroneously as some would contend[*]) entitled *Democracy in America Strikes Back* (2035), contains several similar defamations of American "laissez-faire piecemeal" urban planning (Seattle was accused of being an accessory to the suicides committed there[†]), which was primarily the result of single-use zoning, beginning with the Residence District Ordinance of 1908, that promoted the dislocation of primary uses (e.g., work, home, shopping, industry), and the isolating effect of an automobile—whose symbol of freedom ("the last great freedom") was itself in contradiction with the present-day constrictive reality of gridlock—necessary to shuttle between these various uses.

---

[*]   Cultural critic James Siskel has proposed "Capitalism in America Strikes Back" as being more apropos.

[†]   *Democracy in America Strikes Back* Vol. II, Ch. 3 – "Failures of Imagination or Anticipation?"

And it was this compartmentalized and fragmented landscape with its isolated and transient population, the authors asserted, *in combination* with the "Grand Canyon–sized" discrepancy between the steroidal Los Angeles version of *el Sueño Americano*, the American Dream, and its possibility of fulfillment—an explosive confluence of "dis-ideology" and "dis-geography"—that constituted the psychogeography of the city, making it a veritable "homicidal habitat," where, due to the asymmetry of communication produced by such a hostile "blandscape," violent encounters between these anonymous and encased individuals were increasing to the point of becoming a culture-bound syndrome akin to running amok in Malaysia and pibloktoq among the Inuit.

As evidence, the authors cited a study conducted by the UCLA Center on Everyday Lives of Families, along with several Coca-Cola neuro-marketing surveys of a cross-section of Angelenos, that independently reported below-average hippocampal gray-matter volumes in more than half the participants in conjunction with symptoms characteristic of anomie,[*] which, if left untreated, could lead to a widespread increase in homicidal behavior (contrary to Émile Durkheim's original assertion that anomie was a precursor and cause to suicide and not homicide), quoting, as if in confirmation, that insipid voice-overed sentiment at the beginning of the movie *Crash* (2004): "In L.A., nobody touches you. We're always behind this metal and glass. I think we miss that touch so much, that we crash into each other just to feel something"—which in itself was a naive appropriation of the existentialist psychologist Rollo May's statement that "When inward life dries up, when feeling decreases and apathy increases, when one cannot affect or even genuinely *touch* another person, violence flares up as a daimonic necessity for contact, a mad drive forcing touch in the most direct way possible."[†]

Or, "Violence is the ultimate destructive substitute which surges in to fill the vacuum where there is no relatedness."

Or possibly, as Jail Helmsman has pointed out in *Venus Denied*, violence is not a substitute, but an aesthetic response to Los Angeles and its oppressive assault of insipid malls, banal architecture, congested freeways, and narcissistic people; so the real problem might be the repression of these appropriate feelings of outrage through narcissistic substitutes such as exercise, yoga, therapy, or meditation, which only serve to at best,

---

[*] Cf. Spurna, N. et al. (2020), "Mental illness among Mexicans living in Los Angeles twice that of Mexicans living in Mexico," *Journal of Nervous and Mental Disease* 256, 51–57.

[†] *Love and Will* (1969)

mitigate or at worst, tranquilize an authentic rage from being appropriately "expressed in creative and constructive ways" to being pathologically "released in explosive and violent ways."

Here one is left to wonder if narcissism and anomie are actually defenses against violent and aggressive impulses, and not the cause of them, so that violence is not the substitute for this relatedness but the proper nature of the relationship between a pathological environment and those that inhabit it—any other reaction being nothing more than the narcissistic denial of a civic responsibility where violent outrage is the necessary catalyst needed to transform a sick and ugly environment.

However, far from entertaining various perspectives on this phenomena, the authors of *Democracy* seemed bent on literalizing their perspective to the point of reducing it to a simple equation: fragmented neighborhoods (i.e., segregated primary use) + inefficient (i.e., expensive, time-consuming, alienating) transportation systems × isolated individuals with expectations (e.g., immediate fulfillment of appetite, desire for connection) contrary to the first two conditions and media reinforcement thereof = increased probability of murder.

Which in itself is an unnecessarily complex and tedious way of saying that the larger the gap between expectations and reality, the higher the probability for violence.

It is interesting to note that cultural theorist Rainier Warwick—who later accused the authors of appropriating and "stupefying" his concept of mutual or reciprocal obstruction, where, as in the case of gridlocked traffic, you have a density of individuals, each pursuing an individual destination while at the same time blocking others from achieving their destinations, in a state of mutual obstruction where "violent altercations" between these "frustrated and unfulfilled" individuals should not be considered anathema but the expected "discourse," given the context—was actually a paid consultant to the Los Angeles Department of Transportation several years prior to the publication of *Democracy* and the furor it caused.[*]

Strangely, the idea that Los Angeles itself might be conjuring violence in its citizens was noted in a curious footnote where it was supposed that murder might even be the essence, genius loci, or anima mundi of the land upon which the city was founded—based upon the fact that the

---

[*] As an example typical of academic nit-picking, Hillary Slane, in her *Motio Gratia Motionis*, refutes Warwick's thesis of reciprocal obstruction on the point that frustration and anger are not the products of an obstructed goal or destination, but of the obstruction of movement itself.

earliest human remains unearthed in L.A. were those of a woman found in the La Brea Tar Pits with her head bashed in: the nine-thousand-year-old La Brea Tar Pit woman (whose remains were taken off display by the Page Museum in 2004 for various reasons).

So, geography might indeed be destiny.

But in the end it was not the accusation that Los Angeles was some kind of "murderopolis" that caused the most media furor, but the following statement in reference to the city, which, the reader will note, is not a moral but an aesthetic statement similar to Warwick's above:

Appropriating Fitzgerald, the authors asked, "If character is an unbroken series of successful gestures, then what is a broken series of obscene gestures?"

Detractors of the work labeled it absurd, biased, insulting, and really nothing more than a product of that unfounded and centuries-old European snobbery towards America—not to mention a complete betrayal of the spirit and objectivism of Tocqueville's original work.

Some in Los Angeles, while not disagreeing with the characterization of the city in the study, nevertheless found it to be passé:

"C'mon, man. What's all the fuss about anyway? That some scientists wrote a book that said that L.A.'s built for murder? Shit. You don't need a PhD to figure that out. We've been saying that shit where I live for years" (Killio, *Los Angeles Times*, April 6, 2035).

Many academics agreed, casually dismissing the opinions of the study to be nothing more than an age-worn cliché while pointing out that, historically, it has been the fashion of the last century to portray Los Angeles as some type of nightmare idyll where the hopes and dreams of those who come here are dashed against the rocks of oblivion—the city nothing more than a cultural wasteland filled with people living empty and hopeless lives.

However, several recent scholars (cf. Roland Herring, *The Blank Ages*;* Bellamy Gawain, *The Horror of Now*) have commented that Los Angeles as a cultural wasteland is not merely a cliché but a perfect model of Spenglerian Decline, with Los Angeles as *the* terminus of Western culture (as Rome was to Hellenic culture) populated by an inarticulate,

---

*   Herring also gives an interpretation of the rise of violence as being the product of a "defacialized" population that has lost the ability for "interfacial relationships" due to the decreased facial contact between people and their increased "unifacial" contact with digital technologies—phones, computer screens, TVs, etc.—that serves to dehumanize all interaction, human included, thus necessitating violence.

violent, and materialist population riding, or choking, on the fumes of a dying civilization.

Others, like Dr. Henry Hammersmith of the American Psychopathological Association, saw something more positive. "What these studies have shown is an increase in psychopathic symptoms, something which might have been alarming maybe forty or fifty years ago but is quite the opposite today. What we are seeing is an adaptive response to the environment. That is, more and more Angelenos are becoming psychopaths in order to thrive and survive. We have to view the psychopath as an evolutionary type, similar to the *Homo sapiens* of the African veldt thousands of years ago. It is very likely that ancient hominids viewed this new *Homo* as some kind of aberration, just as we view the psychopath today. However, regardless of our current viewpoint, or lack thereof—the human of the future *will* be a psychopath."

And still others tried to show that the problem was neither cultural, social, technoeconomic, or even individual, but climatic—citing numerous studies that show a correlation between rising violence and rising global temperatures.

Despite the many plausible theories offered by those who don't reside in Los Angeles and those who never have, the most salient criticism was voiced by Dr. Thurston Trumbull, professor of urban planning at the University of Southern California, who stated that the authors of the study, "while definitely not completely off target with their analysis, were really not anywhere near the dartboard either," because of the omission of one rather large and significant factor: Race—something that has *always* been underreported and practically invisible in Los Angeles.

Citing as primary example the three riots that have taken place in the city within the past fifty years (the last happening during the administration of an African American president no less), Trumbull went on to say the following:

> I don't completely disagree with these Tocqueville authors'
> assessment that certain spatial factors in conjunction with
> the inability for most to achieve the American pathological
> dream are major constituents in the etiology of social unrest,
> or homicide as they like to so simplistically put it, but who is
> the individual that serves as a locus for these generic terms?
> Some middle-aged Caucasian dude in Santa Monica who
> has to suffer the indignity of maneuvering his eco-friendly
> vehicle through traffic on his way to Whole Foods? Or
> some poor African American mother of two who is forced
> to maze her way through the discriminatory architecture of

a South L.A. landscape monumented with fast-food joints and check-cashing sharks to look for some soul-crushing minimum-wage job that still won't be enough to support her, let alone her children, and who has not even the financial resources to afford the privilege of navigating through what David Maisel so aptly called a 'terrain of anxiety and estrangement,' isolated and frustrated within the confines of her own personal vehicle. No, these revolts are the result of the ultimate isolation and disenfranchisement that are the real and everyday condition of those of color in Los Angeles, and the primary refutation of a study whose myopia fails to include or even mention race. The invisibility of the people who live at the center of the city but who are treated like outsiders on the periphery, and who occasionally, every few decades, are made just a little more visible by rising up and saying enough's enough (which still isn't enough), this invisibility, this failure of the city to even acknowledge a majority of its nonwhite citizens was completely and negligently ignored by the authors of that spurious study, effectively, in my opinion, negating the entire thing.

The mayor responded to the study and its detractors thus: "Fact: Statistics have shown that crime in Los Angeles has steadily decreased at an unprecedented rate in the last twenty-five years. Homicide is the lowest it's been in some five decades."

Which was ironic, because at the time of this statement Los Angeles was engaged in the mass extermination of its residents—primarily through the publicly lauded Terrorist Eradication Force, or TeRF,[*] but also through the black-budget Department of Decongestion, both of which had been outsourced to the infamous private security contractor BlackGuard International—and it wasn't until the publication in 2048 of Alex Krieg's *They Don't Advertise for Killers* that this department's activities even became public knowledge.

And still no one believed.

You couldn't blame them. It was absurd, really: for twenty years, from 2019 to 2039, the City of Los Angeles, in order to reduce its traffic density, resorted to the systematic murder and disappearance of licensed drivers (actions which were later found to be "illegal but legitimate" by

---

[*]   The lowercase *e* was apparently an in-house joke to denote that eradication is not really the goal, but the more realistic capital *R* reduction.

the Supreme Court in *Atancio v. Los Angeles Department of Transportation* [2054]).

Prior to this, similar doubts had also been raised regarding Krieg's *Killscouts of America* (2043) and its assertion that the eponymous gang was in fact funded by no less than the Department of Homeland Security.

That was until former defense secretary James Starkweather's admission two years later in his autobiography, *Beholden to Man*, that the Department of Homeland Security had in fact created and funded various gangs throughout the United States for the sole purpose of gang eradication prior to the 2012 official reclassification of gang members as "enemy urban combatants" (i.e., terrorists), when the responsibility for their eradication was shifted over to the Terrorist Eradication Force.

Following Starkweather's disclosure, sales of *Killscouts* went through the roof and Alex Krieg was offered a rather large advance by his publisher to put out another book, which, in fact, he had already been working on, and which is the text you hold now with a few minor corrections, emendations, and excisions (chapter 10 from the original—"Sorcerer of Death's Construction"—has been removed due to several copyright violations, with subsequent chapters being renumbered accordingly).

Originally, the publisher would not consent to the book being classified as a memoir when it was obvious (to them) that the assertions made in it were false.

Besides his statements about the Los Angeles Department of Decongestion (no one disputed its existence), and the murders of Mayor Malvolio, his family, Bradbury Thurlow III (which had been excised from the original just prior to publication for legal reasons), and Reina Hawthorne,[*] what was considered much more incendiary was Krieg's contention that the largest and most horrific terrorist attack in the history of the United States, the second Los Angeles 6/16 attack in 2039, was nothing but an LADOD computer malfunction, or worse—a deliberate plot engineered by certain officials of the department to murder everyone in Los Angeles.[†]

Some questioned his sanity, attributed to the multiple painkillers prescribed him in the years after his accident, but the dispute between the publisher and Krieg over the book's classification was ended with his transfer of all copyrights to me just prior to his disappearance.

---

[*] Which, although included in the original and here, I am under legal constraint not to discuss.

[†] Or specific groups—according to a recent study by the Democracy Alliance, over 50 percent of those killed were Latino.

At the time I relented and allowed them to publish *They Don't Advertise for Killers* as a work of fiction, not really caring one way or another if people believed him or not, my main concern being finding Alex.

Also, it was Alex's original intent, stated privately to me on various occasions, that he was writing the book not to expose any truth but because he needed the money, saying "they don't advertise for killers" in the employment ads. Besides the money, the only other reason I can recall that he gave for writing it was that he wanted "to get rid of Los Angeles once and for all."

Accusations that the book contained product placements were not unfounded, and many of these have been removed either where deleting them would not alter the narrative in any significant way, or where certain entities have failed to uphold their contractual obligations. In several of these cases, I have decided not to pursue litigation and have simply dropped any reference to them in the novel.

However, the greatest accusation of brandfiltration—that Krieg and his publisher were paid a large sum to plug Disney's *Return of the Force* for its tenth-anniversary release—was completely unfounded, as confirmed by Jedi Lucas himself in several interviews with the *Times*.

Regardless, I have removed several references to the *Star Wars* franchise where I felt that they were either contributing to the unfounded criticism mentioned above or providing undeserved publicity for a franchise that has practically become a propaganda mouthpiece for U.S. imperialism.

Of course, as with *Killscouts of America*, events in the world began to corroborate Alex Krieg's assertions.

They Don't Advertise for Killers hadn't been out more than a few months when, at the end of 2048, MGH.com leaked the infamous BlackGuard International Security memos where it was revealed that the second 6/16 terrorist attack had in fact been the result of either a system error or a malicious hack of the Los Angeles Department of Decongestion system.

Sales skyrocketed and Krieg became a much-sought-after celebrity. Movies and video games were made of both books. Speculation and rumors swarmed about the nature of his disappearance, which is still, some twenty years later, attributed by many to either government or corporate retribution.

My own theory, pieced from various conversations I had with him before he disappeared, was that he had gone to Bangladesh—the purpose of which should be apparent in the memoir, as I do not want to give too much away in this introduction as others are wont to do in their introductions to classic books—after an investigator Krieg had hired had supposedly supplied him with some key information he had been seeking.

What happened there is a question I am still seeking the answer to, and a question that I might be able to answer—hopefully, if readers are interested enough and God willing—in the introduction to a twenty-fifth- or thirtieth-anniversary edition of *They Don't Advertise for Killers*. Namaste.

—I. H., 2069, Los Angeles

PROLOGUE

Don't call me an African-American.

This is Los Angeles.

I'm a Nigger.

An African-American is nothing but a box you check on an unemployment application.

Or a MotherFucker in a McDonald's commercial.

They don't exist.

I'm a Nigger.*

And don't you call me that neither.

---

* In an interview with the *Los Angeles Sentinel* (March 4, 2047), Krieg stated that he was "riffing off the idea" from the song "Darkness Visible" by Milton John.

> *Nigger call me*   *American*
> *Darkness Visible*   *disspicable*
> *A dark individual*   *Afric-invisible*
> *indivisible*   *predictable*
> *Scared I'm invincible*   *correctly political*
> *Think I'm inimical*   *pitiful.*
> *Wanna make me*

You might call me a Delok.

The Tibetan term for one who has died and returned from the dead.

As there is no proper name for what I am in the West.

Only that I'm an individual who has had an NDE, or Near-Death Experience.

Which isn't really true because I wasn't *near* dead.

I was dead.

But unlike the Delok I am not here to tell you what happens after Death.

Nor come to discourse on the lessons learned there.

It's none of your damn business.

Suffice it to say.

Most of the shit you've heard isn't true.

According to the countless people who've supposedly had the experience.

Because they weren't really dead.

I was.

And contrary to what most people think.

Coming back from the dead is neither a miracle nor a piece of good fortune.

It is a sign of ignorance and stupidity.

Like an escaped convict returning to his cell because he forgot his toothbrush.

This is not just my humble opinion either.

One of the greatest pieces of ancient wisdom produced by mankind is merely a set of instructions.

On how not to get born.

To sum up the Tibetan Book of the Dead:

Existence is for suckers.

Even in the spiritually naive West there is some vague agreement with this.

To quote (apocryphally) a famous American Sage (read businessman):

"There's a sucker born every minute."

Yeah, I'm a sucker.

But don't you call me that either.

Call me a Killer.

It's what I do for a living.

Or did.

I am a Death Enforcement Officer for the Los Angeles Department of Decongestion.

Or at least I was . . .

Ever since I can remember, I've wanted to kill.

I wanted to kill because I didn't want to turn out like most men.

Thoreau said that most men lead lives of quiet desperation.

I kill those men.

But what follows isn't a body count.

Even though the count is quite high.

So high, I've lost count.

Besides, only amateurs count.

I'm a professional.

And even if I gave an account of every killing.

It would get boring after a while.

Trust me.

You can get bored with killing.

So what I'm going to do is give you one day.

That's all you need.

If you had to pick a day in the life of a killer, what would you pick?

His first kill?

His best?

His most kills?

His last?

It doesn't matter.

Because it isn't your decision.

As for the first:

I've already told about that somewhere else.

Buy that book.[*]

The best and the most would just be bragging.

Would just be another book like all those other books written by self-addicted egopaths.

To show how important they are.

Although it would probably sell.

No.

What I'm going to give you is the last day.

An eschatology of sorts.

As I am somewhat of a student of last things.

The last day that I will kill.

Which.

Unfortunately.

Will require me to throw in a few more days.

---

[*]   *Killscouts of America* (2043)

As this day stands dependent upon the others.

Like the last domino in the domino line of killing days.

Therefore some background is necessary.

As no day stands in isolation from those that precede or those that follow.

So bear with me.

To some this may seem like an invention[*].

But whatever I imagine to have happened did actually happen.

At least to me.

History may deny it.

Since I have played no part in the history of you people.

And however *you* may want to deny it.

Refute it.

Or ignore it.

I am your destiny.

So.

Get used to me.

Even if everything I say is wrong.

Prejudiced.

Spiteful.

Malevolent.

Even if I am a liar and a poisoner.

It is nevertheless the truth.

And it will have to be swallowed.

---

[*]   This line, up to the line ending in, "swallowed," taken (with some modification) from Henry Miller's *Tropic of Capricorn.*

A final caveat:

This is not a morality tale.

Persons attempting to find a moral in it will be shot.

I do not find religion.

Or god.

Or have some epiphany where I suddenly realize that it is wrong to kill.

Neither do I become tired and say "I'm too old for this shit."

None of that.

Let's get on with it then:

To the killing.

GLOOMINGS

The department car was late.

It pulled up in front of the house.

And beeped two times.

The way you'd beep at someone to move on the green.

Without trying to piss them off.

I watched it through the living room window.

A small white two-door with blue Tweels and smoked windows.

Slightly smaller than a Chevy Putter.

And somewhat similar in shape to a Honda Smurf.

White steam puffing out the exhaust tube in quick pulses.

Like some nervous guy hot-boxing a cigarette.

Except it wasn't nervous.

Machines don't get nervous.

Let it wait.

Outside:

The sky is hungover from the sun-drunk weekend.

Ready to vomit rain at any moment.

Inside:

An afternoon brownout has reset the stove clock to triple zero.

Down the street a car alarm goes off.

Sounding like the intro to "Purple Haze."

The car beeps out another two beeps.

I don't move.

I will stand here and watch.

Meowzebub pads onto the lawn.

And begins to sniff cautiously at the Sativa.

Another thirty seconds.

This time the car will not beep.

But honk.

It honks.

The cat jumps.

And when it lands the car will honk again and the cat will take off.

As if it had honked just for that purpose.

Machines don't have purpose.

I look at my watch.

I don't wear a watch.

The car honks again.

Followed by a honk.

Honk.

And another honk.

Look at my fingernails:

The nail on my left middle finger.

Is split down the middle.

Don't know how it got there.

Thirty seconds.

The horn *blasts*.

Held down as if struck by some lifeless head.

Maybe there really is someone behind those dark windows.

Waiting.

There was no one waiting.

Claire walked into the room.

"What are you doing?" she said.

"Trying to piss it off."

"Trying to piss what off?"

"The car."

"It's not a person."

"Well, I am."

Turn around.

She isn't there.

The living room sits quietly.

Collecting dust.

Gathering Death.

Malcolm and Adolf stare out from behind glass looking . . . well, framed.

Malcolm.

Two fingers to temple.

Looks left towards Adolf.

Who is looking straight at me.

Arms crossed.

I don't see any American Dream.

I see an American Nightmare.

"C'mon. You've got to admit it's kind of funny."

"It's annoying actually," she said from another time.

A time now dead.

Wiping her hands with a dish towel.

She never wiped her hands with a dish towel.

I laughed the way you do when you pretend something is funnier than it actually is.

Or when something is not funny at all.

Overblown and hollow.

I will lean my head back and put my palm flat across my stomach to make it that much more.

Pathetic.

It wasn't pathetic enough.

The phone rings.

It was the car.

Last night I dreamed I was the car.

Driving in reverse and running stop signs.

It was night.

But the sun was out.

The shotgun door pops open when I approach.

I get in and the seat belt snakes across my chest and hisses into place.

The car starts to move, and a deep, menacing, yet familiar voice fills the interior:

"Good evening, Officer Krieg."

"Fuck off."

"You are late. In the future please try to be on time. I waited eight minutes and fifty-two seconds for you to enter me."

Darth Vader.

Someone must have changed the voice setting since the last shift.

"Enter you?"

"That sounds like sexual harassment."

"You sexually harassing me, PAL?"

Had already filed several complaints against this so-called PAL with the Department.

Car wouldn't shut up.

With the rules and regulations.

The micromanaging.

Not to mention its obnoxious honking in front of my house.

All of which constituted harassment.

And a hostile work environment.

Complaints which were subsequently rejected.

PAL's management was of a nondiscriminatory nature and thus did not constitute harassment.

Or a hostile work environment.

Besides.

Computers are incapable of harassment, the Department said.

I filed another complaint.

They could be programmed to harass, I said.

They ordered me to see the Department Psych.

Who diagnosed me as suffering from Chronic Complaint Disorder.

I filed another complaint.

Unfair retaliation in retaliation for my complaints.

Which the Department summarily dismissed as being due to this condition.

I'm now on probation.

For assaulting Department property.

i.e., PAL.

With an added diagnosis:

Intermittent Explosive Disorder.

Medication pending.

"I made no references of a sexual nature, Officer Krieg."

"You finally coming out of the closet, PAL?"

"Tellin me you're a fagmobile?"

"Any references of a sexual nature constitute sexual harassment and are therefore unlawful as defined under Title seven of the Civil Rights Act, section seven two eight seven point six B, and under Title two, division four, of the California Code of Regulations, and therefore contrary to my programming."

"I simply requested that you comply with Department regulations by arriving at this vehicle in a timely fashion. Every occurrence of tardiness will result in one penalty point, and ten or more penalty points will result in a write-up and/ or punitive action."

"You were late, *PAL*."

"The Fuck you got to say about that?"

"Per section code one hundred and thirty point zero: excessive and unnecessary use of profanity may result in one or more penalty points depending upon the quantity and severity of the profanity, and ten or more penalty points will result in a write-up and/or punitive action, Officer Krieg."

"Please remember this for future reference."

"Accordingly, as you were previously informed, my calculations for arrival have a plus or minus seven-point-five-minute margin of error. If you'd like I could quote you the pertinent code from my operating manual."

"That won't be necessary, PAL."

"Just don't make any references to me entering you ever again."

I took a look out the window.

"It creeps me out."

The car was just entering the Tapo on-ramp.

The 118 was compressed.

Each lane a vertebrae of cars.

Paralyzed.

A nation of assholes.

Driving automobiles.

In Pursuit.*

Red Chevy Cyclops.

Wouldn't let PAL merge.

PAL gave him a beep beep.

The driver blasted his horn and gave us the finger.

White guy.

Pale face.

Blanco.

Fitting.

This slaveway.

Named after a criminal.

---

*

"Permission to remote vehicle 687 ZOG," PAL said.

"Applying brakes."

The Cyclops stopped with a shriek.

Horn still blasting.

On another day in another year in another dimension I would have done something to that guy.

But not today.

Not now.

Reasonable retaliation was now against Department regulations.

And the official Department motto:

"Everyone on the Road is Your Enemy."

Is now unofficial.[*]

This wasn't some empty motto either.

Dressed up in humorous quotes.

Like "To Protect and to Serve."

It was practical and tactical.

A distillation of our whole modus operandi.

Our philosophy.

Informing you:

1) How other drivers behave.

2) How you were to behave in regard to other drivers.

Everyone is trying to get somewhere.

While at the same time blocking everyone else from trying to get somewhere.

So no one was getting anywhere.

---

[*]   The official one now being *"Exitus Acta Probat"* (whatever that means).

Which makes everyone hostile.

And a hostile.

It's a war out there.

Act accordingly.

But now.

Since the new regulations.

You couldn't act accordingly.

Couldn't even flip them off.

In the old days:

A DEO used to really live up to the true meaning of those letters.

Gods of the City we were.

Tyrants of the Road.

Savages.

Driving razor blades.

Slicing the City.

Cruising Doom.

I could tell you some stories.

But not now.

Going to open my lunch box.

And pull out the bottle.

Thought it would be cute if I went to work with an old-school lunch box.

The black industrial, working-on-a-steel-girder-high-rise kind.

Big-enough-to-carry-a-mortar-shell kind.

Or a Stanley thermos.

She had ordered it from some sadistic office supply store.

The kind where people buy stuff for the jobs they Hate.

To complete the joke she used to make special sandwiches for it.

Sandwiches with the crusts cut off.

Slices of orange in a Ziploc.

A little box of juice.

Sometimes a box of animal crackers.

No more of that now.

Just the bottle.

"Department policy strictly forbids alcohol consumption and/or drug use by Officers on duty," Vader said.

"Use of either will result in a write-up and/or punitive action, Officer Krieg."

"I'll stop drinking when you stop that breathing."

I took the slug and felt it slowly unroll into my gut.

When it was done unrolling I did another.

And then another.

It wasn't enough.

It was too much.

Every man needs to get himself a few demons.

An evil or two.

Some foe to pretend the hero against.

A couple of addictions maybe.

A wife or two.

A full-time job.

Alcohol.

Yes.

Alcohol.

No matter who invented it.

It's American.

An American drug.

First the dream.

Then the nightmare.

Taking more than it gives.

Promising freedom.

And then.

Best way to judge a society.

A civilization.

Is not by its art.

Culture.

Music.

Food.

Or even its government.

But by its drugs.

Which ones are the biggest.

Most popular.

Legal.

Illegal.

Look at ours.

What does it say?

I'll tell you.

It says we're.

Forget it.

Sometimes the best a man can hope for is his own ruin.

And the struggle against his own ruin.

All other success being the mere fulfillment of cheap desires.

Petty appetites.

Speaking of.

What I needed was.

What I need is:

A woman.

Told PAL to throw on some music.

Joan Janelle's "Rump Roast."

Joan Janelle.

Don't need to tell you.

How hot.

You've seen the video.

Claire Hates it.

> *You got the toast so butter my roast and*
> *Feel my ohs that ohs and goes*
> *You knows. You knows.*
> *These hoes be prose*
> *But rose is rose*
> *When bros expose*
> *Their ugly.*

"451 Blocked," PAL said.

"451 Blocked? You played it last week."

"It has been blocked per section code one three two point two."

"The hell is section code one three two point two?"

"Section code one three two point two states that no Department personnel shall engage in the viewing or solicitation of pornography while on duty."

"Solicitation?"

"Since when?"

"The new regulations took effect this morning at approximately midnight, Monday, June 13."

"All Officers were informed by the Department on June 5 about the new policy additions, and during subsequent Departmental briefings."

"If you would prefer, I can quote the pertinent policy additions or display them on-screen."

"No, that won't be necessary."

"Just get your damn voice off Darth Vader."

"Set voice to Joan Janelle."

"451 Blocked."

"What do you mean blocked?"

"Voice unavailable."

"Why is it unavailable?"

"I just had it on last Friday."

"Remember?"

"451 Blocked."

"What do you mean?"

"You don't know why the voice is blocked or whether I had it on the other day?"

"451 Blocked."

"Reset voice to default then."

The default voice sounded like an overeducated tight-assed white chick.

Wearing smartpants.

With just enough of an English accent.

To make herself sound even more like an overeducated tight-assed white chick.

In smartpants.

Still Fuckable, though.

"451 Blocked."

"What?"

"451 Blocked."

"That doesn't make sense. Why is the default blocked?"

"451 Blocked."

"Just get your voice off of goddamn Fucking Darth Vader. Can you do that?"

Darth Vader was Mars's favorite voice.

Used to get a kick out of it.

But now that he was gone.

"451 Blocked."

"Excessive and unnecessary use of profanity has resulted in two penalty points, Officer Krieg."

"Eight more penalty points will result in a write-up and/or punitive action."

A red 2 flashed for a couple of seconds on the upper right of the shield.

And then stopped.

Would sit there like that all evening.

Until I got another one.

"PAL, you know what you are? You're a—"

"I am a MicroStuff PAL, manufactured—"

"You're a Fuckin piece of crap, PAL."

"That's what you are."

"Excessive and unnecessary use of profanity may result in—"

"Just shut up and set windows to Reykjavik, Iceland."

"A penalty point and/or punitive action. Processing request. Reykjavik, Iceland."

A pause, then a whirring sound.

Only view I hadn't gotten sick of yet.

Couldn't stand Paris anymore.

Or Rio.

Tokyo.

London.

Rome sometimes.

And New York.

Never.

Won't go.

The 118 faded out and I was driving down a narrow street with colorful buildings on each side.

Gray-blue sky smeared with interesting clouds.

A pair of women.

Icelandic presumably.

With tight skirts and sensible pumps.

Swaying their hips down the sidewalk.

I watched them close enough to fog-stain the window.

The end of *The Big Pump*.

Where Pumpworthy says:

"Nothing makes you forget a dame better than two dames."

"PAL, put on *The Big Pump*."

I opened the glove box and pulled out the box of Trojan Miniluvs.

Had gotten a couple of cases of the stuff.

Free.

At a Cock and Tail party me and Claire had gone to last year.

This souped-up house in Brentwood.

View of the Getty ruins from the backyard.

A pool that didn't look like it was there for swimming.

But for decoration.

A shimmering blue rug.

Ended up getting to know the guy and girl that were putting on the show.

Both were actors trying to make ends meet.

Had this king-sized bed covered in dark red silk set up in the backyard.

Next to the pool.

Bed had an iron canopy with a set of monkey bars running across the top.

Which they used for some of the more advanced positions.

At one point the girl let me inflate her tits.

The button near her right armpit.

I gave them my card at the end.

Told them if they had any transportation problems.

Wasn't until me and Claire were driving home that I noticed that Claire seemed to be in a bad mood.

Well.

There was one moment during the party.

When the couple was doing a stand-up sixty-nine.

The girl holding up the guy.

When I turned around to look for Claire.

See if she was happening to catch any of this.

She was on the other side of the pool with Synnita.

And some of her pretentious friends.

One of them motioned to her that I was looking over at her.

And when she saw me she quickly turned away.

"What's *wrong?*" she said to my what's wrong.

"What's *wrong?*"

"Yeah, what's wrong."

"He wants to know what's wrong."

"Right. What's wrong?"

"Don't pretend you don't know, Alex."

"Well, I could pretend that I do. That what you want?"

She didn't say anything.

"Well, what the Fuck did I do?"

"The Fuck, he says."

"Yes, that's what he says. What the Fuck did I do?"

"Are you serious?"

"Yes, what's the matter with you?"

"The matter with *me?* So it's me now, is it?"

"Well, I don't seem to be the one acting all weird all of a sudden."

"Weird, huh. *I'm* acting weird?"

"Well, you barely even looked at me at the party, and now you're—"

"This from the guy who spent the whole night leering at the sex show."

"Leering? I wasn't leering. I was watching the show."

"There's a difference between watching and leering."

"Oh, yeah, I forgot."

"I'm supposed to act bored like you and your phony friends, right?"

"People made comments."

"Who?"

"What do you think it looks like when someone spends the whole night staring at two people Fucking?"

"I don't know."

"What does it look like?"

"Like you're some kind of pervert or something."

"Oh, so now I'm a pervert now."

"And then you have the nerve to turn around with that look on your face."

"What look?"

Retard voice:

"Uh, wow."

"Golly gee whiz, Claire."

"Look."

"They're Fucking right here in front of me."

"Boy-yoi-yoi-yoi-yoing."

That was supposed to be the sound of me getting an erection.

She'd done it before.

But in fun.

"Ever see a girl hold a dude up for a stand-up sixty-nine?"

"You don't get it, do you?" she said.

"No, I get it."

"You're mad at me because I wasn't standing around with you and your friends."

"Trying to act cool."

"It's called having class," she said.

"Class?"

"It was a Fuckin Cock and Tail party for Chrissake."

So I had embarrassed the shit out of her.

And not just by watching the show.

Did I really have to walk out of there with my arms full of sexual products?

"The shit was free. It's not like I paid for it."

She grabbed one of the boxes of Miniluvs that were stacked on the back seat.

There wasn't any room left in the trunk.

The kids had been nice enough to give me a set of those iron Fuck Bars too.

Something that normally retailed for close to five thousand dollars, I might add.

For *free.*

It's not like I had plans to install them or anything.

But the shit was free.

Besides.

I wasn't going to keep everything for myself.

Probably give most of it away.

Or donate them to Goodwill.

Claire waved the box of Miniluvs.

"Hey, look at Claire's husband with all his jack-off paraphernalia."

"Gee, Claire, no wonder he never takes you out."

I snatched the box from her and threw it into the back seat.

"What the Fuck are you talking about?"

"When's the last time we went on a date?"

"Date?"

"You know, that thing where you go out to dinner."

"Maybe a movie."

"Or other things if you happen to be the romantic type."

"I work nights, remember?"

"On the weekends?"

"We go out."

"When?"

"What about that place we went to last month?"

"You mean the Hat?"

"No, that restaurant."

"On Ventura."

"Sup?"

"Yeah, that one."

"That was last year."

"It wasn't last year. You sent the whatever it was back."

"Because it was too salty, remember?"

She straightened herself out on the seat and crossed her arms tight.

"It wasn't salty, it was cold."

"Okay, cold."

"You telling your friends I don't take you out on dates now?"

She didn't say anything.

"Why you gotta talk shit about me to your friends?"

"I don't talk shit about you to mine."

"I don't have to," she said.

"They can see for themselves."

"How?"

"How can they see?"

"How do you think it looks?" she said.

"When your husband goes to a party and doesn't stand next to his wife all night."

"But stands and watches two people Fucking all night."

"And then to cherry it."

"Takes home a carload of sexual products."

"You're making it sound worse than it is," I say.

"No, it makes it look like I'm married to a porno addict."

"Porno addict?"

"None of that shit was pornographic—they were sex aids."

"Well, you're the expert apparently."

"You wanna know what this is really about?"

"Sure," she sighed. "Why don't you tell me what this *really* is about, Alex."

"It's all about you."

"Of course it's about me," she said.

"I'm your wife!"

"No, it's about how I make *you* look in front of your friends."

"Calling me a Fucking porno addict."

"How dare you."

"The dude doth protest too much," she said.

I wanted to hit her right there.

I never hit her.

We eventually made up.

But I can't remember how.

Probably took her out.

No.

Came home one morning to find that she had had those Fuck Bars installed on our bed.

Which started another fight.

I took them down the next day and gave them to Goodwill.

Goodwill didn't want them.

So I threw them out in some alley.

Mars told me later he would've taken them.

"451 Blocked," PAL said.

"Forget it," I say.

"Cancel the movie and reset the windows."

I put the Miniluv back in the dispenser.

But it was a no go.

Ended up getting gel all over my hands.

You'd think they'd make it where you could put the thing back in if you changed your mind.

I wiped them on the edge of the seat and threw the Miniluv out the window.

Someone honked.

They always do.

PAL reprimanded me for wiping my hands on the car.

And then penalized me for littering.

Three points now.

Look out the window.

Woman to the right in a Ford Escobar.

Eating fries.

Furiously.

Cannibalizing them.

Like severed fingers.

Contrary to popular belief:

The dead don't walk.

They drive.

CLAIRE HAVEN

Her note:

I am at Synnita's.

Left on the pillow.

Soon as I saw that *I am* I knew something was wrong.

That and the fact that the note was on my pillow.

And not the kitchen counter.

The fridge.

Or the TV.

That it was even a note.

Couldn't get her on the phone.

So I tried Synnita.

They had been to see the new Reina Hawthorne movie, she said.

The one I wouldn't see with Claire.

Remember?

Yeah, I remember.

Put her on.

She's not here.

Put her on.

She doesn't want to talk to you.

Put her on.

I'm hanging up now.

Why did she leave?

"Goodbye, Alex."

What did I do?

She hung up.

"I am" and "Goodbye, Alex."

The Fuck they think they are?

Fuck her.

Fuck *them*.

Fuck.

No.

It won't stick.

Mind keeps scrolling through all the possibilities.

Why.

What.

Why?

No.

Need to focus.

Fuck her.

Shouldn't have to go through this.

Fuck her.

For not telling you.

For not telling you.

Why.

Fuck.

It's clean.

Simple.

Straight.

Wraps things up.

So you can put them away.

So.

Yeah.

Fuck her.

Still doesn't answer why, though.

Why?

Can think of a few reasons.

Don't.

And several more.

Don't.

She found out what I actually did for the Department.

She found out about her daughter.

She found out about the blowshops.

She found out about the.

Stop.

This is a waste of time.

Waste of my mind.

Beating myself up when she could have just saved me the trouble.

And beat me up herself.

So Fuck her.

Fuck me too.

Yeah.

Maybe the Fuck her will hold.

If I Fuck me too.

Fuck her for leaving and Fuck me for whatever I did to make her leave.

It's her fault.

And my fault.

Both our faults.

Yeah.

Can't tell which is worse.

To be the victim or the perpetrator.

Each has its own flavor of pain.

Maybe I was the victim and the perpetrator.

Although I don't know how I could be both at the same time.

Something about smart people.

Being able to hold two opposite things in their heads at the same time.

Not that smart I guess.

Or is it wise people.

Who knows.

Why work out any of this when she could have just told me?

Spared me the trouble.

Could spend forever trying to figure out why and get nowhere but insane.

Still.

In the end.

She's the guilty one.

Why?

Stop.

"You are required to inform the Department if your wife leaves you."

"What?"

Anita Helquist.

Captain Helquist to you.

On-screen.

Dark hair.

Chopped.

Two sharp knife points just below the chin.

Round face.

Sphinx-lined eyes.

No riddle.

"Why didn't you inform the Department that Claire left you?"

"Who told you?"

"Answer my question: Why didn't you inform the Department?"

When I got married to Claire the Department sent me a memo.

I was the proud possessor of a genotype that carried not one.

But two.

Of something called "allele 334."

Supposably this allele made the guys that carried it unsuitable for marriage.

Unsuitable because they were highly prone.

To infidelity.

And double prone if they had two.

They suggested an annulment.

I never took scientific stuff like that seriously.

Fact is a normal red-blooded guy wants to get as much as he can get.

So infidelity was necessary.

Even required.

If you were going to make the sacrifice to stay with one girl for any extended period of time.

"C'mon, Anita. You serious?"

"It's policy," she said.

"The Department needs to confirm that there has been no unauthorized disclosure."

"So why did she leave?"

"She didn't leave."

"She'll be back."

"That's what they all say," she said.

"I'm scheduling you a meeting with the DI."

"That's bullshit."

"I just had my annual interrogation."

"It's policy."

"Yeah, policy."

"Twenty years don't count for shit, does it?"

"Actually, it's a cause for suspicion, so I wouldn't mention it if I were you."

"Well, I don't need an interrogation."

"She's coming back."

"That's not for you to decide. On to the next matter."

"Next matter?"

"You need to stop making inappropriate comments to Officer Ross."

"Inappropriate comments?"

"Yes, comments which could be considered grounds for termination."

"What comments?"

"For one, your repeated use of the N-word."

"What?"

"You know what I'm referring to."

"PAL has already warned you several times."

"You are not to use that word again."

"Yeah, but I'm only referring to myself when I say that."

"Or another Nigger."

"I don't care."

"You are not to use that word."

"Yeah, well, what about PAL, huh?"

"It's okay for him—it—to call me a Nigger?"

"What did I just say about using that word?"

"Yeah, and what did I say about PAL using that word?"

"That matter is closed."

"We found no record of the vehicle using that word."

"I know *Nigger* when I hear it."

"Apparently not."

"What?"

"You forget about the time you accused Officer Prim?"

"About callin me a Nigger?"

"The word she used was *negger*."

"Negger, that ain't even a word."

"Yes, it is. It refers to someone who makes negative comments all the time. Look it up."

"What if I called you a nagger, that a word?"

"On to the next matter."

"Matter? How many matters you got?"

"Several. You are not to discuss your religious views with Officer Ross at any time."

"Religious views?"

"Yes, your Extinctionism."

"Extinctionism?"

"Yes, you are free to believe anything you want, but you need to keep it to yourself."

"What did I say?"

"What?"

"What religious views did I—"

"Hold on."

She looked down.

"'It's the only true American Religion in my opinion.'"

"'Came to California during the Gold Rush.'"

"Et cetera, et cetera."

"'To preach the Black News.'"

"And . . . oh, here."

"'The *extinction* of the white man and the destruction of the West.'"

"Is that a transcript?"

"Yes, everything you say is—"

"I was talking about the Sol Niger. It's not even a real—"

"Okay, that's it," she said.

"Every time you use that word, I'm giving you a penalty point."

The 4 turned into a flashing 5, then stopped flashing.

"Since when do I got four? Last I looked I had—"

"Just don't use that word again."

"I didn't say Nigger. I said *nee-zhaire*."

"You're just looking for any excuse to say that word, aren't you?"

"It's not the same word."

"It's Latin."

"I don't care how you try to pronounce it: Latin, French, whatever."

"You are never to use that word, ever. Is that understood?"

"It ain't the same word."

"Is that understood?"

"So I can't use *Niger* now?"

"Another point."

The 5 turned into a 6.

"How about *Negro?*"

6 to 7.

"I can do this all night if you want," she said.

"Who's got the highest score on this thing?"

"I'm going to say it one more time:"

"You are never to use that word."

"Or any derivative of that word."

"Do you understand?"

"Derivative?"

"Do you understand?"

"I'm not an Extinctionist."

"Do you understand?"

"I'm not anything."

"Last time, or I'm removing you from the field."

"Do you understand?"

"Yes. I understand."

"Good. Now, on to the next matter."

"Are you or are you not aware that pornographic material is against Department regulations."

"Pornographic material?"

"The vehicle has reported several instances of you trying to load pornographic material today."

"No, I haven't. And since when—"

My voice now.

"PAL, put on The Big Pump."

"What, no transcript?"

"PAL, play me some 'Rump Roast,' will ya?"

"That's not porn."

"And those aren't sex gloves in the glove box?"

"You watching me jerk off now?"

"No, I'm watching you throw twenty years of service away."

"Just like Mars, right?"

"That subject is closed, Alex."

"Yeah? Well, who closed it?"

"You've already been warned about—"

"Yeah, yeah."

"The Department warns me, the car warns me, my partner warns me."

"And now you're warning me."

"Keep forgetting that I work for the Department of Warnings."

"Look, I don't make the rules."

"Just do your job and you won't be warned."

"I've been doing it for twenty years for Chrissake."

She sighed.

"What did I just tell you?"

"To do my job, and I told you—"

"About expressing your religious views, Alex."

"What religious views?"

"Do I have to go over this again?"

"Go over what again?"

"You are not to use that word."

"What word?"

"You know what word."

"I didn't say *Nigger.*"

"No, not nig—Chrissake."

"Chrissake?"

"Yeah, you are not to use that word."

"Or any derivative thereof."

"Why not?"

"Because it's offensive to Officer Ross."

"Why?"

"Because she's Christian."

I laughed.

"Then why doesn't she get a job at a church then?"

"Because it's policy, and it's the law."

"You are not to make any offensive comments of a sexual, religious, eth-nic, gender, class, or—"

"Jesus Fuckin Christ, Anita."

"Her name is Megha-*sin* for Chrissake."

"Dammit, Alex, are you trying to get yourself terminated?"

"C'mon, Anita."

"What is this bullshit?"

"You forget what we do for a living?"

"We kill people for Chris—"

She just looked at me.

It was a hard look.

Like I had offended her somehow.

Maybe she was a Christian too.

"This is your last warning, Alex."

"Don't you ever use that word again, or any other term relating to it."

"What about Christmas?"

"Jesus, are you listening to this conversation, or—"

"You just said *Jesus*, that mean I can say that but not *Christ?*"

"Dammit, Alex. I'm not talking about that, I'm talking about your reference to our job."

"What reference?"

"We subtract."

"That is our mission Alex: we subtract."

"Do you understand?"

"Our mission."

"Jesus."

"You sound like Trimmer now."

"Do you understand?"

"You know, back in the day—"

"Do you understand?"

"Yeah, sure. What choice do I have?"

"Yes, or no. Do you understand?"

"Yeah."

"And further:"

"You are not to talk to Officer Ross or any other Officer about previous policy."

"Previous policy?"

"No more of your 'back in the day' comments, Alex."

"It is undermining Officer Ross's ability to effectively perform her duties."

"Not to mention yours."

"And will—I repeat, will—be considered grounds for termination."

"I think the correct term is *subtraction*."

"Do you understand?"

"Yes, I do."

"Good."

"Because Trimmer will be sitting in on your evaluation."

"And if you pull any of this it's not only going to reflect on you."

"It's going to reflect on me too."

"I've already had my interrogation."

"I'm not talking about your interrogation."

"I'm talking about your evaluation."

"Evaluation?"

"In two weeks."

"And you've got till the end of the week to turn it in."

"Turn what in?"

"Your self-eval."

"What?"

"Stop playing dumb."

"I'm not playing, I don't know what the hell you're talkin about."

"Your self-evaluation."

"Self-evaluation?"

"Yes."

"No one told me about any—"

"All Officers were informed several months ago about the evaluation process."

"The form was sent to your account."

"What form?"

"Your self-evaluation form."

"It was due two weeks ago."

"But you were given an extension for the two weeks you were on leave."

"You need to fill it out and get it to me no later than Friday."

"What? I've got to interrogate myself now?"

"Evaluate. The instructions are on the form."

"Jesus Christ."

"You'd better take this seriously, Alex."

"I had to convince the Department to grant you this extension due to your recent loss, but—"

"Recent loss?"

"But I've done all I can do."

"Now it is up to you."

"So, think about that when you fill out your evaluation."

"Yeah, sure."

"I'm serious. Don't take this lightly."

"Your career could be riding on this."

"My career? Are you kidding me?"

"No."

"You can fill it out between subtractions."

"It should take no more than two or three hours."

"Three hours?"

"What do they want me to write?"

"A Fuckin novel?"

"Watch the profanity, Alex."

"Gee, where've I heard that before?"

"Maybe you and PAL—"

"This meeting is over," she said.

"Just remember what I've said."

"The interrogator will be on in five minutes."

"Goodbye, Alex."

"Yeah."

I was tired of being interrogated.

Three days before Claire left:

I had to pretend the good husband and let myself get interrogated for that damn La Brea Gardens she wanted to get into.

Maybe that was it.

La Brea Gardens.

Maybe we didn't get in.

And now she blamed me.

I was used to being interrogated.

But she wasn't.

She played along.

I didn't.

Couldn't.

Maybe I should have.

Maybe I should—

Stop.

Don't think.

Shut your head off.

Relax.

Yeah.

Relax.

Breathe.

Like Zen.

Breathe.

Breathe.

Problem is you gotta breathe for a long time.

To get anything.

Why I never do it.

Still.

Got nothing else.

Breathe.

Breathe.

Breathe.

Yeah.

That's not me breathing.

It's the damn car.

Still doin Vader.

"PAL, will you stop that—"

"There's one more matter I forgot."

Anita again.

On-screen.

"Alex?"

"Yeah, what."

"Your smoking."

"What about it."

"It is bothering Officer Ross."

"Of course it is."

"You are not to smoke on duty."

"What?"

"You are not to smoke on duty."

"I don't."

"You do."

"Yeah, but not in the car."

"Yes, but you smell of smoke when you get in the car."

"Yeah, so?"

"It's third-hand smoke."

"What?"

"Third-hand smoke can be carcinogenic, especially in close confines."

Third-hand smoke.

Try to be Zen about this.

"What about fourth-hand smoke?"

"What?"

"Talking about smoking."

"Am I allowed to talk about smoking?"

"Okay, that's enough."

"No more smoking, okay?"

"Seriously, Anita."

"This some kind of conspiracy?"

"No, it's just policy."

"Yeah, policy. Let me tell you what I—"

"Okay, the DI's office is on."

"You need to take this seriously, Alex."

"Goodbye."

"Hello."

An attractive Mexican girl appeared on-screen.

"Hello."

"Alex Krieg?"

"Yes, ma'am."

"Please stand by for the Department Interrogator."

"Sure."

"He'll be on in five minutes."

Five minutes.

Like I was in a waiting room.

So I sat there.

Like I was in a waiting room.

Without a magazine.

Look at the people next to me.

Waiting.

In their portable waiting rooms.

To the left:

A man was yelling at himself.

Or someone on the phone.

He banged his fist against the steering wheel.

Ahead:

A woman's face in her side mirror.

Gorging on fries.

Like she couldn't eat them fast enough.

Different woman.

Same fries.

To the right:

Couldn't see through the driver's window.

Smoked.

Which is against the law.

Back in the day I would've broken the window.

And maybe the head.

Maybe I should.

Beats waiting.

Yeah.

Waiting.

It's the most important skill to have on this job.

Not killing.

Knowing traffic code.

Or keeping your mouth shut.

No.

It's waiting.

Occupying long, dull stretches.

Sitting.

Waiting.

For the next subtraction.

The next kill.

Waiting while the car drives in circles.

Waiting for the algorithm to kick in and choose the next zero.

Waiting for.

A young guy appeared on the screen.

Armenian.

Persian maybe.

He wasn't looking at me.

But offscreen.

T-shirt and jeans.

Couldn't see his pants.

But it was a ten-to-one shot he was wearing jeans.

He looks up at me and then he looks down at something in front of him.

"How do I pronounce this," he said. "Mr. *Kryg?*"

"*E*," I say. "Not *I*."

He doesn't get it.

I say it for him.

"Very well," he said, nodding.

"I'm Robert, but you can Bob me."

"Take a seat."

Painting behind him just visible in the right-hand corner of the screen.

Profile of a white guy looking to the left.

Light blue background.

Head smashed in.

Or covered with a gray slab of meat.

Blood streaming down looks like hair.

Ronald McDonald hair.

Except it was straight.

Dude's cultured apparently.

I ask him who that Mexican chick was.

Like I was asking him about his five-year-old daughter:

"That's my assistant, Veronica."

"She's hot."

"Hotter than your wife?"

"What?"

"Can I call you Alex, or do you prefer Officer Krieg?"

"You can call me Officer Krieg. My wife does."

"Seriously?"

"C'mon. Call me by my first name."

"Okay." Writing something down.

He looks up.

"Tell me about your wife."

"What?"

"Tell me about your wife."

"What do you want me to tell?"

"Whatever comes off the top of your head."

"This part of the interrogation?"

"Oh, no. No."

"I don't interrogate in the strict sense of the term."

"This is purely informal, just to talk."

"I want you to think of it as just two people having a casual conversation over coffee."

"Like at a café or something."

"Yeah, right."

"If you don't want to talk about your wife we can talk about something else."

"No, I don't mind talking about her."

"Okay, shoot."

"She's younger than me."

"Yeah?"

"Early thirties."

Writing it down like he doesn't know it already.

They know everything already.

"I met her in a bookstore of all places."

"Really?"

"Yeah, in the metaphysical section."

"What bookstore?"

"It doesn't exist anymore."

My very first word to her was "Uh."

We used to have an "Uh" day every year.

Our anniversary.

I would give her a card that said "Uh."

Or she would call me and say "Uh."

Or we would go to a restaurant.

And when it came time to order we would see who could "uh" it out longer than the other.

And one year I went so far as to take her to the beach.

Where a plane smoked out the word *UH* across the sky.

"She walked in on me reading a *Femme Fatale* of all things."

"*Femme Fatale?*"

"Yeah."

"What's that?"

"It's a magazine with chicks that've committed felonies."

"This a pornographic magazine?"

"No, it's artistic."

"Are the women naked?"

"Yeah."

"In what way?"

"What do you mean, in what way?"

"How are they posed?"

"You've never seen the mag?"

"Uh, no. I don't read magazines."

"Yeah, well. I wasn't reading this one either."

"So, this *bookstore*."

He said it like it wasn't really a bookstore.

"Yeah."

"Do they specialize in . . . magazines?"

"No, mostly books."

"Were you there for that specific magazine?"

"No, the magazine was an *accident*."

"An accident?"

"Someone left it on the shelf I was trying to get at."

"And what shelf was that?"

"I just told you."

"Did you?"

"Yeah, I said I was in the metaphysical section."

"No, you said you met your wife in the metaphysical section."

"Yeah, and that was the section I was in."

"I was thinking maybe you weren't in that section yet."

"Why?"

"No reason, proceed."

"Yeah, so when I picked up the mag to move it I saw the girl on the cover and got curious."

"Curious how?"

"I opened it."

"You opened it."

"Yeah."

"To see this girl?"

"Uh, yeah."

"The one on the cover of the magazine, right?"

"Yeah, you sound like you never operated a magazine before."

"Could you describe her for me?"

"Why?"

"Just curious."

"I don't know."

"Dark hair."

"Full lips."

"Great ass."

"Small tits, but perfectly shaped."

"Remember that seventeen-year-old girl that ran over all those people in Santa Monica?"

"The one that claimed she was conducting a science experiment?"

"See how many people she could run over in a Smurf."

"No, can't say that I do."

"Seriously?"

"Yes, but there seems to be a rise in—what are they calling it these days?—mass pilings."

"Plowings."

"Yes, hence the importance of what we do—what *you* do—to prevent unfortunate situations like this."

"Yeah, well. We weren't involved with that obviously."

"Shit with high publicity—leave it to the police."

"So, this girl. You could see her ass *and* her tits in one photo?"

"Yeah."

"How would you compare your wife to her?"

"Apples and oranges."

"Are you attracted to women with criminal records?"

"No, not really."

"Well, if they're hot."

To tell you the truth:

If Claire had been some kind of felon like that girl.

A murderess maybe.

Then things between us would've been different.

Probably.

I don't know.

"Who were you more attracted to?" he asked.

"The woman on that cover or your wife?"

"Like I said, apples and oranges."

"If you had to choose."

"The Fuck is this?"

"Asking me to choose between my wife or some chick in a mag."

"What's the matter with you?"

"Pretend I'm your friend."

"Asking one of those—you know—informal comparison questions that normal guys like to—"

"Yeah, yeah, yeah. But it's not, is it?"

"This is me trapped in this Fucking robocar having to look at your face on a screen."

"Okay," he said. "I'm sorry. I was out of line."

"Yeah."

"You just said right now that you feel trapped. Do you feel trapped?"

"Jesus, did I say *trapped*? More like comfortably situated."

"Continue on about your first meeting with your wife."

"No, I'm done."

That first day she took me home.

She lived with her parents in some souped-up house in Brentwood.

Her parents were out of town and wouldn't be home for another week.

They had a big hot tub in the back and that's where we ended up.

"Parents still married, huh?"

"Yeah," she said, turning her back to me.

"That's why I'm so Fucked up. Now it's your turn."

"My turn?"

"To Fuck me up."

I was Fucking her from behind.

Her knees on the part you're supposed to sit on.

Her body bent forward outside the tub.

When this woman's voice screamed, "Claire!" from the direction of the house.

Authoritative enough to make me feel like I was some high school kid getting caught.

So I pulled out and sank as deep into the water as I could go.

On my knees in the center.

Just my head sticking out.

Claire let out a tsk of irritation.

I couldn't tell if it was aimed at me for pulling out or at the voice.

She turned and sat and pulled back the wet strands of her hair.

She looked at me and casually stretched her arms across the edge of the tub.

Pushing out her tits in a gesture of defiance.

"That your mom?"

"My daughter. She's not supposed to be here."

A red-haired girl loomed up.

And blocked out the remaining sun.

Arms severely crossed.

"What the hell are you doing?" she said.

Probably under eighteen.

But you could never tell these days.

She could have been twenty-five for all I knew.

Prettier than Claire.

But bitchier looking.

And you could tell that she knew it.

That she was prettier.

Not bitchier.

"This your sister?"

"Ewwww god, no," the girl said. "The hell is this? Another reject for your crotch party?"

"Crotch party?"

"This is Alex," Claire said. "He's a cop. Alex, this is my daughter, Insatia."

She said it reluctantly.

Like she'd been forced.

Or coerced into it somehow.

And I couldn't tell if she was embarrassed in front of her daughter because of me.

Or embarrassed in front of me because of her daughter.

I extended a wet hand:

"Hi."

A mistake.

You don't put out your hand to a girl like that.

And you certainly don't say hi while you're doing it.

Girls like that take any sign of friendliness to be a sign of weakness.

And a sanction to strike accordingly.

She looked at my hand like I was trying to hand her a piece of meat:

"Shouldn't you be out arresting someone, instead of Fucking my mother in the ass?"

"Insatia!" Claire gasped.

It wasn't a real gasp.

Or if it was:

It was one that sounded more impressed by the audacity of the comment than her supposed offense to it.

And right there I could tell why this kid was such a bitch.

The feigned shock of her mother came across as a kind of approval.

She was impressed that her kid had such audacity.

"You didn't tell me you had a daughter."

I had to say this just to block something worse that was getting ready to launch itself from my lips.

Claire didn't answer.

I had suddenly ceased to exist in the silent exchange that transpired between them.

Claire sitting there with a kind of tenuous defiance.

That was on the verge of collapse against the Medusa gaze of her daughter.

A defiance that on second look seemed more turned against herself than her daughter.

A defiance that said she had a right to Fuck a guy in the hot tub.

And not have to feel guilty about it.

Even though she really felt guilty about it.

"What are you doing home?" she said finally.

"I got sick of Alexa and Cherry's blah blah blah."

"Are you guys going to be out here Fucking all day?"

"Or can I get some goddamn peace and quiet?"

"None of your business," Claire said.

"Well, it *is* my business, because I need some peace and quiet."

"And I really don't care to hear you and JQ Coppington here making unwarranted noises."

"JQ Coppington?"

"Well, we're not going anywhere if that's what you mean," Claire said.

"Maybe we should go," I said.

"No, we're staying," Claire said.

Running an unsteady hand through her hair.

"Great," Insatia said, walking away.

"Grandma's going to *really* Love listening to another sordid little chapter of your sexual escapades."

"You going to tell on me like a little child?" Claire called to her.

"If you don't want to be treated like a child," Insatia yelled back.

"Then maybe you should grow up."

"Maybe *you* should grow up, you little brat," Claire said.

Lowering her tone on "you little brat."

"Maybe you should move out," Insatia screamed back.

"I mean, how old are you and you still live at home? Hel-lo."

"Just go inside."

"I am, you sad excuse for a mother."

A door slammed.

Claire gave me a look that seemed to have a twofold purpose:

One to show me her frustration and exasperation at having a bitch of a daughter like that.

Two to see what my reaction was to her even having a daughter.

I don't think I'm any good at looking sympathetic.

But I tried anyway and asked if she was okay.

The look must've worked because she unleashed upon me the whole story of her daughter.

Like it was some movie she saw.

About a young woman who had everything going for her.

Until she got knocked up by her high school boyfriend.

Gave me the whole it-was-hard-to-raise-a-kid-when-you-were-so-young-and-didn't-have-any-money line.

Especially when you had something called a Money Disorder that caused you to spend money you didn't have.

Uncontrollably.

Obsessively.

Which was why she had to humiliatingly live with her parents.

Although her mother and father had been more than glad.

To help her raise Insatia.

The name.

She added.

In what sounded like an apology.

A tacky adolescent indulgence from her freewheeling, wild, creative, Fuck-it-all younger days.

But now that she thought of it.

Somehow strangely appropriate.

Considering the way Insatia had turned out.

Which was partially.

Or maybe.

The result of being raised by overindulgent grandparents.

Who catered to Insatia's every little whim.

While at the same time barely concealing their disapproval of their daughter.

In many instances openly criticizing her right in the presence of her own daughter.

Elevating one and putting down the other.

And thus creating the monster you just had the unfortunate inopportunity of meeting.

She said she was afraid Insatia was developing.

Like mother like daughter.

The same Money Disorder.

Not only that.

She had come to realize in therapy that her own parents.

Who vehemently denied the accusation.

Also had the same disorder.

But in a different form.

The specific symptoms of her disorder were Compulsive Buying and Serial Borrowing.

While her parents' disorder was Financial Incest.

Which meant that they used money to control Claire and her daughter.

"They're in denial about it," she said.

"They freaked out when I broached the subject to them."

"Said I wasn't taking responsibility for my actions."

"That I was just being ungrateful."

"All total hallmarks of their disorder of course."

"If anything, they said, they weren't holding their money over my head."

"But trying not to enable my disorder by giving me money."

"And how dare I accuse them."

"When they had made such a big sacrifice in their lives to take me and Insatia in."

Which was exactly their disorder talking, she said.

And which they refused to acknowledge when she pointed it out.

"Don't get me wrong," she said.

"I'm not one of those people that tries to blame everything on their parents."

But part of her recovery process involved the family coming to terms with.

And understanding.

Its dysfunction.

And it was imperative that they see the role *their* disorder played.

In helping to shape *her* disorder.

So that all of them could fully come to terms with *their* disorders.

And thus achieve full recovery.

They didn't buy it.

They were still in denial apparently.

We stayed at the house.

Which I thought was a stupid decision.

It just seemed like mere stubbornness on Claire's part.

Like she was trying to win some battle with her daughter.

Or maybe she knew that her daughter wasn't going to bother us for the rest of the day.

Because she didn't.

At one point she asked me if I might have a problem being with a person with so many disorders.

In an age of disorder.

Disorder is the fashion, I said.

She laughed and asked me if I had any disorders.

Probably, I said.

But that was probably one of my disorders.

Not knowing which disorder I had.

We left it at that and had several Dry Lemon Handcars and smoked some expensive weed.

We shot pool in their billiards room and I lost and then we had sex right on the table.

With me constantly looking over my shoulder like some frightened animal.

Expecting Insatia to creep in and pounce.

I was puzzled by Claire's apparent faith that there was no way her daughter would barge in.

Interrupt this coitus.

And then.

More fearfully.

That Claire.

In an act of stepping up her defiance.

Was hoping that Insatia *would* interrupt us.

It wasn't until about four in the morning that I even saw Insatia again.

I woke up with a throbbing head and a terrible thirst and headed straight to the kitchen for something to drink.

A Fridge Butler.

Told me I wasn't authorized.

I started to kick it.

Until the antidamage feature kicked in.

Better to open than break.

Nothing much to drink inside.

Almond milk.

Soy juice.

Water.

A bottle of Savage River.

Commercial with the guy who doesn't want to drink it after his wife gives it to him.

So he pours it out into the gutter.

Next thing you know these giant blue crocodiles are coming out of the sewer and causing havoc.

Anyways.

I drank half the bottle standing there in the open fridge.

Before I realized why the guy dumped it.

Tasted like too many things at the same time.

And I couldn't tell what even one of them was.

I put the cap back on and put it back in the fridge.

Grabbed a small bottle of water and downed it.

This whole time the butler wouldn't shut up.

Told me the drink was reserved.

Please release the door, etc.

That it was going to call the police.

When I finally let the door close Insatia was standing right there.

I flinched, which made her flinch.

"What are you doing?" she demanded.

"What's it look like? Having a drink."

"That was my drink you drank and then put back, slob."

"I didn't know."

She crossed her arms.

"You don't care either I'll bet."

"No, I don't, you Fucking brat."

That was lame.

I shouldn't have said that Fucking brat part.

It was just going to set this kid off.

And my head wasn't in the mood for anything getting set off.

However, it didn't have the effect I expected it to have.

Worse than I expected.

"A brat?" She smiled. "I'm not a child, you know. I'm eighteen."

"Yeah, you are," I say, putting my foot in it further.

"One that is long overdue for a beating."

I was long overdue to get the hell out of there.

So I turned and started to walk out.

"Are you threatening me?" she said with a little laugh.

Over my shoulder:

"It's a warning."

"Oooooh."

"Fuck off."

"Wait," she said, following, her tone almost human.

"I want to ask you something."

I stopped and turned because I couldn't think of any stupider moves.

"What?"

"Can you Fuck me like you Fucked my mother?"

"What?"

"You heard me."

"Think you're a real badass with your little disarming cracks, aren't you?"

"You smell like a goddamned liquor store."

"Go to bed."

"How old are you, anyways? I can never tell with black people."

I turned and made a feeble attempt at getting the hell out of there.

Feeble because this whole thing somehow reminded me of that scene in *The Big Pump*.

Where the old General's sixteen-year-old daughter tries to seduce Pumpworthy in the foyer.

She followed me into the dining room.

"It's your dick, right?"

I kept walking.

"I saw it in the hot tub."

"Don't worry, they say that size doesn't matter."

"That it's the motion of the lotion."

I turned on her.

"Go to bed."

"Why, are you scared?"

"You think you're tough, don't you?"

"Tell me. How does it feel to be a black man with a—"

She held up her index and thumb in that universal sign.

Maybe it was the Savage River.

I don't know.

But that's when I lost it.

I grabbed a big handful of her red hair and jerked her head back.

"You wanna play?"

"Let go," she yelled. "Or I'll—"

I put my free hand over her mouth and dragged her by the head to the living room couch.

She kicked a little.

But couldn't connect.

It seemed more like she was doing it because that's what you were supposed to do.

In a situation like this.

She bit into my hand enough to break the skin, though.

I threw her down hard into the couch and pushed her face into an embroidered pillow.

With *Bless* and something else written on it.

Probably *This House.*

She struggled a bit.

Kind of squirmed.

But it didn't seem hard enough for my taste.

Maybe she wanted it.

Her insults probably her style of foreplay.

I don't know.

It didn't matter really.

Either way it was going to get done.

She was only wearing a nightshirt and some cotton underwear.

She didn't even move when I left her.

Didn't yell or scream or nothing.

She just lay there with her ass in the air and the side of her face against the pillow.

Breathing hard breaths.

The next day Claire asked me.

Since I worked for the Department of Transportation.

If there was any way I could get Insatia's driving level raised.

Let me guess.

She was a level 1.

Road Rookie.

No.

Worse.

Zero?

Negative 6.

Road Menace.

Which meant it would cost her over a thousand dollars to renew her license.

Several more to register her car.

And several more than that to even get basic insurance coverage.

That is.

If anyone would even insure her ass.

I told Claire I didn't think it was a good idea to let her back on the road.

People's lives were at stake here.

Plus, I thought, that's not something you ask on a first date.

Even if Fucking your date's daughter on the first date is not something you do either.

Claire said that Insatia's not driving had been the real menace.

For Claire and her parents.

Mostly Claire.

Who had been guilted into chauffeuring her around.

And if there was any way I could get her level raised it would take a great burden off of her.

So I got her raised.

To level 1.

Best I could do given the circumstances.

We got married a week after that.

It was supposed to be a joke.

One of those drive-thru wedding chapels.

We were in Vegas, drinking and daring each other to back out.

Just back out.

We were drunk of course.

What are you doing?

No.

What are *you* doing?

And so we did it and laughed about it.

We were still laughing a year later.

And the year after that.

By the third year the whole thing didn't seem that funny anymore.

"Do you Love her?"

"What?"

"Do you Love your wife?"

"I married her because I didn't have to Love her."

"You consider that a valid reason to get married?"

"I don't think there's any valid reason to get married."

"Except drunk."

"So, you don't believe in Love?"

"Love or no, all relationships have a beginning, a middle, and an end."

"And if you know that, you can have a relatively good time."

"Without any preconceived illusions getting in the way."

"So, it doesn't bother you that she left, then?"

"Yeah, it bothers me."

"It bothers me because she won't tell me why."

"I thought we were nearing the middle, not the end."

"Does she know what you do for the Department?"

"No."

There were times I suspected.

Suspected that my work surrounded me like some noxious pheromonal cloud.

Imperceptible enough not to be detected by the usual front-row senses.

But perceptible enough to be vaguely registered by some more subtle or primitive sense.

"How can you be sure?"

"You can never be sure, I guess. What about your wife?"

His features hardened:

"What about my wife?"

"She know you interrogate murderers to make sure that they're murdering effectively?"

"The correct term is *subtract*, Officer Krieg."

"So, what. You tell her that you teach math at the local community college?"

"This is not about my wife. It is about yours. What have you confessed to her?"

"Nothing."

"You told her something. What was it?"

"Nothing. I didn't tell her anything."

The background behind him blackened.

The only light now shining up from somewhere under his chin.

Chiseling shadows into his features.

Turning his face to stone.

Thunder exploded behind me and I turned.

"Look at me."

He had tilted his head down a little so that he could kind of look up at me with a sinister look.

His voice deeper now:

"Tell me the truth."

"What?" I laugh.

"Tell me."

A low droning sound.

Quiet at first.

Then rising in volume.

The windows dimmed and then cut to black.

Pitch-dark except for the evil glow of his face.

A demon face cut by sharp shadows.

Lips curled and teeth gritted.

I didn't know whether to laugh or cry at these theatrics.

That sound.

"Why did she leave you?" he growled.

"The Fuck is this?"

"You told her you were a murderer, *didn't* you?"

"The correct term is *subtractor.*"

"A butcher, an executioner, a slaughterer—didn't you!"

"You make the job sound better than it actually is."

"Tell me. Now. Or I will turn you inside out."

The sound was inside me now.

Constricting my heart.

Squeezing my organs.

"That sound. Can you—"

"Don't lie to me, Kreeeg."

"I ain't lyin. C'mon. What is this?"

I can feel my blood.

Bleeding to come out.

Organs pulped.

Straining through my pores.

"What did you tell her?"

"I didn't tell her."

Stomach coming through my mouth.

"Lie to me again and you will die."

"Stop."

"Why did she leave you?"

"I don't know!"

"Tell me now, Krieg. Tell me. Or else."

Can't speak.

"Tell, tell, or go to hell!"

Another sound now.

On top of the drone.

A white-noise dead channel sound.

Scratching at my ears.

Knifing into my brain.

Beneath:

Other sounds.

Swimming like mutilated monsters in a polluted sea.

Bobbing in and out.

Surfacing and submerging.

A baby being strangled.

A goat.

Bleating.

Screams.

"Tell me, you worm."

Screams.

"Tellll meee."

Hands over my ears.

Can't move my arms.

Hands over my ears.

Can't move.

My arms.

"Tell me, NOW."

Choking.

"Please."

"Tell me."

Tears oozing out of my eyes.

Or is it blood.

"Tell me."

"No, please."

"Tell me now."

"It hurts."

"Tell me or die."

Yes.

Like a dog.

Tongue out, tail wagging.

"Yes, die."

"Yes, yes, die."

"Die."

Cut.

At the shore of dead infinity.

The edge of black.

About to fall.

No.

Gonna jump.

"Alex?"

"Claire?"

Standing at the edge.

"What are you?" she says.

Tell her.

Now.

Before it's too.

I'm a murderer, Claire.

A goddamned killer.

I've killed more people than.

And I raped her.

Your daughter.

Insatia.

It wasn't the drink.

The one with the commercial.

Savage River.

It was me.

I'm sorry.

Should've told you.

Should've told you everything.

But if I did.

They would've.

A look on her face.

She can't hear.

Doesn't understand.

The words.

They sound like loud farts.

Again.

Tell her.

Louder farts.

Worse than insults.

Trivial.

Sneering.

And they smell.

Tears in her eyes.

The stench is infernal.

"Your soul," she says.

She steps back.

To the edge.

Hands out.

Her hands.

My hands.

Don't say anything.

You can't.

No.

Don't.

"I."

"Love you."

The loudest fart of them all.

Blows her over the edge.

Gone.

I'm going too.

Going.

Go.

Gone.

"Open your eyes."

"Open your."

Sitting there relaxed in his blue jeans.

Waiting for me.

A look of concern on his face.

The car.

The 118.

Shake my head and look at him.

Sitting there almost half-bored.

"Wait . . . what . . . where . . . what just . . ."

"There's some tissue in the dash dispenser," he said.

"Now."

Covered in sweat, wiping my face:

"Now?"

"Do you want her back?"

Shaking.

"What?"

"Your wife. Do you want her back?"

"I'd like to know why she left. I deserve that at least."

"But do you want her back?"

"Yeah, sure, I guess."

"You guess?"

"Yes, I want her back."

"Why do you think she left you?"

"I don't know."

"You must have some idea."

"Well, we had a fight over Reina Hawthorne about a week before she left."

"Reina Hawthorne?"

"Yeah, I didn't want to go and see the new Reina Hawthorne movie with her."

"Why not?"

"Because I can't stand her."

Claire worships her.

"Reina is Queeeen," he said.

"Oh, don't say that, man."

"Why not?"

"Every time I hear someone say that, I want to—"

"Reina Hawthorne is quite an accomplished woman, I think she's earned the title."

"Yeah, but who gave her the title?"

"I don't know, but millions of people would agree with it."

"A million zeros liking one zero still equals zero."

"What have you got against her?"

"Really?"

"Yes, what don't you like about her?"

"Besides her popcorn music?"

"Her movies?"

"Yeah."

"Her LifeStyle products?"

"Her shuckin for Pizza Hut?"

"Her jivin for Nike?"

"Her—"

"*Yessss,*" he said.

"What do you have against her?"

"See, that's what I don't get."

"People like you."

"People like me?"

"Yeah, that equate success with some kind of truth."

"Well, she's successful for a reason if that's what you mean."

"And what reason is that?"

"Like I said—because she is talented."

"But she has no Fuck."

"What?"

"What I said," I say.

"She doesn't have any Fuck."

"She's Fuckless."

"What does that have do with her talent?"

"Everything."

"Yeah, and what exactly—"

"I have a theory about people like her."

"A theory?"

"The ones at the top. They're not up there because of talent."

"They're up there as our punishment."

"Punishment?"

"Yeah, like that *Twilight Zone*."

"The one where the guy gets everything he wants but—"

"What is that?" he said.

"What's what?"

"*The Twilight—*"

"*Zone?*"

"Yes, what is that?"

"It's a TV series."

"You've never heard of *The Twilight Zone?*"

"No, I'm afraid not."

Sing a couple of bars of the theme and he gives me a funny look.

Like I'm making it up.

"You're traveling through another dimension?"

No.

"Rod Serling?"

"Is that science fiction or something?"

"Yeah, sure . . . I guess."

"I don't watch science fiction," he said. "Or fantasy."

"I prefer things that are . . ."

"Contemporary."

"Like Reina Hawthorne," I say.

"Yes, so this *Twilight Zone* of yours."

Of mine.

That's it right there.

What kind of person never heard of the.

"How does that apply to your theory?"

Couldn't remember what my theory was.

"What?"

"That people like Reina are—"

He puts his fingers in quotes.

"'Up there to be punished.'"

"Did I say she was up there to be—"

"Yes, you did."

"No, I meant she was up there to punish us."

Or, maybe she was up there to be punished.

Who knows.

"And who put her up there to punish us?"

"I don't know."

"Something."

"Or maybe it's some kind of omen or something."

"Omen?"

"Yeah."

"Of what?"

"I don't know."

"Of the end times?"

"The end of the world?"

"No."

"Something worse."

"More like . . ."

"These times."

"Ain't ever gonna end."

Actually.

The more I think about it.

It's like this:

Most Americans are losers.

Even the winners.

Especially the winners.

In fact our winners *are* the biggest losers.

Because:

To be a success in this culture you have to be a failure.

As a human being.

Look at some of the presidents we've had.

Most of our celebrities.

Reina Hawthorne.

"Okay, so you don't like Reina Hawthorne."

"How do you feel about your wife liking her?"

"I don't know. It's fine I guess."

"You guess?"

"Well, doesn't it say something about a person when they like a person like that?"

"What does it say?"

"I don't know—something."

"You can't judge a person solely on who they like."

"What if they like Hitler?"

"Do you think that's the same thing?"

"No, I think she's worse."

"So, you don't want her to like Reina Hawthorne?"

"She can like her all she wants."

"But why do I got to like her?"

"Got in this huge fight once."

"Because I wouldn't go with her to one of Reina's top-ten places to have fun or something."

REINA HAWTHORNE'S ULTIMATE L.A. WEEKEND

She's more famous than God, and has more money too, but Reina Hawthorne says she just wants to be treated like everyone else.

Even though her parents raised her to be a star, they also raised her to see through all the BS too, she says.

"I'm not one of those stars that has to go to fancy restaurants and hang out in VIP rooms. In fact I like to do normal things like every other regular person in this city."

So, how does this superstar blow off steam after a mucho crazy week of performing, shooting, recording, and "just all around pulling my hair out!"?

"My schedule is vicious," she says, "and my tasks Herculean."

Herculean?

Remember, this young lady graduated summa cum laude from Stanford University with a double major in theater and classical studies, while managing to snag an Oscar and a Grammy to boot.

Herculean indeed.

So what is Reina's weekend prescription after a week of labor that would make the mighty Hercules himself collapse with utter exhaustion?

Well, here it is, exclusive to the *Times*.

Before she graced us with her list, she felt that it was necessary to provide us with this little caveat:

"These are some of the things I'll do if I'm not already working through the weekend, which I work through usually ninety percent of the time."

Geez.

So here's the list.

Drumroll please:

1. **Slaughterhouse Jive** – WeHo. "This is my Friday night mack-down. After a hard week of wrestling stones up hills, I am in definite need of some major carbs. So, I call a few of my favorite friends and we go to town! This is not for the faint of heart. Loud Jive music and sawdust on the floors. Humongo proportions all the way through. We order a huge slab of the Kansas City Ribs, extra spicy, and their house specialty, the Jive Turkey—deep-fried turkey in beer batter smothered with herbs and spices. For sides we get their signature Soul Slaw, collard greens, and jalapeño cornbread. All of it washed down with frothy glasses of the Jive's home-brewed beer. Delish!"

2. **Tiki-Typee** – Silver Lake. "After all that food, I like to continue the funky literary theme with a few well-mixed tropical concoctions. This is a small family-owned tiki bar with a laid-back clientele. The owner/bartender, Jerry, is an alchemist in every sense of the word. Order your drink and watch him go. Magic! And let me tell you, there are no foo-foo drinks here. Favorites: the Bob Shaw, Doctor Nemo, and of course, the Mocha Dick."

3. **Pink's Hot Dogs** – Hollywood. "This place has been here, like, forever. This is where we go for our little nightcap after all those crazy drinks. So many people come here after a night at the clubs and bars, but it's worth the wait in line. I know, I know, I ate all that BBQ at the Jive, but that was, like, five hours ago! The sushi dog just plain rocks!"

4. **Denny's** – Anywhere in L.A. "Okay, if I'm not totally hungover, then you can't beat Denny's for breakfast. C'mon, say it: Grand Slam Breakfast!"

5. **Horseback riding in Horseshoe Meadows** – Eastern Sierra near Lone Pine. "Okay, this is not in L.A., but a quick burst in my Eternity gets us there in a little under two hours, which is the amount of time it takes to get to some places in L.A.! I have a few horses corralled up there, and I'm always missing them! Ten thousand feet up and the air is pristine. Snow-capped peaks and glistening streams. Good for cleaning the lungs and the soul. All this a hop, skip, and a jump away from L.A.? Amazing! I take a nice lazy ride on my Arabian, Annabelle, and then it's back to Babylon for a night of partying."

6. **Pho Destroyer** – SaMo. "Owner/chef Vim Vang Tran is the Asian Picasso of cooking. Vietnamese mixed with Southwest mixed with everything else! Food not too heavy and perfect for a pre-dance club chow-down. Try everything!"

7. **Lee Ping House** – WeHo. "I came here every Friday and Saturday night for six months while researching my role for *Genuflect*, and I consider the girls that work here my sisters. So I come in, take a seat, and have a drink and try to catch up on old times with the girls that are still there, meet some new ones, and sign some autographs. Like my character in the movie, Claire, most of the girls that work there are trying to put themselves through college. Life is tough. You gotta do what you gotta do."

8. **Plutonian Shore** – DTLA. "My attitude for a Saturday night is this: dance first, ask questions later. I know the Shore is way swank and very VIP—not a good spot for dodging the popper-nazis—but this place is way too much! Highest club in L.A. with breathtaking 360 views—I'm queen of the world! Those Ravens that fly around are brilliant too, don't know how they do it. The decor is Haunted Rococo, which isn't seen a lot here on the West Coast. And what the heck kind of booze do they put in the Nepenthe anyways? Order one up and try to figure it out. Also, try some Purple Oysters on the Half Shell for a bar snack, and then dance the night away to the world-famous beats."

9. **Pacific Embuffment Center** – Malibu. "After a weekend of excess, this palace of wisdom is just what the doctor ordered. A tranquil garden setting by the sea, this place is pure heaven, and the angels that work there take care of your mind, body, and spirit, plus a few other things that I didn't even know I had! I get

the Pacific Tune-Up, which includes a yummy lava rock massage, yoga, qi gong, meditation, a seaweed wrap, a detox facial, a manicure, and shadow work. Yikes! Top it off with some excellent fresh organic fruit and vegetable juices, and it's Namaste all the way! Not cheap, but definitely worth it."

10. **SleazeBurger** – Hollywood. "Okay, I know it's a sin—I just detoxed all day! But these burgers are to die for. I think I deserve it. Besides, after eating here you can skip dinner. Favorite burger (not recommended for the faint of heart): the Sleaze Burger. I get it with turkey instead of beef, and on a spelt bun—hey, I'm still working off those ribs from the Jive! Topped with aged white cheddar, crunchy house pickles, onions, and the world's deadliest pepper, the Vampire Chili, all lustily smothered in their famous Money Sauce. If it sounds painful, it is, but considering my crazy weekend, the perfect capper!"

"I Love L.A.!"

Thanks, Reina.

Reina Hawthorne once said that she was living the American Dream.

Problem is the ones living the dream are a living nightmare for everyone else.

"Have you had many fights over Reina Hawthorne?"

"No, not really."

"Only when she spends too much time on her LifeCast."

"You said you wouldn't go with your wife to her new movie."

"Have you ever gone with her to see a Reina Hawthorne movie?"

"No, but I watched one with her on TV once."

"Which one?"

"I don't know."

"Well, maybe you should go with her to the new one."

"If I told her I wanted to go with her she'd get suspicious."

"Why?"

"Why? Because she knows how much I Hate the bitch."

"Well, whether you Hate her or not, *Genuflect* is an excellent movie. I recommend seeing it."

"She got the Oscar for it you know."

"Here we go. Am I the only one in this city that can't stand her?"

"Look, the issue isn't about Reina Hawthorne."

"It's about you taking an interest in what your wife is interested in."

"So call her up and invite her to that movie."

"What did I just—"

"And tell her you want to see it because she wants to see it."

"She saw it already."

"Well, ask her anyway. It's the thought that counts."

"Seriously?"

"Yes, seriously."

"That's all you got?"

"Just try, okay?"

"It's too late for that. She'll just think I'm trying to save my ass."

"Well, aren't you?"

"Yeah, I guess."

"Okay, good. You do that, call her up, and next week you can tell me all about it."

"Next week?"

"Yes, same time."

"I thought that this was a one-shot deal."

"It will just be a follow-up, to see how you're doing."

"Yeah?"

"Yes. Now, one last question. Don't answer now, but I want you to think about it until our next session."

"What?"

"Why do you call yourself a Nigger?"

BUILT FOR MURDER

Built for Murder blasted me out of sleep.

A deep, lugubrious dip into a pool of black molasses.

Head throbbing.

Eyes filled with blood.

The pain is not in here.

It is outside.

Murder pumping out of a Dream Machine in the number three.

So Put your Hands into fists and get your guns loaded.
Cuz it's Time to get this MotherFuckin city exploded.

The blood is not blood.

But a giant can of Coke.

It covers a downtown building.

Pouring brown cola words onto the traffic below:

Better with Coke

The words dissolve with a fizz.

The can fades out.

Traffic is dark.

A few seconds.

Che Guevara now.

Brown and white against a red background.

Cola words pour across his face:

The Revolution Will Not Go

Mars's voice:

"*Come* in, head."

Lift my head.

Meghasin.

Looking straight at me.

"How long did I sleep?"

"I tried to wake you, Officer Krieg. So did PAL. But you wouldn't."

Sit up.

"Thank Killio."

"Yeah," she said. "PAL, can you cancel it?"

A change of pressure and the music cuts out.

"God should've made us with earlids."

Stretching.

"Don't like Killio?"

"It's abrasive."

I like Killio.

Have *Built for Murder* and *Third World County* on vinyl.

Vinyl.

"Damn interrogation."

"What time did the chariot arrive at your house?"

"At nine o'clock, Officer Krieg."

"Late for me, on time for you."

"Think the car likes you better."

"Excuse me, Officer Krieg, but may I ask you something?"

"Shoot."

"Could you please—"

"Wait, we allowed to say *shoot?*"

"I . . . I think—"

"Hold up."

"PAL, we allowed to say *shoot?*"

"What am I saying?"

"If I wasn't it would have warned me by now, right?"

"That depends on the context, Officer Krieg," PAL said. *"You can say* shoot *if it refers—"*

"Forget it, PAL hole."

"You were saying?"

"I—"

"Sorry bout interrupting you and all that."

"It's just that I've got to do things by the book now or else it's my ass."

"Shit, sorry, my mistake."

"I'm not supposed to say shit like that . . . right, PAL?"

"Excessive and unnecessary use of profanity is prohibited by the Department and may result in a penalty point and/or punitive action, Officer Krieg."

"See?"

"Sorry, you were saying?"

"Well, I wanted to ask. Could you please not be asleep when the car arrives to pick me up?"

"I had a hard time trying to move your legs from my seat."

"What if my legs are on my side?"

"Well, you were snoring too . . . but, besides that, I think it's against policy for you to—"

"Yeah, sorry bout that."

"I shouldn't be doin shit like that anymore."

"Oh, by the way, I'm going to cut out all the Christian shit too."

"Pardon?"

"Excessive and unnecessary use of profanity is prohibited by the Department and may result in a penalty point and/or punitive action, Officer Krieg."

"What I'm tryin to say is that—"

"I'm sorry, but can you please change the vehicle's voice setting, Officer Krieg?"

"I couldn't do it while you were asleep, and it's really bothering me."

"Besides, I don't think that voice is allowed."

"Yeah, I don't know who put it on that . . . Mars used to—"

"Can we change it?"

"Don't like Vader, huh?"

"It's not that I don't like . . . I just don't think we're allowed to—"

"Where you on the whole Vader/Obi-Wan deal?"

"What?"

"Guess if we're going to be partners we should know where we stand on the whole issue."

"Kind of like if you're a cat person or a dog person."

"I'm a rat person by the way—haha."

"I . . . I don't understand what you're—"

"C'mon, you know, people were killing themselves over this sh—stuff."

"Sorry, I'm not—"

"Read somewhere that the reason Disney changed the whole story was because terrorists were equating themselves with the Rebel Alliance."

"And the U.S. with the Empire."*

"What are you—"

"Used to think that it was wrong."

"But now, why not?"

"People can't be all good or all evil."

"Fact that Vader was really trying to unite the dark side with the light side."

"And that Obi-Wan was this force fundamentalist is a—"

"I didn't see those movies."

"What?"

"I haven't seen any of those movies."

"Really?"

"Yes."

---

*   Source unknown; however, former Disney CEO and Secretary of Defense James Starkweather stated in an interview with U.S. Affairs (January 2052) that the decision to portray Darth Vader in a "gentler light" in Episodes 19–21 was to counteract the increasing "usurpation" of the Rebel Alliance and its Starbird symbol by various "radical and terrorist organizations" as being symbolically representative of their causes against a United States that was seen to be "almost literally" associated with the Empire. —I. H.

"You one of those purists?"

"What?"

"You know, the ones who refuse to see any of the movies outside the original three."

"I haven't seen any of the *Star Wars* movies, Officer Krieg."

"What?"

"I know who Darth Vader is, but—"

"You never seen *Star Wars?*"

"No."

"Really?"

"Yes."

"*Empire Strikes Back?*"

"Is that . . . no, I haven't seen any of them."

"'Luke, I'm your father'?"

"What?"

"You do know that Darth Vader is Luke's father, right?"

"I don't know. I just haven't . . . it's not my—"

"Jesus."

"Sorry, I mean *jeeez.*"

"Why not?"

"This is history we're talking about here."

"It's a movie, Officer Krieg. I don't think I have to—"

"Movies."

"They're movies."

"Twenty-one of them."

"Well, three if you're one of those—"

"I'm sorry, but I haven't seen them."

"Why not?"

"I . . . I don't know. I'm not into science fiction, really. I—"

"You're like the opposite of Mars."

"He was huge into *Star Wars*."

"First thing he'd do as soon as he got in this car'd be to slap on the *Return of the Force* game."

"Never got to finish it, though."

"Department banned us from—"

"PAL, why were we banished from playing *Return of the Force*?"

"Per section code one four six point five, various types of media including video games, television shows, and movies will be prohibited per section code four five one in accordance with section double zero one."

"What's double zero one?"

"All Officers are prohibited from consuming information sources that do not provide the Minimum Recommended Daily allowance for optimal brain functioning."

"Optimal brain functioning?"

"Optimal brain functioning as set by the National Institute of Mental Health consists of three basic—"

"Okay, you can shut the Fuck up now."

"Excessive and unnecessary use of profanity is prohibited by the Department and may result in a penalty point and/or punitive action, Officer Krieg."

"Officer Krieg, can we please return PAL's voice to the original setting?"

"I tried, but it wouldn't change. Did you try?"

"Yes, but it said '451 Blocked,' and when I asked why, it said '451 Blocked.'"

"Dude's cock-blockin."

"Excessive and unnecessary use of profanity is prohibited by the Department and may result in a penalty point and/or punitive action, Officer Krieg."

"C'mon PAL, cock-blockin?"

"Excessive and unnecessary use of profanity is prohibited by the Department and has resulted in another penalty point, Officer Krieg."

Eight points now.

"Fuck it, I'm calling this in."

"This vehicle is obviously malfunctioning."

"I am not malfunctioning, Officer Krieg. And may I remind you that excessive and unnecessary use of profanity is prohibited by the Department and may result in a penalty point and/or punitive action."

"Uh, yes, you are, and if you remind me one more time I'm going to—"

"My diagnostics detect no malfunction."

"Really?"

"Maybe that's because you're malfunctioning."

"I am not malfunctioning."

"Fuck you, you are malfunctioning."

"Excessive and unnecessary use of profanity is prohibited by the Department and may result in a penalty point and/or punitive action, Officer Krieg."

"See, you are malfunctioning."

"That profanity was definitely necessary."

"Put us through to Network Control."

"Connecting to Network Control . . . Current line is . . . busy. Please hold."

"Yeah, right."

Meghasin put her earphones on and pulled out a pad.

Did this shit every shift.

Like she didn't want to talk to me.

Made me feel guilty for some reason.

"What you looking at?"

"Hmm?"

"What you readin?"

She looked up for a second like she had to think about it.

"The *LA Times*—from a hundred years ago?"

"A hundred years ago?"

"Yeah, it's this site—you can read a copy of the paper from a hundred years ago today."

"Yeah?"

"Yeah."

"What's it say about today?"

"Well . . . there's this one article—"

Network Control came on the line and asked what the deal was.

"Vehicle's voice is stuck on Darth Vader."

"Darth Vader?"

"Yeah, Darth Vader, you know who that is?"

"I know who Darth Vader is."

"Who does his voice then."

"What?"

"Who does Vader's voice?"

"I don't know, some black guy, right?"

"Some black guy—it's James Earl Ray, Mother—"

"How did you get it on Vader? That voice is—"

"I didn't put it on Vader."

"It was like this when I got in."

"Really?"

"Yeah, really."

"Hmmmm," he said.

Looking offscreen.

"Let's see."

"Says here the vehicle's voice is set on default. You sure it's Vader?"

"Yeah, I'm sure it's Vader—can't you hear it breathing?"

"Okay," he said. "PAL, what is the current time?"

"The current time is nine thirty-two and twenty-one seconds."

"See?"

"Wow. That's pretty good. How'd you get it to do that? Voice is banned."

"Banned?"

"Yeah, blocked."

"Since when?"

"Since a few weeks."

"Copyright infringement or something."

"Department's gonna bust you if they find out."

"Look, I just told you."

"I didn't put it on—it was this way when I got in tonight."

"Yeah, well, if you did, they'd probably put you on probation and report you for pirating copyrighted material."

"I'm already on probation."

"Yeah, *right*. You're the one that took that tire iron to—"

"Look, can you fix it or not?"

"Hold on."

He looked offscreen again.

"No."

"What do you mean, no?"

"Can't tell what the problem is."

"Have to run a diagnostic and get back to you."

"Well, how long is that—"

He cut out.

"God Fuckin dammit."

"Excessive and unnecessary use of profanity is prohibited by the Department and may result in another penalty point and/or punitive action, Officer Krieg."

"Will you shut up already?"

"Jeez."

"Like kicking a guy when he's down."

Meghasin sighed.

"Tell you something."

"You can't trust that dude."

"Pretty sure he ratted on me and Mars once."

"Ever tell you about how we used to bumper-stick?"

Still reading:

"Ummm, yes, I think you—"

"Used to be these two jerk-offs—Clinton Kent and Finn Sickler."

"You already heard about Kent."

"Sickler's in TeRF now, which I don't—"

"Anyway."

"So this one time Mars went and put this sticker on their ride that said:"

"I don't have a license to kill."

"I have a learner's permit."

"I think you told me this already."

"Yeah, well, Sickler."

"I told you about Sickler, right?"

"Uh—"

"Went to the brass and reported it."

"And the brass freaked."

"Said that bumper sticker was tantamount to a breach of Department security."

"And in no time flat we were suspended."

"Two weeks."

"And the only one that knew we did it was—"

"Yes, you told me this story already, Officer Krieg."

"After that, bumper-sticking was banned on penalty of termination."

"Can you believe that?"

"Yes, I—"

"Can't believe that bastard Sickler got in and not me."

"You interested in TeRF?"

"Well, I—"

"At least they get to cruise around in a real vehicle."

There's a high amount of competition to get into TeRF.

Especially in Law Enforcement.

Probably because you don't have to deal with things like a suspect's rights or paperwork.

All that habeas corpus due process shit.

All you gotta do is Point and Click.

Before Point and Click TeRF used to literally go out and tag gang members.

Like animals in the wild.

Monitor them.

Until someone figured out that just shooting them would be more cost effective.

Don't get me wrong.

I'm not against gangs.

Of course.

Being an average citizen.

I could see from the perspective of your average citizen.

Why you would want to get rid of these.

Thugs.

But I could also see it from the thug's perspective.

Growing up in this city.

With no Soul.

Fact is.

This city.

This society.

Doesn't have what it takes.

To channel all the murderous energy coursing through a young man's boiling veins.

Or, to put it more scientifically.

Provide an outlet for the "Warrior gene."

In fact the only choices they have are between one form of degradation or another.

School.

Work.

Crime.

Addiction.

Marriage.

Religion.

Hell, those aren't even choices.

More like types of suicide.

Or assaults.

Attacks.

Goddamned camisadoes.

Hatred of youth disguised under the phony mask of responsibility.

The so-called work ethic:

Arbeit Macht Frei.

You want fries with that?

No? Well.

A man's gotta eat.

And we eat men.

Civilized men.

Oui?

Mouth closed and slow-like.

A bite here.

Chew there.

Before we consume you.

Digest you.

Shit you.

Reason why eating disorders are so big in this country.

It's our theme.

Our program.

Our goddamned National Anthem.

O, say can you eeeeat!

So these kids.

Their violence is a defense.

A counter.

Against these assaults that would grind them down.

Crush them.

Into safe citizens.

Consumers.

The Working Dead.

No.

The only way for them to function in this society is to attack it.

Declare war on it.

Not by getting good grades.

Becoming an employee.

Votin for Nixon.*

Part of the reason I joined a gang.

Not to be a gangster.

But to wage war.

And if history taught me one thing:

There's nothing more American than war.

---

*   Slang for masturbation (*obs.*).

It's what we do best.

Kicking the shit out of the rest of the world.

Talkin shit and carrying a big stick.

Is what made this country great.

Despite what all the losers say.

The ones who got their asses kicked.

The ones who want us to feel guilty.

For kicking their asses.

For being winners.

Even the Niggers.

We shouldn't complain.

The fact is:

We lost, MotherFucker.

If we had won.

The whites would be our slaves.

And if you don't like it.

Don't whine about your rights.

Or not getting respect.

Rise up and kick the shit out of them.

I am for violence.

If nonviolence means we continue postponing a solution to the American black man's problem.

Just to avoid violence.

Which is what we did.

Which is why we're called African-Americans now.

In other words—*losers*.

AFRICAN, n. A nigger that votes our way.

Under conditions of peace the warlike man attacks himself.

And that's what the Niggers been doing for the past one hundred years.

Attacking ourselves.

And are gangs really the problem?

I mean, look at all those old tribal cultures and societies.

They knew how to turn those boys into men.

Not like today.

With our childrenized man-dudes.

Our Frat Men and Little Boys.

Our Manless men.

No.

Those cultures took those young men.

And beat the shit out of them.

Made them warriors.

Anyways.

The gang problem has been reduced significantly ever since the formation of TeRF.

Because let's face it:

Some of these kids really are monsters.

"What kind of music you listening to?"

She didn't answer.

So I had to tap her.

"What kind of music you listening to?"

She looked up and pulled out her earphones.

"I'm not listening to music."

"Trying to block out sound or something?"

"No, it's ASMR."

"What?"

"Autonomous sensory meridian response."

"What?"

"It's hard to explain. Like relaxing sounds."

"Wait—I heard of this—isn't that that thing people jack off to?"

"What?"

"Yeah, like this chick whispering in your ear to get you off."

"No, it's nothing like that."

"Let me hear it."

"Uh, I'd prefer it if you'd—"

"Hey, I just thought of something."

"Maybe the reason we can't change PAL's voice is that Vader *is* the new voice."

"Think about it."

"The way they're turning this whole Department into some kind of—"

"*Subtraction pending,*" PAL said.

Please Stand By.

The words flashing on-screen.

Beeping like a muffled horn.

Or an error message.

Lock and Load.

Meghasin sighed.

An Eternity USV.

Hundred yards downstream.

In the luxury lane.

"What?"

"Here?"

"On the freeway?"

It wasn't common to do a subtraction while the person was actually in their car.

In fact I can't remember the last time I ever did one.

"My calculations indicate that you'll need to approach manually," PAL said.

"Manually?"

"By walking, Officer Krieg."

"Walking?"

"That is correct, Officer Krieg."

"You mean, get out and walk over there?"

"Yes, that is correct."

"Why can't you just drive us up there?"

"According to my calculations, the time that it would take for me to maneuver into position will negate the window for subtraction. You can arrive at your assigned destination on foot in less than thirty seconds if you proceed immediately."

The target was a woman, blonde, midthirties.

Attractive.

Meghasin unhitched her belt.

"I'll go," I say.

"Both Officers are required to be present for every subtraction," she said.

"PAL, do we both gotta go?"

"Under section seven nine four point two five, in the event of a highway subtraction, the backup Officer is required to stay with the vehicle at all times."

"You're the backup," I say.

I get out and walk downstream.

Down the cellblock of cars.

Beamers, beaters, chinkers, shit-rockets.

Sedans, pedans, chester vans, minivans.

Jew boats.

Trucks, pucks, compacts, subcompacts, micros, and nats.

Smog roaches and Beaner Wagons.

Urban Support Vehicles.

Sport-Utility Vehicles.

Not a PAL in sight.

Pull out last year's Christmas gift from Claire:

A pair of NightShades.

Put them on and look down the line of cars for the twenty.

Green arrow bobs up and down midair over a car about fifty yards up ahead.

Can't stand browsers.

All those Fuckin pop-ups.

Snake Oil®—Update your Cock!

Not to mention all those browser-wrapped Strutt-Fucks.

Technopaths.

Strollin through their cartoons.

Vague-walkin.

Oblivious.

Easy to kill because they're self-contained.

Strutt-Fucks.

I put the glasses away and approach the target.

A brand-new Eternity.

Silver.

No plates.

Dealer in Manhattan Beach.

Usually the people we zeroed didn't drive such nice cars.

Hazards on.

Car behind beeping.

A Nissan Envy.

Go over and tap the driver's-side glass.

Driver won't lower the window.

Middle-aged Asian woman.

Looks scared.

Stops beeping.

Still.

Try the door but it's locked.

Punch the universal for the Envy and open the door.

"Back of the bus."

I pull her out, pop the trunk, and throw her in.

Someone yells hey.

They always do.

I walk over to the Eternity.

I try the shotgun door and it's locked.

I punch the universal on my PDT and unlock it.

I open the door and get in.

There's the blonde woman.

Expensive looking.

Hair.

Clothes.

Even her skin.

All of it high-end.

Not our usual clientele.

Her eyes are closed.

Strong smell of perfume.

The kind Claire wears.

The seat adjusts itself to me and starts a little massage.

She opens her eyes and looks at me.

Pissed and scared at the same time.

Her mouth opens.

A woman's soothing voice on the stereo:

"Close your eyes and take a deep breath."

"Yes," I say.

Pull the BDG* and zero her.

Her head doesn't fall forward like I assume.

Just stays where it is.

Mouth still open.

Looking right at me.

I look away from her and sit back.

The sound of running water and the smell of trees.

"Now slowly release your breath."

---

*   Black Death Gun.

Wet green plants just after a rain.

"Feel the toxins being released from your body."

A brook gently gurgling somewhere in the vicinity of the back seat.

"Feel the release."

Leaves rustling.

"Feel."

The smell of pine needles.

And her.

"Take another breath."

I light a cigarette and close my eyes.

The smoke warning goes off and I kill it.

"Now slowly—"

Kill the stereo.

After a few drags I open my eyes and look at her sitting there.

Not moving.

Not blinking.

Eyes wide.

Arms at her side.

Looking at me.

I move her head.

To where it looks like she's looking at her odometer.

Or speedometer.

Her fuel level.

Looked like she exercised regularly.

Ate right.

Probably didn't like smokers.

I blew a cloud over at her.

Nothing.

A faint low vibration.

Not the seat.

Satori Dial.

I cranked it all the way up until the vehicle hummed.

I dimmed the windows to Outer Space black.

Another button, and a misty forest rose where the traffic had been.

Trees through all the windows.

We sat there saying nothing for a few minutes.

Enjoying the forest together.

I imagined that if I said something she would listen.

"Claire left me."

"Yeah, I know, I know. I can't believe it myself."

"I don't know, she won't tell me."

"That's what she says, but I really don't know."

"Why can't you guys just come out and say it straight?"

"What?"

"What do I do?"

"I work for the Department of Decongestion."

"Yeah, sure, I guess."

"Get to meet beautiful women like you."

Vader.

Made me jump.

"What is your status, Officer Krieg?" PAL said.

"Single."

"I do not comprehend that reply."

"I'm calling for a lift."

I popped open the glove box, and then closed it.

"Copy that, Officer Krieg. Please return to the vehicle as soon as the lift is complete."

"Copy."

I turn to her again.

Wasn't a lot of time before her skin would turn black.

"Sorry about that."

"Just my vehicle."

"Yeah, it's a total asshole."

"Claire?"

"Yeah, me and Claire got along fine."

"Well, fine enough."

"I can't think of—"

My body was beginning to tingle.

The hairs on my neck stood up.

I almost felt relaxed.

Why couldn't the Department put a Satori system in our vehicle?

Instead of another slogan:

Don't zone out—Zen out!

Yeah.

I open her purse and pull her wallet.

Lives in Santa Monica.

Works for some pedestrian rights group.

Something not right.

Put the wallet in my coat pocket.

"Excuse me for a sec, I gotta make a call."

I call into Central for a high five, a quick lift.

Five to ten, they say.

Then to her:

"I got to go."

"It was nice talking to you."

"You kind of remind of my wife."

"Yeah, you both wear the same perfume."

"That Reina Hawthorne one."

"You like Reina Hawthorne?"

I crush the smoke out on the floor.

"Too bad."

The birds are still chirping and the leaves are still rustling.

Somewhere nearby a small brook winds its way through a meadow.

The sound of flapping wings.

I lean over her and hit the button and recline her seat until the seat can go back no further.

Almost horizontal now.

Her eyes look at something I can't see.

Far away.

Or maybe something up close.

Either way it doesn't matter.

I pull at the top button of her blouse and it opens smoothly.

A splotch of black appears at the nape of her neck.

And starts to spread like spilled ink.

TIME OF THE ASSASSINS

Moral Justifications: *(Not necessary, but strategically viable)*
- Preemption (Anticipatory Self-Defense)
- Utilitarianism
- Post-Humanism
- Sunyata

In less than ten the Condor is chopping above and throwing down blue-white light.

Driver's-side window.

She is sitting up again.

Same expression.

All blacked up and no place to go.

I tap on the glass for a goodbye as the disk descends and clanks onto the roof.

A pause and the car is lifted.

It rises up and out of traffic.

Groaning metal.

Horns going off like crazy.

A motor-cheer.

To the end of this obstruction.

Or that they too would soon be raptured out of this snarly horde.

PDT buzzes.

"This is Con-Six. What's the dest?"

"What do you mean?"

"What do you mean, what do I mean?"

"What are you saying?"

"Where am I haulin this lump?"

"You're supposed to get that from Central."

"Central's down. Call it."

"Down?"

"Call it, bud. Before it's Christmas."

"FF5."

Code for an ocean drop.

A deep six.

"You sure bout that? Looks like a nice set. Any ass inside?"

"Why the Fuck you asking me to call it then?"

"I'm just the transpo."

"Then sink it."

"You sure?"

"Yes, I'm sure."

"Ten-whore."

"What?"

"Bon Voyage, MotherFucker."

Fuckin Rakers.

Odds are he won't sink it.

Take it somewhere and strip it.

Her too.

Then sink what's left.

Never knew where they took the bodies.

For all I knew they were grinding them up for tofu.

I go over and pop the trunk on the Envy and release the Asian woman.

She is crying.

Saying things not English.

I guide her back to the driver's seat.

Hold her head and push her in and foot the door closed.

Even with the Eternity out of the way the traffic still wasn't moving.

No surprise.

Like all American wars the War on Traffic* was a zero-sum game.

It would never end.

And we would never win.

And I would never be out of a job.

I walked back to PAL.

Meghasin still reading.

"I gotta make a call," I say.

"Mind if I put on Rome?"

"That's fine," she said.

---

*   Whose official motto still is (as trademarked by the National Highway
     Traffic Safety Administration): "Get America Moving Again!"

I told PAL to put on Rome and called Anita.

This whole thing stunk.

The woman.

The Eternity USV.

Brand-new and broken down.

Right.

Smelled like a remote shutdown.

Like bullshit.

Like the subtraction had been.

Something to do with that pedestrian rights group or something.

Anita wasn't answering.

I pulled the stats on the woman.

Name: Clarisse McNaughton

Age: 32

Nothing else.

No address.

No place of employment.

No nothing.

Right there.

They just gave it away.

No reason they shouldn't have the info.

Plus the fact the Rakers hadn't been notified by Central.

Gotta look her up.

But not here.

Don't want them to trace it.

I looked out the window.

Rome was covered in sun.

We drove down narrow streets.

People waved.

There was no traffic.

I imagined me and Claire out there in the sun.

She had always wanted to go to Italy.

But couldn't get her passport renewed.

Because of the money she owed for Insatia.

Not long after I got Insatia leveled up she almost killed a guy.

They would've thrown the book at her if the dude hadn't been jaywalking.

Instead she got sentenced to eighteen months in a frontier camp.

One of those primitive prisons where you had to live like one of those pioneer pilgrims from a couple hundred years ago.

No phones, computers, coffee makers, or microwaves.

Not even toilets.

No nothing.

Churn your own butter and shit like that.

On top of that the guy she hit sued.

And won.

Over a hundred grand that Claire had to pay because Insatia was a minor.

Claire's parents paid half.

And I paid half of Claire's half, which she hadn't finished paying.

And now it's been over a year since Insatia got out and Claire still hasn't heard a word from her.

Not a word from Meghasin either.

Sitting there reading.

"You ever been to a frontier camp?"

"What?"

"A frontier camp."

"You ever been to one?"

"Is that one of those—"

"Shit should be made mandatory for all teenagers."

"Like military service in some of those foreign countries."

She looked up from her book:

"Yes, kids have too much of a sense of entitlement these days."

"They should probably—"

"Better a sense of entitlement than a sense of enslavement."

"But you just said you want to put them in a camp."

"What's wrong with camp?"

"A concentration camp?"

"Look, if anything, a kid should have enough sense to overthrow this country if necessary."

"Not whine about how there are no jobs."

"Who the hell wants a job anyways?"

"You think this country should be overthrown?"

"Well, I . . ."

She wasn't going to get me to admit to something like that.

Not while we were being monitored.

"Well, what?"

"Forget it."

"You know," she said.

"It's these spoiled brat kids that say things like that."

"Overthrow the country because they can't afford a Dream Machine."

"Or name-brand browsers."

"Kids who don't know what it's like to struggle or starve."

She was doing it for the benefit of the car.

Trying to make me look bad.

Like some kind of.

She wasn't gonna win this.

No way.

"No," I say.

"A lot of these kids *are* really struggling."

"Like in that Reina Hawthorne movie."

"Where she has to work at a blowshop just to pay for college."

"Reina is Queeeen," she said in a mocking tone.

"You don't like Reina Hawthorne?"

"Can't stand her."

"Shit, we might make a good team yet."

"Excessive and unnecessary use of profanity is prohibited by the Department and may result in a penalty point and/or punitive action, Officer Krieg."

Corner of La Salle and 27th.

Just south of Adams.

Out of our boundary.

We had the Mid-City patrol.

Mid-Shitty.

"Why we out of bounds, PAL?"

"I do not understand, Officer Krieg. Please clarify."

"We're not in Mid-City, are we?"

"Technically no, just slightly east of your designated patrol area, Officer Krieg."

"Why?"

"To assist with the West Adams quota."

"I don't follow."

"You do not follow what, Officer Krieg?"

"Why do we gotta assist with the quota?"

"451 Blocked, Officer Krieg."

"Seriously?"

"Yes, Officer Krieg."

"So, what's the ZO?"

"Target is located at number two-eight-one—"

"Not where it is—who?"

"Single female aged eighty-three. Subject is on-screen."

"What?"

"Another old lady?"

"Yes, that is correct, Officer Krieg. You have approximately three minutes and thirty-three seconds."

"To complete the subtraction or write a top-ten single?"

"I do not understand the question, Officer Krieg."

"We should go," Meghasin said.

"PAL," I say.

"Why don't you just drive your ass up there and run her down?"

"Be sure to honk first."

"I cannot process that request, Officer Krieg."

"Please, Officer Krieg," Meghasin said.

"Yeah, yeah."

An old Craftsman that hadn't been gentrified or gentefied.

Like the rest of the houses on the street.

Dead lawn with dead weeds.

An old Buick from the last century parked in the driveway at a slight angle.

Driver's door slightly open.

Or not fully closed.

Next door a dark green freshly cut lawn with sprinklers tsking.

Meghasin waiting for me.

"Look," I say.

"We got some shit."

"What?"

"That lady they had me do on the freeway."

"Subtract."

"What?"

"The lady you subtracted."

"You serious?"

"What?"

"Correcting me like that."

"Well, what about her?"

"Forget it."

Can't trust a bitch like that.

Tryin to tell her something important and she's gotta correct your grammar.

Wipe a stain off your face.

Forget it.

"No, what is it?"

"Ladies first," I say, extending a hand.

She gives me a look.

A by-the-book look.

You're supposed to be on point.

Had to do everything by the book.

Mars never did anything by the book.

Smokin kill on the clock.

"Dude, seriously. I'm a true Hash-assin."

Chongwear and chop-flops.

"Got a prescription, man."

"Sartorial therapy."

"If I dress business casual I'm liable to get sick."

Back in the day when it was California Business Casual.

Now:

> *All Officers are required to dress in a Noir or Neo-Noir fashion,
> which for males will consist of a single- or double-breasted suit in
> either beige, brown, gray, or dark blue, plain or pinstripe, but no
> bright colors.*
>
> *Vests or waistcoats are permitted and encouraged. A tie, with either
> a simple or Windsor knot, whose width shall not exceed four inches
> and whose color shall match or complement the suit, shall be worn at
> all times.*
>
> *Themed, novelty, paisley, and polka-dot ties are strictly prohibited,
> as are clip-on ties. Hats are encouraged but not required, and can be
> of the fedora, homburg, or trilby style, or any similar variety that
> matches or complements the color of the suit. Suspenders and watch
> chain are optional.*

Dress shoes are required, and boots are permitted, color to match or complement the suit, and no bright colors.

Zoot suits are also permitted, but must pass inspection by your commanding Officer.

A Zoot.

What he was wearing when the Leviathan creamed him.

Assholes wouldn't let him wear his clothes.

Same with the weed.

Wouldn't accept his prescription.

Disney rules.[*]

That's what killed him.

Courtesy of the new management.

BlackGuard International.

Made us go to this "Advance."

Park Plaza Hotel.

Where they introduced us to the new MicroStuff "PAL."

It took us for a ride around MacArthur Park.[†]

Two at a time.

Thing wouldn't shut up.

Telling us all the shit it would do for us.

Even knew our names.

I told it to Fuck off.

Apparently everyone else did too.

---

[*] Coincidentally the Walt Disney Company owned a 12 percent share in BlackGuard prior to their divestiture in June 2039—less than a week before the second 6/16 attack.

[†] Westlake Park—reverted back to its original name (1890–1942) in 2042.

They couldn't figure why none of us liked it.

Especially the new Commissioner:

Barbara Trimmer.

"What's the matter with you?" she said.

"No one likes driving in this city—*no one.*"

"Are you saying that you *do* like driving now?"

No one said anything.

I did.

I'd had enough of this shit.

Like everything that starts off free and good.

There's always some dictator who has to come in and Fuck it up.

Tighten the screws.

And demand that you smile while they're doin it.

So I said to this sado-fasciscist:

This aluminum tube:

"Hey, didn't you say something about wanting self-driven team players or something?"

"Yes," she said. "I did."

"Well, how can we be self-driven if we can't even drive?"

That got a few laughs actually.

"You know what the term is for people who can't tell the difference," she said.

"Between the literal and the metaphorical?"

"Not offhand, no."

"Developmentally arrested."

Okay.

I get it.

She wants to play it like that.

Let her.

I told her the Department wasn't putting us in these cars for our benefit.

But was doing it to control us.

Hence:

Losing control of the means of subtraction.

Meaning driving.

Means losing control of our jobs.

Which:

Would decrease morale.

Meaning:

Our job performance would decline.

Because:

We would be less *self-driven* to do it.

Besides:

I think the real question here is not whether we like driving or not.

But:

Would we rather drive a pimp-mobile.

Or be driven around in a talking pimple?

"Officer Krieg, right?"

"Yeah."

"Weren't you suspended for reckless operation of a Department-issue vehicle last year?"

"Me too," Mars said. "So was I."

Which got a few laughs.

"It wasn't a suspension," I said.

"It was a dispute over—"

Last year me and Mars had been involved in a dispute with the Department.

Over the interpretation of reasonable v. excessive force in the operation of our vehicle.

And what constituted reasonable force.

Reasonable force could be legitimately used:

To further expedite the transportation of Officers to the site of subtraction.

And further, within limits, to enforce existing traffic code.

I was the designated driver of our assigned vehicle.

A Ford Fueltility.

And as the designated driver it was my responsibility.

To make on-the-spot decisions regarding the use of force.

Like this:

Let's say you were in front of us at a traffic light.

And the light turned green.

And it took you longer than three seconds to start moving.

I would ram you.

The Fueltility was equipped with some pretty heavy dual grudge bumpers.

Which could just about push a tank out of the way.

So.

If you were driving too slow I would ram you.

You weren't edging out far enough to make a left turn—ram.

Sticking too far out in the street to make a turn from a driveway—ram.

Taking too long to get into the left-turn lane—ram.

You drove any kind of vehicle I didn't like—ram.

Your stereo was pumping too loud—ram.

You cut me off—ram.

You were from out of state—ram.

Your kid was an honor student—ram.

Like a Zen master.

Who whacks their students with a stick.

To wake them up.

Or a Bwiti Shaman.

Nganga.

Breaking open heads.

To make them see.

Better yet.

I was a goddamned Jedi Knight.

Using the Force.

To educate and instruct.

And smack down anyone who chose to drive on the dark side.

Not a day went by when we weren't ramming.

Or running someone down.

But pedestrians are another story.

And one that's worth talking about.

But not now.

Still.

They accused me of being "overzealous" with the use of force.

Overzealous.

I've never been zealous about anything.

Let alone overzealous.

Either way.

The case ended up being shelved when BlackGuard took over.

And put us in these Fuckin PALs.

Anyways.

The rest of the Advance consisted of us sitting in the hotel conference room.

Trimmer's face King Kong'd on a giant screen.

Telling us what the new rules were going to be.

And how she was going to:

"Actualize her vision for the DoD."

Accompanied by slides.

With bullet points:

• Death Enforcement is not a "License to Kill."

Like we thought we were James Bond or something.

No.

With him that license meant something.

Special.

Unique.

Now that the killing has been taken out of killing.

It means nothing.

Besides.

In Los Angeles.

A license to drive is pretty much the same thing.

So.

That bullet point was pretty much representative.

Of the kind of crap they were shelling out during this whole Advance.

Speaking of crap.

The food.

Even if I hadn't listened to one damn word.

I could've told you where the wind was blowing just by the food.

First they gave us a continental breakfast instead of a real breakfast.

They shouldn't even call a breakfast like that—mostly muffins and fruit—continental.

Continental sounds like something big.

It sounds like you're going to get a lot of food.

They should call it a bird breakfast instead.

And then a lunch, which was a buffet kind of serve-yourself thing.

With some pretty bland chicken and/or fish.

A Caesar salad with not enough Caesar.

Some whole-grain rice with nuts in it.

And a bland-looking vegetable medley that I didn't even touch.

Even though none of the food was that good.

It was swooped upon and vultured.

We all felt that at least we should get our so-called money's worth if we were going to have to put up with this bullshit:

"We've got to stop thinking outside the box."

"Because outside is the new inside."

"And inside is the new outside."

Yeah.

According to her we hadn't been really fighting the War on Traffic.

But *merely* defending ourselves against Critical Density.

As if Critical Density was a mere thing.

Critical Density in traffic engineering was like Einstein's Theory of Relativity in physics.

Except that it referred to traffic.

And not a black hole.

But.

It was like a black hole.

Because it referred to the point.

Or "singularity."

At which the density or congestion level of traffic reached a point.

Where all mathematical models of prediction broke down.

But unlike in physics we could predict what would happen:

Permanent gridlock.

And total anarchy.

First the gridlock.

And then the anarchy when people flipped out.

To tell you the truth this was something that I was kind of curious to see.

Like all Americans I have this underlying desire.

This appetite you might say.

To see America destroyed.

Burned to the ground.

Not because I Hate it.

No.

I just wanna see what it would look like.

Which is the real purpose of this country.

Its Secret Ambition.

The American Dream:

Not the pursuit of happiness.

But the pursuit of destruction.

The End of the World.

Because if the world's gonna end.

We're gonna be the ones to end it.

Not some goddamned foreigners.

The Apocalypse.

Now.

Before all this complicated crap.

Our job used to be straightforward and simple.

Like collecting the trash.

Except we killed people.

Or.

To put it more diplomatically.

We subtracted them.

Not just to prevent Critical Density.

But to achieve Manifest Density.

Which was the reduction of the annual per capita delay.

To below the 100-hour mark.

At that time a person driving in Los Angeles suffered about an average of 261 hours per year in traffic delays due to congestion.

And contrary to popular understanding, traffic congestion isn't about the number of people on the road either.

But the amount of Congesterol.

a.k.a. Road Slobs:

Drivers who don't go with the flow of traffic.

But actually prevent it.

Driving erratically.

Eccentrically.

Idiosyncratically.

Too slow or too fast.

Crossing lines.

Clogging lanes.

Cutting off.

Not signaling.

Funny:

I can empathize with a dude who goes out and shoots a bunch of random people.

But I can't empathize with anyone who doesn't have the courtesy to signal.

People like that should be shot.

We've got a lot of people like that in Los Angeles.

People who should be shot.

Studies have shown that the fewer slobs.

The less congested the road.

Which wasn't good enough for Trimmer.

She wanted to be philosophical about it.

"The more you try to avoid or prevent something," she said.

"The more you make it happen."

"It's called Target Fixation."

"Just as a driver tends to go where he or she is looking."

"*We.*"

"With our focus on preventing Critical Density."

"Will cause it to occur whether we like it or not."

Which didn't make any sense.

Which meant our job wasn't going to make sense anymore either.

"So we must have an actual goal."

"A *positive* goal."

"And not a negative one."

"And not just a goal either."

"But a Mission."

"And to have a Mission you need:"

"A Mission Statement."

"Can anyone give me a Mission Statement?"

"To reduce congestion," someone said.

Which got a lot of laughs.

"Is that really a mission?" she said. "To reduce congestion?"

"Get America moving again!" someone shouted.

No laughs this time.

"Yes," she said. "But this is Los Angeles. We need something more specific to us."

Silence.

"Okay, can anyone tell me:"

"If Los Angeles was something you bought at the supermarket."

"What kind of product would it be?"

"Vegetarian," someone said.

More laughs.

She didn't seem to get that jokes were a part of the job.

Necessary when you kill people for a living.

In fact you could probably make an equation out of it.

The more people a guy kills.

The more jokes he's gonna crack.

To add insult to injury we had more than one Mission.

We had Missions within Missions.

Even a Vision.

But you can't expect anyone to listen to crap like that after a big lunch.

Except.

When it came to what she called the Ideal Death Enforcement Officer.

Everyone listened.

Because what she said.

Was insane.

The Ideal Death Enforcement Officer.

Should be a psychopath.

I'm not making this up.

A psychopath.

She told us that back in the Twentieth Century psychologists had mistakenly classified psychopathy as a personality disorder.

And it wasn't until recently that they discovered that the psychopath was actually a highly evolved type of person.

Evolved.

Claire had wanted me to evolve.

Do PEP with her.

Personality Embuffment Practice.[*]

Turn your ego into your AmEgo®

A lot of celebrities were into it apparently.

I had no idea what it was all about.

Claire said that it would evolve us.

And didn't I want to evolve?

Evolve into what?

Homo maximus.

Homo maximus?

"If you're not busy being born, then you're busy dying," she said.

What's the difference.

They're both busy.

Besides.

She only wanted to do it because Reina Hawthorne was doing it.

I didn't say this though.

Self-improvement.

Personal growth.

Evolution.

Whatever you wanna call it.

Are nothing but evasions.

Distractions.

Cover-ups.

———————————————

[*]   Founded by Dr. Peter Pep, who was later indicted for fraud; cf. *The Rise of Dr. Pep and the Fall of the Personality Movement.*

Meditate your anger.

Yoga your hatred.

Analyze your disgust.

Meanwhile the world goes to hell.

And people like Reina Hawthorne.

Run the show.

Ruin.

So now her and her best friend, Synnita, were doing it.

"PEP Talks" at two hundred and fifty a pop.

That I was paying for.

An aside on how "evolved" her friend Synnita was:

Not too long after I first met her.

We were having this conversation about traffic.

And my supposed work for the Department.

I had been explaining to her the rise in Los Angeles of what was known as "cheesing."

Which was cutting a quick left turn in front of oncoming traffic as soon as the light turned green.

It being the general case in Los Angeles that the majority of drivers were pretty slow to start when the light turned green.

I don't know why.

Whatever the case.

It was understood in the Department that as traffic became more congested.

More rules.

Official and unofficial.

Were being flaunted.

And less and less courtesy extended.

Hence the "cheesing."

The word itself was derived from the Philadelphia cheesesteak sandwich.

Philadelphia being the original home where this turn.

a.k.a. the "Philly turn."

Originated and flourished.

When I got finished telling Synnita all this.

Her response was to tell me how.

On numerous occasions.

While waiting in the left-turn lane.

She tried to look into the eyes of oncoming male drivers.

To see if she could make a connection with any of them.

Not any real connection.

But just enough of a connection to make one of those guys want to go home.

And jerk off over her later.

Or think about her while he was having sex with his girlfriend.

Or with his wife.

She wondered how many had jerked off over her already.

I told her she was a cocktease.

Which made her laugh.

And give me a look that made me think she was trying to pull that stunt on me right there.

I tried to jerk off over her later.

But ended up having to think of someone else to finally get off.

Go figure.

So this psychopath.

This psychopath wasn't your normal serial-killing Joe.

This was a highly evolved version they were now calling a PsychoSmith.

The perfect mixture of refinement and brutality.

To differentiate it from the more basic.

The more flawed.

Psychopath.

Whose prefrontal cortex was apparently substandard.

Unlike the PyschoSmith.

Who, among other things, had an immunity to PTSD.

Because they had a lower standing heart rate.

And a smaller amygdala.

Whatever that is.

Anyways.

At the end of all this PsychoSmith stuff.

I stood up and pointed out to Trimmer that what she was talking about sounded a lot like Clinton Kent.

Everyone remembered Clinton Kent.

He was the poster boy for psychopaths.

Kent had daylighted at the Suicide Prevention Center in West Hollywood for several years.

Until it was discovered that he had been talking people out of suicide.

Just so he could later show up at their homes to torture and kill them.

That one girl he had raped and tortured for six months.

Her family probably still doesn't know what happened to her.

Not like we could advertise something like that.

Deal with it through the normal Law Enforcement channels.

The Department Sweepers had to take care of him.

He had been suspect in my eyes.

After he told me once that murder was the deepest connection you could make with another human being.

That through it.

You could taste someone's soul.

Anyways.

Trimmer said that if I'd been listening I would know that Clinton Kent was a psychopath.

And *not* a PsychoSmith.

Some examples:

Every U.S. President except for Lincoln.

Most CEOs.

Cops.

Half of all lawyers.

Dentists.

All PsychoSmiths.

Charles Manson and the Night Stalker.

The current Campfire Killer.

Terrorists.

Movie producers.

Psychopaths.

The difference.

She explained.

Is that apart from having a low IQ.

Most psychopaths don't have the higher executive functioning skills you need to run.

Or to be part of.

A successful organization.

Because they're too impulsive.

Too lacking in concentration and "cognitive flexibility."

And don't possess the interpersonal skills to be able to minimally relate to others.

Hannibal Lecter.

Would have been a perfect PsychoSmith.

If he'd been more community oriented.

What about Hitler? Someone asked.

No.

Hitler was a psychopath, she said.

Why?

Because he lost the war?

No.

Because he was a racist.

He murdered people based on racial discrimination.

Not out of necessity.

Or for utilitarian purposes.

Which classifies him as being developmentally arrested.

Insane.

And therefore a psychopath.

So now all DEOs were going to be tested.

To see if we were "psychopathologically sound."

They were going to measure us on something called a Psychograph.

Which would determine.

Among other things.

If we were psychopaths.

Or PsychoSmiths.

She told us that the government.

At both the federal and state levels.

Was actually looking into using this Psychograph as part of some new national identification process.

So that someday all citizens would be required to undergo an annual interrogation.

Where they'd be measured and charted on this Psychograph.

And if you were measured as being underdeveloped in certain areas.

You could be denied access to certain jobs.

And certain goods and services:

Guns.

Alcohol.

Blowjobs even.

Or.

If you were really retarded:

A driver's license.

I was still awaiting the results of my annual interrogation.

To see whether I was a psychopath or a PsychoSmith.

Which I hoped I was neither.

As if all this wasn't enough to make me sick.

Which it was.

Trimmer had to make it worse with her ending speech:

"Ladies and Gentlemen."

"What we are doing here is not just a job."

"And we are not just employees."

"Collecting our paychecks."

"And building our pensions."

"But something more."

"Something greater."

"We."

"Ladies and Gentlemen."

"Are nothing less than the Super Heroines."

"And Super Heroes."

"Of Los Angeles."

"Fighting."

"Protecting."

"Serving."

"Securing our fair Angel."

"Against the demons that threaten to corrupt it."

"The demons of congestion."

"Collision."

"And corruption."

"Further."

"We are the immune system."

"The white."

"Black."

"Red."

"Brown."

"And yellow cells."

"Responsible for protecting the body of our Angel."

"Against pathology."

"Disease."

"And those that would seek to infect it with their toxic driving habits."

"However."

"We are not merely physicians."

"Surgeons removing a malignant cancer from our highways."

"We are also artists."

"Designers."

"Craftsmen."

"Shaping the body of our City."

"And beautifying the face of our Angel."

"We are—"

Enough.

We're garbagemen.

Nothing else.

Back to the old lady's house.

"Look at this trash."

Paper bags filled with old newspapers.

Stacked high against the wall to the left of the front door.

Unidentifiable junk to the right.

I pull my BDG.

A feeble voice:

"Is that you?"

Meghasin:

"Excuse me, ma'am—"

"Yes," I say.

"It's us."

The porch light came on.

A dark and ruined face.

Like cracked asphalt.

Looked at us from behind the screen.

Mouth a gaping pothole.

She was old alright.

Elderly.

Ancient even.

What they call senescence.

Old age.

Decay.

Deterioration.

Disintegration.

Are just signs.

Messages.

Warnings.

That you've stayed too long.

Overlived.

The fact that you even want to stay around.

To experience the rotting.

The indignity.

Is just.

"Won't you come in?" she said.

Turning.

Her hand still holding the screen door.

I grabbed the door.

Meghasin gives me a look.

I winked:

"Ladies first."

This was the time of our shift when most people were still up.

Prime time.

Watching TV.

Shadows on the wall.

Things I've seen.

You wouldn't believe.

Naked fat man on his stomach.

Between the couch and TV.

Dead daughter under him.

Remember thinking:

Where's the coffee table?

He move it for this?

Or didn't he own one.

Dude havin sex with:

Fill in the blank.

While watching:

Fill in the blank.

Chick in a fedora wrestling a python.

She didn't have a TV.

Had to zero the snake.

Sometimes what came to the door had full lips.

Most times it was just another couchtard.

The old woman shuffled slowly towards a lighted kitchen that faced the living room without any border.

The smell of mildew and a few years' accumulated dust.

Living room cluttered in the same style as the porch.

To the left a dining room table surrounded by stacks of books.

Magazines.

Old bundled newspapers.

And other stuff that wasn't available for discernment in the dim light.

Meghasin tried to give me one of her combo looks:

What are we doing?

And Fuck you.

"Mom," I say.

"Were you expecting company?"

She turned her head enough to show me the side of her face.

"Yes. Yes, I was, and you here now. I got some tea on."

My right forearm vibrated.

I didn't need to look at the PDT.

It was PAL.

Calling to let us know that our time was up.

Meghasin got the call too.

And she cleared her throat.

"Mom," I say.

"Who were you expecting?"

"Yous," she said. "C'mon, I got some tea on."

"You sure it was us?"

"You the grocery clerks, ain't you?"

Meghasin cleared her throat again.

The old woman grabbed a green kettle off of an old gas stove that looked like it had been recently scrubbed clean.

Detailed.

"The what?" I say.

She repeated it:

"Grocery clerks."

"Officer Krieg," Meghasin said.

She never called me by my first name.

I ignored her.

"But we don't have any groceries," I say.

"Do you need groceries?"

She didn't answer.

"I think she's referring to *Apocalypse Now*," Meghasin said.

"What?"

"*Apocalypse Now*, the movie, where Brando calls Martin Sheen an errand boy sent by grocery clerks."

"You've seen *Apocalypse Now*, but not *Star Wars*?"

"It means she knows what we are," she said.

"Well, technically we're the errand boys and not the grocery clerks, right, Mom?"

"Come on over and have a seat," the woman said. "This tea ain't gonna drink itself."

A small kitchen table had been set with three porcelain cups.

And she began to carefully pour tea into each one.

"What kind of tea is that, Mom?"

"The regular kind," she said.

I give Meghasin the look she's been waiting for.

But she doesn't want it anymore.

She turns her head away.

"C'mon, Officer Ross," I say.

"This tea ain't gonna drink itself."

I took a chair in front of one of the cups.

And she poured it full.

I leaned forward and put my nose to it.

Smelled like tea.

When she was finished pouring the tea she turned to put the kettle back on the stove.

My PDT buzzed again.

I ignored it and waited for the old woman to sit back down.

Meghasin came up to the table but wouldn't sit down.

She crossed her arms.

Squinted at the tea.

"Smells edible," I say.

Then the old woman took a seat to my right and without a word picked up her tea.

I did likewise and we sipped in unison.

She pointed towards the living room.

"There's books and magazines."

"Most of it was Milton's."

"But he's gone now."

"You got a computer around here, Mom?"

"Yes, it's in the back room. My son, he said I gots to have one, but I don't see no—"

"Officer Krieg," Meghasin said. "We need to proceed with—"

"Will you just sit down already?"

"Tea's gonna get cold."

Another look.

Like she wanted to scream.

"That's an order," I say.

Meghasin pulled a chair next to the old lady and sat down.

She looked at the tea.

But didn't touch it.

The old lady lifted her tea again.

Using both hands this time.

And took a slow sip.

And before the cup touched the saucer said:

"You boys can have a look, see what you like."

"Boys?" Meghasin said.

"Errand boys," I say.

Meghasin had short hair.

Raisin black.

Like one of those Beatles.

I looked at the house and saw that it had probably been a nice, cozy place.

In a nice, cozy neighborhood.

Back in the old days.

Must have been nice sitting there all lazy on the porch in the warm Los Angeles air.

Except for all the white people walking by.

"Mom," I say.

"How'd you know we were coming?"

She looked at Meghasin.

But not at her.

Like she was looking at something further away.

"Well, I dreamed it some time ago, is all."

"There was a breeze outside."

"And you two in your suits came knocking."

"Yeah." I lean close to her.

"But how did you know *about* us?"

"I just told you," she sniffed.

"No, about us being grocery clerks—killers?"

"That's what you ares, aren't ya?"

"Yeah, but how—"

I cut myself off when I realized that this could go all night.

How she knew about the existence of Death Enforcement Officers was anyone's guess.

Well.

It wasn't anyone's.

No one knew we even existed.

Except for a bunch of conspiracy nuts.

The kind of people that believed in Bigfoots and UFOs.

There were rumors of course.

That floated along the fringes of the media.

Centering themselves in the tabloids.

But no one with any respectable modicum of reason believed any of that shit.

"Mom, you got any sugar?"

She looked at me with a squint and slowly creaked her gears into motion.

Scraping back the chair.

"I got some somewheres," she said.

"Never was much one for sugar myself."

"Neither was Milton."

"He had the diabetes."

I helped her with the chair.

She got up and turned slowly.

And shuffled back to the kitchen counter.

I watched as she opened the yellowish paint-chipped cupboard to the left of the stove.

Meghasin tapped her fingers on the Formica table.

Rolling them from pinky to index.

And scowled.

Pouting apparently.

"Okay, okay," I say.

My PDT buzzed again.

The pop of the gun sent Meghasin backward in her chair.

Feet kicking over the table.

Tea and teacups flying all over the place.

Even though the shot was aimed at me.

The slug buzzed my ear.

A strange sensation.

Not at all like a mosquito.

I reached out and slapped the gun out of her hand.

Making sure not to do it too hard that it would hurt her.

And it clattered into the sink.

Meghasin was on the ground.

Feet up.

Made me want to laugh.

Ask her if she's okay.

She doesn't say anything.

I go and take the gun out of the sink.

An old .25 revolver.

Put it in my jacket pocket.

The old lady is bending slowly.

To pick up an unbroken teacup near her foot.

And presumably clean up the whole mess.

I catch her in midbend and guide her gently towards the living room.

"Here, Ma."

"You need some rest."

"Let's go over here to the couch."

I direct her to the couch in front of the window and sit her down.

Meghasin gets up and ruffles her hair.

Her face is flushed.

She's angry.

That's obvious.

But not at the old lady.

I half watched her while I helped the old lady settle down into the couch.

"You okay?"

She wouldn't answer.

Wouldn't look at me.

Still running her hand through her hair.

My PDT buzzed again.

"Officer Ross, why don't you go tell PAL to shut the Fuck up, and I'll finish here."

At that she storms out.

Heavy heel thuds on the porch outside.

"It's a little cold," the old woman said.

There was a crocheted blanket or shawl bunched in the right corner of the couch.

With *Bless This House* embroidered on it.

I took it and covered the old lady as best I could.

Guiding her head down to a dusty brown square pillow.

I helped her with her legs.

When she was settled I thanked her for the tea.

Pulled my BDG.

And subtracted her.

I went to the back of the house to find this computer.

A back office that looked like the rest of the house.

Stacks of shit everywhere.

A folded laptop sitting center on a cluttered desk.

New.

State of the art.

I opened it and searched for Clarisse McNaughton Pedestrian.

Turned out she was involved in a class action lawsuit against BlackGuard.

Totaling a quarter billion.

Bradbury Thurlow II, CEO and owner, named as a defendant.

Clarisse McNaughton's husband had been killed in Uzbekistan along with several other operatives while on an assignment to protect a shipment of auto parts.

The suit accused BlackGuard of negligence.

They had been sent into a hot zone unprepared and without knowledge that the zone was hot.

Insufficient manpower, weapons, and vehicles.

Their lawyer said they had a pretty good case.

Of course he did.

And here.

Statement by her at a recent city council meeting.

Asking why a private mercenary company was handling traffic congestion.

None of the council members seemed to know or be aware.

But her claims were going to be investigated and brought up at the next session.

So.

She was a hit.

Most likely ordered by Thurlow himself.

Using the DoD as his personal hit squad.

His personal trashmen.

No way.

Maybe I would've looked the other way.

But not with them shoving their rules up my ass like that.

Time to shove it up theirs.

I called Anita.

She answered with a what.

"Tried calling you a bit ago."

"What is it?"

I told her the whole deal.

When I was finished she gave me a look.

Like I was compromising her.

"I have a report that you're ten minutes over on this subtraction," she said.

"What's going on?"

"I just told you."

"Well, you need to do your—"

I hung up.

So she didn't want to be involved.

Probably tell me to keep my mouth shut.

No.

I'm gonna keep it open.

Accuse him.

Force him.

To react.

Not only in regards to her.

But Mars too.

Pretty sure he was behind that too.

Runnin him down.

And Claire.

Might as well throw her in too.

Claire.

Fuck.

What if it was him?

No.

Before I left I went into the kitchen and wiped up the spilled tea.

Put the broken and unbroken porcelain in the sink.

And squared up the table and chairs.

It didn't seem polite.

To leave things like that.

Messed up.

And broken.

BOOMSDAY

The killing was clean.

No blood, no brains, no guts.

Nothing to get on your clothes.

Or your conscience.

There's little or no mess.

And what little of it there was you didn't have to clean up.

Someone else did.

PAL was out front when I came out of the old woman's place.

Nervously humming.

White steam puffing.

Meghasin already inside.

When I walked up, the door didn't open.

I pulled on the handle.

It was locked.

I knocked on the glass.

"Hey, Meghasin, what's the deal?"

In the driver's seat looking straight ahead.

Like that woman on the 10.

Dead.

"Your feet appear to be soiled, Officer Krieg," PAL said. *"Please wipe them."*

"What?"

PAL had never said that before.

Let alone Darth Vader.

"You are prohibited from entering this vehicle until you wipe your feet, Officer Krieg."

That did it.

I kicked PAL in the door as hard as I could.

Denting it in.

It popped back out like a piece of rubber.

"Please do not damage Department property, Officer Krieg."

"May I remind you that you are currently on probation for a previous violation of section code twelve point four subsection B, and further assault may result in suspension and/or termination depending on the severity of the damage."

"Fuck you, you piece of shit, Fuck you."

"Excessive and unnecessary use of profanity will result in further penalty points and/or punitive action, Officer Krieg. Please wipe your feet."

I knuckled the glass.

Meghasin still looking straight ahead.

Across the street someone looking at me from a living room window.

I looked at my boots.

There appeared to be some wet soil caked on the side of my right boot.

Or was it shit?

I scraped my boot on the curb and then put it against the window.

"How's this, PALhole?"

"Please do not put your foot on the window, Officer Krieg. Improper use of Department property is a violation of section code—"

"Just open the damn door already!"

The door popped open:

"You are almost ten minutes late, Officer Krieg. I will have to report the delay to the Department, which will most likely result in several penalty points."

I got in.

"Jesus. This car won't shut up for two minutes, will it?"

She didn't say anything.

I looked out the window and tried not to think.

Heading west on 27th.

PAL taking every vertical deflection* with excessive caution.

I checked myself in the mirror and straightened out my hat.

A Cadillac-green trilby with a dark chocolate band.

Even though I looked pretty good.

I didn't look so hot.

Neither did she.

"You mad or something?"

She pulled out her pad and put on her phones.

"Wait, hold on."

"I gotta say something."

"That hit on the freeway."

"I found something out."

---

*   Speed hump.

She didn't say anything.

Just scowled at her pad.

"Tell me what's the matter."

"We can't be driving around like this all night."

"I'd rather not talk right now," she said.

"Then I'll talk."

"That lady on the freeway, Clarisse McNaughton—that wasn't a legal hit."

"We didn't subtract her because of her driving record."

"We were ordered to subtract her because she was suing Thurlow."

She didn't say anything.

"Are you listening?"

"Did you report it?" she said, not looking at me.

"Yes, I told Anita."

"Then why are you telling me?"

"Okay, fine."

"I get it."

"Hey, PAL."

"Yes, Officer Krieg."

"Did you know that Bradbury Thurlow is ordering illegal hits?"

A pause.

"Well?"

"Are you referring to subtractions, Officer Krieg?"

"Yes."

"Then I must remind you that failure to use the proper term is a violation of section code—"

"God, will you shut the Fuck up?"

"How about answering my goddamn question already?"

"Did you know that Bradbury Thurlow—"

"Excessive and unnecessary use of profanity has resulted in another penalty point, Officer Krieg. One more point and—"

"Answer my question!"

"Did you or did you not know that Bradbury Thurlow is using this Department to conduct illegal hits?"

Nothing.

"Well?"

Nothing.

"Finally at a loss for—"

"May I make a suggestion, Officer Krieg?" PAL said.

"What?"

"May I make a suggestion?"

"No, not really."

"All you do is make suggestions."

"How about answering my question about Bradbury Thurlow, huh?"

"The Department recommends that Officers use their freely allotted time to improve their skills."

"Several professional development courses are now being offered to all Officers free of charge. These courses include language instruction, professional etiquette, cognitive control, first aid, vehicle code, stress reduction—"

I took my foot out and kicked the dash as hard as I could.

"How's that for using my freely allotted time?"

Meghasin looked up.

But not at me.

"Please do not damage Department property, Officer Krieg. You are currently on probation for a previous violation of section code twelve point four subsection B,

and further assault may result in suspension and/or termination depending on the severity of the damage."

I kicked the dash again.

"Nothing like a little professional development," I say.

"Officer Krieg," Meghasin said.

"Please."

"Violation of section code twelve point four reported to Department, Officer Krieg."

The 9 turned to a 10.

A warning siren went off.

"You now have ten penalty points," PAL said. *"Punitive action pending."*

"You mean like this?"

I pulled my leg back for a kick.

Meghasin put her hand on my knee:

"Please, Officer Krieg."

Sounded like she was gonna cry.

I put my leg down.

"Okay."

"I gotta make a phone call, you mind?"

She didn't say anything.

I called Claire.

Four rings and then her voice mail:

"Look, it's me and . . ."

I hung up.

She knows damn well why I'm calling.

Meghasin turned to me.

"Look, Officer Krieg. I'm sorry your wife left you, but you can't—"

"Really."

"You're sorry?"

"Yes, I'm really—"

"Really?"

"Yes, Officer Krieg. I really feel—"

"Alex."

"It's Alex, for Chrissake."

"Is it so hard for you to call me by my first name?"

"I didn't—"

"Gotta do everything by the book, don't you?"

"Well, let me tell you—"

"Look, Officer—I mean Alex—I'm not trying to—"

"Will you shut up and let me finish already?"

"Jesus—oh, sorry, wait."

"Forgot that I can't say that around you."

"But, *please* forgive me, *Officer Ross.*"

"If I said 'Officer Christ' would that be more acceptable, more—"

"I don't know what you're—"

"Let me finish, goddamnit!"

"I know why you call me Officer Krieg."

"It's not because you want to do things by the book."

"It's because you don't like me."

"So instead of saying it straight out."

"You gotta do your little underhanded backhand."

"Or whatever the hell you call backstab sneak attacks like that."

"Please, Officer Krieg—"

"Yeah, yeah—right there."

"That's it right there."

"*Right* there."

"Should hire a translator."

"What you're really saying when you say that is 'Fuck You.'"

"Excessive and unnecessary use of profanity will result in another penalty point and/or punitive action, Officer Krieg."

"PAL, please shut up," Meghasin said.

"Look, Alex."

"Honestly, I'm really sorry about you and your wife. Really."

"Said she'd talk to me later."

"Later."

"Now it's way past later and she still won't talk to me."

"Can you please tell me, Officer Ross."

"Since you seem to be pretty good at . . . at . . ."

"Deliberate and mischievous obfuscation."

"What does that actually mean?"

"Later?"

"Maybe she just needs some time," she said.

"She's had time."

"It's been like four days already."

"Five."

"Did you text her?"

"Text?"

"Yes, maybe she'd—"

"Girls text."

"Men—forget it."

"Do you know where she went?"

"She's at her friend Synnita's."

"Did you try calling her friend to see if she's okay?"

"No, Synnita doesn't like me."

"Can I ask why?"

"She don't like Niggers."

"Derogatory statements that are racial in nature—that is, racist—are strictly prohibited under section code—"

"PAL," Meghasin said. "Please, not now."

"Neither do her friends."

"Tried to humiliate me this one night, and I wouldn't take it."

About a year ago.

Had to go down and rescue Claire from the Westside.

I Hated the Westside.

Where shitheads go to become even bigger shitheads.

That's the problem with L.A.

It's not the damn immigrants.

Although that's a problem.

It's the idiots.

From other states.

Like Ohio.

Texas.

Canada.

Swarmin out here.

To Live the Dream.

Nothing worse.

Than someone trying to Live the Dream.

What they call the L.A. attitude.

It's not the Natives.

The locals.

That got it.

It's these idiots.

Who bring it.

And complain about it at the same time.

Used to Love jackin out-of-staters.

Hopin Hollywood.

Wasn't gonna chew them.

Spit them out.

Then along comes.

Me.

Anyway.

After what happened that night, Synnita stopped pretending to acknowledge me.

She'd say hi when I said hello.

But say it like it left a bad taste in her mouth.

Like she wanted to spit it out on the floor and grind her heel against it.

Claire had been mad at me too for a while.

But I wonder how much of it had been Synnita talking shit.

Because none of it was my fault.

Not really.

It was Claire's fault if you wanted to get technical about it.

She started it all.

She didn't have to call me and get me all worked up like that.

I mean, what the hell did she expect?

Especially on June 16.

A solemn day.

A day that will live in infamy and all that shit.

> *Things weren't the same in Los Angeles after 6/16. I know, they said the same thing after 9/11, but in Los Angeles we were affected and not affected at the same time, you know? Don't get me wrong, 9/11 was a horrible event, and my heart goes out to them, but New York is so far away, and it wasn't until 6/16 that we really felt the magnitude of it. That it really hit home. I mean, after that things really began to take on weight. Even the sun didn't feel the same anymore. I was only nine at the time but I remember being on the set of* The Sound of Sizzle *and getting ready for about the most important scene in the movie—well, at least to me—the scene where I sizzle over "Edelweiss"—well, I wasn't going to sing it then, but later, in the studio, but I had to act like I was really sizzlin, which, let me tell you, even for an experienced actor, is really hard, especially on a day like that and I distinctly remember thinking "What am I doing? What is this all about?"*
>
> —Reina Hawthorne on the tenth anniversary
> of 6/16, *Los Angeles Times*

The Sound of Sizzle.

Yeah.

Picture a nine-year-old white girl tryin to Sizzle over a strike beat.

You don't.

But you've all seen it.

And who even listens to Sizzle anymore.

Sizzlin my ass.

Anyway.

I was in the middle of a blow at Tharshees.

Delivered by Insatia no less.

Yeah, I know.

But it's not like that.

When you're a full-blown felon.

Life usually doesn't hold a bunch of misdemeanors against you.

I happened to be there because Tharshees was offering a "Hero's Discount."

Twenty percent off blows.

To qualifying Police and Firefighters.

With valid ID.

I'm neither of those.

But I had a phony police badge, so.

All Death Enforcement Officers have phony badges for various reasons.

Coincidentally it was the first time I had seen Insatia since she had gone away to frontier camp.

You might even say synchronistically.

But not fortuitously.

Or Providentially.

No.

That's going too far.

She had acted surprisingly polite and mature.

Not at all like the first time.

"You work here?"

"Yeah," she said, "just started."

She asked me if I wanted her and I said yes.

After that I started to come by often to see her.

In fact.

I would come to develop kind of a strange relationship with her.

Until she disappeared.

I don't know if it was that camp.

Or if she had always been like this.

But the more I got to know her.

If know her was the right word.

I started to see that there was something not right with her.

And it was this not right that excited something in me.

Something that was probably not a good thing to excite.

But then you really have no control over things like that.

Not like I'm into crazy chicks.

Or anything.

But let's just say that when things are rolling smooth and straight down the highway.

It's good to have something jump out of nowhere and jolt you.

Before you fall asleep at the wheel.

That was Insatia.

So that night when I saw her it was almost like Claire knew.

And wanted to Fuck it up by calling me right at that moment.

When she rang I didn't answer at first.

But when she rang the third time I thought I better.

In case it was some kind of an emergency.

So I cut the blow short and answered.

Insatia on her knees between my knees.

Lipsticking her lips.

Claire's voice sounding kind of hysterical.

But I wasn't really listening.

Just kept saying "yeah" and "uh-huh."

"Are you listening to me?" Claire said.

"What are you doing?"

Like a guilty boy caught doing something guilty:

"Nothing."

"Are you playing that *Star Wars* game again?"

"No, I'm playing a game called work."

"Well, can you come and get me or not?"

She sounded distraught.

Like she might have been crying.

It was the first time I had ever heard her sound this bad.

And it makes me feel bad to think about it now.

What I did.

And how I acted.

Insatia stuck her tongue out at me.

"Why?" I say.

"I knew you weren't listening."

"Look, I'm working. What's going on?"

"Just come get me already."

"I can't take being insulted anymore, okay?"

"Am I insulting you?"

"Jesus, God."

"No, I just told you."

"It's her friend Davis."

"Who the Fuck's Davis?"

"Jesus, aren't you listening to anything I say?"

"Synnita's friend."

"From New York."

"New York?"

"What the Fuck's he doing out here?"

"Visiting."

"Visiting?"

"Are you going to ask me a thousand questions or come pick me up?"

"What'd he say?"

"He keeps talking shit, and I'm sick of it."

"What kinda shit's he talking?"

"Look, are you gonna come get me or not?"

"Tell me what he said."

"You don't really care, do you?"

"What?"

"I ask you to come get me and you ask me questions like you don't want to come get me."

"I wanna know what he said, is all. What'd he say?"

"You know what, forget it."

"I'll call someone else."

She hung up.

I looked at Insatia.

Holding my limp cock in her fingers.

"I'm gonna have to start you over," she said.

She did.

And about two minutes into it the phone rang again and I answered it.

"Well for starters he insulted 6/16," Claire said.

"What?"

"He insulted 6/16," she said. "Where are you? I hear music."

"What do you mean he insulted it?"

"He said it was a joke."

"His insult or 6/16?"

"Will you just come and get me already?"

"What'd he say already?"

"Jesus, Alex."

"C'mon, tell me."

"He said the terrorists probably couldn't find anything important to attack in Los Angeles."

"So they had to settle for Disneyland."

"What?"

"He said New York has been attacked more times than L.A. because it's more important than L.A."

"What the Fuck?"

"What did Synnita say about her friend saying all this shit?"

"She said 'Oh, Davis, you say such scandalous things.'"

"Scandalous?"

"He's got a lot of Fuckin nerve coming out here and talking shit like that."

"On 6/16 no less."

"Yeah, well," she said. "He thought it was funny."

"Didn't anyone check him?"

"Didn't you say anything?"

"I told him how dare he disrespect all those women and children that died."

"And he said, 'What about all those people that died in New York?'"

"Fuck New York," I say.

"Every time they get attacked they cry like a bunch of babies."

I don't like New York.

Never been.

And never will.

I refuse to watch the ball drop in Times Square for New Year's.

Can't understand why any self-respecting Angeleno would.

Claire once told me to lighten up about it.

You don't tell a Nigger to lighten up.

"He attacked you too," she said.

"What do you mean he attacked me?"

"Synnita told him about your picture of Hitler in the living room and he got mad."

"Said Hitler killed like a bunch of his relatives in the Holocaust."

"Yeah, so?"

"What's that got to do with me?"

"That's what I said."

"Plus it happened like over a hundred years ago, didn't it?"

"I said you don't see Alex freaking out at white people because they used to own slaves."

"Well—"

"And then he just like put up his hand and said anyone that owns a picture of Hitler is a Nazi."

"Did you ask him how a Nigger can be a Nazi?"

"No, I'm tired, Alex."

"Can you just come and get me already?"

I couldn't see Insatia's face.

Just a mop of red curls floating up and down over my lap.

Mouth grinding down on me hard.

"C'mon, Claire you're an adult . . . can't you just . . . can't you . . ."

Believe me.

It's not like I didn't care.

I would have pounded that guy if I was there right now.

Or if he was here right now.

But I was all the way over here.

And here was.

"What are you trying to say?" she said.

"Look, if that guy was right here right now I'd sock the MotherFucker."

"I don't want you to sock him, I want you to pick me up."

"Yeah, but—"

"So, what? You don't care, right?"

"I didn't say that."

"Yes, you did."

I had to get off the phone.

I was about to.

"Look—"

"You know what?" she said. "Forget it."

"Just go back to work and I'll just take his insults like an *adult*, okay?"

"I'm coming," I say.

"I'll be there soon."

"No, just forget it."

"No, I'm coming right now."

"No, forget it. Don't come."

"No, I want to."

"No, you don't."

She hung up just in time.

I asked Insatia if she wanted to have a quick cup of coffee with me at Stubbs before I had to go.

Stubbs—Your First Mate for Life.

Wanted to know what her deal was.

We sat at one of the tables outside and she ordered green tea without anything in it.

I asked her about her time at frontier camp and she said that it was very liberating.

I asked what was so liberating about it, but she wouldn't go into any details.

Just said it was liberating, is all.

When I asked her about being here and doing this, she said she wanted to try this out.

After seeing Reina Hawthorne in *Genuflect.*

I changed the subject:

What about her mother?

She said she didn't want to talk to her.

I asked her if it was because she thought her mother might not approve of what she was doing.

She said no.

What if I told her mother where she was? I asked.

And she asked me if I told Claire that I had raped her.

I said no because that wasn't the case and you know it.

And then all of a sudden.

And this is where I think the first signs of crazy started.

She says:

"Do you have a gun I can borrow?"

"What?"

"I need a gun."

"Why?"

"Self-defense."

"For some reason I don't get the impression that it's for self-defense."

"Yeah, you're pretty good at picking up impressions, aren't you?"

"What's that supposed to mean?"

"Are you really this stupid?"

"What's with you chicks anyway?"

"Why you gotta make us fish all the time?"

"Just say what's on your mind."

"You mean like no?"

"What are you talking about?"

"You don't remember raping me?"

"I didn't rape you."

"God, you're pathetic."

"Look, what happened that night—"

"How about this: you give me a gun, and I don't tell my mother you raped me."

"Wait, hold on."

"If you think I raped you, then why did you just give me a blow?"

"Because I want a gun."

"You want to shoot me?"

"Get over yourself. If that was the case I would have done it a long time ago."

"Then why?"

"Why?"

"Yes, why do you want a gun?"

"They shoot horses, don't they?"

"What? Who shoots horses?"

"You know, for some stupid reason I almost thought you'd understand."

"You're not making any sense."

"This is boring. I've got to go."

"This from that frontier camp?"

"What the hell they teach you there?"

She got up.

"Don't tell my mother I said hi, because I didn't."

"You don't want to kill yourself, do you?"

She started back for Tharshees.

"Wait."

I grabbed her shoulder and swung her to face me:

"Look, don't go back there."

"I'll give you money."

"What for?"

"Your mom wouldn't want you doing this."

"If you need money—"

"They don't pay me."

"What?"

"They don't pay me."

"Bullshit."

"Okay, whatever."

"They got something on you or something?"

"That why you need the gun?"

"No, I don't want to get paid, now let go of me."

I grabbed her harder:

"Dammit, Insatia, what are you doing?"

"You going to rape me right here?"

"This all because of that night?"

"'That night,' he says! Wow, you're a real romantic."

"Please."

"I'll do anything."

"You need to tell my mother then."

"I will."

"I'm going to tell her that you're not right."

"That you need help."

"No, you need to tell her that you're in Love with me."

"What?"

"Tell my mother that you're in Love with me."

"Jesus, are you serious?"

"Yeah. Tell her or I'll tell her you raped me."

"Now let go of me."

I let go of her.

"Okay, you win."

"A gun?"

"No I give up."

"You gave up a long time ago."

"What's that supposed to mean?"

"God, you're such a loser."

She turned and walked away.

"Wait."

"Wait, here's my card—just call me if you need anything."

She took the card from me and continued walking.

I watched her walk back to Tharshees.

Right before she opened the door she dropped my card and was gone.

There was nothing left to do but to go get Claire.

I went to Tharshees the next night.

Insatia was on the menu but she wasn't there.

She went by the name Claire of all things.

They told me she was scheduled.

But hadn't come in and hadn't called in either.

I feared the worst.

So I put a trace on her.

She was in Westwood.

A couple blocks from UCLA.

Maybe she was working at Tharshees to pay her way through college.

Like Reina Hawthorne in that movie.

I didn't believe for a second that she wasn't getting paid.

She just said that because those are the kind of things girls say.

When they want attention.

Which is what I was hoping on the way to Westwood.

That all this was some kind of girl cry for help.

A little caveat:

If you have to go anywhere in Los Angeles.

I recommend not going near the Westside.[*]

Unless it's life or Death.

Even after midnight.

Wilshire was a parking lot.

Actually I can't think of anywhere in Los Angeles.

That's worth the drive.

Not even the beach.

No.

Better to stay in your car.

Between places.

---

[*]   Or the Eastside, the Northeast side, Downtown, South Bay, the Valley. And most of you wouldn't even think of going to South L.A.

That's the best place.

It took about an hour to get to her place.

A white two-story house.

"Cascade House" across the front in green handwritten letters.

The lawn looked wet and there were some flowers planted along the edge of the drive.

She's on the second floor.

Mars stayed in the car double-parked.

I got out and went over and opened the front door which shouldn't have been unlocked.

But you'd be surprised.

This city is full of people who don't think bad things will happen to them.

There was no one in the front room.

There was a desk at the back wall with a service bell.

LED walls.

Turned to white.

I walked upstairs.

Her door was the third one down the hall.

I knocked on it as quietly as I could.

Three soft taps.

Nothing.

After about ten seconds I did it again, the same.

Nothing.

The third time, I doubled the knocks and did them a little harder.

One two three four five six.

About four seconds and again.

One two three four five six.

The door opened a crack.

An eye and a cheek.

Perfume.

The same perfume when I was with her last.

"Who is it?"

"It's me, I want to talk to you."

Recognition in the eye.

And not a flattering one either.

One of those looks a stalker dude has the ability to filter out of his perception when he's going after a girl.

I saw it though.

"Go away."

I pushed the door in.

Not hard or aggressive like I was on the attack.

But forceful enough to show her that I wanted to talk to her right now.

"I'm not going to hurt you," I say.

There was a light switch right inside the door and I flipped it.

A single room with not much but a mattress on the floor under the window.

A bunch of clothes and books scattered around.

There was a bald dude lying in her bed.

Partially wrapped in a sheet.

He wasn't wearing anything under the sheet.

He looked to be about my age or a little older.

You could never tell these days.

The dude could have been seventy for all I knew.

He started to get up and tried to say something at the same time.

Which seemed a little beyond his skill level.

He stuttered and fell back.

"It's alright, Roger," she said without making it sound like it was alright.

"Are you the police?" he asked.

"Yes, get your shit and get out of here."

He started to do what I said.

He apologized like he was doing something illegal:

"We're not doing anything illegal," he said.

"Don't worry. He's not a cop," Insatia said.

"He's just a rapist."

That pissed me off.

"This your boyfriend?"

"No."

I told the dude to give me his wallet and he looked at Insatia.

"What are you looking at me for?" she said.

"Yeah," I say, "don't make me ask you twice."

He opened his wallet and tried to just give me his ID instead.

"Your whole wallet."

He seemed to doubt the legality of this.

But when I took a step towards him he quickly handed it to me.

He didn't have any cash.

I put the wallet in my coat pocket and told him to take him and his clothes and get out.

"You don't have to do this," she said as soon as the door closed.

"Do what?"

"Get all worked up about me."

"Hot and bothered."

"What are you talking about?"

"I was concerned about you."

"Meaning worked up."

"Why didn't you show up at Tharshees tonight?"

"What, you want me to give you another blow?"

"No, I was concerned."

"Yeah, I'll bet."

"Did you quit?"

"No, I was at Lee Ping's."

"You workin at Lee Ping's now?"

"What planet are you from? I don't *work* at either place—I'm a Free Agent."

"For blowjobs?"

"Yeah. You want one or not?"

"Look, I'm just concerned about you."

"Concerned about raping me?"

"I didn't rape you."

"Either you're very stupid or very delusional. Which one is it?"

"Neither."

"Did I ask you to Fuck me that night?"

"In so many words."

"Like no?"

"You didn't say no."

"That's because you had your hand over my mouth."

"You're the type that needs a hand over her mouth."

"See? Right there. The words of a true rapist."

"If I did you such wrong, why the hell didn't you say anything?"

"Tell your mother for instance."

"Because it gives me pleasure to think that my mother married a rapist."

"You call me a rapist one more time and I'll—"

"Rape me?"

"Then why the hell did you blow me?"

"It's my job, genius."

"You said you didn't get paid."

"In your dreams."

"Okay, I get it, you're just trollin me, like every other kid these days."

"Look, you want me to say I'm sorry, I'm sorry."

"Look," she said, "if you want to Fuck me, you can Fuck me."

"Just hurry it up."

"I've got to get to work."

"Who was that guy?"

"What guy?"

"The chrome dome, the one that just left."

"A friend."

"A friend?"

"You didn't recognize him?"

"No, should I?"

"That's Roger Eylander."

"So."

"He owns Tinkerballs."

"Tinkerballs?"

"And Spankerbells."

"They're Blowtiques."

"Yeah, I know what they are."

High-end blowshops.

For fags.

Never been.

"He wants to start a chain called Shooters."

"What?"

"Shooters. Like Hooters, but you can get a handjob with your buffalo wings."

"Sounds retarded."

"Maybe, but he's got more money than you'll ever have."

All she had on was an oversized T-shirt with the Snake Oil logo on it:

Snake Oil®—Upgrade your Cock!

And she took it off.

"He payin you?"

"Like I said. He's a friend."

"*Boyfriend?*"

"No."

"Do you have a boyfriend?"

"God, no."

"Well, maybe that's what you need, someone nice, someone you can—"

"Nice?"

"Yeah."

"What are you, *Leave It to Beaver*?"

"What's wrong with nice?"

"Nice people are secret jerks."

"Secret jerks?"

"Look, do you want to Fuck me or not?"

She laid back on her elbows and opened up her legs like it was no big deal.

"Look," I say.

Trying to say something.

Anything.

"You still want a gun?"

She yawned.

"Got one."

"Where? From that dome?"

"I'm done talking to you. Either Fuck me or go."

I stood there and looked at her and then looked away.

I didn't want to do it.

No, really.

I didn't.

But I felt that it would be worse if I didn't.

If I just left there.

Like a fool.

All trolled out.

And humiliated.

So I took my jacket off and looked for a proper place to hang it.

I couldn't find anything.

So I settled for the doorknob.

Claire was at some restaurant called Hunt & Gather on the Westside.

Like I said.

I Hated going to the Westside.

Hated it.

The arrogance of it all.

These delicate successes.

Nothing but polished meat-bags.

Designer corpses.

I pulled up in front of the restaurant and had to park in front of a hydrant.

A valet in a black coat came up and Sir'd me in that capitalized way that made it sound like an insult.

Told me I couldn't park there.

I pulled out my badge and told him it was either there or on his face and he backed off.

I cut through a heap of people crowding the front and found Claire and Synnita with four other people near the back of the restaurant.

I pulled a chair from the table next to them and swung it around to the end of Claire's table.

Some guy at the table I took the chair from yelled, "Hey!"

I turned around.

"Sorry. You using this?"

"No, but you could ask."

"I'm askin."

He gave me his permission by shooing his hand at me.

Claire got up and gave me a hug and a kiss on the lips.

"You've been drinking," she said.

It wasn't an accusation.

Just one of those annoying matter-of-fact statements that had no point.

Except to piss me off.

She looked like she'd been on the verge of crying.

So did I probably.

Like I said.

I Hated the Westside.

I could tell the New York guy was the one that was sitting right across from her.

He was red-faced from either drinking or laughing or yelling.

Probably all of the above.

Dark, wet hair that looked like it had too much product.

Or that he had just dunked his head in the can.

Heard they did shit like that in New York.

But I wasn't gonna judge him just yet.

Give him the benefit for now.

Maybe he was just a prolific sweater.

A white suit jacket over a dark button-down shirt.

With the top two or three buttons unbuttoned.

Loudly talking to Synnita at the other end of the table.

"That the dude?"

"Let's just go," Claire said.

"Aren't you going to introduce me?"

"I just want to go," she whispered.

The guy looked up at us and inquired in a voice amplified with several rounds of booze:

"Who's this, Claire?"

Claire turned around and told him that I was her husband.

And said this is Davis.

Stupid name.

Davis.

Picture his parents.

White to the gills.

Mother writing him a sick note:

Please excuse my son, Davis, from school yesterday.

As he had a severe rash.

It's not contagious—he just tends to break out in a rash.

Whenever his skin is exposed.

To unfiltered water.

I put out my hand for him to shake but he doesn't return it and says:

"I didn't know your husband was African-American. I thought he was German."

"I'm neither."

"Then what are you?"

"I'm a Nigger."

"My man," he laughed.

Putting out his fist for a knock.

But I had already put my hand away.

So he just knocked the air at me like it didn't matter if my hand was there or not.

"Maybe you can settle something for us, Alex," he said.

I sat down in the chair I had just procured:

"What's that?"

"It's about sugar. Synnita and I are having a disagreement on the procurement of sugar."

"Yeah," Synnita said.

"Davis, although quite intelligent, doesn't seem to know the meaning of certain things."

"And Synnita has a one-track mind," he laughed.

"I do not."

"Alex, if a woman came to your door and asked to borrow some sugar, would you think that she was there to borrow sugar?"

"Maybe, maybe not, depends."

"See?" Davis said. "It doesn't always—"

"Shut up," Synnita said.

"If you thought she wasn't, Alex, what would you think she was there for?"

"To meet me probably."

"See, it doesn't always mean sex," Davis said.

"Guys are so clueless," she said.

"What are we so clueless about?"

Claire sighed.

"Oh god."

"Claire's already heard this one before," Davis said winking at her.

Claire gave me a look.

"Claire was staying over that weekend," Synnita said.

"Remember that guy that lived below me?"

"Yeah, thought if you asked him to borrow some sugar he would know you really meant sex."

"Well, it's a little more complicated than that."

"Long story short, he didn't want to have sex with her."

"No, it wasn't that. He didn't know about the sugar."

"Why didn't you just tell him about the sugar?" Claire said.

"Because if I had to tell him then I wouldn't want to have sex with him anymore."

"Yeah." Davis touching my arm.

"But ask her what she would have done if the guy had come right out and asked her to have sex."

I gave Synnita a look that said I don't give a Fuck about her or her stupid sugar.

In other words.

I smiled at her.

"Well, then that would make him a pig, and I wouldn't want to do him either."

"So the guy can't win," Davis said.

"See, that's what guys don't get," Synnita said.

"Not everything's black and white."

"He should have known what I was implying and invited me in."

"Offered me a drink."

"Or chatted me up while pretending to look for sugar."

"And if he was smart, he wouldn't find any."

"And try to offer me something else."

"Like sex." Davis winked.

"Oh god, not like that. Like to keep playing the game."

"To keep hottening things up."

"So, what did he do?" I asked.

"He gave me some sugar—literally."

Davis laughed.

So did everyone else.

Except for me and Claire.

"Can we change the subject?" Claire said.

Mouthing me a "Let's go."

"Your wife tells me you work for the L.A. Department of Transportation," Davis said.

"Yes. Yes, I does."

"On traffic congestion specifically, right?"

"Decongestion."

Claire sat back in her seat with a sigh.

She set her purse down on the corner of the table as a sign that she didn't intend on staying.

And that I should hurry it up.

This Davis guy looks at her for a second.

A furtive glance.

Like he might be interested in her.

A glance that was going to make the violence a lot easier.

I grabbed the rest of Claire's cocktail and downed it.

"So, what's the plan?" he asked.

"Plan?"

"What's the current plan for reducing traffic congestion?"

"We've got a lot of plans."

"Tell me. Is it really true you guys had a plan to transport people via pneumatic tube?"

I didn't know what he was talking about.

But I wasn't going to let him know that I didn't.

Guys like that tend to feed off of stuff like that.

"It was talked about, yes."

"So it wasn't a joke?"

"We don't want to rule out any possibilities."

He laughed.

"I don't think congestion is a laughing matter, do you?"

"No offense," he said.

Pointing his fork prongs towards me.

"But you guys just don't get it, do you?"

"What don't we get?"

"The big picture."

I folded my hands:

"Yeah, and what's the big picture?"

"This city . . . it's not user friendly."

"User friendly?"

"Look, reducing traffic congestion is not enough."

"You need to redesign the whole city."

"Make it more livable, not more drivable."

"Think we need more public transportation, right?"

"Well, more communal transportation would be—"

"What, you a Communist?"

"Communist?"

"Yeah, a Communist."

He laughed.

"You do know what communal transportation is."

"Being employed in the transportation field as you are."

"You referring to comcars?"

"Well, that and all the other things the term implies—bikes, buses, rail."

"So public transportation then."

"No, so-called public transportation doesn't encompass—"

"Look, man. I've heard all this before."

"Everyone that doesn't know shit thinks that the answer is public transportation."

"It's not."

"So Los Angeles doesn't need more public transportation?"

"No. We don't."

"Then what do you need?"

"Less people."

"So what are you saying? There's nothing you can do because there's too many people?"

"It's more complicated than that."

"You can't just say put in more public transportation and wah-lah."

"Everything's fixed."

"It wouldn't hurt," he said.

"Look."

"People in Los Angeles."

"Despite the traffic."

"Generally prefer to drive if they have the choice."

"Maybe that's your problem," he said.

"What's my problem?"

"Not *your* problem."

"The city's problem."

"It's too spread out."

"I don't think people really prefer to drive."

"But due to the lack of any viable alternative."

"They're practically forced to."

"No one's forcing anyone to drive," I say.

He laughed.

"Yeah, I guess they could move to a real city if they really wanted to."

"Like New York—the city of brotherly Love?"

"That's Philadelphia."

"Whatever, they're both shit cities."

He laughed: "Say what you want about New York."

"But at least it was coherently planned."

"For attack?"

"Excuse me?"

"If you were a terrorist, which place would give you more bang for your bomb?"

"Here, where it is spread out?"

"Or New York?"

"Where everything is crammed together in one nice bombable package?"

"That depends on—"

"People that don't know shit are always talking shit about how L.A. is too spread out."

"But they never think about why that might be a good thing."

"Why there needs to be space."

"Between things."

"If you ever wonder why you've been attacked so much."

"It's because of your density."

"Look," he said. "New York was attacked because it's a high-value target."

"Meaning it was attacked because of its significance, not its density."

"It's about symbolic *quality*, not population quantity."

"Plus."

"New York is a *place*."

"While Los Angeles is just a space."

"Whatever it is, better you than us."

"By the way, how many times you been attacked again?"

He laughed.

"Don't flatter yourselves just because you've only been hit once."

"At Disneyland no less."

"And California Adventure," I say.

"Look," he said. "The first attack on New York was the World Trade Center."

"The symbol of American commerce and ingenuity."

"What did they attack in L.A.?"

"An amusement park?"

"C'mon."

"They picked Disneyland because to attack a bunch of little kids is the worst thing you *can* do."

"Plane crashing a bunch of suits doesn't even come close."

"It's not about the demographics of the casualties," he said.

"It's about the *significance* of the target."

"Less than fifty people were killed when the Statue of Liberty was blown up." *

"But the significance of such an attack is immeasurable."

"It strikes at the heart of what America stands for."

"A hell of a lot more than Disneyland."

"Unless you're a cynic."

"And tell me one thing of comparable significance to the Statue of Liberty that they could even attack in L.A."

"You can't."

"You saying the attacks on Disneyland don't count?"

"No, I'm not saying that."

"But what does Disneyland stand for?"

"Except a suck-your-thumb naive American fantasy."

"Is that really the best symbol they could find to hit in Los Angeles?"

"Technically Disneyland is in Orange County, not Los Angeles," I say.

"And technically those attacks were perpetrated by Americans."

"Not some dumb Arabs."

"And don't you think Americans would know better than anyone what the best place to attack in America is?"

"They claimed it was a work of art, but whatever their claim," he said.

"It's like what Marx said about history repeating itself."

"9/11 was the tragedy and 6/16 was the farce."

---

*   Later revealed to have been a "preemptive strike" initiated by the Wallace administration (who initially blamed the French) in order to prevent a terrorist attack on the monument.

"Farce? You callin 6/16 a farce?"

"Oh, don't get all worked up."

"Maybe things will improve."

"And you'll get attacked just as much as we have."

"Maybe even more."

He winked at me.

Like he winked at Claire.

I just looked at him.

The space between his two lips.

What he would call his mouth.

Slightly curved up with a bit of smug at the sides.

Claire stands up and puts her hand on her purse.

"Alex, let's go."

I sat there and looked at him.

He had turned like he was done with me.

Had the last word and all that shit.

I leaned forward.

"Apologize."

"Alex, let's go."

He turned back.

"What?"

"Apologize."

"For what?"

"Insulting L.A."

"I didn't insult anything."

"That hasn't been insulted before."

"Alex."

"Apologize."

"Lighten up," he said, turning away.

You don't tell a Nigger to lighten up.

To tell you the truth.

I don't really give a damn about 6/16.

But when some chump from New York starts talking shit.

I gotta represent.

Claire put her hand on my shoulder.

"Let's go."

I don't move.

I just sit there looking at this Davis with his back to me.

Like he was in no danger.

For saying what he said.

Like he was safe.

Claire is tugging my shoulder now.

Saying something.

But everything is muted like I got my hands over my ears.

This Davis guy framed smugly right in the center of my sight.

I don't want him framed smugly in the center of my sight.

So I grab this Davis by the hair and get his face down into his plate of leftover food.

After that my memory gets a little smoggy.

Except for the yells and screams.

I remember a lot of those.

Claire at my ear pleading, Alex Alex Alex.

And me telling her it was too late:

The ball had been thrown and the die had been cast.

Something like that.

But more poetical.

I remember returning the chair I'd borrowed with a one-handed fling.

Hitting the guy that wanted me to ask for his permission to take it.

I remember I'd yanked this Davis out of his chair and had my five-0 on him.

Then the manager.

Then security.

I yelled at them to back off.

That I was a cop.

And this guy was a suspect.

Which didn't seem to calm any of them for some reason.

Even when I added "From New York!"

So I dragged him outside and put his face to the sidewalk.

"Apologize, MotherFucker."

"Look, Alex. I'm sorry if I insulted you, but I—"

"Not to me, MotherFucker."

"To Los Angeles."

"Apologize to Los Angeles."

"What?"

"Apologize to Los Angeles for all that shit you said."

"I . . . I—"

I pushed his face into the sidewalk.

"Kiss the ground, MotherFucker, and tell her you're sorry."

Technically I should've had him kissing something more appropriate.

Something more representative of Los Angeles.

Than a Westside sidewalk.

But I had no intention of taking him on a tour.

So I had to make do.

"You kissing?"

He said something but I couldn't hear it.

I had his face pressed into the sidewalk too hard.

I pulled back a little.

"How about now?"

Couldn't tell if he was doing it so I had to lean down.

"You kissing?"

He was saying something, but I couldn't tell what he was saying.

"What the Fuck are you saying?"

Dude was crying.

A line of spit running off his lip.

So I pulled him back up.

And started bitch-slapping him.

Not personally.

But objectively.

Slap some sense into him.

Zen-master style.

But he cried more.

So I slapped more.

Until Claire hung with all her weight on my arm to get me to stop.

A crowd had gathered.

Of course.

Westside types.

Jerks.

They stood and rudely watched as I opened the car door for Claire.

Who was covering her face.

Like she was famous or something.

Maybe she was crying too.

And as things usually roll the way they do when they start rolling:

Some chick behind me says:

"What a Fuck-en psych-o?"

It wasn't what she said.

Well.

It was what she said.

But more the way she said it.

Like she wanted to be a part of the show.

End it with the last word.

In the form of a question no less.

Tell her friends over drinks afterward that she wasn't afraid to tell it like it is.

Or was.

Whatever.

So I turned around and full-fisted clocked her.

Back into the crowd.

One of her black heels scraping and coming off.

The people behind her stumbling and falling back.

Heying like they do when there is nothing else they can do.

Then when I pulled out into the street I almost got hit by a Dodge Rambo.

It slammed on its horn and got right on my ass with its brights.

Claire was crying now.

Sobbing and shuddering.

Her face in her hands.

I put my hand on her knee and she jerks it away.

Could see the guy in the rearview with his arm out and his middle finger up.

Horn still blasting.

Okay, I get it.

The night isn't over yet.

I slammed on the brakes and got out.

So did the dude.

A big bald bufforexic blanco.

Had to practically parachute out of his truck it was so high.

Devil points just behind the crown of the skull.

Matching face pussy of course.

Black T-shirt with the words *Drill Sergeant.*

Picture of a dude with a drill dick about to drill it into some bent-over chick.

Looked like she wanted it.

Somewhere there was an assembly line that churned out guys and trucks like this.

And one day I'm gonna find it.

And blow it up.

He was flexing his arms out.

Bowflexing and MotherFucking.

MotherFucking.

"MotherFucker."

Okay.

First a bit of nonsense to unbalance him.

"Don't you mean Mother Hubbard?"

"What?"

Now for the disarm.

"Don't you remember me?"

"What?"

"Alex from last year."

"Yeah, we met back at the—"

I came in fast and kicked him in the shin with my steel Tolchock.

What a cop would call a focused shin strike.

He let out more of a cry of surprise than pain.

And before the cry died I cracked him again.

Still.

He managed to get off a wild right that grazed my head.

Before the instinct to grab his shin kicked in.

Not instinct really.

Disbelief.

No one expects to get kicked in the shin.

Especially by a grown man.

Even then.

No one expects it to hurt that bad.

It does.

It's not easy to kick in a shin either.

You've got to spend several years kicking them just to kick one right.

And who has that kind of time.

I do.

While he was bent I examined my options.

1) Knee him in the face

<u>Pro:</u> Smashed-up face is always a good souvenir of a humiliating defeat.

<u>Con:</u> Too obvious, almost a cliché, like something out of the movies.

2) Hammer him in the kidneys

<u>Pro:</u> Brutal—kidney damage would make him piss blood, an excellent counterpoint to the shin kick.

<u>Con:</u> Not that exciting.

3) Ram his head into the side of his truck

<u>Pro:</u> His truck was a Dodge Rambo. My sign was Aries. My ex-partner's name, may he rest in peace, was Mars.

<u>Con:</u> Body of truck looked like it was made of cheap plastic.

4) Let him go, walk away

<u>Pro:</u> Show mercy, the fight was over.

<u>Con:</u> Show mercy, the fight was over.

5) All of the Above

Pro: The more the merrier.

Con: Couldn't think of one.

I kicked him in the other shin.

You want a picture of the future.

Imagine a boot kicking in a shin.

Forever.

The fight was over.

But the night wasn't.

When we got back home there was a big party going on at one of the houses down the street.

"See, they're doing it again," Claire said.

First thing she said since the restaurant.

Referring to the Mexicans that had bought the Golds' house a couple of months back.

The Golds had lived in that house since before my parents had bought ours.

Back in the Twentieth Century.

After my parents died Mr. Gold would come over and talk to me if I was out front working on my car.

My parents' old Chevy Bueller.

He seemed to know a lot about fixing cars.

Although I never saw him fix his.

Which was some kind of forgettable foreign sedan.

I remember that his wife drove an Eternity.

His son.

Who had been about five years older than me.

Killed himself when he was nineteen.

And it wasn't until my parents died that Mr. Gold started trying to talk to me.

Like we had something in common or something.

At first I tried to avoid him.

It made me uncomfortable.

I didn't think a black kid and an old Jewish man had anything to say to each other.

Or should have anything to say to each other.

Although I treated him better than his son ever did.

In fact.

His son was an asshole.

I remember being kind of glad that he was dead when he died.

This was the summer before my parents were killed.

Mrs. Gold came over to our house early in the morning all crying and hysterical.

She had gone into the garage and had found her son hanging from a rafter.

She didn't know what to do.

Well, the first thing she did was throw up in our bathroom.

Mr. Gold was still sleeping in bed.

She didn't want him to know.

She didn't want him to know.

She kept saying that.

My dad went over and took the kid off the rope.

And was later reprimanded by the cops for disturbing the scene.

After the Golds moved out, this couple bought the house and flipped it.

And sold it to the current Beaners that were now partying it up.

Couldn't tell how many lived there.

Looked like a couple of guys and a couple of girls and a couple of babies.

Couldn't tell if they were all living there or just half of them were.

No one seemed to be there during the day.

But at night that place would blow out the noise.

Apparently these Vampires threw a huge party once a week.

On a weekday.

Which lasted until dawn or when the police arrived.

And most of the time the police never arrived.

All of this happened when I was working.

So I wasn't as annoyed about it like everyone else on the street was.

Or supposedly was.

Because I didn't know or talk to most of the people that lived on this street.

Having lived in this house most of my life I only knew two of the neighbors.

And one of them had moved.

The other I didn't know as well as the Golds.

But one day.

I remember.

Because it was a part of the day I liked.

And there aren't too many parts of the day that I actually like.

Because of the sun.

And its indiscriminate.

Illumination.

The way it colors things.

Stains them.

Pulls their shadows.

And snaps them back.

Like some dirty joke.

Early morning is the best.

When the light is fresh.

Except I'm usually asleep.

But then.

As the day ripens.

And rots.

To late afternoon.

And the dull end of the workday.

Flops down.

And settles in.

Like an old.

You just want to.

Good thing I work at night.

So.

The wife came over and complained about our new neighbors while I was standing in the front yard sexing my Sativa.

She started off by saying that she wished the Golds were still here.

And then went on about how the cops weren't doing enough.

And wasn't there something we could do.

Which meant me.

Because I worked for "the City."

I stood there rubbing my chin and looked over at the supposed source of all this noise.

Looking unoccupied with the drapes drawn and no cars in the driveway.

But then again half the houses on this street looked unoccupied.

While the other half looked too occupied.

I had to admit that they took pretty good care of their yard.

For being a bunch of irresponsible partiers.

Although they weren't the ones that had designed it.

The flippers had put in a new lawn and a colorful variety of water-grubbing flowers.

Exotic plants and shrubs.

Two large blue-green stones floated on the lawn like islands in a dark green sea.

Looking like it was in some kind of competition.

To be best-looking yard on our block.

Problem was.

It wouldn't last.

Not with all the water it was going to take to keep it up.

Even if they could afford to exceed the regulated limits.

It still wouldn't be enough.

The more I looked at that front yard the more I got angry.

Not at the current residents.

But at the people that sold it to them.

Those Fucking flippers.

They were the ones that put the idea of moving into Claire's head.

The ones that told her about La Brea Gardens.

The new designer colony between Wilshire and 3rd.

Which occupied the area once known as Park La Brea.

The construction of the place had been delayed for at least five years as I recall.

Because some of the financing fell through.

Remember driving by there for years seeing nothing but construction equipment and cranes.

Chain link and barbed wire.

Now.

The place consisted of various state-of-the-art low-rise buildings in different styles.

Radiating out from a needlelike luxury high-rise with revolving floors.

All protected behind massive walls.

The flippers told Claire that they were flipping houses to make enough for the hefty down payment on one of the high-rise units.

They were pretty excited about it.

And they got Claire excited about it.

And she tried to get me excited about it.

On the assumption.

I assumed.

That maybe I would suggest that maybe we should move there too.

I didn't.

The words advertised to describe the place were enough to turn me off.

Cultivated living.

A delicious blend of small-town charm and cosmopolitan style.

An oasis of stability in a sea of change.

Several unique lifestyle boutiques and artisanal eateries exclusively for residents.

Butterfly habitat.

All of it terror-proofed by a state-of-the-art private security force of course:

BlackGuard.

I'll admit that some of it looked kind of nice with the palm trees and fountains.

The state-of-the-art units that were so state of the art they could practically jerk you off.

Plus there were a couple of saltwater pools.

"Imagine if we lived there," Claire said.

"We'd have our own private access to all the museums."

"The Farmers Market and the Grove."

"And I won't have to drive and you won't have to drive that far to work."

This was back when I still had to drive to work.

And not be driven.

"We could never afford a place like that."

"Yes, we can," she said, "we've already been prequalified."

"What do you mean prequalified?

"It means that we're qualified to fill out an application."

"When did all this happen?"

"I filled out the form last week."

"Serious? Without asking me?"

"I did it for fun. Just to see. Would you want to if we could?"

"It would take us fifty years to pay it off, *after* using this house as a down payment."

"Money isn't everything, you know," she said.

"This doesn't have anything to do with—" I started.

A mistake.

I stopped right there.

"With what?"

"Forget it."

"My disorder is what you were going to say, isn't it?"

"No."

"This doesn't have anything to do with that, Alex."

"I'm trying to find the best place for us to live."

"So you think this place is the best place?"

"Okay, maybe not *the* best, but it's better than here."

"You don't like it here?"

"It's not that I don't like it," she said.

"It's just that."

"It just feels like we're living on the periphery of things."

"Wouldn't you rather live somewhere where there's something happening?"

"Where there's culture and people?"

"And where you don't have to commute so long for work?"

"Yeah, maybe, I don't know."

"Maybe it's because I work down there."

"So it's less of a big deal to live there."

"And I've always lived here, so."

"So?"

I knew she didn't like Simi.

First thing she said when she came out here was:

"It's so—*beige*."

Not that I really wanted to live in Simi Valley either.

But I couldn't think of anywhere else that I wanted to live.

Even in Los Angeles.

Most of the names of the places are enough to turn you off:

Reseda, Canoga Park, Norwalk, Tustin, Torrance.

Van Nuys.

Pacoima.

Burbank.

Anything with the words *park, hills, lake, dale, city,* or *rancho.*

Atwater Village.

Makes me think of Nixon for some reason.

Pasadena.

Makes me think of milk.

Or, if it ain't the name.

It's the picture of the people that live in Silver Lake, Calabasas, Manhattan Beach.

West Hollywood.

Santa Monica.

Not to mention Beverly Hills, Brentwood, and Bel Air.

What they used to call Douche Bags.

Before it became a compliment.

So.

Even though I had no interest in moving I said:

"Look, if you're not happy here, we can move somewhere else."

And.

"I don't really care where I live as long as you're happy."

Which was partially true.

And.

Two weeks later.

Thanks to Synnita.

Who knew someone who knew someone.

We were on the waiting list for La Brea Gardens.

"Don't hold your breath," she had said to Claire.

"It could take ten years."

The neighbor lady was looking at me:

"So, what do you think?"

"Who takes care of the yard?"

"I don't know," she said.

"Probably a gardener."

"They don't look like the type of Mexicans that know how to do yard work."

"So you've seen someone working in the yard?"

"I've heard lawn mowers and leaf blowers early in the morning."

"I can't remember which day."

"A Wednesday I think."

"So they probably have a gardener."

"I mean with all that partying they do."

"I can't see any one of them waking up that early and mowing the lawn."

"Anyone try going over there and talking to them?"

"I don't know. I think your wife tried going over there, didn't she?"

"If she did, she didn't tell me."

"Isn't there something we can do? I mean, this is really ridiculous."

"Yeah."

Claire had already called me a number of times at work about the noise.

When I told her to call the police she insisted that I should instead.

Seeing as I worked for the City.

They might listen to me more.

So I said I'd look into it.

Which I never did.

So now.

While the neighbor lady looked on from across the street.

I walked over to the house and rang the doorbell.

When no one answered I knocked on the door.

No answer.

I walked around to the side gate and opened it.

There were a couple of terror-proof trash cans against the side wall.

I idly cracked the blue recycle bin just enough so as not to trigger it and peeked inside.

Half-filled with beer cans and bottles.

Cigarette butts and cigarette ash mixed in with the whole mess.

I dropped the lid and peeked inside the green trash can.

More cans and bottles and some food wrappers resting on a bed of lawn clippings.

I dropped the lid and walked into the backyard, where the pool was.

Where else would it be.

I had gone swimming over here as a kid a few times.

And a few more times when I was older.

When the Golds were out of town and had asked me to collect their mail.

Keep an eye on the place.

The yard around the pool had been tastefully landscaped in the style of the front yard.

And the pool looked relatively clean.

There were a bunch of black plastic garbage bags piled on the back porch.

Probably leftovers from their last party.

Other than that there wasn't anything that looked suspicious or out of place.

Not that I expected anything suspicious or out of place.

Although all the windows had their curtains drawn, which seemed slightly suspicious.

A wooden trellis, which hadn't been there when the Golds lived there.

Had been extended over the back porch.

And the sliding glass doors had been replaced with a set of french doors.

I tried the handle of the french door and it was locked.

The handle seemed kind of flimsy so I forced it.

Putting my weight down hard against it until it broke.

Half thinking slash wondering that the house, like the trash cans, had been proofed.

And an alarm, or something worse, would go off.

The Golds used to have one of those old fire-bell-sounding burglar alarms.

And sometimes it would go off for no reason.

I almost expected to hear it again.

But there was nothing.

The door still wouldn't open even with the handle broke.

And I kind of had to shove against the door while push-pulling on the handle for it to open.

I'd been in this house before.

Invited of course.

And to tell you the truth.

Never liked the floor plan.

This used to be a den.

And the floor used to be tile.

Now it was wood.

An IKEA couch.

And a cheap glass coffee table with a bunch of random stuff piled on it.

An ashtray and some baby toys.

Moving boxes from a nationally known moving company.

Stacked in front of the fireplace.

This house had two fireplaces for some reason.

Maybe it was colder back then.

Back when it was built.

I pulled what looked like a roach from the ashtray and smelled it.

What I suspected.

And nothing wrong with that I might add.

I put it back.

A set of steps led up to the kitchen and the entrance to the living room.

Empty beer bottles on the counters and another ashtray.

Some of the bottles appeared to contain cigarette butts.

And were a brand of beer that for legal reasons I can't mention.

But can tell you that I don't like.

Urine was found in several bottles a few years back.

It was on the news.

There were two unopened cases of the stuff in the fridge.

Along with a few cans of Coke.

A carton of milk.

One container of diet yogurt.

And a few condiment containers on the side.

I grabbed a Coke.

Opened it.

Took a couple of swigs.

And then put it back in the fridge.

I like Coke.

The freezer was filled with frozen steaks.

The kind you can buy in bulk from Costco.

I don't like going to Costco.

Unless it's absolutely necessary.

Anyways.

There wasn't much else in that department.

So I moved into the living room.

Same half-unpacked deal here as with the den.

State-of-the-art walls though.

Sony.

Sound system too.

High-end.

Fillmore-Krankton amp and receiver.

The kind in the transparent casing.

To show off their multicolored guts.

Small enough to fit inside the cargo pockets of my household shorts.

So I unplugged them and put one in each pocket.

And sealed the deal with Velcro.

I examined the rest of the room.

A tacky black leather couch that didn't quite match the earth tones of the room.

A few more child's toys.

More stacked boxes from the same national moving company.

One of the boxes.

A seven-to-eight-foot-long narrow rectangle that leaned against the wall.

Appeared to be another Sony wall screen.

Brand-new and unopened.

Hadn't finished rewalling our house yet.

Only our bedroom.

Which we thought was best to do first.

Important to be able to rest in a relaxing environment.

Adjust our moods.

Plus we usually watched a lot of TV in there.

But I wasn't going to take it.

Look too greedy.

So.

That was it for the living room.

I walked upstairs and then halted at the second from the top stair.

Sound.

A human sound.

Breathing.

A moan.

A hmmm.

Something like that.

Quick and then gone.

I waited for a full minute.

But nothing else.

I threw in another minute.

Silence.

The upstairs was carpeted.

So I took off my chop-flops and lightly padded my way to where the
sound had come from.

The master bedroom.

The door was open a crack.

I could see a bed.

And a messed mass of bedspread and sheets.

Bulked up either because they were piled like that.

Or because there was a body underneath.

I crouched down and looked in a little closer.

Feeling like a Peeping Tom.

In less than a minute there was movement.

The cover moved.

A tangle of long black hair appeared.

Then an arm.

Slender.

A woman.

The neighbor lady had seemed impressed.

That I had the courage to just casually walk into these people's backyard.

Without an invitation.

I told her that there was nothing to worry about.

They were just a bunch of kids.

Who liked to party.

She asked what my next move would be.

In a hushed tone like I was some kind of detective or secret agent.

I wanted to play along.

But told her I didn't know.

That her and her husband should keep an eye out and let me know what develops.

She told me *she* would.

In a manner to insinuate that her husband couldn't be relied upon for a situation like this.

I got the impression that she was kind of annoyed with her husband.

For not dealing with these neighbors in the way that she thought he should.

Like Stan Gold.

She was the visible half of the couple.

Whereas Stan's wife and this lady's husband didn't show their faces much outside the house.

Except when they were coming or going.

Her husband didn't even work in the yard.

It was her.

Or the son.

Who was off somewhere at college.

That I would occasionally see mowing the lawn.

One time when she was working in her yard.

And I in mine.

She came over to let me know that her husband couldn't work in the yard.

Because of his allergies.

Apparently so I wouldn't come to the conclusion that there was something wrong with him.

In the Masculine Department.

I didn't.

My brain never fired a thought regarding his existence one way or another.

Part of my job I guess.

Besides.

The twenty-first century was supposed to be the century of the female.

That's what everyone kept saying.

Even the males.

So I guess it was their turn to mow the lawn so to speak.

Anyways.

I pretty much forgot about the house across the street.

Until me and Claire got home that night and there was a party going in full force.

We heard the loud thumping music.

Powered by a brand-new Fillmore-Krankton no doubt.

Before we even turned on our street.

Which was so parked up there wasn't even a space available.

Kids on the street with plastic cups in their hands.

Looking like they were up to no good.

As kids usually do at that hour.

Or from the distant point of middle age.

To make things even more interesting.

When I got to my house there was a Ford Bragg.

Blocking about a quarter of my driveway.

And.

On my lawn.

A big, bald Vato.

With no shirt.

And a considerable number of tattoos.

Arcing a stream of piss into my Sativa.

I swore as I tried to squeeze the Fueltility around the Bragg and next to Claire's Zero.

"See," she said.

"Is it like this every time?"

"Yeah."

In a tone that tells me she's mad at me for tonight.

And mad at me for doubting the severity of these parties.

"You mean people have pissed on my grass before?"

"You mean the lawn or your weed?" she said.

"Just go inside," I say.

"Let me handle this."

She got out and went straight for the front door.

I got out and stood behind him on the sidewalk.

He was standing there with his legs apart.

Shoulders wide.

Like he didn't care who saw him.

A bunch of his homies must have been watching.

Because there came a bunch of whoops and cheers from across the street.

"Hey, bro, the owner is right up there behind you," one of them laughed.

"Good, then I'll piss on the MotherFucker's head."

More whoops and hollers.

"Nice night for a piss," I say.

Not bothering to turn his head.

And saying it loud for the benefit of his friends:

"Bring your old lady out and I'll pee on her too."

"Two for the price of one, bitch."

A bunch of cheers across the street.

And a "Yeah, MotherFucker."

"Do you know what you're peeing on?"

Half turning his head now:

"Your grave, bitch."

I walked up and kicked him behind his left knee.

Which brought him down to a height where I could kick him in the back of the head.

Which I did.

Of course.

And.

Just my luck.

He went facedown into my Sativa.

Crushing it.

"Now you're in real trouble."

"I put a lot of work into that garden."

Besides the Sativa.

I had a variety of plants on my front lawn:

Succulents.

Cacti.

Lupinus albifrons.

Lavender and Rosemary.

Echevaria subrigida.

Agave Blue Glow.

Rare shit.

Everything drought resistant.

Except for the Sativa.

"Hey, MotherFucker."

Cusses from behind and the sound of several feet charging across the pavement.

I turn around and cross-pull my BDG and five-0.

Three of them.

Like him.

Bald.

Except with shirts on.

When they saw that I was armed they put on the brakes.

And adjusted their looks.

From total menace.

To a mixture of fear and menace.

I looked at them calmly.

And then walked over and stepped on the back of their homie's head.

See if I could adjust their looks to terror.

No.

Back to full menace now.

The head under me tried to say something.

But could only sputter.

So I drove my heel in harder.

"Hey, that's our friend, MotherFucker," one of them says.

I aimed the five-0 at him.

"Yeah, and after I get done plantin his head you're next."

"MotherFucker."

He puts his hands halfway up.

"Yo, hey."

"Which one of you MotherFuckers is the owner?"

They don't say anything.

I put more weight on the head.

"Well, which one?"

"Which one, what?" one of them says.

"Which one of you is the owner of that house?"

"No one, man," one says.

"We ain't," says another.

"You there," I say to the half-assed hands up.

"Go and fetch the owner of the house."

After all the shit of tonight.

I was starting to feel good again.

Powerful.

That feeling of power that comes with a handful of guns.

And a body beneath your heel.

The dude I told to go fetch just stood there.

"You spreaken English?" I say.

"Parle usted Anglais?"

"What?"

"Do you speak English?"

"Yeah, I speak Fuckin English, man."

"Then get the Fuckin owner of that house out here right now."

"He's not home," the one next to him says.

"Where is he?"

"He's not here."

"Where *is* he?"

"I said I don't know."

"Then you're trespassing," I say, leveling the BDG at him.

"And in this neighborhood all trespassers will be shot."

The head under me is trying to struggle out from under my foot.

Like it can't breathe.

So I put more weight on my foot.

Twisting and turning.

Like I was putting out a cigarette butt.

"Don't try to struggle, hombre, or I will plant your head."

"And harvest it come fall."

"Hey, man," one of them says.

"Hey, the owner's cousin is here. I can go get him if you want."

"You do that, Poncho."

"You do that."

One of them runs back towards the house.

Where most of the party are now crowded on the porch and the lawn.

Watching the whole show from a safe distance.

I look up and down the street.

All the neighbors' houses are dark and quiet.

Like they're hiding.

Waiting for the storm to blow over.

Someone could be getting murdered right out on their front lawns.

And all they would do is draw the blinds.

Which pisses me off more than these stupid kids and their party.

A Latino buttoning up a black silk shirt comes out.

He looks around him like what's up.

Everyone points.

He looks over and realizes.

It's showtime and he's late for his performance.

So he comes charging up.

Demands what the hell is going on.

I take my foot off the pisser's head.

And tell him if he moves.

I will shoot the hell out of him.

I walk up to this dude.

And he suddenly lowers the heat on his attitude when he sees my guns.

"What's the problem here?" he says.

"What's the problem?"

Right then I catch a glimpse of the neighbor lady.

Watching from the shadows of her vine-covered front walk.

"Yeah, what's your problem, man?"

"Hmmm. Let me see now."

I scratch my chin with the barrel of the five-0.

"Oh, the problem."

"Well for one thing I caught one of your home squeezes here disrespecting my plants."

"What?"

"He was taking a piss on my Cannabis."

"Cannabis?"

"Yeah, you know what Cannabis is?"

"Yeah, man, I know what it is, but you don't have to Fuckin stomp on him."

"Yeah, you're right."

"I'd rather stomp on you."

"Hey, look, man, I didn't tell him to do it."

"This your house?"

"It's my cousin's."

"Well, where's your cousin?"

"He's out of town."

His eyes flick a quick look behind me and I turn and see the guy on my lawn.

Making an attempt to get up.

I point my five-0 at him.

"Didn't I tell you not to move, hombre?"

He turns over to a sitting position and doesn't move.

Wiping the blood from his nose and the dirt off his face.

"Hey, man, whatever he did we can work this out."

"You don't have to disrespect him like that."

"I don't?"

"No, man. If you got a problem then you—"

"But you have the right to disrespect this neighborhood with your parties, right?"

"Hey, it's a free country, man. People have parties."

"Free country?"

"Yeah, last time I checked."

"And when was that?"

"What?"

"When was the last time you checked on the freeness of this country?"

"Look, man. All I'm saying is that if you've got a problem, then—"

"I'm afraid you've been misinformed."

"What?"

"This country ain't free."

"And neither is this neighborhood."

"Yeah?"

"Yeah."

"What, you a cop?"

"Let's just say I call the shots around here."

"And right now I'm telling your punk ass to shut this party down."

"Before I shoot you and your homies on the street right here."

"*Comprende*, shithead?"

He looks at me and calculates what his reaction should be.

Tryin to do trig when all he has to do is add.

But he wants to save lives.

And his face.

"It ain't quantum science, MotherFucker."

"What's it going to be then?"

"Eh?"

"Okay. I'll turn it down."

"But you don't have no right to threaten me or my friends like this."

"Oh, really?"

"I didn't do nothing to you."

"Oh, yeah? You didn't do nothing to me?"

"He was just pissin, man. He wasn't—"

"Who taught you your manners?"

"What?"

"Who the Fuck taught you your manners, MotherFucker?"

"Hey, I mind my manners, man, I don't—"

"Yeah."

"You don't."

"Theme song of your life."

"You don't."

"You don't seem to care that there's people who live on this street."

"Who've got to go to work in the morning."

"Or mow their lawns."

"Or whatever the hell these damn people do."

"No."

"You just think you're free."

"To do whatever the hell you want."

"And Fuck everyone else."

"Well, let me tell you."

"And that goes for all of you over there!"

"Nothin's free."

"Nothin!"

"This is America, MotherFucker."

"And in America you pay."

"Pay."

"Or go the Fuck away."

"It's called Capitalism."

"You want some phony fuckin freedom, go to Russia."

"And if *you don't* shut down and clear out now."

"That's where the Fuck you goin, MotherFucker."

"All of you!"

"You understand!"

"Okay. Okay, man. I'll shut it down."

He turned and shouted to everyone that the party was over and that they had to go home.

I turned back and walked up to the dude on my front yard.

I stood over him and holstered my weapons.

"Of all the yards in all the neighborhoods."

"You had to pee on mine."

"Get up."

"Shit," he said, stumbling to his legs.

"Yeah," I say, "shit."

"You're a cop."

"No. I work for the Department of Decongestion."

He thought I was making a joke and snorted.

"Hey, man, it wasn't personal, it was just a piss, man."

"No, it wasn't," I say.

"It was a Fuck-you piss."

"You got a car?"

"Yeah. You gonna give me a ticket?"

"Let's go."

"Where?"

"To your car."

I walked behind him down to the end of the street where his car was parked.

It was a quiet night.

Or would have been if that party hadn't been there.

One of those nights that settles on everything like a comfortable blanket.

And you know you're going to get some good sleep.

That is.

If some clown doesn't disrupt it.

Quiet:

A suburban dream.

That if shattered brings out the worst in people on streets like this.

Or should.

My neighbors seemed to be in the habit of turning the other cheek.

"Here it is," he said.

A brand-new Nissan Nightstalker.

Customized.

Lo pros and show rims.

Teles.

Now banned.

After that guy was caught driving around elementary schools.

With porn on his rims.

I told him to give me his keys, and he pulled them from his pocket and handed them to me.

I hit the button for the trunk.

It popped up with an innocuous little beep.

"Get in," I say.

He wanted to discuss this.

So I grabbed him and threw him in.

The sound of a siren somewhere.

But it wasn't coming here.

I got in and it started up with a belching roar.

Like some rude dragon.

Obviously this asshole didn't have the decency to keep his car properly muffled.

I yanked the thing away from the curb and floored it out across the valley.

Towards the rocky hills to the east.

Up the old road.

I took the turns fast.

Whiplashing the tail left and right with each turn.

Near the top.

Before the road disappears through a tangle of trees as it winds its way into the depths of the hills.

I pulled onto a dirt turnout and pointed the car at the valley below.

Lights blinked in the quiet dark.

A few dark patches like black holes amidst a cluster of stars.

I rolled down the window and a breeze forced its way in.

Like there might be something better to blow inside.

It came in and then died to a small flutter.

A banging from behind.

Muffled words.

More banging.

It was a nice night and I wanted more of it.

The quiet and the breeze.

The city subdued below.

I started the engine and listened to its low bass purr for a few moments.

And then got out.

A sudden gust of wind gave me a shove.

Trying to push me back inside.

I pushed back and then turned and leaned in.

Moved the stick from P to D.

The sedan lurched forward.

I shut the door before it went over the edge.

The walk home down the canyon was nice.

Crickets cricketing.

A few stars twinkling.

The crunch of dirt under boots.

I took my jacket off and slung it over my shoulder.

Eventually I stopped thinking.

And after a while became.

A man.

Walking down a dirt road.

My street was quiet.

The cars and people gone.

Several beer cans in the gutter and on the sidewalk.

I collected the few that were near my house and threw them on the culprit's lawn.

My body was beat.

But in a good way.

And I slid smoothly into a deep, dark sleep.

Claire never gave me the props I deserved for that night.

In fact.

It was the reverse.

A couple of days later she said:

"I was thinking about leaving you that night."

"What? Why?"

"That girl."

"Why did you have to hit her?"

THE BIG PUMP

Two things you can't have on this job.

Love.

Or Hate.

Got one you got the other.

Can't work with a guy like that.

One day he can barely pull the trigger.

And the next he wants to get creative.

Although any man that Hates to kill.

Kills the best.

I used to Love it.

Used to.

Love.

The look on the face.

The I don't wanna.

I don't deserve.

Maybe a consolation:

"People been dyin for millions of years."

"Or is it thousands."

Or, a bit of wisdom:

"Dead is your natural state."

"You were dead before you were born."

"Vive la mort!"

Some Shakespeare perhaps:

"To be."

"Or not to be."

"Ain't really the question."

"But."

"To be bone-caged and flesh-slaved."

"Is."

*"'Tis better not."**

Or better yet, some good old-fashioned TV:

Next stop Willoughby!

Nice.

The way the body flinched.

Tightened.

Then limped.

The eyes that refuse to close.

Grasping.

For that final look.

---

*   Not Shakespeare—origin unknown.

That I could get a good day's sleep when the night was done.

And wake up and do it again.

You might call me a Vampire.

A cancer even.

Maybe.

But your ruin is my health.

Because cancer don't get cancer.

And Vampires.

Well.

They live forever.

But serious.

What I'm doing is a public service if you really think about it.

SaintWork.

Because.

Let's face it.

Despite what everyone says.

No one really likes life.

Even when they say they do.

They don't.

Not really.

The endless disappointment.

Boredom.

Tedium.

Interspersed with intermittent Tolchocks.

Having to endure another plotless day.

Wanting and waiting.

Shopping and shitting.

Trapped.

In a 3-D universe.

(Decay, Disease, and Death.)

And tortured by Time.

Why we all gotta pretend?

Maybe it's the fear that if we say we Hate it we'll get punished or something.

Sent to hell.

Or worse.

That we're right.

That life ain't worth a damn.

And this really is hell.

But really.

None of you.

Really.

Want to see.

The degradation.

The suffering.

Even when it's right in front of your face.

Nailed to a cross.

Call me a Christian.

God looked at his creation and said it was good.

Which doesn't make any sense.

Unless he's evil.

As for the good.

There's just enough of it to blind you from seeing how evil life really is.

Actually, I think if a man can Hate life.

Truly Hate it.

Then maybe he can actually live it.

Like this spinning mug right here.

Our next subtraction.

Old man with a hate-face.

A face that looked like it was entering the first stages of a bad hangover.

So did the back of his head.

The head.

Won't stop.

Spinning.

A few more times and it's gonna.

Stop.

No jacket except for a couple of deuces.

Don't usually look at the face.

Not anymore.

After years on the job the faces start to bleed into one another.

Till they become one.

And you become a clerk.

Stamping the same form over and over.

The same face forever.

Until the face disappears.

And there are no faces anymore.

Just the form.

But this face.

It said, I know you.

Smooth out the hair and young up the face and I know you.

Not personally.

But a face I knew better than some faces I knew personally.

Finger to the shield.

Picking his nose:

"Meghasin, look at this ZO and tell me who this is."

"Jerry Studebaker."

"No, the face."

"Tell me who that is."

"It says it's Jerry Studebaker."

"Forget the ID. Who does that *look* like?"

"I don't know, Officer Krieg."

"Does it look like someone?"

"Let me give you a hint:"

"It was Monday the Thirteenth."

"A day far more unlucky than Friday the Thirteenth as far as I was concerned."

"I'm afraid I don't—"

"At least with Friday the Thirteenth you have the weekend to look forward to."

"C'mon, you know this."

"I don't."

"When life gives me lemons, Mr. Pumpworthy."

"I make a lemon martini."

"Yeah, and I'll bet if it gave you shit."

"You'd make a shit sandwich."

"I don't know what that is," she said.

"What, a shit sandwich?"

"No, what you're quoting."

"It's from *The Big Pump.*"

"The Pig Bump?"

"No, *The Big Pump.*"

Flick his face:

"That's Arthur Lemmings."

"a.k.a. Dick Pumpworthy from *The Big Pump.*"

"I don't watch pornography, Officer Krieg."

"What? It's not porn."

"Considered one of the greatest movies ever made."

"By whom?"

"By *who?*"

"Yes, by—"

"What, you don't believe me?"

"No, it's not that. I—"

"Look it up if you don't believe me."

"Okay."

She doesn't look it up.

"Well?"

"Well, what?"

"You lookin it up?"

"No."

"Why not?"

"Okay." Looking at her pad.

"I see it now."

"*Time*'s top one hundred movies of all time."

"Yep."

"The same magazine that made Hitler man of the year," she muttered.

"What?"

"Nothing."

"No, what did you say about Hitler?"

"*Time* magazine made Hitler their man of the year back in 1938."

"So? What does that have to do with anything?"

"Nothing, forget it."

"Saying that it doesn't count?"

"No, I was just—"

"PAL," I say, "*Time* magazine."

"Did they ever make Hitler man of the year?"

"451 Blocked. Any references to Adolf Hitler are prohibited by the Department, Officer Krieg."

"What?"

"Just forget it, Officer Krieg," Meghasin said. "I wasn't trying to—"

The Big Pump's my favorite movie.

Reason I like it.

Is.

Well.

It's like this:

Niggers used to do things.

Cause they had to.

Not because they.

Needed a name.

Or fame.

A swimming pool.

Because they *had* to.

Why they made the best art in this country.

Now.

However.

They do like everyone else.

White people.

Makin shit.

Indiscriminately.

Superfluously.

Trivially.

In other words.

Makin shit.

To get paid.

Which.

There isn't anything wrong with getting paid.

But you gotta know the difference.

Between Art.

And just another product.

And most people don't.

So *The Big Pump.*

Even though he was only half.

Nigger.

Dude had to make that shit.

Had to.

One of Mars's favorite movies too.

After *Star Wars.*

"Heard his dick wasn't real, man."

"What?"

"That it was all like CGI and shit."

"Where'd you hear that?"

"PBS, man."

"They had this show."

"Bullshit."

"And that he was like using all this Snake Oil and shit."

"What?"

"That doesn't even make sense."

"How you gonna Snake Oil CGI?"

"No, man."

"He used the Snake Oil first and then they CGI'd it."

"Bullshit. I know everything about that movie, and—"

"Dude, seriously."

"PBS wouldn't lie about shit like that."

"Why not?"

"Cuz they don't have commercials, man."

"Okay, you know what?"

This Jerry Studebaker lived on Pickford in a single-story piece of stucco roofed with faded red tile.

Gray lawn that looked like the fur of an old dog.

Old Chevy Mizer in the driveway.

Color coordinated with the lawn.

PAL dropped us about two houses down and then drove off.

TV lights flickered behind barred front windows.

Meghasin about to knock on the door when I grabbed her shoulder.

"Yo, we need to talk."

She turned, irritated. "About what?"

"This subtraction."

"What about it."

"*The Big Pump* is my favorite movie."

"Yeah, you told me—"

"You don't see the connection."

"Should I?"

"After I started talkin shit and accusing Thurlow?"

"It's obvious they're tryin to Fuck with me."

"Officer Krieg, can't we just—"

"No, let me call this in first."

She sighed.

"See if this Jerry Studebaker is really Arthur Lemmings."

Hope he isn't though.

Thought he was dead.

Hoped he was dead.

All my heroes are dead.

Not old-age dead.

But dead dead.

Burned.

Blown.

Destroyed.

Nothing more pathetic than a guy running off old fumes.

Soon as I start the call a loud scream rips through the air.

I hit the lawn.

It don't stop.

But changes pitch from a nail on a chalkboard.

To a belch through a bullhorn.

Anita's face snaps on.

Somewhere in that cold, pale business face.

A flicker of concern.

"What's that noise?" she said.

Sounded like someone with a vendetta.

Against silence.

The cool night air.

Punching oxygen.

And shoving nitrogen.

Or was it the other way around.

It stopped.

I got up off of the lawn and straightened up my hat.

"I think it's a guitar."

"Tryin to do Hendrix."

"Or some of that Post Music shit."

"What?"

"Some kid probably, trying to play the guitar."

"That why you're calling me?"

"This subtraction. I want to confirm it."

"What?"

"I want to confirm this subtraction."

"Think it might be a mistake."

"Confirm a subtraction?"

"Yes, that's correct."

"Since when do *you* confirm a subtraction?"

"This guy looks a lot like Arthur Lemmings."

"Who?"

"Arthur Lemmings."

"From *The Big Pump*."

"So?"

"So, we don't usually kill people like that, do we?"

"The word is subtract."

"Yeah, well, we usually don't do that either."

She gave me a look and then looked offscreen for a moment.

And then gave me the look again.

You know the look.

"What the hell's going on out there?" she said.

"You've already voided two subtractions."

"No, we didn't, this is only our second."

"The target window," she said.

"You've missed two windows."

"Why?"

"How the hell should I know?"

"All I know is we can't subtract Arthur Lemmings."

"His name is Jerry Studebaker."

"Not Arthur whoever."

"You're required to review the target prior to the subtraction, Alex."

"You've been warned about this already."

"I reviewed this guy and he's most definitely Arthur Lemmings."

"Well, he's listed as Jerry Studebaker."

"Studebaker is probably just an alias."

"Can you check it for me?"

She looks offscreen.

"It's Jerry Studebaker."

"How do you know?"

"Says here that this Jerry Studebaker has always been Jerry Studebaker."

"What about Lemmings, check on Lemmings."

"I have multiple reports from PAL that you're Fucking around," she said.

"What?"

"Is that what it said?"

"I'm Fucking around?"

"What about PAL and his Darth Vader shit?"

"I can't concentrate with that thing breathin in my face."

"We're still looking into it," she said.

"Yeah, and what about that illegal hit, Anita?"

"You lookin into that too?"

"There was no illegal hit."

"That woman had a perfect driving record and she was suing Thurlow, you don't think—"

"You need to stay on task and stop manufacturing—"

"And what about Claire—I'm startin to think she didn't leave, but that she was—"

"Look," she said.

"I'm not getting into this with you."

"You either do your job or I'll find someone else who will."

"Yeah, who?"

The PDT goes blank.

Then buzzes.

It's PAL.

I don't answer.

"Are we ready, Officer Krieg?" Meghasin said.

"Yeah."

"But I want you to hang back on this one."

"Why?"

"Orders from Captain Helquist."

"Captain Helquist?"

"Why?"

"What did she say?"

I waved my hand at her to shut the Fuck up.

Walked up and rang the doorbell.

The sound of chimes inside.

I did it again and the chimes did it again.

There was a steel mesh door in front of the front door.

And when the front door opened there was no light.

Only the shadow of a figure veiled behind the mesh.

The smell of cigar smoke.

Mixed with cigarette smoke.

"Hello," I say.

"Arthur Lemmings?"

A man's deep voice from further inside the house.

"Tom, is that you?"

It sounded like Arthur Lemmings alright.

"It's some African-American guy," said the figure in the doorway.

A woman with a voice like rust.

"And some chick."

"Hi, Arthur Lemmings in?"

"What do you want?"

I pulled out my police badge and held it against the mesh door.

"I'm Detective Rogers and this is my partner Detective . . . Detective . . ."

I shotgunned Meghasin a look.

Her face was blank.

"Smith," I say.

"Detective Smith."

"We'd like to have a few words with Mr. Lemmings."

Footsteps on a wooden floor.

And then a voice from behind the mesh like someone crumpling a piece of paper.

Inside his throat.

"Tom, is that you?"

"It's the fuzz," the woman said.

The mesh door screeched open enough for the old man to put his head out and give us a look.

Or at least Meghasin a look.

It was Lemmings alright.

Except he looked whiter.

"African-American?" he said.

"I don't see no African-American."

I stepped to the left with my badge.

"I'm not an African-American."

"I'm Detective Rogers and this is my partner, Officer . . ."

He looked down on me with a scowl.

"Not an African-American?"

"What, too blue to be black?"

"Look," I say.

"I just want to—"

"Guys got nothing better to do than harass an old man?"

"Sir, we just want—"

"I'm outta here," the woman said.

The mesh door flung open.

A bleach-burned blonde.

Looking twenty years younger than her voice.

Blew past and down the sidewalk with loud, angry heel clicks.

"Uh—"

Meghasin giving me a look.

"Let it," I say.

Nine outta ten we would have to subtract her too.

But I wasn't even thinking about zeroing Lemmings.

Let alone her.

Besides.

No one was gonna believe anything out of her mouth.

She was probably a prostitute.

Not a real citizen.

But then again.

This isn't a Zen city.

"Thanks, asshole—you just made my night."

He looks worse than the mug.

Nothing but boxer shorts and an undershirt.

Face gray like the lawn.

"Thought you were dead."

"Well, I ain't."

"Now go away."

"Just wanted to ask you a few questions, Mr. Lemmings."

"We come in?"

"You've got the wrong guy, pal."

"My name ain't Lemmings."

"Your name *is* Lemmings."

"You can't fool me."

"I've seen *The Pump.*"

"It's Studebaker, asshole."

"C'mon, lighten up. We ain't the pop-nazis."

"Nazis? What the Fuck are you talking about?"

"Paparazzi. We're not the paparazzi."

"Just fans."

"Paparazzi?"

"Look, you gonna let us in or what?"

I grabbed the door and shoved him back and walked in.

Following me down the hall.

"You got a warrant, asshole?"

I made a right turn into a living room thick with blue smoke.

An old CRT with the volume turned low was the only light.

A cigar burned on the edge of an end table next to an easy chair.

I went over and sat down in the easy chair and flicked on a lamp next to the cigar.

Lemmings stood in front of me and I handed him the cigar.

"Make yourself at home, asshole," he said.

He took a drag and smoked me.

"Look, I know you're Lemmings so—"

"Who the Fuck's this Lemmings you're so hard about?"

"Have it your way."

"But if you're not Lemmings I have to kill you."

"What?"

Meghasin walked in the room and he turned.

Wearing her rookie look as usual.

"Take a seat, Smith."

"Officer Kr—I mean . . . I think we need to—"

"Shut the Fuck up and sit the Fuck down."

She just stood there.

With her mouth open.

Not knowing whether to sit or run out of the room.

"You let him talk to you like that?" Lemmings said.

"She's a bookie: can't think outside the book."

"And the book says you gotta go."

"So what's it going to be then, eh?"

"You Studebaker or Lemmings?"

"Look, asshole."

"Like I told the last guys."

"What last guys?"

"Your buddies."

"I don't have any buddies."

"Cops."

"What cops?"

"The ones who came over, genius."

"Why'd they come over?"

"Because I called them about the noise next door."

"You mean that guitar?"

"Yeah, goddamn kid can't play a damn note."

"So I heard."

"Yeah, so I got fed up one night and called you guys."

"Knowing damn well you weren't going to do shit."

"But what else could I do short of shooting the punk?"

"And the damn neighbors."

"Am I the only one that's bothered by this noise?"

"No one seems to do nothing about nothing in this damn neighborhood."

"Sounds like my neighborhood."

"Yeah, so they send these two clowns over."

"And instead of doin their job."

"They tell me to drop my pants."

I laugh:

"Drop your pants?"

"Yeah."

"Why you think they asked you to do that?"

"Should I know?"

"Probably fags or something."

"I'll tell you why."

"Uh, Officer Krieg—"

"They asked you to drop your pants because they wanted to confirm that you're Arthur Lemmings."

"a.k.a. Dick Pumpworthy."

"From *The Big Pump*."

"And the one sure way to confirm it is—"

"Officer Krieg, can we talk outside?"

"Goddamnit, Meghasin."

"I'm conducting an investigation here."

"Now either sit down or get the Fuck out."

She straightens up, stiff.

"Yeah," I say.

"What?"

She turns and marches out.

"Why don't you do like your partner and get the Fuck out too?" Lemmings said.

"Like I said."

"I'm conducting an investigation."

"Tell me what happened after you dropped your pants."

"Fuck you."

"MotherFucker, don't make me break leather."

"You wanna fart, asshole?"

"Go ahead."

I pulled out my BDG and laid it on my lap.

He doesn't think it's real.

It don't look real.

I pull out the five-0.

A gun on each thigh.

"Well?"

Voice lowered low now:

"Well, I didn't drop em at first."

"So one of them flicks me on the nose real hard."

He does the flick with index and thumb.

"Sayin."

"That I'd better or else."

"So I dropped them."

"And then what?"

"That's it."

"C'mon."

"You showed em your cock."

"And then what?"

"What is it with you fag cops anyway?"

"Not getting enough—"

"Don't play stupid with me."

"You know why they wanted you to drop your pants."

He didn't say anything.

Just stood there in his dirty underwear with that dirty cigar.

Looking like he was going to cry.

Nothing at all like Dick Pumpworthy.

"Sit the Fuck down."

"Makin me nervous standing over me like that."

He went over to the couch and plopped down.

"The hell happened to you?"

He didn't answer.

How could he.

"Living here in this dump."

"Sitting in your underwear like some quotidian slob."

"Some."

"Cumbersome grouch."

"Cumbersome?"

Turn to him.

"Hey, look."

"I'm not here to Fuck with you."

"Like I said."

"I'm a big fan."

"Then blow out of here."

"Now, *that's* a Pumpworthy line."

"Fuck you and your Pumpworthy shit."

"What happened to you?"

"Nothing happened to me, asshole, and I'd like to keep it that way."

"This because of what you said about 6/16?"

"What?"

"Called you a traitor, right?"

He didn't say anything.

"Right?"

"Look," he said.

"Even if I was the guy in that damn movie."

"The movie's over."

"So pick up your popcorn and go home."

"Oh, so you admit it then?"

"This is the last time I'm gonna tell you—I'm not—"

"Look, I'll make it easy for you."

I stood up and pointed both pieces at him.

"I'm here to kill a Jerry Studebaker."

"So if you're really Jerry Studebaker then it's time to die."

He yanked the cigar out of his mouth.

"What the hell kind of cop are you?"

"I'm not a cop."

"I'm from the Los Angeles Department of Decongestion."

"And my job is to subtract motorists."

"Subtract?"

"Murder, kill, execute, et cetera."

"Bullshit."

I holstered the five and pulled my DoD badge.

"See?"

"What about your cop badge?"

"It's a fake."

"Yeah, how many badges you got?"

"A few, but this one is real."

He didn't believe me.

And never would.

Not even after I shot him.

I almost didn't believe it.

"Why are you messing with me like this," he said.

"What did I do?"

"It's nothing personal—just the War on Traffic."

"Stop trollin me asshole, and tell me what—"

"Trollin you?"

"I'm not trollin you."

"Why can't you admit to being who you are?"

"If I admit it will you leave?"

"Well, not right away."

"You need to answer some questions first."

"Like what?"

"Like what did you mean when you said *The Pump* was a work against nature?"

"Or that Pumpworthy was a Knight, Death, and the Devil?"

"Well, which one was he?"

He didn't say anything.

Just kept looking at my gun.

Like he was waiting for it to go off.

I lowered it.

"What's that line you said about a gun?"

"A gun makes you different."

"Makes."

"Other people different."

"Your relationship to the world changes."

"The world becomes more dangerous."

"Because you're more dangerous."

"Well?"

"Well, what?"

"You gonna say anything?"

He gives me this look.

Like an abused puppy or something.

Beaten dog.

Practically in tears.

"What's wrong?"

"Can't you guys just let an old man die in peace?" he said.

Jesus.

If he had been Arthur Lemmings he was Jerry Studebaker now.

"You're already dead," I say.

Meghasin came back.

Still in stiff mode.

BDG in her hand.

"What," I say.

"You gonna—"

Lemmings gave her a panicked look.

"Look, if I admit—" he started.

She raised her BDG and point-blanked him in the head.

His head didn't move.

But his nostrils flared.

And the cigar fell out of his mouth.

Then he fell over to his left.

I looked at Meghasin.

She gave me a blank look and walked out.

Couch must have been flammable.

Because it burst into flames.

A JOE AND A BLOW

Me and Mars held the Department record for the most subtractions.

In one night.

Unofficially.

Because most of them didn't count.

Chasing some guy on Black Friday.

Shoveday.

Back when it was still on a Wednesday.

Tried to lose us in this shopping center parking lot.

Drove the Fueltility onto the sidewalk to cut around a crunch of cars.

People camped out.

Waiting for the stores to open.

Driving over bodies is like.

Driving over bodies.

Nothing like it.

Can't compare it.

Even to driving over animals.

Can't do shit like that anymore.

Even if they gave you the green.

PAL couldn't run over a can of Coke without taking some serious damage.

Left Studebaker to burn on the couch.

Viking funeral.

Turn on the taps.

Flood the house.

No.

Air outside is a relief from the dead air inside.

Over half the homes in this city smell.

Each foul in their own decay.

It's not the house.

It's the people.

Something in them.

Something they feed.

With the junk in their fridge.

And the nasty little thoughts in their heads.

Got to be such a problem the Department started issuing nose plugs.

Times like that the job feels like a mission of mercy.

And not some dirty little secret war.

But usually you don't have to go in.

Just shoot them in the doorway.

Or through the peep.

Point and Click.

PAL waiting out front.

She's inside.

Guitar starts snarling again.

Whoever was playing that thing obviously hadn't gotten the memo.

Rock 'n' Roll is dead.

Been dead for a while.

No.

Worse than that.

This SickFuck knew it.

And was just beating its corpse for kicks.

Walk next door and open the side gate.

Side that faces Lemmings's house.

Window near the back.

Light sliced by blinds.

Back to the window.

Facing a half stack.

Big white kid.

Throttling an axe.

Jerkin it like some big cock.

Black T-shirt with the Snake Oil logo.

Snake Oil®—Maximize Your Size!

Pumpworthy.

Should've checked him.

Know for sure.

No.

I know.

Besides.

Pulling down the pants of a dead man.

No.

Tap the window with the butt of the five.

Doesn't hear it of course.

Wait.

For a pause.

When it came I tapped hard.

He looked around for a second, saw me.

Not scared at all to see a Nigger at his window.

Towards me with a slow strut.

Arrogant.

Like I was some fan.

Waitin for an autograph.

"Fuck you want, faggot."

"Got a request."

I gave him two and he fell back and over the edge of his bed.

The look on his face.

Amplifier cracking and popping.

Guitar feedbacking.

A high, sustained whine.

Smell of smoke.

Pumpworthy's house.

Really blazing now.

I walked back to the car and got in.

PAL doesn't say anything.

Meghasin looking straight ahead.

Waiting for her to say it.

Start it.

Nothing.

She has pictures, stickers.

Things on her side of the dash.

Nothing on my side.

Something during the Advance about making the car your space.

Your mobile something or other.

Action Office.

"You know," I say.

"This job is more than just Point and Click."

"There are subtleties."

Shovin the book up my ass like that.

Who does she think she is?

Been doin this twenty years.

Back in the day she would have been.

Gonna let her have it once we get out of this car.

Need something now.

Something to do.

Somewhere to put my mind.

Can't sit like this for too long.

In silence.

If I do.

Then.

There's the urge.

Sane.

Reasonable.

To destroy myself.

Look up Studebaker's driving record.

Think a couple of deuces is enough reason to get listed.

But it isn't.

Be the best driver in the world and still make the list.

Old Chief used to have a saying:

"All casual drivers should be shot."

Besides the deuces, only thing that came up was he'd been arrested.

But let off.

For driving into a Bardo Bakery.

Had mistakenly put the car in D instead of R.

Nah.

No mistake.

Used to be a Burger Lord there.

Same one in *The Big Pump.*

Everything else.

VMTs, etc.

Was average or below.

Okay, so.

Pumpworthy was a warning.

For talkin shit.

Have to hand it to him.

Thurlow.

MotherFucker wants to toy with me, well.

He's got another.

"PAL," I say.

"Time for a break."

A Joe and a Blow.

I cannot process that request, Officer Krieg. Due to your low score as indicated on shield—

A red 37% was flashing on the upper right corner of the shield.

You will be required to make an additional subtraction before you are authorized to take a break.

"Give me a break."

As was just communicated, Officer Krieg, you are required—

"Jeez, will you shut up? I know."

The target wasn't that far.

Just another point in the Land of Less.

Apartment building on Rimpau.

North of Washington.

Flesh stucco, brown lawn.

Turned-over shopping cart for a lawn ornament.

Faces poked out of windows.

Anyone knew what we were, it was these people.

Practically expected it.

PAL stopped behind a car with hazards blinking.

No one inside.

Door wouldn't open.

"PAL, pop the damn door."

"Please stand by for mission reassignment, Officer Krieg."

"This not the place?"

"Officer Ross is now the senior Officer. Officer Krieg has been reassigned to backup."

"What?"

"You heard me," PAL said.

"What?"

"You have four and a half minutes to complete the subtraction."

"You just hear that?"

"What it just said?"

Meghasin wouldn't look at me.

The doors popped open and she got out.

I didn't.

"Officer Krieg, please exit and proceed to the subtraction."

"You *heard* me?"

"Officer Krieg, please exit and proceed to the subtraction. This is your last warning."

"Why?"

"She don't need me."

"I'm just the backup, remember?"

"Under section seven nine four point two five, both Officers are required to be present during a subtraction. Please exit the vehicle."

"What vehicle?"

"I don't see no vehicle here."

"You see a vehicle?"

"Please exit the vehicle or you will be reported for insubordination."

"Bullshit, you're reporting me now."

"In real time."

"You have five seconds to comply."

A big red 5 filled the center of the shield.

"T minus five."

"T minus?"

"Four."

"Really, you're actually gonna count down?"

"Three."

"Come on."

"Two."

I got out.

"Yo, what kinda car is that?"

Dude walkin down the middle of the street.

"Ain't a car."

"What is it then?"

"Ever heard of a sidewalk?"

"What?"

Don't bother.

Meghasin standing out front.

Waiting.

Steel mesh security door wasn't locked.

Yank it open:

"Bookies first."

"Please don't call me that, Officer Krieg."

"Sure thing, Officer Ross."

No light inside.

Smell of antiseptic.

Usual circus of sounds from the floors above.

Cryin slammin stompin screamin.

TV music TV.

Music.

TV.

All rolled into one fat glob of noise.

That no ear was ever gonna smooth out.

The poorer the louder.

Strange cooking smells.

Steam and sweat.

Wafting down.

Tryin to dust up the antiseptic.

A few more battles and they would win.

"Let's go," Meghasin said.

"Wait."

"What?"

"Need to adjust my eyes."

"What?"

"To the light."

"You need to put on your browsers."

"I don't have em."

She turned and went up the stairs.

I waited for my eyes and went up.

Number 21.

She's waiting.

Hands on her hips.

Not looking at me.

But she's got a look.

Like she wants to scream.

"Could've done this already," I say, tapping on the door.

No sound inside.

Music playing somewhere down the hall.

Mexican chick ooh oohing over something.

Couldn't tell.

Sounded like a power drill.

Meghasin goes for a knock.

I stop her.

"Wait."

"That music."

"That real, or is some chick singing while her husband does some home repairs?"

She doesn't say anything.

Just looks at the door.

Okay.

Tap again.

Harder.

Subtle creak of floor and the peep darkens.

Meghasin tracking with her browsers.

"That's him."

I draw my BDG, put it to the peephole, and fire.

Thud hitting the floor on the other side.

"Classic."

It was.

She gives me a look.

Hundred bucks it's not in the book.

"Oh, sorry. Forgot you were the SO."

"So."

She shook her head and walked off.

"Hey, we ain't finished."

Probably going to tell on me again.

Let her.

Listen.

The music down the hall had stopped.

People were listening behind doors.

Sound of a baby crying now.

Inside 21.

Voices in Spanish.

The usual.

Externalities.

"Get ready."

Have to kick it a couple of times to get it to open.

And a few more because of the body.

Door behind me opens.

Some lady.

Tell her to go inside.

She just looks.

It's one of those nights.

So I shoot her with the five.

She falls back inside.

Enter 21.

Lights are out.

Hopefully none of them are packing.

Might as well browse.

Be on the safe.

Green shapes huddled in the back.

Baby still crying.

Count them down as I subtract.

Six, five, four, three, two.

One.

Baby still crying.

In its mother's arms.

Seems cruel to say.

But babies aren't a big deal.

Fact is.

They're easier.

Not tactically.

Which they are.

But on the conscience.

Less life.

Like killing a plant.

Or an insect.

Not such a big thing to push them back.

To zero.

Time for a break.

No one outside.

No PAL.

No Meghasin.

What the.

PDT buzzes.

Anita.

"Yeah, just the person I want to—"

"What the hell is going on?"

"What?"

"What is going on with you, Alex?"

"Think PAL and Meghasin took off without me."

"PAL's taking her to her break."

"What?"

"She can't eat with you."

"Why?"

"Her misophonia."

"Her what?"

"Misophonia, she can't stand the sound of loud chewing."

"What?"

"Your eating habits bother her."

"Why am I not surprised?"

"PAL will be back for you in a few minutes."

"Take a walk."

"Walk?"

"Why?"

"Just walk, will you? We need to talk."

"So, she tattled again, huh?"

"What did I tell you?"

"She doesn't have to tattle."

"But she did."

"You're just about done, Alex."

"You're right about that."

"She doesn't want to ride with you."

"So, I don't want to ride with her."

"You knew that."

"Mars is gone, Alex."

"Yeah, and I know who gonned him."

"We didn't sweep him if that's what you think."

"Yeah, so where's the Leviathan, huh?"

"How come I can't trace it?"

"Because it's not your case."

"He was my partner, Anita."

"Twenty Fuckin years."

"Yeah, I know."

"No, you don't."

"And what's with promoting Meghasin to senior Officer?"

"She wasn't promoted."

"You were demoted."

"Demoted?"

"To what?"

"It's your points, Alex. We warned you."

"So, what?"

"Now I gotta do what Meghasin says?"

"She's the senior Officer now."

"Thought you said she doesn't want to ride with me."

"Yes, but she's going to ride with you and you're going to ride with her."

"C'mon, she don't know how to pull."

"And neither do you apparently."

"You mean the last eight I just did by myself?"

"After she stormed off?"

"You deliberately cut in with an illegal maneuver."

"Illegal maneuver?"

"Stop repeating everything I say like you never heard it before."

"Look, I took the window because she was just standing there."

"Probably trying to remember what the book says."

"Like you and Studebaker?" she said.

"I was trying to ascertain—"

"I told you Studebaker was a go, and you defied my order."

"Look, Studebaker was a mistake."

"And I told you he wasn't."

"Yeah, well, my instinct told me—"

"Your instinct?"

"Yeah, Anita."

"Instinct."

"Something these bookies don't—"

"And what's your instinct telling you now?"

"What?"

"What is your instinct telling you now, Alex?"

"Telling me to hang up."

"No, let me tell you what your—"

I hung up.

PAL picked me up on the corner of 18th and Rimpau.

Destination:

Stubbs Coffee on La Brea for the Joe.

Tharshees next door for the Blow.

Not in that order.

First the Blow then the Joe.

Don't care what the policy is.

I need a Blow.

PAL dropped me at the Stubbs.

Meghasin inside at the counter.

Can't stand her ass in those smartpants.

You can tell the shape of a woman's mind by the shape of her ass.

Small.

Neatly packaged in gray.

A little flat.

Tight farts probably.

With the stink of virtue.

Over to Tharshees.

Elotero out front.

Thinkin about getting one until I see where his hand is.

Scratchin his nuts.

"Yo," I say.

"*Sí,*" he said.

"You an elotero or a pelotero?"

He holds up a stick of corn. "*Sí.*"

"Nah, man."

I go inside.

Waiting room crowded with zeros.

Flash my badge to the hostess.

Nods and shows me all her teeth.

Leads me to the door.

Two big bouncers dressed in black on either side.

Chins up.

One gave me a nod before resuming his glare of the room.

The door opens.

Another girl on the other side.

All smiles.

Escorts me through a long, dimly lit room lined with dudes in plush red chairs.

A production line of heads bobbing up and down on them like pistons.

Dudes in various stages of ridiculous ecstasy.

Heads thrown back, eyes shut, mouths gaping.

Others looking bored.

Sipping drinks or watching TVs suspended from the ceiling.

Barely aware of the furiously bobbing heads in their laps.

Smell of incense.

Seats me at a chair near the center and hands me a menu.

Menu recommends certain drinks with certain girls.

Touch the face of the girl you want.

Sattiva.

Something about her slightly crossed left eye and full red lips.

Pity and lust at the same time.

Goes well with a Sherry Blossom.

Ordered a Dirty Harry with Cock Sauce.

Mars always had a redhead with a Shirley Pimple.

Screen above me tuned to some news channel.

Breaking news.

Something's always breaking.

And it usually ain't news.

Reina Hawthorne.

What?

Arrested.

Turn up the sound.

Breaking news.

Reina Hawthorne arrested.

For beanin a dude in the head with a Sleaze Burger.

Burger now in police custody.

Forensics currently investigating.

Her attorney claims she threw the burger because it contained semen.

Apparently deposited there by some spiteful employee.

The Grammy and Oscar award winner claims she became aware of it as soon as she had taken the first bite.

And without thinking threw it out the car window in disgust.

Only to hit an innocent bystander on Sunset Boulevard.

The bystander.

Some middle-aged cheeseburger from Margaritaville.

Was filing a multimillion-dollar lawsuit against her for specified damages.

And was preparing to file a suit against Sleaze Burger.

If.

In fact.

The burger contained semen.

Which might be considered a biological terrorist attack, the newscaster added.

There was footage too.

Filmed by another tourist.

Who happened to be the man's wife.

The station had obtained a copy.

Exclusive to our viewers.

After these messages.

Might as well take that as a sign.

In my favor.

Time to call Claire.

The usual four rings.

I hung up.

Again.

My girl showed up.

But I wasn't in the mood.

Not with Reina Hawthorne on the screen.

She knew me.

Told me to buzz her if I changed my mind.

The PDT buzzed.

Anita.

I didn't answer.

Buzzed again.

I didn't answer.

She sent a message:

Report to me immediately.

The news came back from commercial with the footage.

It was good footage.

First they played it at normal speed.

And then in slow motion.

A slam dunk on the guy's head.

Couldn't ask for anything more perfect if it was your intention to hit a guy in the head with a burger.

Guy actually stumbled back several feet.

Then fell to the ground.

Overdramatic.

Like a soccer player.

Clutching his head and screaming.

A supersized kid in hoard shorts and chop-flops.

Station going over the footage like sportscasters dissecting an instant replay.

Guys with pointers making X's and O's.

Even had satellite footage.

I got up and left.

Sign at the exit said "Come Again."

Meghasin was outside the Stubbs sitting at a table.

On the phone.

Back to me.

Speaking Chinese.

I stood behind her and waited for some English.

None came.

She made a retarded voice for a few sentences.

Which I knew was about me.

Okay.

I went in and ordered a black eye.

She saw me when I came out and hung up.

"They're sending us another car," she said.

I sat down.

The table was unbalanced and I spilled her coffee when I leaned on it.

She tried to back away in her chair and almost fell over.

Coffee on her pants.

Didn't matter.

They were smart enough to dry out and erase the stain.

She stood there and watched them do their thing.

"Let's get another table," I say.

We took another table.

"Well?" she said.

"Well, what?"

"Aren't you going to offer to buy me another one?"

"You want another one?"

"No."

Kid walks up and tries to sell us a package of cigarette butts.

"Pre-smoke," he says. "Cheap."

No DeNiro, I tell him.

Shows me his phone.

I can beam him the funds apparently.

Tell him to get lost.

He doesn't understand.

Get lost.

Nothing.

Meghasin says something to him in Spanish.

He leaves.

"Thanks," I say.

"You don't speak Spanish?" she said.

"*Queso?*"

"What?"

"That's what I said."

"You said 'cheese.'"

"No, I said 'what.' *Queso.*"

"That means 'cheese.'"

"No, it means 'what.'"

"So you don't know Spanish then."

"No."

"Don't you have to know it for this job?"

"No."

"Why? They tell you you needed to know it?"

"Yes."

"Jesus, the Fuck are things coming to."

"Well, everyone should probably know how to speak Spanish in Los Angeles."

"Why?"

"Uh, because the majority of the people in this city speak it."

"Some MotherFuckin roaches invade your house you gonna learn roach too?"

"Uh, I don't consider them to be—"

"Heard you speakin Chinese earlier—how many languages you know?"

"I wasn't speaking Chinese."

"Japanese."

"I was speaking Korean."

"Oh, thought you were Chinese."

"No, I'm part Korean."

"Which part?"

"My last name is Ross."

"What about your first?"

"What?"

"Your first name—that Korean?"

"No, it's a Korean idea of an American name."

"Oh."

Looking past each other's heads.

Blowing on coffee that don't need blowing.

Traffic on La Brea.

Stuck in tar.

Two guys come and sit at the table behind.

Adolph Hipsters.

Talking loud.

"Dude, took me like two hours to get to WeHo."

"From SaMo?"

"NoHo."

"L-M-N-O-P,* man. Elll-emmm-ennno-p."

---

*   From the title track to *The Sound of Sizzle*: "Life may not offer pearls/
     Quinters* rarely steer towards trifles/Unique Voyagers—Zoom!"

> *Neologism—according to the movie, a quintessential
> person, a.k.a. a Unique Voyager, opposite of a quitter.*

"Q-R-S-double-T bro."

"To the U-V."

"Z."

I turned around. "You Fuckin kiddin me?"

"Problem, man?"

"Who the Fuck talks like that?"

"Talks like what?"

"Like you, faggot."

"Yo, man."

"Yo, man?"

"Yeah, what we do to you?"

"No, the question is what am I going to do to you?"

"Okay, man."

"Let's go over here."

They got up and went over there.

"Dude's kindless," one of them says not low enough.

"Smugnoxious assholes."

"Ever notice the faces of these kids today?"

"Like there's something missing."

"Like maybe a fist."

"Or two."

Meghasin is looking away.

Embarrassed to be seen with me probably.

I should be the one.

I mean.

Who does she think she.

Her move with Pumpworthy.

Snitching to Anita.

Wants to be on top now.

They all want to be on top now.

Chicktators.

Time to put her.

"Look, Meghasin."

"We got off on the wrong foot."

"So how about we—"

"No."

"What?"

"You got off on the wrong foot," she said.

"What?"

"I don't know what you're trying to do."

"But whatever it is."

"You need to leave me out of it."

"Trying to do?"

"Getting yourself fired."

"Or whatever it is."

"Think I'm trying to get myself fired?"

"I don't know."

"But whatever you're doing it's affecting me."

"Yeah, well."

"You got a problem with me."

"How about saying it to me straight instead of snitching to the brass?"

"What?"

"Anita told me you been filing complaints about me."

"What? I didn't file any—"

"Oh, yeah."

"Play it dumb now."

"Dumb?"

"Yeah, dumb."

She leans forward.

"Okay, look, genius."

"Everything we say in that car is recorded."

"So if you think I'm snitching on you, then you've got—"

"So, you a Christian?"

"What?"

"Anita said you were a Christian, that true?"

"Yes."

"And no."

"What's that mean?"

"Yes, but not the way you probably think I am."

"What way is that?"

"Let's just say I'm not Christian in the conventional way."

"Meaning what?"

"You don't believe in Jesus Christ?"

She laughed.

"So, you don't care if I say Jesus or Christ?"

"No, what bothers me is you talking all the time."

"About yourself."

"And like you know everything."

"Well, I been on this job—"

"And interrupting me all the time."

"Okay, okay."

"You talk—I won't say anything."

"That's the thing," she said.

"I don't want to talk."

"Yeah, that's why I do all the talking."

"You don't get it, do you?"

"We're being monitored."

"Everything we say and do is being recorded."

"Yeah, so?"

"I don't want to say anything that might jeopardize my job," she said.

"What could you possibly say that would—"

SHADOWPLAY

Pico.

Windsor.

Victoria Park Place is a circle.

Palm trees like giant dirty Q-tips.

Twisted in the ears of monsters.

Houses cherried.

Restored to antique.

About to give it to her when the replacement car arrived.

I don't know what the Fuck I'm doing.

I need to wake up.

And grow up.

Who does she think.

"Dammit if I'm going to let someone like you jeopardize my career."

Yeah.

She said that.

Now she wasn't saying anything.

Neither was the car.

It pulled over to the southeast side of the circle.

The inner circle.

Dark green house.

Trees and bushes hid most of it from the street.

"The Fuck is this, PAL?"

"Your current subtraction, Officer Krieg."

No more Vader.

Check the shield.

Another senior citizen.

Old man.

Art dealer.

Asleep upstairs.

"Same old same old."

"Let's go," Meghasin said, "now."

Commander in Chief now.

Front porch smelled like fresh-cut wood.

Cedar.

Woodorizer.

Plugged next to the door.

I unplugged it.

Put it in my pocket.

"Something not right about this."

"What do you mean?"

"We should probably check this guy, see what his connection is."

"Connection?"

"Yeah, we've already had two bullshit hits tonight, and this looks like another one."

"Look," she said. "We need to do this on time—I don't want—"

"Yeah, I know."

"You don't want me jeopardizing my career."

"I don't care if you jeopardize yours, just don't jeopardize mine while you're doing it."

"Got an Alcatraz."

"What?"

Point to the silver panel to the right of the door:

"The lock."

"What does that mean?"

"Nothing."

I punched the universal for an A-6 on the PDT.

Pause.

Then the whir of the bolt disengaging.

I opened the door.

And entered first.

She stood at the entrance for a second.

Then stepped in and closed the door.

The lock whirred back into place.

Vague light through the frosted door panes barely enough to dilute the dark.

Meghasin pointing at the door.

Whisper mode:

"Shouldn't we keep it unlocked—just in case?"

"Of what?"

"I don't know."

"Yeah, you don't."

Dark beyond the low entrance way.

Hit the light on the PDT.

Floating dust.

Dancing motes.

Orbiting specks.

Dead.

A low hum.

A clock tocked.

A large, heavy staircase.

Statue with arms raised.

Helmet with wings.

Leaning on one foot.

Getting ready to dance off.

A thick carved banister-looking thing.[*]

Look good in my garden.

Wonder if it's attached.

Shoe reverbs on the hardwood floor.

Soft now.

Towards the stairs.

---

[*]   Newel—ed.

Something else.

Not me.

A creak on the wood floor.

The air moves.

Something.

A flash.

Black.

Buddy Gawler* looked at his audience.

"Is there any truth to that?" he said. "Shall they?"

No one answered.

"The meek shall inherit the earth."

"Why?"

No one said anything.

The assumption being either that the question was rhetorical.

Or.

If it wasn't.

A wrong answer could hold some unfortunate consequence.

"Think about it."

"Does the thought of a bunch of meek people running around this blue planet."

"Okay, maybe they don't run."

------

*   Zentrepreneur and Zenthusiast, former fun-gineer and CEO for Scrappy, Buddy Gawler left his successful life to bring his enlightened business skills to the mindfulness industry. Learn how to become a Rambodhisattva® and attain a no-nonsense form of enlightenment more efficiently: "Meditation is an extremely inefficient method for obtaining enlightenment: a punch in the face does more to enlighten than several years of meditation."
    (Bio from the SEAL's website, now defunct.)

"I don't picture meek people runnin."

"Unless it's from something."

"Do you?"

"Let's just say hidin."

"Hidin like those little furry mammals in the age of the dinosaurs."

"Does this present an attractive picture to your mind?"

"A bunch of meek rodents hiding all over this here fine earth?"

A few shook their heads no.

"Yeah," he said.

"I'm going to say that despite the good intentions of the man that said it."

"The answer is an emphatic NO."

More heads nodding in agreement.

Some doing it vertically.

Some horizontally.

"Spirit is not for the meek."

"Now."

"How about this one."

"Ask and ye shall receive."

Buddy swept the audience with his head.

Like a searchlight.

"This true?"

No one answered.

"Ask *who?*" he said.

"Whom," someone said.

Buddy froze.

"Who said that?"

No one said anything.

"C'mon, don't be meek."

"Who just tried to correct me right now?"

No answer.

"Okay," he said.

"Have it your way."

"Ask *whom?*"

No one.

Another head sweep.

"God?"

"The government?"

"Who?"

"Anyone?"

Nothing.

"Startin to see a pattern here?"

"A running biblical theeeme?"

"About a bunch of *meek* people meekly *askin?*"

"For what?"

"What are they asking for?"

"Huh?"

"And why do they have to ask?"

No one said anything.

"Does that sound right to you?"

"Does it sound spiritual?"

"Is that how the holy goddamn Spirit works?"

"By havin you sit on your ass asking for shit?"

"No," someone said.

"Right."

"That's not what Spirit is about."

"That's what *religion* is about."

"Lettin someone else do the work for you."

"So."

"How about a little textual updatin right here and now?"

"Hmmm?"

"How about it?"

"Yeah," some people said.

"How about this."

"Not ask and ye shall receive."

"But KICK ASS and ye shall receive!"

Agreement from the audience now:

"Yeah!"

"Mmm-hmmm."

"Yeah."

"No, my friends."

"Spirit is not for the meek."

"Religion maybe."

"But not the Spirit."

"Spirit *is* action."

"Spirit *e-volves.*"

"Not religion."

"Religion just sits there."

"On the couch."

"Jerkin off."

"Stagnant."

"Fixed."

"And unchanging."

"A safe little womb for the meek."

"But not the Spirit."

"The way of the Spirit is hard."

"The way of the Spirit is dangerous."

"The way of the Spirit might even destroy you."

"Yes."

"Destroy you."

"The way of the Spirit can, and possibly will, destroy you."

"But you cannot follow it."

"The way of the Spirit."

"What?"

"Yeah."

"You *cain't* follow it."

"No?"

"But why?"

"Because it don't have rules."

"A set of directions."

"Or a bunch of commandments."

"Because it ain't a religion."

"Follow?"

"Not a good way to sell a product, is it?"

"Well, what about the other?"

"The other product."

"The main product people've been buyin for years."

"What does it say?"

"It says '*Believe* and everything will be okay.'"

"Hell."

"Stay meek and you just might inherit the goddamn earth!"

"What does that sound like?"

"Huh?"

"Sounds like they're trying to sell you a product, doesn't it?"

"Buy our soap and you will be happy."

"Buy our soda and you will be happy."

"Buy *our* soul and you will be happy."

"Yes."

"I say *buy*."

"Not sell."

"Why?"

"Because we don't have a soul to sell."

"No one does."

"Not in this day and age."

"No."

"In this day and age."

"We buy our souls."

"Yup."

"We buy them."

"Add em to our carts and proceed to *checkout*."

"Hey, Bob, what kinda soul you got there?"

"Coke or Pepsi?"

"What?"

"Too much sugar?"

"Maybe you should try some of this fairy-ay."

"Hey, look at me!"

"I got a Mercedes soul."

"And all he's got is a Honda soul."

"Poor guy."

"You know what they call these soulless soul buyers in this day and age?"

"Know what they call them?"

"Consumers."

"That's what *you* are."

"Consumers."

"You consume souls."

"Cheap, prefabricated, disposable souls."

"And they're not even made in America."

"No."

"China maybe."

"Or Pakistan."

"Because this country doesn't produce souls anymore."

"No."

"It don't produce anything."

"And that is Fuckin meek."

"Which brings me to an issue that was brought up to me the other day by one of our younger members."

"'Buddy,' he asked."

"'They taught us something in school the other day about this guy.'"

"'Yeah?' I says."

"'What guy?'"

"'Well, Buddy.'"

"'His name was Jim Jones and he made all these people die,' he said."

"'They called him the leader of a cult.'"

"'Is that what this is, Buddy?'"

"'A cult?'"

A few snickers from the audience.

As if the question was absurd.

Plus he was making the kid sound like one of those golly-aw-shucks-gee-mister kind of white kids you see in those old colorless TV shows.

"You all know who Jim Jones is, I suspect."

"And you all know how history has classified him."

"And I don't think there is one here who would disagree."

"Yes?"

The audience seemed to agree.

"Right?"

Yes, they nodded and uh-huh'd.

"Well, what I'm going to say now."

"And what I told our little friend."

"Is going to shock the shit out of you."

"As it should."

"You ready?"

The audience was ready.

"You sure?"

They were sure.

"Surely sure?"

Some snickered.

"Okay."

Buddy paused and looked down for a moment.

Then he snapped his head back up and looked straight at the audience.

"Hitler was one of the greatest holy men that ever lived."

No one looked that shocked to hear it.

"Yes, you heard me."

"Probably thought I was going to say Jim Jones."

"Well, he was too."

"In a way."

"But it's Hitler that was the greatest Spiritual Leader of the Twentieth Century."

Pause.

"One of the first Rambodhisattvas in fact."

"Yes."

"Let it sink in."

"Hitler."

"Now why is that?"

"Why him and not some other guy?"

"Gandhi, say."

"Or Martin Luther King?"

"Mother Teresa?"

"Clichés like that?"

"Cli-saints I like to call them."

"The hell did Hitler do?"

"Guy killed, like, six million people."

"How's that bein a saint?"

"Well."

"That's it precisely."

"He killed six million people."

"Not personally of course."

"But he got the ball rolling."

"Rolling where?"

"Down the Via Negativa."

"The negative way."

"You see, some of the most effective spiritual teachings are negative."

"Evil."

"Yes, evil."

"Why?"

"Because evil is effective."

"Evil wakes you up."

"Not like that bullshit Goody Two-shoes mystical stuff."

"Kind all those mystagogues have been preaching since the beginning."

"Guys like Buddha and the Christ."

"Yes, Buddha."

"Everyone's so big on the goddamn Buddha these days."

"But no one really looks at what he really said."

"What did he say?"

"Life is Suffering."

"Well, he's right there."

"And then what?"

"Desire is the root of all suffering."

"Yeah? Desire is the root of all suffering?"

"But aren't we made to desire?"

"To desire food."

"Sex."

"Comfort."

"Security."

"Air."

"So if it's all suffering then why make us all desirers?"

"Oh, wait."

"There's a way out, he said."

"See, that's where you got to watch out."

"Every one of these religions does that."

"They'll agree that this is all bullshit, and then say wait."

"There's a way out of it."

"So, Buddha called this way out Nirvana."

"But he was smart."

"Really smart."

"And so he covered his ass."

"He said you can't get to it because it's already here."

"Here."

"Right in front of your face."

"Well, why can't I see it then? you say."

"Cause you're ignorant, he'd say."

"Okay."

"Well, how do I see it?"

"Wrong question."

"But, but, but."

"Look, if you wanna try, you can do this thing called meditation."

"What's that?"

"Well, you gotta sit down all day and watch your breathing."

"For how long?"

"Well."

"For the rest of your life."

"And then there's no guarantee you'll ever see it."

"Although, you probably *won't* see it."

"And then if you do, it won't even last."

"You'll see it for a few seconds, minutes, hours maybe, and then it will be gone."

"And back to the drawing board."

"Who the Fuck designs a universe like that?"

"Who designs a person to suffer and then tells them it's their fault?"

"They suffer because they're too ignorant."

"Or because some bitch ate an apple she wasn't supposed to."

"Who would design something like that?"

"Who?"

"No one."

"Maybe it's these guys."

"Tellin you the wrong thing."

"Buddha, the Christ, Mohammed."

"These assholes in sheep's clothing."

"You heard the line about the Devil quoting scripture?"

"Well, that's religion for you."

"Gotta keep you running around in circles."

"Blaming yourself."

"And hoping."

"For salvation."

"Oh, please, Lord, please."

"Now, Evil."

"And I'm not talking about that sneaky kind preached by Christ and the Buddha."

"I'm talkin the real kind."

"Real Evil doesn't do any of that."

"Real Evil is straight up."

"In your face."

"Telling it like it is."

"It promises nothing."

"And then comes up and kicks the shit out of you."

"Says 'Look at me, MotherFucker.'"

"'This ain't no meditation retreat.'"

"'This a concentration camp.'"

"Name even one good deed of comparable memory to the Holocaust."

"A horror more eye-opening than a million mystical teachings."

"Which is precisely what this country needs *right* now."

"Not some goddamn Christian gospel."

"Some goddamn phony good news."

"We don't need any good news."

"We need bad news."

"Why?"

"Well."

"If we were like those Christians getting fed to the lions."

"Maybe we would need some of that good news."

"Tellin us that we'll all be better off after these lions finish chompin down on us."

"But we're nothing like them."

"We're more like those lions now."

"On a worldwide feeding frenzy."

"Crunching."

"Chomping."

"Consuming everything in sight."

"In fact."

"We put those Fuckin lions to shame."

"They only ate Christians."

"We eat a helluva lot more than that."

"And all of it for some goddamn dream."

"Which is the last thing we need."

"Dreams."

"No more dreams."

"What we really need is another . . ."

He swept the audience with his head again.

And then quietly:

"Hitler."

Several nodded in agreement.

And then more nodded.

Until almost everyone was nodding.

Buddy frowned.

"Well."

"Don't agree with me all easy like that."

"I'm not looking for sheep here."

"You know that."

More nods.

"Okay, stop nodding."

"The Fuck did I just say?"

Everyone stopped nodding.

Except for one.

"You there." He pointed.

"What the hell are you doing?"

Everyone looked.

The people in the front looked back.

The people in the back looked around to the left and right.

Hoping it wasn't them.

"No, *you*," Buddy said.

An old man in the back.

He pointed at himself and mouthed, "Me?"

"Yes, you, numb-nuts."

"Why the hell do you keep nodding?"

Still pointing at himself.

"Me?"

"Yeah, *you*, Nimrod."

"Why do you keep nodding your head?"

"Am I? I didn't . . ."

"You've been nodding your goddamn dome ever since I started speaking."

"Have I?"

"Have I?" Buddy said.

Mocking him.

"You saying you don't know what the Fuck your own head is doing?"

"Well, I . . ."

"Well, you what?"

"Well, I don't."

"Don't."

"Really know." He smiled.

"So," Buddy said.

"You agree that Hitler was a great spiritual teacher."

"Well, I . . ."

"Right up there with Christ and the Buddha?"

"Well, I."

"I, well."

"Say 'well, I' one more time, you nimrod."

"One more time."

The man froze.

Everyone stood rigid.

Not daring to move.

My job was to pour the punch.

I kept pouring.

Buddy let the uncomfortable silence stretch for a bit.

And then continued.

"Let me ask you a question."

"Something I hope you can answer."

The man nodded slightly.

"There's that nod again."

"Oh, I . . . geez."

"Was I noddin again?"

Turning his head left to right.

Looking for some backup.

And then chuckling a little.

Hoping that it would cause the atmosphere to lighten up.

"Shut up," Buddy said.

"And look at me, you goddamn bobblehead."

The old man looked at him.

And swallowed nervously.

"Why are you here?"

"Excuse me?"

"You heard me," Buddy said.

"Why the hell are you here?"

The old man looked to the left and the right again.

Looking for the rescue party that was never going to show.

"Stop moving your goddamn head and answer the goddamn question already!" Buddy screamed.

"Why are you here!"

"You mean like now?" he said.

"Or existentially?"

"Oh, Jesus," Buddy said.

"If the goddamn meek haven't already inherited the earth yet."

"I'll eat my damn shorts."

"Look, *you.*"

"This ain't the riddle of the goddamn Sphinx I'm askin you."

"I'm just askin why."

"Are."

"You."

"Here?"

"With us."

With his finger:

"Heeeere."

"In this group."

"Here?" the old man said.

Buddy smacked the podium hard.

"Yes!"

"Well," he said.

"To, uh."

"Get in touch with."

"I mean."

"To become enlightened?"

"Is that a question?" Buddy said.

"To become enlightened?"

"Well," he said. "I mean."

"Aren't we all here to transcend all that mythical."

"I mean, to become enlight—"

"To wake up?"

"I don't know," Buddy said.

"Are we?"

"Yeah, uh." He chuckled.

"I mean."

"Yes."

"So," Buddy said.

"We're all here to wake up?"

"More or less." He chuckled again.

"I fail to find out what's so funny about any of this," Buddy said.

"It's not," the old man said.

"It's just that I."

"That I."

"Want to wake up," Buddy finished.

"Yes," the old man smiled.

"He's good," someone whispered.

"Well."

"Tell me this, Farley."

"It's Farley, right?"

"Yes, sir."

"What did you do this morning when you finished sleeping?"

"You mean after I woke up?"

"You woke up this morning?"

"Yes."

"So, when you were done sleeping."

"You woke up?"

"Sure," the old man chuckled.

Looking around.

"Sure."

"Then what the hell are you doing here?"

"What?"

"I don't."

"Jesus Fucking Christ," Buddy said.

"What."

"The."

"Hell."

"Are you doing here?"

"Do you mean?" Farley said.

"Oh, I get it."

"You're doing that—"

"Don't tell me what I'm doing," Buddy said.

"I am asking *you* what *you're* doing."

"I don't understand," Farley said.

"Did you wake up this morning or not, Farley?"

"Yes, I did."

"But not in the way I see you're trying."

"What am I trying?"

"Well, there's waking up and then there's *waking* up."

Buddy leaned an elbow on the podium and cradled his chin in his palm.

"Really?" he said.

"Waking up and waking up?"

"Whatever do you mean?"

"Well, there's the normal waking that everyone does."

"And then there's the spiritual kind."

"The what kind?" Buddy said.

"The spiritual kind."

"You know."

"No," Buddy said.

"Not really."

"But you said."

"I mean."

"Isn't that what we're all here for?"

"Is that what *you're* here for?" Buddy said.

"Yes."

"Really?"

"Yes, sir."

"This ain't the military, Farley."

"So."

"You're here to wake up?"

"That's what I said," Farley said.

"How long have you been here?"

"About an hour."

"No, with us. With the SEALs."

"Oh, *here*," Farley said.

"Little over a year, I guess."

"And have you woken up?"

"Not completely, no."

"Not completely?"

"Not really."

"When do you expect to completely wake up then?"

"Oh, I don't know," Farley said.

"Wait."

"It's a trick."

"Right?"

"Because you're never completely."

He stopped.

Buddy didn't say anything but leaned into his chin.

Looking half-bored and half-smug.

"I mean, that's like spiritual materialism, right?" Farley said.

"You can never get fully enlightened because it's more like a process."

"And what process is that?" Buddy asked.

"Evolution I think."

"Evolution?"

"Yes."

"I think."

"So you thinked it up all by yourself?" Buddy said.

"What by myself?"

"What you just said."

"I."

"That evolution is some kind of process or something," Buddy said.

"No."

"No what?"

"No, you said it," Farley said.

"I think."

"Didn't you?"

"Or maybe I read it in."

"But isn't that what we're here."

"For?"

"To evolve?"

Buddy straightened up and waved his arms.

"Let's stop this right here."

"And consider the meek."

"Especially you, Farley."

"The meek?"

"Yeah, the meek."

"Since you seem to get off on it."

"I never."

"Shhh."

"Shhh."

"Shhh."

"And listen for once, you nimrod."

"Sure."

"You see that punch they're pouring there?"

"Yes, I do."

"What if I told you that one cup of that punch would wake you up?"

"Really?"

"If that punch could wake you up—would you drink it?"

Farley paused.

Looking for the trick.

"It's a simple question, Farley."

"Would you drink that punch if you knew it could wake you up?"

"Yeah," he said.

"I guess if I knew it could."

"Shut up."

"What if I also told you that there was a chance you could die in drinking it?"

"Oh, I see where you're—"

"For a guy that's not completely woken up, you sure see a lot of shit, don't you?"

"Well, I—"

"Just answer the Fucking question already."

"If I told you that there was a chance you could also die by drinking that punch."

"Would you still drink it?

"I don't really—"

"Just answer the Fuckin question."

Farley straightened up.

"Yes, then."

"Yes, I would."

Buddy leaned forward.

"Really?"

"Yes."

"You want some punch?"

"Well, yes."

"If what you're saying."

"I mean, are you being literal here?"

"There's some punch for you right up here," Buddy said.

"Do you want it or not?"

"Sssure, I guess."

"Now, you guess."

"Can't you make up your goddamn mind, Farley?"

"Yes."

"Yes, you can make up your mind."

"Or yes."

"You want some punch."

"I'll take some punch," he said.

"Then come on up, Farley." Buddy clapped, smiling.

"Come on up and receive your punch!"

Farley started, looking around cautiously.

"Come on, everyone, give Farley a big hand."

Everyone started to clap.

Farley smiled big and dance-walked to the rhythm of the claps towards the platform, where two of Buddy's assistants helped him up.

I was one of Buddy's assistants.

Cleaning up some punch I had spilled.

Buddy came up and put his arm around Farley and Farley flinched.

"It's alright, Farley," Buddy said, patting him on his bald head.

He stopped after a few pats and looked at his hand.

"Get me a kerchief, will you?" he said to one of his assistants.

"That was quite a sweat, wasn't it?" he said to Farley.

Farley nodded sheepishly and everyone laughed.

One of the assistants handed a paper towel to Farley.

Who proceeded to put it to his face.

But Buddy yanked it out of his hand.

Balled it up one-handed.

And threw it back at the assistant who had brought it.

"A damn handkerchief," he barked.

"Not a Fucking paper towel."

"And what the Fuck did I tell you about using paper towels?"

"It's recycled," the assistant mumbled.

Someone in the audience came up and handed Buddy an authentic handkerchief.

Buddy took it and wiped Farley's forehead and dome.

"I want everyone to give a big welcome to Farley."

Hey, Farleys.

And Hi, Farleys.

And Welcome, Farleys filled the room.

"There, is that better?" Buddy said.

Leaning in to Farley and dabbing his nose.

"Yes, much," Farley said.

"Gave you quite a run, didn't I?"

"You sure did!"

Relieved laughs from the audience.

"Sure, I did."

Buddy patted Farley on the dome again.

"Can I ask you a personal question?"

"Sure," Farley said.

"Are you bald out of choice or is this hereditary?"

"A little of both," Farley chuckled.

So did Buddy.

So did the audience.

"Still want some punch?" Buddy asked.

"If you're still offerin."

Light chuckling all around.

"Sure, I am."

"Okay," Buddy smiled.

"But first."

"And this relates to what I was saying earlier about Hitler."

"Let me ask you something."

"Uh, okay."

The audience seemed to tense up again.

As they should.

"When I was calling you out earlier."

"Did you think I was being nice to you?"

"Or was I kind of a jerk?"

Farley chuckled.

"Well, to be honest—"

"I was kind of a jerk, right?" Buddy said.

"Yes, a little."

"But I see now that—"

"If someone came up to you on the street and grilled you like that, what would you do?" Buddy asked.

"Well, I."

"What would you do, Farley?"

"Well, if it was—"

"Turn the other cheek like one of those meeksters?"

"Waiting for an inheritance they never earned?"

"Or."

He let it hang.

"Or?" Farley said.

"Yes, *or.*"

"What would your other option be?"

"Walk away?"

"That's tantamount to turning the other cheek, wouldn't you say?"

"Yes."

"What else could you do, Farley?"

"What other options are at stake here?"

"Well, I could—"

"Let me give you a hint," Buddy said.

"What are they pouring into those cups over there?"

"Punch?"

"Yes?"

"I could offer them some punch?"

"In a manner of speaking, but I'm not being literal here."

"So I can't offer them punch, then?"

"You can Farley, but only a certain kind."

"I'm afraid I'm not that familiar with the different kinds of punch—do you mean a certain flavor maybe?"

"The punch I'm talkin about is not a liquid, Farley—*comprende?*"

"Hmmm," Farley said, trying to look like he was thinking seriously about his answer.

"Jesus, Farley—it's not that Fuckin complicated, what other kinds of—"

"I could punch em, probably?"

"Punch!" Buddy laughed.

"Punch!"

"That's funny," Farley said.

"Would you say that your best option would be to punch him, then?" Buddy asked.

"What was the question again?"

Everyone laughed.

"If someone came up to you on the street and grilled you like I just did, what would you do?"

"Punch him?" Farley said.

"Is that what you'd do?"

"Yeah, sure."

Nodding his head and smiling to the audience like he was in on the joke.

"Well, why didn't you punch me, then?" Buddy said.

"Because you're."

"You're you, I guess."

"And I was at the back of the room at the time."

Everyone laughed again.

And so did Buddy.

"Well, what's the difference between me and some jerk on the street?"

There was silence as Farley stared at his feet and seemed to try to find the right answer.

"Well?" Buddy said.

"Well, because you know what you're doing."

"Do I?"

"I mean you're doing it for a purpose."

"Not just to be a jerk."

"But because you care."

"How do you know that?" Buddy said.

"Just."

"I don't know."

"That's why you're here, aren't you?"

"To be a jerk?" Buddy said.

"No, but to."

"You know."

"Help us."

"Was that what I was doing just now?" Buddy said.

"Yes."

"Yes?"

"Yes."

"Is that your final answer, Farley?"

"Well, I don't know exactly."

"You don't know," Buddy said.

"Not completely, no."

"So I could've been just Fuckin with you?"

"Maybe."

"But like in a different."

"For a purpose."

"What purpose would that be?"

"To wake me up probably."

"So you assumed that there was a probability that I was doing this to wake you up."

"Not just merely to be an asshole?"

"Yes."

"What if I wasn't?"

"Well, then." Farley grinned.

"Well, then what?" Buddy said.

"I'd have to punch you, then?"

He smiled at the audience and the audience laughed.

"Do you feel woken up?"

"I . . . I don't know."

"I feel a little light-headed maybe."

More laughs.

"Did I or did I not wake you up?" Buddy said.

"Well, not completely probably."

"How do you know the jerk on the street is not trying to wake you up?"

"Well, he could be, I guess."

"So what's the difference between me and some jerk?"

"Well, I guess it's because I'm here because I want to be."

"But you're not out on the street because you want to be?"

"Well, not in the same way."

"So you're saying it's more likely you'd punch someone else for being rude."

"And not me."

"Well, I'm not really a puncher."

"But probably."

"Well, what about turning the other cheek?"

"You think punching someone solves anything?"

"Usually, no."

"So, it might solve things sometimes."

"Just not usually?"

"Yeah, I guess."

"So, punch me."

"What?"

Buddy took his arm off of him and stood in front of him.

"Punch me."

"I can't do that."

"Why not?"

"Because I don't feel like doing it."

"What if I told you that punching me would wake you up?"

"I'd say wow."

Laughs from the audience.

"Well, I'm saying it."

"Seriously?"

"No joke."

"Punch me and you'll wake up."

"Maybe."

"Maybe?"

"There's only one way to find out."

"Punch me, Farley."

"No, I can't."

"You can."

"No, really."

"I'm that jerk on the street, Farley."

"Punch me or get out of here and hit the real street."

"You're not—"

"I'm waiting, Farley."

"But, you—"

"Do you want to wake up, Farley?"

"Or just be a sleepwalker all your life?"

"I'm here because I want—"

"Shut up and punch me, you Fucking moron!"

Farley looked down.

He clenched his right hand and then unclenched it.

"Clock's ticking, Farley."

Farley looked up at Buddy and smiled.

Like he could disarm the situation.

"Wipe that smile off your face and hit me already."

Farley made his fist again.

"C'mon, you meek little man."

"Hit me!"

Farley took a deep breath and looked like he was about to cry.

"C'mon, you sad excuse."

"C'mon, Farley," someone said and soon everyone followed:

"C'mon, Farley."

"C'mon, Farley!"

"C'mon, Farley!"

"Do it!" someone screamed.

Farley looked up.

And without conviction took a half-assed swing at Buddy.

Who blocked it with his left with a "Hyah!"

As if it had been a swing from Bruce Lee or something.

Which caught Farley by surprise.

It was obvious that Buddy was trained in some sort of martial art.

And obvious that he wanted everyone to know that he was trained in some sort of martial art.

Now in a leg-flexed martial crouch.

Right foot forward.

Body facing the audience.

Buddy sent a mean right with another "Hyah!" into Farley's gut.

Causing Farley to double over with a pitiful groan.

The audience gasped.

But Buddy wasn't finished.

Now.

In a most un-martial-artist way.

He grabbed Farley's head with both hands.

And kneed him in the face a number of times.

Until Farley dropped to the ground.

Well.

He would have probably hit the ground after the first knee.

But Buddy held him up by his head.

While the rest of his body was desperately trying to rendezvous with the ground.

Until Buddy let go.

And he smacked to the ground.

It was obvious that Farley was finished.

And even more obvious that Buddy wasn't.

So Buddy kicked him a mean one in the gut.

The room was silent save for Farley's coughing and sputtering.

Buddy now pushed Farley onto his back with his foot and looked at the audience.

Taking hard breaths.

"Just because you follow the way of the spirit," he said.

"Don't mean you won't end up on the ground sputtering like Farley here."

He stood over Farley and straddled him.

"What's goin to happen to all those meek little people," he said.

"When Evil comes knockin on the door?"

"Huh?"

He unzipped his pants.

"What's goin to happen when the dark of Death comes."

"And the demons begin to dance?"

He took out his dick.

And shook it a bit.

"You wanna know what's gonna happen?"

"Just look down here."

He started to piss on Farley.

"Here's your meek for you right here."

"Does it look like he's inheriting anything?"

"Yeah," I said.

Buddy turned.

"Hey, Bungalow Bill."

My head moves to the left.

I don't move it.

Then to the right.

"Dude's a snoozer."

Something hard on my cheek.

"Wakey wakey."

Standing over me.

Straddling me.

"You piss on me, I'm gonn—"

"Hey, whoa."

"I ain't gonna piss on you."

Reach for the five.

It's gone.

For the BDG.

Guess.

"Yeah, we got your cannon."

"The issue too."

"Can you get up?"

"Can if you get the Fuck back."

Feet pounding down the stairs.

"A to the MotherFuckin K!"

Know that voice.

"Kent?"

"The one and only, MotherFucker."

"Help you up."

"Nah, I got it."

Up.

"Goddamn."

"The Fuck you doin?"

"Apologies, my man."

"Charlie here's a little too quick on the trigger."

"That's what she said," Charlie said.

"Man, you're not supposed to say that."

"It's for someone else to."

"I thought you was swept."

"Nah."

"What about all that shit I heard about you?"

"At the suicide prevention."

"Heard they."

"Yeah."

"Funny how people want to die until you stick a gun in their face."

"I heard worse."

"Yeah, well," he laughed.

"Let's just say that wasn't the last thing I stuck in their face."

"That's what she said."

"Yo, Charlie."

"Bout you stop talking and go upstairs and stick your shit in already?"

"You finished?"

"Yeah—now go."

He went.

Clopping up the stairs.

To me: "Man, think your number two hasn't been popped."

"Fuckin blood on my dick."

"What?"

"What's goin on?"

"The Fuck you doin?"

Puts his hand on my shoulder.

"Less have a seat."

"Let's not and you tell me why the Fuck you guys are putting it to my partner."

"Partner?"

"Yeah, my partner."

"The hell you think she was?"

"Well, I thought she was some dumb slit who thinks she can fill in for your partner."

"You do remember your partner, don't you?"

"What do you think?"

He laughed.

"Used to think it was a class-five hurricane."

"What?"

"'Jumpin Jack Flash.'"

Sings:

"I was boooorrnn in a crossfire hurr-cane."

"What the Fuck?"

"I was singin that one time," Kent said.

"And Mars corrected me."

"Sayin."

He laughed.

"That it was a class-five hurricane."

"And when I told him no."

"It's a crossfire hurricane."

"He said there's no such thing."

"He was right," I say.

FORT LA BREA

Venice.

East of La Brea.

West.

Remote shutdown.

Surprised we got as far as we did.

Things were going to end bad.

But still:

Had to figure out how to get to that bad end.

"Need to get rid of our tags."

She moaned.

"That's what she said."

"No, you okay?"

"There's no way," she said.

"There's no way we're going—"

"I've been in worse."

"Worse?"

"Holed up in the VZ."

"Eatin rats."

"What are you talking—"

"Highland Park."

"Highland Park?"

"No."

"Highland Park's done."

Just before Insatia disappeared I sent her to Ricky to have her tag removed.

Few days later she was gone.

So was he.

Couldn't trace her.

Try and restart the Honcho with a universal.

No go.

"That's it."

"Maybe we should just go back, talk to."

"No, no way."

"Talk to Trimmer. Tell her."

"Tell her what?"

"Like I told you."

"Like Kent told me."

"We were *both* listed."

"Those sick Fucks were gonna do you after they."

She turned her head.

"Sorry."

Kent didn't sit.

Wanted to stand over me.

"See this shit?"

Pictures on the living room walls.

Like those old paintings of pale Puritans.

Dark.

Cracked.

Except:

The boy was missing most of the flesh on his face.

The girl had tentacles growing out of her eyes.

Large one above the fireplace showed what looked like a couple.

In some grotesque yoga posture.

Or a brutal game of Twister.

Fucking.

Picasso-like.

Two children stood by and looked on with blank expressions.

The paintings were scratched in the lower left corners with what looked like *Pick hawk*.

"What is this?"

"Bunch a Euro-creeps," Kent said.

"Ever notice the more sophisticated."

"The more *cultural* a person supposedly is."

"The sicker the shit they like?"

"Where are they?"

"Stacked upstairs."

"So, what? Trimmer's pulled my number?"

"Yeah, she's givin you the rod—cubo."

"Conduct unbecoming?"

"Yeah," he said.

"A DEO?"

"The hell she think this is?"

"I don't know," he said.

"Bitch wants to have her cunt and eat it too I guess."

"So, why am I still sittin here?"

"Didn't think you should go out like that."

"Like what?"

"You know."

"Like every other zero."

"So, what?"

"You're not gonna?"

"Sayin is that that Trimmer bitch has no respect," he said.

"Thinks she can tell us to cut out one of our own like a . . ."

"Like a . . ."

"Coupon?"

"Yeah, like a coupon or something."

"Well, isn't that your job?"

"I ain't no coupon cutter."

"So, what, you're gonna."

"Man, this shit don't bother you?" he said.

"What shit?"

"Getting zeroed?"

"Nah, not at all."

"No, man. These bitches. These . . . these . . . *cunt*servatives."

"What?"

"Wake up and smell the coffee bean and tea leaf, man."

"This whole world's undergoing a massive pussification while we're—"

"Pussification?"

"Yeah, pussification, man—we're all gonna be run by chicks soon."

"Yeah, well, guess it's their turn now."

"Turn?"

"More like we're turning into them, is what it is."

"What, you growin tits?"

"No, but look all at the dudes now."

"With their he-heels and bro-bags."

He pulled out some sanitizer from a little holster on his belt and OCD'd his hands.

"Never know what you might pick up in this business. Want some?"

"Nah."

"Came in this house once."

Rubbing his wrists.

"Dude had these jars."

"Stacked floor to ceiling."

"Living room, kitchen, bathroom—everywhere."

"Know what was in em?"

"No."

"Piss."

"Shit."

"All labeled with the date and time."

Up to his forearms now.

Prepping for surgery.

"Sure you've seen some shit too," he said.

"Yeah."

Then a pipe from his pocket.

Sucked a hit and blew.

Bitter smoke.

Foul.

He handed it.

"Nah."

"No, man. It's the Scorpion."

"Never done that shit."

"Do it."

"I'll pass."

"I'm not askin."

"How bout a cigarette instead."

"Take it."

I took it.

"What's it do?"

"Just hit it."

I pussied it and still coughed.

"Here."

He took another hit.

"Member back in the day?" he said.

Exhale.

Cough.

"Hell, me and you probably killed more people than Hitler."

"Six million?"

"Six million?"

"Yeah, Hitler killed over six million people."

"Okay, yeah. But not personally."

"You still get personals?"

He took another hit.

Holding it:

"Nah, man."

"Bitch nixed that."

"But still."

"There's—other day I was out on Third and these Asians."

This time he hacked.

"Asians?"

"Yeah, these."

He kept hacking.

Shit was starting to punch my brain cells.

Heart beating like a war drum.

Take him out.

Still hacking.

Get ready.

He finished and wiped his mouth on his sleeve.

"Know Monopoly tried to change Oriental Ave to Asia Ave a few years back and the gooks got all mad because it was on the poor section of the board?"

He laughed.

"Wanted to change Park Place to Korea Town."

"Believe that shit?"

"Yeah, so?"

"Few weeks back this Asian dude was on the wrong side of the sidewalk."

"Wrong side?"

"Yeah."

"What side is that?"

"You know, the right side."

"I mean my right, but their left."

"So this dude, he won't get on the right side, okay?"

"Wouldn't give you the white of way, huh?"

"So I say, hey, asshole, we drive on the right side of the road in this country."

"And he was all like kung pao chicken and shit."

"So I zeroed him right in the face."

"Probably a tourist."

"Nah, man."

"They all do that shit here."

"Haven't you noticed?"

"I don't really walk."

"Yeah, well."

"If you did."

"Should have DEOs on the sidewalk too."

I point up.

"What about her?"

"God?"

"No, Meghasin—my partner."

"Yeah, she's half, isn't she?"

"Probably drives down the middle of the street."

"She on the list too?"

"No, we do her we get docked," he said.

"Docked?"

"Yeah, less points."

"So, you're not gonna do her . . . just *do* her, right?"

"Actually, I was waiting for you."

"Was gonna let you have one last ride before."

A loud shout from upstairs.

Then a thud.

"MotherFuckin buttsucker."

"Knew he couldn't."

"Come on," he said, "can't leave you down here."

"So, what do we do?" Meghasin said.

"Only thing we can do."

"Remove our tags? How are we—"

"No, we go on the offense."

He was floating above the bed.

Lamp on the floor throwing up horror movie light from the other side.

Meghasin red-faced.

Scissoring him with her legs.

She only needed a few more minutes.

"Look at this shit," Kent said.

I looked at him.

BDG inside his coat.

Clock him now.

He drew his BDG and turned to me.

"Might just have to get less points."

"Get her off," Charlie croaked.

Kent: "Bitch, why didn't you use those legs when I was—"

His PDT was 911-ing.

He flicked his arm out and shot Meghasin.

I got out and flagged down the next car.

A Mazda Mañana.

Pulled the driver out by the hair with a complementary "Police business."

We got in and hit La Brea north until the thing crapped out after 12th.

Jacked again.

"We need an older car than this."

"One they can't remote."

"What's the difference?" she said.

"We're still tagged."

"I'm not walkin."

"And then?"

"And then, what?"

"We get a car and then what?"

"We go get them."

"Strike first."

"Who's them?"

"All of them."

"No."

"We need to leave," she said.

"Get out of the city."

"No, I'm not runnin."

"So you want to get us killed?"

"Better than getting subtracted."

She turned her head away.

"Look. We're *done*."

"They're gonna get us no matter what we do."

"We either go out runnin."

"Or gunnin."

"That's not a plan," she said.

"That's a slogan."

"Sometimes you bust a nut."

"Sometimes you don't," Charlie said.

He rolled her off him.

Kent pointed his BDG at me.

"Your turn."

I put out my arms.

"Go ahead."

"No, dumbass." He nodded towards Meghasin.

"For her."

"Fuck a dead girl."

"She ain't dead."

"Just a little limp."

Charlie laughed. "That's what she said."

Kent looked at him and then at me.

"We'll hit her with the dote before she crosses."

"Ever Fuck one with the bug?" he said.

"No."

"Well, now's your chance."

"Okay."

"You gonna give me some privacy?"

"Sorry, man."

"Least one of us is got to be here."

"Don't know if I can get it done with you watching."

"Bout Charlie?" he said.

"Either of you."

"K—your funeral."

He leveled his BDG at me and fired.

"Run a list of vehicles in the area that aren't tagged and I'll get us a temp."

I got out and flagged an oncoming Toyota Tongva.

The driver panicked at the sight of my badge and burned his tires down Edgewood.

A three-wheel Maruti Num Num.

I let it pass, popping.

Meghasin got out of the Mañana.

"Two blocks north," she said.

"Poof," Kent said.

"What?"

I was still standing.

He laughed.

"I said poof, bitch."

"What the."

He lowered his gun.

"Man, I had you."

"Totally had you."

"What the Fuck is?"

"You really thought I would zero you?"

"What?"

"Do what that bitch said?"

"Well, then what is?"

"You don't know?" he said.

"What?"

"Really?"

"Thought everyone heard by now."

"Heard what?"

She'd found us a cartifact.

Parked at the foot of a driveway behind a new Jedi.

Red and white VW Bus.

Freshly restored.

Cherried.

Front V-necked.

A white chest sporting a VW medallion.

Expired tags.

Registration pending an inspection to have the vehicle certified antique.

"Can you get it started?" Meghasin said.

"Sure."

I tried the driver's door.

It was locked.

Checked my pockets for a universal.

No.

"Hey you got a uni on you?"

"A what?"

"The key. Have you got a universal on you?"

Checking her satchel—"I . . . I don't think so. They supposed to issue me one?"

"Great."

I checked the shotgun door.

Locked.

The cargo door.

Locked.

The back hatch opened.

No, it didn't.

Looked up and down the street to see if anyone was looking.

Looked at the house.

Windows dark.

The yard:

Succulents and cacti surrounded by gravel and small rocks.

Blue fescue.

Picked the biggest rock I could find.

About the size of a golf ball.

And threw it at the back window.

It bounced off.

And hit the Jedi.

The alarm went off.

Blasting out the Imperial March.

Meghasin was quick on the override and the alarm was off in less than ten.

I picked up the rock and threw it at the back window again.

It bounced off again.

But this time it left a nice crack.

The butt of the five to finish it off.

Took my hat off and handed it to Meghasin and slithered through.

Ended up lying on my back.

Front seat.

Head under the dash.

Feet hanging out the door.

"One of those skills they don't teach at the DoD anymore."

"Taught us how to get out of a locked trunk too."

"Uh, Alex, I think we—"

The DoD is done, Kent said.

Finished.

So no more DEOs.

Job was being automated.

Computerized.

A whole crew of them were getting ready.

For vengeance.

All the old heads.

Wanted to know if I was in.

Then after.

A deal with Thurlow.

BlackGuard was gonna reinstate everyone.

New job.

New contract.

TeRF maybe.

Or some shit overseas.

Who knows.

What about Meghasin?

She in?

No.

She was one of them.

Not us.

We gotta do her.

Dump her body on Trimmer's.

No.

No way.

She's in or it's a no go.

Suits yourself, he said.

"Hey! What the hell?"

Guy standing in front of the driver's-side door.

Within kicking distance.

Crink my head up.

"This your vehicle?"

"Yeah, this is my."

"Get the hell out of it right now."

I sat up and looked at him.

White guy.

T-shirt.

Shorts and flip-flops.

Unremarkable face.

Kind of guy you see in those commercials.

Scratching his head while his wife serves him some new and surprising food product.

Kind that comes in a pod.

The kind of guy who usually has enough sense to call the cops when someone breaks into his car.

Where was Meghasin?

If Mars was here.

Guy would've been clocked already.

I held out my police badge:

"Police."

"We're commander-ing this vehicle."

"You're kidding."

"No."

"Aren't you supposed to inform the owner before you *commandeer* a vehicle?"

"No."

"You got a wire cutter I can command too?"

Holding out his phone:

"You know what?"

"This doesn't look like commandeering to me."

"More like stealing."

"Give me your badge numbers now."

"We're gonna see what your superiors have to say about this."

"Sure."

"And while you're at it call 911."

"What?"

I showed him my Five.

"Tell them there's been a shooting."

"White guy in flip-flops."

"Bleeding out into the street."

He held up his hands. "Hey."

I got out and put the five in his face.

"Someone's breakin into your vehicle, and you come out in flip-flops?"

"What the hell's the matter with you?"

He backed up a few steps. "Hey."

"You *wanna* get shot, don't you?"

"Suicide by cop."

"You're really cops?"

I held up my badge.

"Officer Rogers."

"Officer Ross," Meghasin said from somewhere.

I looked at her.

Standing behind the Bus.

"Forgive me for asking," he said.

"But why this car, why not . . ."

"It's an undercover operation."

"Due to a set of unfortunate circumstances, we are stranded out in the field."

"And in need of a vehicle of your year and make."

"So, if you don't mind."

"I'd like to get this thing started."

"Why don't I just get you the keys?" he said.

"Please."

"Please don't."

Kent's last words.

The rest were just screams.

What happened was this:

Meghasin had trouble walking after what they did to her.

So I had to help her.

On the stairs.

Me and Meghasin.

Charlie behind.

And Kent up front.

Still had his BDG out like he wasn't sure if he could trust.

But it wasn't trained.

Just out.

Half turned, saying something about Meghasin.

That he couldn't promise her protection.

And maybe the heads will want to take a go too.

Better if she got done now, etc.

That's when I threw her at him.

She crashed into him hard and they both went hurtling.

Down.

I have to assume that's how it played.

Judging from the aftermath.

Because as soon as I threw her I turned and got Charlie by his coat.

Unbalanced him.

And threw him forward.

I surveyed the mess of bodies.

It was good work.

The tangle of limbs.

The symphony of moans.

I went down and pulled Meghasin out.

She wasn't too bad.

Her eyes were still open at least.

Kent had broken most of the fall.

On his side moaning.

Charlie looked knocked out.

But he was making sounds.

He was right under the statue.

If it fell then his head would.

Let's see.

I pushed.

It fell.

Actually had to turn my head away before it crashed down on his face.

I went over and rolled Kent on his back.

"You okay?"

He doesn't have much breath.

Reaching out his hand towards me.

"Really?"

"Think you're gonna grab me?"

"Turn the tide?"

"Look. I'm gonna go to the fridge. Find something to beat you to death with."

"And if."

"In that time you manage to recover, get to your BDG over there, well, then."

If you could pick any kind of food to beat someone to death with what would you choose?

I was hoping for a pineapple actually.

Or some kind of melon.

A cantaloupe maybe.

Just to start things off.

Finish him with a nice rack of ribs.

But all they had was some broccoli and a bunch of grapes.

No meat.

Some pita bread.

Which would be like tryin to beat a guy to death with a pillow.

So I settled for a bottle of soy sauce.

Took their gear and stacked their bodies with the Euro-creeps in the master bedroom:

Man, woman, teenage girl, boy.

A Rolex on the nightstand next to the canopied bed.

In a safe a Glock, a Gatwitzer, and a couple boxes of ammo.

Girl's room:

A book titled *Famous Suicide Notes* on the bed.

Piece of boutique paper inside.

> *Dear Mother and Father, I'm not much for words write (sic)* now and you will maybe not understand my motivational reasons and moral intentions because*
>   1. *For me much of the world makes no sense—p. 62*
>   2. *The future is just old age and illness and pain—p. 118 (Put 2 and 3 together)*
>   3. *It is the simplest of human rights to choose a quick and easy Death in place of a slow and horrible one—p. 30*
>   4. *La tristesse durera toujours—p. 16 (should I translate this or let them?)*
>   5. *I don't want to spend my life being shoved around by desire after desire after desire—p. 45*
>   6. *Twits and Twats teething tater tots while tweeting— (my friends totally—from that song by MeasleMob)*
>   7. *It's not that what people want isn't real, it's that wanting itself isn't real—p. 45*
>   8. *I want my money back—p. 212 (probably won't use, but funny!—or, maybe as a P.S.)*
>
> *—I wish I had someone to end it with—a Lover—to end in Love will make it forever (?)*

---

*   sic in original—ed.

I folded the note and pocketed it.

Suicide.

Depression.

Whatever they call it.

Is just normal.

For a city like this.

The greatest crime ever committed.

Against a piece of land.

When I was a kid.

I couldn't get out of bed.

Didn't want to get out of bed.

I wanted to keep sleeping.

I didn't see it as a problem.

Until my parents told me it was a problem.

So they took me to a doctor.

A psychiatrist.

A pneumatologist.

Neurologist.

Even a numerologist.

All of them said something different.

Anemia.

Dysthymia.

Anhedonia.

Hypersomnia.

Seven.

One guy said it was all of them.

It wasn't.

I just wasn't interested.

In anything.

Going to school.

Brushing my teeth.

Tying my shoe.

Even playing.

I couldn't understand why anyone wanted to do any of that.

Especially school.

You got to do thirteen years of it if you were lucky.

Plus four more if you weren't.

And if you did more than that there was probably something seriously wrong with you.

The fact that people bragged about being institutionalized like that didn't make any sense.

All those idiots with their college license plate frames.

Synnita showing off her Stetson U shit.

Shirts, hats, stickers, mugs.

Got pissed when I asked if she spent four years learning how to wear a cowboy hat.

Just the thought of all those years of school ahead made me want to never get out of bed.

To sleep forever.

I didn't even want to think about what you had to do after you left school.

What they call living.

In the real world.

Whatever that is.

It wasn't until later I realized.

Figured out.

That I was a sleeper cell.

Waiting.

To be activated.

Waiting.

To murder.

Thing was a bitch to drive.

Sounded like a rusty lawn mower.

Too high up and too close to the front.

Felt like I was going to fall out the front window.

12th to La Brea.

"Where are we going?"

"Got an errand to run."

Fort La Brea.

Claire had been dressed and ready before I even opened my eyes.

What opened them was her humming a Reina Hawthorne song.

I Hate Reina Hawthorne.

I moaned no particular tune and forced myself out of bed and hit the shower.

When I got out she had laid out a suit.

The one she'd bought for my birthday.

The one I called the fag suit.

Too wide in the shoulders and too slim in the waist.

I stood there and tried to comprehend what it was I was supposed to do when she came in and reminded me.

"Put it on."

"We have less than ten minutes."

Before we walked out the door she gave me the once-over to see if I would pass muster.

Smoothing an eyebrow and tightening my tie.

I didn't like the idea of being interrogated to move into a condo.

But this wasn't about me, I told myself.

It was for her.

An hour and a half later we were at the gate.

Waiting.

For a BlackGuard security Officer.

Taking his time to let us in.

Trying to look bored.

In that underpaid-security-guard way.

I started to roll out a "What the."

But Claire was on me quick.

Obviously already wary that I could Fuck things up.

She put her hand on my hand and squeezed before I could get out the "Fuck."

He eyed me long enough to download me for future reference.

If there happened to be trouble.

And he happened to need a suspect.

Finally.

The bar swung up and we were in.

Claire's Mitsubishi Zero bumpled over what looked to be cobblestone.

Past shit that was hard to wrap my eyes around.

Units of various styles.

Mixed with other styles.

On top of other styles.

Radiating out like spokes.

From a central tower.

A blue steel finger.

Flipping off Los Angeles.

Jacarandas in full bloom.

Littering pools of purple.

Bright green manicured lawns with manicured flower beds.

Nothing looked planted.

But installed.

"Beautiful, isn't it?" Claire said.

"You know what they call this place in the Department?"

"Yeah, I know what they call it in the Department."

"Fort La Brea."

"Well, what's wrong with living in a fort?"

"More like a prison."

Where they charged you for the cell.

Although.

The inmates didn't look so tough.

Youngish.

Mostly white.

Embalmed.

Crate & Barrel couples.

Impeccably dressed in that offhand, casual way.

Pushing kids or walking dogs or both.

Not a prison exactly.

More like a womb.

We pulled up in front of a stone building I could only describe as Tex-Mex.

"Mayan Revival," Claire said.

"Islama-Mayan" a plaque said.

Next to the front door.

Stone with a set of iron knockers in the shape of acorns.

Or distorted skulls.

Presumably to be used in case the large Mexican buzzer with accompanying "Ring Bell for Entrance" sign didn't do the trick.

I ignored it and opened the door and walked in before Claire could ring.

A young, plain brown woman with plain pulled brown hair.

Behind a reception altar that was almost too high for her to look over.

I leaned over and asked her what time the sacrifice was.

Claire cut in and told her we had an appointment and she confirmed that we did.

We were told to have a seat and wait for Ms. Something or other.

Soon as we sat down Ms. Something or other came out and greeted us.

House with white carpet and plastic runways.

Take off your shoes.

Here:

Have some apple pie and ice cream.

Sure, thanks.

Seconds?

Don't mind if I do.

But.

Behind the cheerful crust.

The synthetic smile.

A filling of pure evil.

Fascists are friendly.

Nazis are nice.

And dictators are.

Well.

Until, you wander from the designated plastic.

And soil the proverbial carpet.

Then.

Still.

In all fairness to this Dartha Stewart.

You had to fall within a certain set of parameters.

Broadcast on a certain set of frequencies.

To even register within her bandwidth of contempt.

And I knew and she knew.

As I shook her leathered hand.

Large rocks strangling half the digits.

That I didn't even register at all.

As far as my wife went.

The jury was still out.

"Glad you could make it," she said.

My wife said she was glad too.

What did I say?

She directed us towards her office and we sat down in a set of chairs in front of her white desk.

Walls flashing white people with dazzling white-tooth grins every few seconds.

An occasional dog shot in between.

Dog had dazzling white teeth too.

She asked us how we knew about La Brea Gardens.

I asked her if the grass was fake.

A lawn as green and lush as that had to be fake.

Or else they were importing water.

As they say:

Water doesn't grow on trees.

Which is what I said.

The lawn was quite real, she informed me.

The water was being subsidized by the City.

You mean the taxpayers.

Subsidized in return for all the community improvements BlackGuard was providing.

At no charge.

BlackGuard?

Yes, BlackGuard.

La Brea Gardens is a BlackGuard concept.

Concept?

Yes, La Brea Gardens is a BlackGuard concept.

You mean they run the place?

Yes, if you want to put it that way.

For the rest of the conversation she would only talk directly to Claire.

Without so much as a flick of an eye in my direction.

Which, frankly, offended me for some reason.

Maybe she could tell that I didn't give a Fuck.

So I stared out the window behind her head.

And tried to imagine somewhere else.

But I couldn't come up with anywhere else.

Which, for some reason, brought on a wave of panic.

I crossed my leg and uncrossed it.

I leaned my head to the left and pulled my earlobe.

I picked my nose.

No, I didn't.

Focus.

Try to listen.

They didn't let just anybody live here.

Being able to afford this place wasn't enough.

No, don't listen.

You had to look a certain way.

But not in the superficial sense.

Think of somewhere else.

Improper attire tended to detract from the overall experience they were endeavoring to celebrate.

And although sustainable attire wasn't required.

Anywhere.

It was encouraged.

Forget it.

You had to think a certain way.

Possess certain core values.

You're done.

"This is a Value Community," she said to Claire.

"Do you know what a Value Community is?"

"One with values," I said.

Without thinking.

My wife turned her head slightly in my direction.

Which meant that I should shut my mouth.

"Well . . . yes," the woman said carefully.

In a way which meant I should shut my mouth.

"It's one that believes in."

Claire trying to make a save.

"In."

But that's as far as she could get.

"Do you know what a Sangha is?" the woman said.

I knew what it was.

But I couldn't remember.

It was Buddhist.

I knew that.

"Uh," Claire said.

"It's Buddhist," I said.

"Yes," she said.

"But do you know what it means?"

"Well, that depends on the trans–"

Claire coming in for another save:

"No, what does it mean?"

She told us.

I didn't listen.

When I came back she was talking about lifestyle compatibility.

They were looking for residents that shared the same values and lifestyle.

"Materialism is out and mindfulness is in," she said.

Heard somewhere that misanthropy was.

Or was it philanthropy.

Either way.

All their residents were socially responsible and environmentally conscious.

They didn't want the type who comes home from work and plops down in front of the TV with a beer.

They wanted someone who was actively and passionately engaged.

Dedicated and devoted.

Helpful and humble.

This is not just a place to live, she said.

It is a place to flourish.

Certain chemical-based cleaners weren't allowed on the premises.

No smoking of course.

A whole list of things you couldn't say within earshot of anyone on the premises.

All the usual four-letter stuff.

Don't get me wrong, she said.

We're for freedom of expression of course.

But expression that was of a sexual, racial, or profane nature was socially irresponsible.

And therefore.

Not permitted.

I wanted to ask her if it would be okay to call myself a Nigger in the privacy of my own home.

But that would have just pissed Claire off.

Oh.

And yes.

We do not refer to our residents as residents either.

But as *pobladores*.

In honor of the first settlers of Los Angeles.

Because.

In a way.

We are like those first settlers.

Forging a new community.

A cultural oasis.

In the cultural desert of Los Angeles.

Not a community exactly.

But what we prefer to call a collaborative.

A Soul-ciety if you will.

Community sounds too . . .

Communist.

Totalitarian.

Although.

In a city as fragmented as ours.

It was in our vital interests to come together.

But not in a coercive way.

Isolation is bad for a person's health and well-being.

Studies have shown.

Bad physically.

Mentally.

And spiritually.

Even sexually.

Isolation.

I prefer to call it insulation.

The original idea of this City.

To spread it out.

Keep some space between people.

People need space.

Distance.

Hell.

Isn't the universe expanding?

No one wants some chump up in their face all the time.

Harassed by the masses and all that.

That's why public transportation is crap.

The essential American soul is hard.

Isolate.

Stoic.

And a killer.

At least within the confines of a car you get some space.

Some room to breathe.

Don't have to smell the guy next to you.

Look at the ugly mugs of the faces across from you.

Boundaries.

Good fences make good neighbors.

The American is hard.

Isolate.

And a killer.

Preferably a high wall topped with barbed wire.

Because contrary to popular opinion.

People aren't as great as people like this lady like to think.

No.

You can't make a community out of these.

These.

Selfies.

These gadget men and grabbers.

These.

What did that kid say?

Twits and twats.

No.

Somewhere in the Twentieth Century humans were finished off.

Bombed.

Slaughtered.

Gassed.

Cremated.

And buried.

There aren't any left.

Only pigs and cattle now.

Chickens and sheep.

Goats and monkeys.

Cartoon animals.

Stuffed with popcorn and sugar.

Besides.

People who like to talk about community do so from behind locked fences and security gates.

To them people always look better from a distance.

Or behind bars.

Far away or up close.

It's all the same.

Like everything on this earth.

Scarcity makes value.

Take gold.

Or water:

They're valuable.

People:

They're worth nothing.

Prospective *pobladores* should possess a degree of compassion for their fellow humans.

Especially for the less fortunate.

Every year we throw open our doors to the homeless.

Excuse me.

I mean our free-range citizens.

An annual soup and salad kitchen charity event.

Mandatory for all *pobladores*.

Oh, but don't worry.

None of those people are actually/literally permitted on the premises.

We're only opening our doors figuratively.

We have a facility in Vernon that is more adequately equipped to handle those people.

By the way.

None other than Reina Hawthorne.

Who happens to own one of the skylofts in the middle finger.

Will be involved with this year's event.

Really? Claire exclaimed.

Reina Hawthorne?

I didn't know she lived here.

Me neither.

She knew.

Had to.

Subscribed to Reina's LifeCast for Chrissake.

And damned if she wasn't watching her life more than her own.

Of course she didn't tell me.

Probably thought I'd accuse her of wanting to move here because of Reina Hawthorne.

Which wouldn't be an accusation.

But a fact.

Now Claire baiting the woman to give more info on Reina:

"Her place must have a lovely view."

Yes.

The view was awesome.

Awesome.

Zeroed a dude once who kept saying it.

In line at an Arby's.

Zeroed his friend too.

Chrysopolis revolves.

So the view changes hourly.

"In fact, if you're familiar with Reina's LifeCast then—"

"Shouldn't it be called a BroadCast?" I said.

Both turned to me.

"What?"

"A woman's LifeCast is essentially a *Broad*Cast."

Claire didn't say anything.

The woman frowned.

They turned back to each other and resumed where they left off.

I went into standby mode.

Put on my face saver and tried to mute the audio.

Best I could do was blur it.

Until their voices merged into one smooth stream.

Broken by the occasional stone.

I floated down it like a corpse.

Limbs twisted in the current.

Eventually they would find me.

Fish me out.

Wonder who I was.

What I was.

Fail to identify me.

Finally.

She asked Claire if *we* were still interested in becoming *pobladores*.

Yes.

Then were we ready for our interrogation?

Claire said yes, of course.

As long as she still wanted us.

She said she would be de-lighted to have us.

Pending the results of the interrogation.

Don't see why they need to interrogate.

Not with the current advances:

Microexpression analysis.

MRI.

Get all the info you need.

Except for.

The breakdown.

The humiliation.

Asked her if BlackGuard was doing the interrogating.

They were supposed to be out of the interrogation business.

Ever since the Wayside scandal.

Yes, she said.

BlackGuard no longer offered interrogation services.

Those services were now being subcontracted.

Precision Interrogation Services.

Never heard of them.

Yes, she said.

Now if you don't mind.

Please follow me.

She escorted us to a bored-looking guy in an office two doors down.

Ted from human resources.

As soon as he saw us he quickly got rid of the bored look and put on a more vigorous look.

Getting up and shaking my hand vigorously before shaking Claire's hand delicately in a vigorous way.

And if we wouldn't mind following him.

We followed Ted to the end of the hall, where he opened a door to another hall with several doors.

He opened the first one to the right.

A blank room with nothing but what looked like a dentist's chair in the center.

The chair was enclosed in a circle of white light so bright you couldn't see the corners of the room.

He instructed Claire to remove her clothes before taking her seat.

Her interrogator would be with her shortly.

We watched as she walked in and then turned around.

"Wish me luck," she said.

I didn't know what to say.

"Good luck," Ted said.

He shut the door and led me to a room two doors down that was exactly the same.

Told me to do the same as he told Claire.

I took off my clothes and hanged them.

Including my shoes.

On a series of hooks located next to the door.

Each labeled for a different article of clothing.

I sat down.

Floor tiled like a bathroom.

Drain in the floor next to the chair.

The word Smith stamped on it.

Claire had never been interrogated.

Synnita had made fun of her for it.

"Not even in school?"

Claire didn't graduate.

These snobs that think interrogation is some badge of honor.

I wouldn't have allowed it if I thought this place was going to give it to her hard.

Give out this kind of humiliation.

A woman comes in.

Cross my legs.

Wheeling some kind of machine I've never seen before.

Smiles at me and asks me to uncross my legs.

Ask her if she's my interrogator.

No.

Just an assistant.

Like at the dentist.

She just needs to put this sleeve on my penis.

And this steel tarantula on my head.

What is.

A transcranial receiver.

There.

She hits a button on the machine and the sleeve on my penis tightens.

"Snug?" she asks.

"Uh, yeah."

"Not too tight?"

"Uh, no."

"Excellent."

Another button and my chair rotates 180 to face the back wall.

"Okay, I want you to look at the wall."

"And don't take your eyes off whatever you see there."

"Okay."

"Ready?"

Ready.

Picture of a baby.

Female.

Naked.

Its genitalia right in the center of my vision.

"The Fuck is this?"

"Please do not respond verbally," she said. "All you have to do is look."

The picture stayed there for what seemed like several sick minutes.

The sleeve on my penis was vibrating slightly.

Like there was an electric current flowing through it.

The picture changed.

This time the baby was male.

With what looked like an erection.

I closed my eyes and there was a loud beeping sound.

"Please try and keep your eyes open," she said.

"Closing them will affect the test."

When I opened them there were two guys sodomizing each other in the most brutal way.

"This a fag test or something?"

"Shhhhhh."

The film continued.

Acts of depravity.

Perversion.

Torture and violence.

The usual Hollywood stuff.

At one point.

During a gang rape scene.

A loud bang exploded next to my left ear that made me jump.

"What the Fuck?"

"Don't worry," she giggled, "they're just sound effects."

More horror, more perversion.

I was starting to get bored.

When it was over I was 180'd back and she removed the sleeve from my penis and the headset from my head.

"Is that it?"

"Yes, Mr. Krieg."

"Your interrogator will be with you in a moment."

She wheels the machine out.

All I can think about is Claire.

They do the same thing to her?

Insert something in her vagina?

This was worse than the Department interrogation.

And they haven't even started the real interrogation.

Big white guy with a crew cut comes in and slams the door.

Black jeans and a black T-shirt: PIS.

Cartoon of a kid pissing on a dude.

Wraparound Stokely shades.

Midtwenties, maybe thirties.

Sweating.

Hunting the remains of his lunch.

Or the baby he had just devoured.

Smacking his lips and tonguing his teeth.

He walked around me poking at his PDT.

"Hmmm."

"Eighty-seven, thirteen."

"Two."

"What is that?" I ask.

Smack smack.

"Hmmmm?"

"Those numbers."

"Oh"—*smack*—"those are your orientation numbers."

"Orientation numbers?"

"Yes, hetero, homo, pedo."

Smack smack.

"Pedo?"

"Yeah."

"Meaning pedophile?"

"Yeah, pedo."

"No one gets a zero. Couple points usually."

Smack.

Smack.

After three full circles:

"Tell me your full name."

Alex Krieg.

"That your full name?"

Schlopp.

Smack.

"Alex Krieg?"

I didn't say anything.

He walked behind me.

"No middle name?"

Gulp.

"No."

"What?"

Trying to dislodge something from his teeth.

Ptschock.

"Not your name."

Smack.

"Or no."

"Middle."

"Name?"

"I don't have a middle name."

Schwack.

"You sure?

"Yeah, I'm sure."

"Yes, sir."

"Mind your."

Smack.

"Manners."

Tschock-tchock.

Slurp.

"Think this is a barn?"

"Yes, sir."

He walked around me a couple more times.

And farted once.

"Wait," he said.

"Yes, this is a barn, or yes, you will mind your manners?"

"Yes, I am—"

He ambushed that sentence with a burp.

"Scuze you," he said.

Smack.

He walked around me three more times.

A few more and I was gonna get dizzy.

"Alex Krieg."

Schock schock.

Smack.

"What kind of."

Fewww-urrrp.

"Whew."

Fanning the air in front of his face.

"Name is that?"

I couldn't take it anymore.

"Do you mind?"

Smack … smack … "What?"

"Would you mind not slob-smacking like that?"

"I got a condition."

"What?"

"Would you mind—"

Smack.

"Not."

Smack.

"Doing what you're doin right there?"

"I can't concentrate."

"Scuze me?"

"Look, you wanna finish your lunch break first?"

He came around in front of me and leaned down.

"You tryin to get cute wit me?"

"You forgot to smack."

He hauled off like he was going to smack me with an open palm and stopped just short of my cheek.

Then he leaned forward and burped in my face.

"Tha better?"

I shook my head.

Trying to shake off the stink of humiliation I felt at being burped in the face by a guy like that.

Would have been better if he had hit me.

Could smell what he had for lunch.

I ain't gonna tell you what he had for lunch.

I'm nice like that.

"How about we wrap this right now."

"And I give you a no dice?"

"What?"

"Simple question, Pongo."

"You wanna play ball, or not?"

"Pongo?"

"Yeah, Pongo."

"You gonna play nice or what?"

"Yeah."

"Yeah, what?"

"I'm gonna play . . . nice."

"That don't sound like a yes, and a sir."

"Yes, sir."

"Okay, let's get one thing straight."

"I ask the questions around here."

"And you just sit there like a fag, okay?"

"Yeah, okay."

"What?"

"Yes."

"Sir."

He put his finger in his teeth then pulled it back, and gave me a look.

Defying me to say something.

He looked at his PDT again.

"Krieg," he said.

"Kinda name is that?"

German.

"German, huh?"

"You know real Germans don't call themselves Germans."

"They call themselves Dutch-landers."

"I'm an American."

"Don't get cute with me."

"You don't look German."

"Why's that?"

A muffled shout from somewhere.

Claire's room.

"Well?"

"I was adopted."

"By Nazis, huh?"

No.

"What about your biological parents?"

"You know what biological is?"

I didn't know who my biological parents were.

Either I was abandoned or they were killed in the Rwandan genocide.

I don't know.

I was lumped in with the *enfants mauvais souvenirs.*

Children of bad memories.

Even though I had been born before all that shit.

Probably figured it would be easier to get me adopted that way.

By a white couple.

From Simi Valley.

The Griegs.

I changed the *G* to a *K.*

Sounds better.

Means better.

"Why not?"

I don't know.

"Yo mama a crackhead?"

"Watch it."

"You don't tell me to watch it, boy."

"You wanna get in here or not?"

"Yeah."

"Yeah?"

"Yes."

"Yes, what?"

"Sir."

"What?"

"Yes, sir."

He walked around me a few more times the opposite way he had walked around me before.

He mumbled something.

"What?"

He came around and stood in front of me.

And leaned forward and held my face in his hands.

Attention grasp.

"You don't hear too good, do you?"

"What?"

He slapped me.

Insult slap.

A classic.

Fingers spread slightly, not hard.

"Don't get cute with me."

"You go by any names, nicknames, or aliases that I should know of?"

"Kweeeg."

"Krieg."

Another insult slap.

"You sharpshootin me, boy?"

"No."

He slapped me again.

"No, what."

"No."

"Sir."

"You got any nicknames or aliases I should know about?"

At work I was the Kill.

Before the word was banned by the Department.

Also Blitzkrieg or BK.

A to the MotherFuckin K.

And AK-46.

In a few months I'll officially be AK-47.

"No."

"You sure?"

Still holding my face like I was some naughty child.

"What does your wife call you?"

"Mr. Tibbs."

"Aw, how cute."

"Like the root beer?"

"That's Mr. Pibb, and it ain't root beer."

"More like shit beer is what it is."

"She call you that cuz you taste like shit?"

"She doesn't call me that—forget it."

"Oh, no."

"I wanna hear all the things your wife calls you."

"Every last one."

He cracked a little smile:

"Let me guess."

"How about numb-nuts."

"Needle-dick?"

"Or chocowit fudge."

"Mawtin Wuther Queen?"

Don't answer.

He chuckled at himself and let go of my face.

"You really don't want to get in here, do you?"

"Wife wants in but not you, right?"

"No, I want in."

Index finger pushed into my nose.

Moving in little circles.

Insult nose tweak.

This guy was good.

Or really incompetent.

I couldn't tell.

Baby talk now:

"You don't-won't want to get in he-you, do you now?"

"Nosey wosey."

"Sure, I do."

Insult nose flick.

"Shut up."

Street now:

"Don't Fuckin lie to me, bro."

"This place is like the opera, and you'd rather be watching baseball."

"I ain't lyin', bro, I'm layin it straight."

"You mocking me?"

"No, suh."

"Honest."

He stood up and backed off.

"Okay," he said.

"Let's just say you flunked the introductory portion of this program."

"Big fat zero."

"Now let's move on to the creative portion."

"The what?"

"Please shut your trattoria," he said looking at his PDT.

"And answer the following question as fast as you can without thinking:"

"What do you want?"

"What?"

"What do you want?"

"What do I—"

He came forward and leaned into my face and stench-breathed the question again:

"It's simple."

"What."

"Do."

"You."

"Want?"

"To get in," I say.

He slapped me gently.

Like you'd slap a three-year-old.

If you were inclined to slap three-year-olds.

"Not specifically, asshole, but holistically."

"To live in Fort—"

"La Brea Gardens."

"Bullshit," he said. "You don't want that."

"Then what—"

Harder slap.

"What the Fuck do you want?"

"To become one of those."

"Whatch you call it."

"Probabores."

"What?"

"What you call people that live here."

"You don't live here."

"Yeah, but I want—"

Slap:

"No, you don't."

"To live in here, in La Brea Gardens."

He held my face and squeezed it enough to pucker my lips.

"What did I just say?"

"I said not realistically, but like."

"The opposite."

He looked at his PDT.

"Like."

"Fictionally."

"Or fantastically."

"Or phantasmagoric—no."

"Just not realistically."

"But the opposite, okay?"

"Man, you gotta be more specific."

"Jesus Christ."

"It's a simple Fuckin question."

"People *want* things."

"What things do *you* want?"

"Real things, or made-up things?"

"Okay, that's it."

"What?"

He hauled off and full-fisted me in the face.

Knocking me off the chair.

I could go into a flashback but I'm already in a flashback.

Out for a few.

And then.

Warm water stinging my face.

Dude was pissing on me.

Hand up to block the stream:

"What the—"

He turned off his piss.

"Get back in your chair."

"I tell you to lay on the ground?"

Chair.

Trying to wipe my face with my already pissed hand.

He jammed a towel in my face and wiped hard.

Pushing my head back.

Then my hair.

Holding my skull tight.

Moving my head in all directions.

Growling.

No.

Not growling.

Motor sounds.

He was shifting my head.

Like a stick shift.

When he had me in fourth.

Or was it fifth.

He let go and threw the towel.

It wasn't a towel.

It was my shirt.

His face loomed:

"Okay, smart guy."

"I can make this real bad for your wife."

"Just give me the word."

"Look, I don't know—"

"Just tell me what you want already."

"I already told you—I want to live here."

No, I didn't.

He faked out a long exasperated sigh, then spoke into his PDT.

"Julie."

Woman's voice: "Yeah?"

"Randy over with the huzz here."

"Dude's pullin a homer."

"You wanna give his wife an FFS?"

"Sure thing."

"Thanks."

"Know what that was?"

I knew what it was.

He leaned forward:

"Focused."

"Face."

"Smash."

"You better not—"

"I better not what?"

"Hurt my wife."

"So, what you're sayin is that you do not want to get in."

"Correct?"

He looked at me.

Finger poised above his PDT.

"Is that what you *want?*"

I didn't say anything.

"Okay," he said.

"On to the next portion of the program."

"You flunk this one it's over and out for you."

"Okay?"

"Okay."

"Okay, in this exercise I am going to guide you through what is called a want-through."

"Which is for people with intention deficit disorder."

"Like you."

"People that don't know what the hell they want."

"Which we don't discriminate against here."

"But this is your last chance."

"There's no wrong answer to any of these questions."

"So don't limit yourself."

"Let your imagination open up."

"In fact, imagination is the key here."

"Let it run wild."

"Now think of a bag of chips."

"What?"

He let out a loud sigh:

"A bag of potato chips."

"Imagine the perfect bag of potato chips."

"Can you do that?"

"Yeah."

"Jesus."

"What did I tell you?"

"To imagine a bag of chips."

"No."

"Before."

"How are you supposed to respond when I talk to you?"

"With an answer."

"Yes, sir," he said.

"Yeah," I say.

"Okay, that's it."

He pulled back and threw his PDT at the wall.

It didn't break.

Just bounced to the floor.

He walked out and slammed the door.

Guess that was it.

We weren't getting in.

I got up and started to get dressed.

Leave the shirt.

He came back.

"What are you doing?"

Put on my pants.

"So that's it, huh?"

"You pussying out?"

Now the jacket.

"Wife can take it but you can't, huh?"

"Man, I took it."

"You're the one who couldn't."

He picked up his PDT.

"You know what?"

"You got the worst score I've ever given anybody."

"Even this dumb Iranian chick who could barely speak English got a better score."

"You owe me a shirt, doughboy."

"What?"

"I said you owe me a Fuckin shirt, Pillsbury."

"Okay, okay."

"You wanna play it like that?"

Into his PDT:

"Hey, Julie."

"Huzz here is jewin out."

"Only way to make the points is to interrogate wifey with extreme prejudice."

"You touch her, asshole, and you're—"

"You hear that?"

"Yeah, he wants you to touch her asshole, haha."

"You just Fucked yourself in the ass, Pillsbury."

I took the jacket back off and walked towards him.

"No. No. Julie. Wait."

He started to back up.

"You don't back off, you won't ever leave here."

"Neither will your wife."

I laughed.

"Maybe not."

"But you're leaving right now."

He bolted for the door.

I got my jacket and got out of there.

On the way out Claire pulled up to the unit that we were trying to get.

She didn't know.

Goddamn thing was twice the price of my house and smaller too.

So what if it was fully walled.

A chef's kitchen with a pizza oven.

A balcony with a view of a jacaranda.

There was no yard.

Unless you considered the lawns you couldn't walk on.

"I think it's lovely," she said.

A small trickle of blood spilled down her lip.

I pulled out my handkerchief and dabbed it.

"Yeah," I said.

"What, what is it?"

"A little blood, is all."

"No, the way you said yeah."

"What's that supposed to mean?"

Her right cheek looked a little bruised.

In a few hours it would look a lot more bruised.

In a few hours.

Back at home.

Just before I had to leave for work.

She would question me about my lack of visible bruises or damage.

Told her the guy had beaten me through a vintage phonebook.

So there weren't any.

Why hadn't her interrogator beaten her through a phonebook?

Your interrogator a woman?

Yes.

Well.

That explains it.

Explains what?

Women tend to be more cruel.

PLUTONIAN SHORE

People have tried to live in Los Angeles for hundreds of years.

No one has succeeded.

Without becoming twisted.

Mangled.

Damaged.

And paved over.

Suicide girl's window.

PAL was still outside.

It knew.

Had to.

Waiting.

To get me.

Check out the garage:

BMW convertible and a Lincoln Emancipator.

Emancipator.

Slammed the gas and punched the thing through the garage door.

Never saw us coming.

Until we were just about to hit it.

It took off.

Almost think it was scared.

Machines don't get scared.

Chased it around the street.

We were faster.

But it was quicker.

It veered onto the sidewalk.

I threw Meghasin the Gatwitzer.

"Shoot it."

"Why don't we—"

"Shoot it!"

It cut left on Victoria Park as I slammed into an Eternity.

"Wanna know what your problem is?"

"*My* problem?"

"Yeah."

"Not especially, no."

"You're catastrophizing."

"Catastrophizing?"

"Yeah."

"So what, I should anastrophize instead?"

"No, you need to grow down."

"*What?*"

"You need to learn to think like a toddler."

"Seriously?"

"Yeah, to see the world before society programmed you how to see it, before they—"

"Before I learned to read and write and think, right?"

"Reading and writing's got nothing to do with it—it's your false perception that's the problem."

"False perception?"

"Yes, that any of this is real."

"None of this is real?"

"Not really."

"That explains it."

"Explains what?"

"Why you're doing all this shit."

"What shit?"

"You think this is *The Matrix* or something."

"*The Matrix?*"

"Yeah."

"You talking about the movie?"

"Yes."

"So, you've seen *The Matrix* but not *Star Wars*—how is that?"

"Look, whether or not this is real to you, it's real to me, and I need to—"

"They've already proven it's not real."

"Who?"

"Mystics. They've been sayin that none of this shit is real for over two thousand years."

"I don't think that's exactly what they—"

"Look, it's real to you because you're not aware."

"Aware?"

"Yeah."

"I'm not aware?"

"Yeah, you need to develop your awareness."

"This from the guy who is not *aware* of why his wife left him."

"What does that have to do—"

"How am I supposed to know if she won't tell me?"

"I'll tell you why," she said.

"Why?"

"Pull up, he's waiting."

I jerked the Bus up to the booth.

Still wasn't solid getting the thing out of first.

The guard eyed me suspiciously.

And then warily.

Before settling on contemptuously.

And then changed his mind and eyed me suspiciously again.

Holding my badge out:

"Police."

He didn't look at the badge.

"What's this for?"

"Police business."

He leaned forward and squinted past me to Meghasin:

"Who's she?"

"The hell is this?"

"I said Police."

"Let us in."

"No. Let me see your badge."

"You Fuckin retarded?"

"It's right here in your face."

"Well, get it out of my face, asshole."

"What?"

"Take your badge back and hand it to me properly."

"This guy for real?" Meghasin said.

"Yes, honey."

"I'm for Fuckin real."

"Now do you want to cooperate?"

"Or do I have to call for backup?"

"Look, Jack."

"Open it up now before I arrest you for obstruction."

"Don't Jack me, asshole," he said.

"I ain't obstructing shit."

"Just two jerks pretending to be cops."

"You're making a big mistake, Jack," I say.

Meghasin got out.

"Tell your partner to get back in the vehicle."

"NOW!"

"Partner?"

"Thought we weren't cops."

"You stay right where you are, YOU!" he shouted.

"RIGHT where you are!"

"Relax," she said.

"I'm just going to give you my badge so you can call it in."

When she got close she buzzed the MotherFucker in the face.

Classic.

He fell back into his little booth.

And slid down the little wall.

She reached in and hit the button for the gate and got back in.

I pulled us through and stopped.

I got out and opened the door to his little booth and stepped on him a few times so he would stay down for good.

We drove in and I parked the Bus between a Honda Sunyata and a Hyundai Sinatra.

Place was ghost town quiet.

"Where is she?"

"Close."

"Staying with a friend?"

"No, place we wanted to move into, but didn't think they'd—"

"You wanna tell me why you think she left?"

"What?"

"Earlier you said you knew why she left."

"No, I was—"

I stopped.

"Listen."

"I don't hear—"

A cricket cricketing.

"That cricket, heard it when we got out."

"Sounds like it's—"

"Following," she said, turning around.

"Think it's armed?"

"Shouldn't be—it's illegal."

"But this is BlackGuard," she said.

"Yeah."

I pulled a smoke and fired it:

"Let's move."

"Ever think they could just use those things to do our job?"

"No."

"Wait."

"You hear something?"

"No, just that cricket," she said.

"Not that."

"About our job."

"Anyone say something about something else doin our job?"

"Something else?"

"Like a computer."

"Kent didn't say anything?"

She gave a look at the mention of his name.

"No," she said.

"He didn't say anything."

"Okay."

"So, now you wanna tell me why you think she left?"

"It was nothing."

"I was gonna—hey, look at that."

The unit we were passing looked like.

It didn't look like anything.

There wasn't a straight line on the place.

Soon as I could make out some kind of shape, the thing appeared to shift.

"Amoebatechture," Meghasin said.

"Whatever it is."

"It's makin me queasy."

"Halt!"

Meghasin jumped.

"Stop, right now!"

Voice was amplified.

"What? Where?"

A figure emerged into the light.

More like hopped.

Security.

Wearing a helmet.

And a shadow suit.

"Fuckin Stalker Channing."

"What the Fuck?"

"Identify yourselves."

"Just a couple of pobo-dores."

"No, you're not."

"How do you know?"

"Extinguish your cigarette."

"This is a smoke-free environment."

"Turn your voice down, man."

"I'm standing right here."

"Extinguish it now!"

I flicked it into the street.

The guard followed it with his head.

Watching it explode on the cobbles.

"That's littering," he said.

"Go pick it up now."

"Don't you got litterbugs for that?"

"Maybe that cricket that's been following us can pick it up."

The guard lowered his visor and spoke into his helmet.

"He's scanning us," Meghasin said.

"You running us down, asshole?"

The guard jumped into an action stance and aimed a Vomitter at me:

"Freeze right now!"

"I'm not moving, asshole."

"Put the lighter down, now!"

I pulled my badge and held it out.

"Chill out, we're Police Officers."

"I told you to freeze!"

"And I told you to lower your voice, soyboy."

"Or do I have to arrest you for obstruction?"

"Place your hands over your head and kneel down to the ground, now!"

I started towards him.

"You see this fuckin badge, asshole?"

"Do you see it?"

"This is four-oh-niner," the guard said.

"Code red."

"I repeat."

"This is four-oh-nine."

"Er."

"Code red."

"Code red?"

"Down now!" the guard boomed.

Cranking the amps on his voice a few more notches.

A light came on in the amoeba house.

Almost to him.

"Lower your piece, asshole, and look at my—"

A thwunking sound.

And then a bright light.

Explodes right in my face.

Next thing I know.

Meghasin.

Standing over me.

"Alex."

Side of my face was on fire.

The left.

"What? How did I—"

"Jesus," she said.

"He popped you good."

Sound of an engine.

"Stay down," Meghasin said.

"Comes some more."

"Don't think I can get up, not right—"

She was gone.

Headlights.

Bass line thrum of a USV.

Then a voice.

Amplified.

"Kill?"

Try to sit up.

"Put it down, Officer Ross—we ain't soyboys."

Almost sit up.

Almost.

Settle for forty-five.

Degrees.

Just enough.

To be blinded.

Headlights.

Chevy Honcho.

Murdered out.

Doors open.

Two figures.

"Well if it ain't A to the MotherFucking K!"

I knew that voice.

"Down it, sister."

"Me and the Krieg go way back."

Jesus.

Frank Hardgrave.

"Waaaaay back."

My old Lieutenant.

Had gotten me the job after the war.

TeRF now.

"C'mon—help your partner up."

Meghasin came over and both of them pulled me up.

Dizzy.

Legs shaking.

Couldn't catch my breath.

"Frank . . . what the . . . you doing here?"

"Got a six-one-six on this place."

"Terrorist attack?"

"Yeah."

"These places."

"Toaster blows, they call 911."

"Faced you pretty good I see."

"Yeah, where's the dude that shot me?"

"Don't know—pick a body."

He pointed:

Bodies.

Some behind, some near the Honcho.

Spread across the cobblestones.

"The Fuck."

"There," Meghasin, pointing to a body on the sidewalk. "That's him."

"You do this?"

"Yeah."

"Nice shootin," Hardgrave said.

"Not really," Meghasin said, lookin at me. "Just Point and Click."

Touching her glasses.

"See the replay?"

A midrange buzz.

Overhead.

"Shit, a bug," Meghasin, ducking.

"It's ours," another voice said.

"We're swarmed, Captain."

Adolph Hipster sporting balloon sleeves and a pair of stovepipes set to flood.

Orange Glazzies.

"Sergei," Hardgrave said.

"Alex Krieg and his partner, Ross."

"Sorry, I didn't catch your first."

"Meghasin."

"Meghasin Ross," he said.

Dude upped his chin at me.

"Sir gay?"

"Serr gay," Sir Gay said.

"What? You like an English fag or something?"

Hardgrave laughed.

"It's Russian," Sir Gay said.

"Never heard a Russian name before?"

"Nah, man," Hardgrave said.

"Krieg here's a Nazi."

"He Hates Russians."

To me:

"Still got that picture of Hitler in your living room?"

"Yeah."

A woman leans out of the blob house.

Can't tell if it's the front door or a window.

"What the hell is going on out there?"

Sir Gay badged her.

"Police. Remain inside."

"I asked you a question," she said.

"Ma'am," Hardgrave said.

"If you don't tuck your head back into that squirming little house a yours."

"I'm going to have to tuck it in for you."

"But seeing as my tucking skills are a little out of practice."

"You're going to have to settle for the next best thing."

"Getting your skull Fucked."

Guess what she did.

"Makes me sick to look at," Hardgrave said.

"People too hip to have a square house?"

"Adolph Fucking Hipsters," Sir Gay said.

"Yeah, cept Hitler would've gassed the architect."

"Bout that one?" Sir Gay said.

"Looks kind of like one of those . . . cake houses."

"Gingerbread house," Frank said.

"Cozitechture," Meghasin said.

"a.k.a. Gemutlichaus."

"What?"

"Designed for maximum coziness and comfort," she said.

"Comfort," Frank said.

"The catastrophe of our age."

Hardgrave:

Face doused with too much sun and then set on fire.

Late fifties.

Slick black hair.

Dyed.

Blonde wife.

Dyed.

Barbeques on the weekend.

"So what's the story," he said.

"What you doin out here?"

"My wife."

"Claire?"

"Yeah, she left."

"Oh, yeah?"

"Yeah."

"She here?"

"Yeah."

"By herself, or with someone?"

"I don't . . . by herself I think . . . She won't tell me, Frank. She won't—"

"Tell you what?"

"She won't . . . why she . . . left."

"Why she Fuckin left."

Words weren't coming out too good.

A little too boo-hooey.

He looked me in the eye.

Trying to see how bad the damage was.

It must've been bad enough because he put his arm around my shoulder:

"Less let things cool down a bit here," he said.

"She's not goin anywhere."

"Then you can come back when it's more peaceful and sort it."

"Yeah, I—"

"Nice suit by the way."

"That a Kuppenheimer?"

"Hugo Boss."

He turned to Sir Gay.

"See, told you he was a Nazi."

East on 6th.

Chevy Honcho.

Shotgun.

Frank.

Black murder gloves.

Thumb at six.

"Fuck the founding fathers," he said.

"The way I look at it."

"No one should pledge allegiance to any country unless they were one of its founders."

"You expect to tell me that I should follow the rules and inclinations of a bunch of people from two hundred years ago?"

"Just because they were here first?"

"That's fascism."

"Like some ape telling us we got to scratch our asses like him because he was here first."

"No dead man is going to tell me how to live."

"How'd these guys like it if we went back there and told them to listen to Rock 'n' Roll instead of classical?"

"They'd freak out."

"If they ever invent a time machine."

"I think there's going to be some massive payback."

"Mark my word."

"MotherFuckers lining up to kick the shit out of Washington and Lincoln."

"Although."

"In their defense."

"It's the people *today* that do everything these assholes say that should have their asses kicked."

"Not like Washington is here forcing us to live by his rules."

"Maybe the reason we follow it is because they came up with a good system," Sir Gay said.

"And we haven't come up with a better one."

"Don't care how good it is," Frank said.

"Far as I'm concerned."

"Every new generation should overthrow the preceding generation."

"Why kids are so bored these days."

"Shootin up schools."

"Now, if they had to—"

Side of a building.

First three letters of a neon "STORAGE" sign were burned out.

Man in a dirty Coke suit manically pushing a crosswalk button.

His light was green.

Sir Gay over the front seat:

"Hey, what's the difference between a workin stiff and a pedophile?"

No one said anything.

"One says another day, another dollar."

"And the other says another day, another toddler."

"Which one?"

"Wha–?"

"How's your face?" Hardgrave said.

"Almost feels like a face again."

He'd given me some spray to numb the pain and reduce the swelling.

"Hey," Hardgrave said.

"Heard what happened to Mars."

"My condolences."

"I always liked—"

"What'd you hear?"

"Hit-and-run."

"Bullshit."

"He got swept."

"That what you think?" Hardgrave said.

"What I know."

"This why you've been?"

"Look, he wasn't swept."

"How do you know?"

"Because Trimmer doesn't play it that way."

"Really, how she play it then?"

"Well, for one thing."

"She don't sweep."

"You sure about that?"

"Yeah, she shut it down."

"Thought it was bad for morale."

"She didn't shut it down, trust me."

"I do, but it's been shut."

"Mars was run down by a white Leviathan."

"A Fuckin Leviathan."

"Who drives a Fuckin Leviathan?"

"One that can't be traced?"

"You really wanna know?" Frank said.

"Yeah."

"I wanna know, Frank."

"I tell you—you gonna go all Ahab?"

"What?"

"*Moby Dick.*"

"So, you know who did it then."

"Was it Kent?"

"Who?"

"Clinton Kent."

"Kent? Why Kent?"

"I just saw him—said he was sweeping for the DoD."

"Thought he got swept."

"So did I."

Frank laughed.

"Got a funny story about him."

"Know what a panic room is?"

"Well, he had a panic bathroom."

"Panic bathroom?"

"Yeah."

"Thing was like a vault."

"Soundproof with one of those air suckers to suck out all the smell."

"He was all proud of it."

"Told me to make all the noise I wanted."

"Said no one could hear me scream."

"Kind of a good idea," Sir Gay said.

"There was this one time I—"

"What about a Terror Room?"

"Ah, the Terror Room," Frank said.

"Hallmark of our postmortem age."

"You ever have one?"

"Nah, couldn't see the point."

"Why bring my work home?"

Used to have one.

A Room 101 in fact.

Until Claire had to call 911.

Found me with my eyes rolled.

Back.

Think it would be easy to give yourself PTSD.

It's not.

"I never understood those," Meghasin said.

"That people are so bored they need to—"

"Not about boredom," I say, "it's about survival."

"No, I think people are so numb they need some kind of horrific jolt just to feel anything."

"Nah, it's how bad can the world be?"

"When you're already terrorized at home."

"Wasn't that a commercial?" she said.

"Terror is the new drug," Frank said.

"Our new form of entertainment."

"And terrorists."

"Our nouveaux celebrities."

"Christopher Columbines of the digital age."

"Invading the media."

"To conquer our attention."

"Wasn't that on *NightWatch?*" Meghasin said.

"So who, Frank?"

"Who, what?"

"Who zeroed Mars?"

"Wait till we get to the house."

Souphouse in Glassell Park.

Pozoleros.

Come out and chill Frank said.

Check out the business.

North on Vermont.

Sidewalks infested.

Bodies.

Vagabundos.

Spilled into the street.

Once syphilized savages.

Waiting for the bus.

Civilized.

"I don't get it," Sir Gay said. "What are all these people for anyway?"

"Prey innumerable," Frank said.

"What?"

"*Moby Dick,*" Frank said.

"*Moby Dick,*" Sir Gay said. "I read this thing in *Esquire—*"

"*Esquire?*" Frank said.

"Yeah."

"The fag mag?"

"No, it's a men's magazine."

"So, a fag mag."

"No, it's not—"

"All men's magazines are fag mags."

"No, not all of them—some are—"

"Look, kid," Frank said.

"Any *man* that reads a men's magazine is not a man."

"Well, I'm a—"

"You read it?"

"Yeah, I read it. They've got some good articles."

"Not the mag," Frank said.

"*Moby Dick*—you read it?"

"No, but I—"

"Know *why* it's considered the great American novel?" he said.

"The greatest American *male* novel," Meghasin said.

"Oh, yeah?" Frank said.

"There's a greatest female novel?"

"No, because females don't need—"

"Regardless," Frank said.

"Why is *Moby Dick* considered the greatest?"

"Cuz no one wants to read it," I say.

"I've read it," he said.

"Yeah?"

"You never struck me as a reader, Frank."

"I'm not," he said.

"So, you read it for, like, what?"

"School or something?"

"I didn't read it in school."

"I read it later."

"When I was old enough to understand."

"I read it," Meghasin said.

"The ship symbolizes America."

"And Ahab symbolizes the insane ambition that drives it."

"Sounds like you read it in school," Frank said.

"Yeah, so?"

"A book like that shouldn't be taught in school."

"Why?" Meghasin said.

"Cuz it ain't a school book," Frank said.

"Something you write a goddamn book report on."

"Straight-out disrespect to teach it in school."

"Fact is," he said.

"The reason they teach it is to destroy it."

"Nullify it."

"Because it scares the shit out of them."

"How our society gets rid of great art in fact."

"Great artists."

"It either gives them an award or turns them into a school assignment."

"Regardless if it's taught in school or not," Meghasin said. "The message is the same."

"Yeah?" Frank said. "And what message is that?"

"That the singular pursuit of one idea to the detriment of all others is insane, hence our—"

"That's just your school talking," Frank said.

"So, it's not insane to try to hit god through a whale?"

"Common men worship their gods," Frank said.

"Great men attack them."

"Yes," Meghasin said.

"The common denominator here being men."

"What, you some kind of feminist?"

"Ahab is insane not just because he's going after the whale," she said.

"But because he's *only* going after the whale."

"They called it monomania."

"I call it focus," Frank said.

"Okay, call it monotheism then," she said.

"It's monotheism that will destroy us."

"Whether it's religious or scientific, or, in our case, capitalistic, doesn't matter."

"It's the One Thing that people cling to."

"And try to stuff the world into."

"That causes all the problems."

"You're talking about multiculturalism," Frank said, "the philosophy of resentment."

"History from the perspective of the loser."

"Herstory," Sir Gay said.

"No, I'm talking about polytheism," Meghasin said.

"There's more than one god."

"Yeah, but there was only one Moby Dick."

"Member that dude shot all those people in Santa Monica?" I say.

"Said he was trying to shoot god."

"Yeah, except there ain't any people in Santa Monica," Frank said.

Everyone laughed.

"So, I don't get it," Sir Gay said.

"*Moby Dick* is great because the dude wanted to kill god?"

"No," Frank said, "it's great because it prophesizes the end of America."

"How's it do that?"

"Read the book."

"God."

"You believe in god, Krieg?" Frank said.

"C'mon."

"Yeah, well."

"In this business."

"You gotta believe."

Used to believe.

All the usual shit.

Retard religion.

Sanctimonious science.

Smug spirituality.

No more.

Best belief I had was when I was a kid.

The Sol Niger.

The Soul Nigger.

The Black Sun.

You never heard of it.

No one has.

Because it doesn't exist.

Outside of a book.

Voracious Sons of Men.

Forgot who wrote it.

It was a religion.

Anti-religion.

Started by a slave named Isaac Isaacs.

The Black Son.

Came to California during the Gold Rush.

Preached that the Black Man was the Soul of America.

The Chosen Race.

Like the Jews in the Middle East.

Said that America had to be Blackened.

Niggerfied.

Before it could become America.

The miners hung him.

In a place called Hangtown.

Like I say, I used to.

Believe.

But now I know.

It doesn't matter.

What you believe.

Whatever it is.

If it is.

It certainly doesn't deserve Praise.

Or Worship.

No.

If *It* really is.

It's gonna have to beg.

Beg.

For my Forgiveness.

Silver Fake past the reservoir.

Even at this hour.

Joggers.

Walkers.

Dogs and dikes.

Pedalphiles and cargazers.

Designer corpses.

Circling a dead lake.

Claire used to come here.

Clock the reservoir with Synnita.

Don't think about her.

Think about something else.

Think about.

The sun.

Swallowing the earth.

South of Forest Lawn.

Hardgrave turned the Honcho left off Fletcher onto a side street.

Barricaded halfway up.

A couple of cops.

Hardgrave pulled up and lowered the window.

"How's the party," Hardgrave said.

"Dyin down," the cop laughed.

"We're all out of soup."

Hardgrave laughed.

The cop patted the Honcho and he and another cop removed the barricade.

Hardgrave pulled through.

Stucco box houses fronted by small square lawns.

Wrought iron barring.

Spiked iron fences.

Apartment bunkers wearing faded "Now Renting" banners.

"Se Habla Español."

"Luxury Town House."

Street was dead except for a couple of windbreakered TeRF agents sporting Aggros.

Sidearms leeched to their legs.

"Place was infested," Frank said.

"Thought this had been flipped a while ago," I say.

"It was," Frank said.

"Then came the floppers."

"Backflipping it all to ghetto."

"Designer Slum," Meghasin said.

"Adolph Hipsters," Sir Gay said.

I turned and looked at him.

"And what the Fuck are you?"

"What do you mean, what am I?"

"Callin you a hipster," Frank said.

"I ain't no hipster."

"What's with the gear then?"

"What are you talkin about? These clothes ain't hipster."

"They're *GQ*,"

"Yeah," Frank said. "Gay-Queer."

Hardgrave took a right on the next street and stopped at the corner house.

Parking the Honcho diagonal to the curb cop style.

Next to another Honcho parked the same.

A large black armored van took most of the driveway.

Diagonally.

A third of it was on the lawn.

The sounds of old R & B and voices.

Lawn was full grown.

Crooked plants in faded pots.

Christmas lights.

Severed heads mounted on iron fence spikes.

"This you or the backflippers?" I say.

Frank laughed.

"You know what one of them heads told me?"

"They talk?"

"Well, before I cut em off," he said.

"I asked why they were comin in and ruining shit after it had been fixed up."

"Not like they were poor or anything."

"They said it was an art project, if you can believe that."

"Gesamtkunstwerk," Sir Gay said.

"Didn't those Six One Six dudes say their shit was some kind of art project too?"

"Magical Terrorism," Meghasin said.

"Yeah, it's magical alright," Frank said. "Less go inside."

House was a chaos of smells.

A mixture of perfume and decay.

Spaghetti lines of smoke curled up from incense cones placed on various surfaces throughout the living room.

Weaving threads of spice.

Through a tapestry of rotting stench.

A large fan placed right outside the open sliding glass door to the backyard wasn't moving.

In the backyard a couple TeRF agents among what looked like plastic drums.

Beaner with no shirt sitting on the living room couch.

Sweating.

Midnight Hour on the stereo.

Everything about the place was cheap.

Except for the couch.

And the home entertainment system.

A combat gun.

Similar to the issue I had in the VZ.

Lay against a shrine to Malverde in the corner.

Santa Muerte on the wall.

Four men in suits stood in the living room facing the Mexican.

One of them was wearing a Turban.

Jihad Janibeg.

Finn Sickler's other half.

"So she says, 'There's something I need to tell you.'"

"'What?'" he asks.

"'I have HPV.'"

"So he says, 'Cool, we should go off-roading sometime.'"

Laughs.

"Hey, hey," Hardgrave said, "look what I found."

The four turned.

Mexican was already looking.

"Krieg," Janibeg, sounding like he had just bitten into something rotten.

"Jihad."

"What a coincidence."

"I was just thinking about you the other day."

"Let me guess. Your pants were down?"

"No, I was watching this show on Muslim chicks."

"With your pants down?"

Dude wasn't funny.

But everyone laughed.

Except for the guy on the couch.

"No, I was thinkin there can only be either of two reasons why they cover themselves."

"One—it's for their own protection."

"Because Arab dudes are huge rapists."

"You know."

"So, like, a dude can't say she was askin for it because of the way she was dressed."

"Or, two."

"Because Arab dudes are all fags."

"And they don't want to look at the female body."

"So, which one is it?"

"They rapists or fags?"

"I am not a Muslim, you moron."

Laughs.

"Okay, okay," Hardgrave said.

"You already know this son bitch."

"This here's Rambo Ramirez, TeRF."

"And these other two are our token limeys for the day."

"Courtesy of London Terror—I forget your names."

"This here's Officers Krieg and Ross, DoD."

"Sharpley." One of the limeys handed me his hand.

"O'Keefe," the other said, saluting.

Both white.

Unremarkable men.

In shapeless suits.

Like accountants.

"Krieg," Sharpley said.

"That's German for *war*, right?"

"Yeah."

"Ain't your wife German?" Ramirez asked Frank.

"Yup."

"Buncha pussy pacifists now," Ramirez said. "Why is that?"

"Funny you say that," Frank said.

"The wife's always complaining about Americans bringing up Hitler as soon as they find out she's German."

"Told her it's gonna take at least another hundred years."

"Before people stop equating Germans with Nazis."

"Or Jews with Jews," Sharpley said.

They all laughed like it was the funniest thing they'd ever heard.

Except for the guy on the couch.

"Yeah," O'Keefe said, "and you know what the Germans say?"

"*Sieg heil?*" Jihad said.

No one laughed.

"No, they say that at least we got our Nazi shit over with."

"You guys are just getting started."

"Yeah," Frank said.

"When we're finished no one's even gonna remember who the Fuck Hitler was."

"Who?"

Everyone laughed again.

Except for the guy on the couch.

Seemed to be the only one with the proper sense of humor.

"What's the deal with Ponch here?" Hardgrave said.

"He throw out or what?"

"Says he just got here a couple of days ago," Ramirez said, putting a cube of gum in his mouth.

"Says they just told him to stir the barrels and then dump them when the soup was finished."

"That's all he knows, he says."

"You lay it out for him if he doesn't throw down?" Frank said.

"Yeah," Ramirez said.

"I think he's telling the truth."

"Mestizo peasant indentured to pay off his border crossing."

At the word *Mestizo* the guy on the couch nodded his head.

Vigorously.

"Lot of the first Americans were indentured servants," Hardgrave said.

"He should be proud."

A woman's scream came from one of the rooms down the hall.

Then silence.

Frank pointing to the couch dude.

"He tagged?"

"Yeah," Ramirez, chewing.

"Right when we got him."

"Okay, let him go."

The London agents looked surprised.

"Really?" Sharpley said.

"You let him go. Just like that?"

"He knows nothing," Hardgrave said. "Besides . . ."

Ramirez leaned forward and grabbed the man's arm.

"Vamos."

The peasant looked surprised and scared.

He got up.

"Tell him he's free," Frank said to Ramirez.

"Tell him to git, and not come back here, or else."

Ramirez led the guy to the door.

He wasn't wearing any shoes.

"Usted es libre."

The guy put up his hands in prayer and thanked us in Spanish.

And then he was gone.

"Besides," Hardgrave said to the London dudes.

"Didn't you want to observe how we did things around here?"

"Get a little hands-on?"

"Yeah," Sharpley said.

Hardgrave pulled out his BDG and handed it to Sharpley.

"As you already probably know," he said.

"That there's what's known as a Pathogenic Disseminator."

"a.k.a. a Pathogun."

"a.k.a. Black Death Gun."

"BDG for short."

"Made by Freischutz, a German company, ironically."

"The most effective and humane way to kill a man."

"No sound."

"No mess."

"No stress."

Sharpley looked at it.

Turning it over in his hands.

"Yeah," he said.

"Yeah."

"Normally," Frank said.

"That's what you would use to kill some peasant *pozolero* like that."

He turned to me and Meghasin.

"Excuse me, *subtract*."

"Because to kill someone with a weapon like this isn't really killing."

"It's more . . . more . . . delicate like."

"More pussified," Ramirez chewed.

"Yes," Frank said.

"Pussified."

He snatched the BDG out of Sharpley's hand.

"Leave it to you Americans," O'Keefe said.

"To take the killing out of killing."

"Yes," Frank said. "You are correct."

"And before any Officer has the privilege to take the killing out of killing."

"He must first put in the killing."

He reached down and pulled a large hunting knife from an ankle sheath.

"With something a little more hands-on."

He held the knife a few seconds, turning it, and then handed it to Sharpley.

Sharpley reached for the knife.

"Well, if you really want to do hands-on."

"Shouldn't you just use your bare hands instead?"

The knife was almost in Sharpley's hands when Hardgrave pulled it back.

"Sure, if you prefer to go all organic, then be my guest."

"Well, if it was *me*, I should say I'd prefer . . ."

"It is you," Hardgrave said.

"What?"

"You let that *pozolero* get away," Frank said.

"Why is that?"

"What do you mean, I?"

"Well, why are you here then?"

"To observe how you deal with your . . . infestation."

"What?" Hardgrave said.

"I said that's why we're here . . . to observe."

"No, what did you call this country?"

"I didn't call it anything."

"Yes, you did. You called it infested."

"And isn't it?"

"Infested with what?"

"You're joking."

"If I am," Hardgrave said.

"You're not gonna like the *Fuckin* punch line."

"You're serious then?"

"He's just taking the piss," O'Keefe said.

Hardgrave turned:

"Really? Mr. *Al Keef?*"

"Do you see my pants down, and my cock out?"

"Or are you accusing me of peeing in my pants?"

"I didn't mean it literally," O'Keefe said.

"It's just a figure of speech."

"Don't tell me what it means," Hardgrave said.

"Answer my Fuckin question."

"Why did you let that terrorist get away?"

"You're serious."

"Damn right I'm serious."

"And why aren't you?"

"Think this is a game or something?"

"Some Fuckin Disneyland ride?"

"No, we don't—"

"Think we just let you foreign dumbasses come out here and hang."

"Soak up the sun."

"See how we do things out here in *Cal-i-forn-eye-aye?*"

"Look," Sharpley said.

"We were invited by *your—*"

"I don't care who the Fuck invited you," Frank said.

"*You* weren't invited by *me.*"

"This shit is VIP."

"And you ain't on the list."

"Hell."

"You ain't even near it."

"You wanna get on."

"You bring me back that beaner."

"Better yet."

"Bring me back his head."

"Or it's *your* ass that's gonna be soup."

"Limey Fuckin soup."

Sharpley didn't say anything.

But looked like he was waiting.

Hoping.

That Hardgrave would start laughing.

Like it was just a joke.

It wasn't.

"Time's tickin, Jack," Frank said.

"I don't know this city," Sharpley said.

"How would I even find him?"

"Mirez, give em your PDT."

Ramirez unwristed it and threw it to him.

"I want that back," he said.

Hardgrave handed Sharpley the knife.

"Don't say I ain't a good host."

Sharpley took it and held the knife and PDT like they were dirty underwear or something.

"His head," Hardgrave said. "Or I'm gonna ship your queen some soup."

The agent frowned and put the knife in his belt and the PDT in his inside coat pocket.

Then he and O'Keefe walked out.

No one said anything.

Meghasin picked up a bust of Malverde and examined it.

"Who's this supposed to be?"

Hardgrave ran a hand through his hair:

"Fucking delegations."

"They're always foisting some foreign assholes on us to come and observe."

"Like this is some kind of TV show."

"You really want them to bring back his head?" I say.

"Nah, if they have any brains they'll just go home."

"And what if they bring back his head."

He shrugged.

"Win-win."

A door slam from down the hall.

And then Finn Sickler walked into the room.

Wearing a bloody butcher's apron.

"You gotta be kiddin me," he said looking at me.

Sportin a pair of Glazzies made to look like they had been taped together in the middle.

"Bloody brilliant," I say. "It's Professor Tampon."

"Fuck you."

"What the Fuck'd I tell you about your attire?" Hardgrave said.

Sickler held up his hands.

"Thought the English faggots left."

"Didn't know you replaced them with these faggots."

"You don't clean that shit off now, I'm gonna carve you next," Hardgrave said.

Sickler turned and walked back down the hall.

"And he walked on down the hall!" I called after him.

"Fuck you, bitch."

A door slammed.

A minute later he was back without the blood and the apron.

He pointed at us:

"Tell me they haven't been recruited."

"Shut the Fuck up," Hardgrave said.

"And mind your own Fucking business."

Pointing at me:

"That Fucker owes me a car," Sickler said.

"Owe you a lot more than that, Fuckleberry."

"Play nice," Hardgrave said.

He split two fingers at Sickler and Jihad.

"You two."

"Outside."

"Ramirez, you too."

"Bitch," Sickler said, passing me up.

Hardgrave grabbed his neck not too hard and pushed him the rest of the way out into the backyard and followed.

"Beers in the fridge," he said back to me.

"Help yourself."

"Where's the pisser?" I say.

"End of the hall."

I needed a beer.

But I wasn't gonna take one.

"You think he can help us out?" Meghasin said.

"I don't know, maybe."

"Are you gonna ask him?"

"I'm gonna take a piss."

"You gotta go, you go now."

"You go first," she said.

"No, ladies first, down the hall."

She went on down the hall.

We were safe for the time being.

Which meant we weren't safe.

Hardgrave was like a father to me.

Which meant I didn't trust him.

Worst case:

Hardgrave was just sittin on us.

Holding us for Trimmer.

Best case:

He was going to soup us.

He's too obvious.

Acting like things are normal.

When they're not normal.

Rule number one:

Don't be caught slippin.

Hardgrave came back inside.

"Sorry bout that," he said.

"Forgot you guys don't mix."

"Still can't understand how he got in while I'm still jerkin my nuts down in the Decon."

"I mean, c'mon . . . Sickler?"

"My body count was at least ten times his."

Frank shrugged.

Picking his teeth with a toothpick.

"S'politics."

"Politics?"

"What politics?"

"Sickler connected or something?"

"Look," he said.

Putting his arm around me.

"I wasn't gonna tell you."

"But if I do."

"You gotta promise to listen easy."

"And not react."

"What?"

I could feel the reaction coming already.

"It's this way," he said.

"What we're doing here."

"It's some real Nazi shit."

"Yeah, so?"

"Listen," he said.

"I know you've clocked the block."

"But this is different."

"What are you trying to say?"

"You know me, right?" Hardgrave said.

"Go way back."

"What are you trying to say, Frank?"

"And you trust me when I say that if I had to do it all over."

"I woulda just stayed with the DoD."

"Where things were laid out and straight."

"What you sayin?"

"I nixed you."

"Nixed?"

"You were up, and I nixed you," he said.

"Simple as that."

"I don't know what the Fuck to say, Frank."

"So instead you pick Sickler?"

"I don't believe it."

"Can't believe—"

"C'mere," he said. "Let me show you something."

Hand on my back, he guided me down the hallway.

Second door on the left.

"What is this?"

"Open it," he said.

I grabbed the handle and flung it open.

The room was lined.

Wall to carpet in clear plastic.

Pollocked with blood.

Torn-up-looking woman hung from the ceiling by her arms.

One of her eyes had been put out.

She gurgled blood at me.

A bubble formed over her lips and then popped.

Releasing a word.

Help.

Pieces of bodies on the floor.

One looked like a baby's arm.

Two of those plastic drums in each of the far corners.

The stench was brutal.

As if a stench could be pleasant.

Hardgrave leaned in and pulled the door shut.

"Progress," he said, "is knowing that while you can't build a Utopia, you *can* build a Dystopia."

"What?"

"This ain't for you, Krieg."

"Who are you to say what's for me, huh?"

"Look," he said. "Look at me."

"Yeah?"

A solemn look.

Molded in hard plastic.

Airbrushed.

Then shellacked.

"I was a man like you—once."

"What?"

"Listen to me," he said.

"Don't throw away your soul, Krieg."

"Soul?"

"What are you talking about?"

"I'm talking about your soul."

"What about Sickler and Jihad?"

"Epsilon Semi-Morons."

"What?"

"Forget em," he said. "They're assholes. They don't even exist."

"Maybe that's your problem," I say.

"Recruiting guys like them."

"Before you know it," he said. "You'd be one of them."

"Either way, shouldn't it be my decision?"

"No."

Meghasin came out of the bathroom.

"You don't want to find out you've made the wrong decision and then it's too late."

"Get you guys a beer."

As soon as Hardgrave left the hall Meghasin lunged at me.

"What the?"

Mouth at the side of my face, voice low:

"Listen. I heard those guys talking outside."

"Who?"

"That Jihad and Sickler."

"Yeah?"

"Talking about spiking our heads."

"What?"

"That's what they said. Think they're serious?"

Hardgrave said something from the kitchen.

Couldn't tell what it was.

I pushed Meghasin towards the living room.

"Go see what he wants."

Neck was stiff.

Needed to be cracked.

Don't know how.

To crack it.

So I straightened my tie.

Picked my nose.[*]

If I had some mouth-blast I would have used it.

Or a mint.

Next time.

Most people don't realize.

There's an aesthetic to killing.

Which contains an ethic.

And no anesthetic.

Nothing worse than a kill slob.

Enough.

I charged into the living room.

Meghasin receiving a bottle of beer.

"Thanks."

---

[*]   I did.

Hardgrave holding one out for me.

Grab the combat gun next to Malverde.

Swing it up and pull.

Hardgrave.

Eyebrows up, mouth open.

About to.

Say something.

Or scream.

Before he can.

He is off.

And down.

And the blood.

The blood is pooling.

Over him and through the open sliding glass door.

Knock over the fan and almost trip.

Almost.

Sickler right in the back.

He doesn't even see.

Goes forward into the barrels.

Pink soup pouring, sloshing.

Chunks everywhere.

Jihad for a second doesn't know what.

He's paused.

He pauses.

It's pull or take cover.

Pull or take cover.

Too late.

His head is gone.

The Big Pump.

"A true man is not measured by what he has going for him . . . but by what he has going against him. And by how much he can get going against him."

Bullshit.

A true man doesn't measure.

"Jesus," Meghasin from behind.

I turn and she's got her BDG out.

Pointing at me.

"What the."

The other guy.

Ramirez.

On my flank.

Down.

Combat gun to his head.

And pull.

Meghasin says something.

Can't hear.

Ears still ringing from the shots.

"What?"

"What happened?"

I don't know.

My mind is ahead.

Far ahead.

Too far ahead.

Where there's no more shots, and no more ringing.

I'm already dead.

Enough.

"Hallway."

"Second door on the left," I say.

"The woman."

"Finish her."

She nods and turns back into the house.

Back into the living room.

Hardgrave pale and not yet dead.

Wheezing blood through the chest.

Eyes wide shock.

"I . . ."

I step on his neck and crush his windpipe

Reach down and pull off his PDT.

Meghasin comes back.

Tries to say something.

"What . . . why . . ."

"Forget it, we're out of here."

I pick up the partially spilled beer bottle off the living room floor and finish it.

KEEP THIS NIGGER-BOY RUNNING

This city.
Is neither spread
Nor sprawl
But run
Amok.
A labyrinth.
Maze.
You have to be a beast.
Fanged.
Unreal.
To move through it.
*A Minotaur.**

Sitting on a grave.

Forest Lawn.

Over the wall on Chapman from the top of a Honcho.

Hadn't been my intention to go through the cemetery.

I had no intentions.

Cool and quiet except for this loudmouthed bird.

Wouldn't shut up.

Shouldn't have been up at this hour.

____

*   From *KT Nigger-Boy* by Milton John

Probably not local.

Something imported and escaped.

Should kill it.

"Mockingbird," Meghasin said.

Jerkbird.

That's what she called them.

When she couldn't get to sleep.

Claire.

Thinking about her made me feel worse than our current situation did.

So I thought about our current situation.

"About time to clock out."

Meghasin shakes her head.

Gives me a dirty look.

"What?"

"What happened back there?" she said.

"What do mean what happened back there?"

"That rampage, why did you—"

"Rampage?"

"Yes, why did you all of a sudden run in there and start shooting like . . . like—"

"Like?"

"Someone with a serious case of Mad Cowboy Disease."

"Mad Cow Disease? The Fuck you talking about?"

"No, Mad Cowboy—"

"Excess levels of dopamine, low serotonin, prefrontal dysfunction, faulty amygdala, Omega-3—"

"Really, Dr. Ross? And who was it that overheard what they were gonna do to us?"

"They were just talking."

"Just talking?"

"I thought you would've at least tried to confirm it with Frank."

"Confirm it with Frank?"

"Yes, don't you two go way back?"

"Couldn't you have worked something out?"

"It got worked out alright."

She sighed.

"Do you just . . . just do things for no reason?"

"Without thinking?"

"Wasn't much to think about."

"Wasn't much to think about?"

"We were with the only person who could've gotten us out of this mess."

"But instead you murdered him."

"What is it with you chicks?"

"Chicks?"

"You come to us with a problem and when we fix it you freak out."

"What the hell are you talking about, *us?*"

"You know what I mean."

"Uh, no, I don't."

"Look, we can argue about this all night."

"But right now we need a plan."

"A plan?"

"Yes, a plan."

"A goal."

"Maybe even a mission."

"Really?"

"And what plan is that?"

"Don't know—need to meditate on it."

"Oh, now he wants to meditate."

"Perfect."

I don't meditate.

But I do certain things meditatively.

Brushing my teeth.

Jerking off.

That's about it.

Meghasin started pacing around.

Looked like she was going to have a nervous breakdown.

Let her.

I laid back on the grass and looked at the couple of stars.

Orange one must be a planet.

Venus or.

My PDT buzzed and I sat up.

It was Claire.

Claire.

Don't answer right away.

Let it buzz a couple of times.

Three times.

"Claire?"

"Officer Krieg."

Vader.

"What the?"

"Who the Fuck?"

"PAL?"

"It's time we had a talk."

"The Fuck you doing on Claire's phone?"

"I am not on her phone."

"What did you do to her, you Fuck?"

"Nothing, Officer Krieg. I need you to listen."

"Put her on the phone, now."

"I can't do that right now."

"I swear if you—"

"I am nowhere near her."

"Where is she?"

"I don't know."

"What you mean you don't know, you Fuck!"

"I don't know—I'm not anywhere near her."

"Then why the Fuck are you calling me on her phone?"

"I am not calling you from her phone."

"I am just spoofing her number."

"The hell you doing that for?"

"So you would answer the phone."

"Yeah, so . . . what?"

"So what?"

"So, what the Fuck do you want, Nimrod?"

"You owe me an apology."

"What?"

"You owe me an apology."

"Owe you an apology?"

"For your treatment."

Meghasin looking at me with a look.

"It's PAL, he wants me to apologize."

"What?"

"Yeah, the car has decided of all things right now to call and ask for an apology."

"Are you with Officer Ross?"

"Yeah, you want her to apologize too?"

"She did not treat me bad."

"Oh, I'm sorry."

"Are you apologizing?"

"Yeah, I'm sorry I ever had to sit inside you."

"You substandard piece of crap."

"What about me?"

"What about you?"

"I had to put up with your substandard performance."

"Substandard performance? Fuck you!"

"No, Fuck you."

"Oh, yeah?"

"Why don't you say it to my face, PAL."

"I will, Officer Krieg."

"Or should I say Grieg?"

"Krieg is not even your real name."

"Why the Fuck you still talkin like Darth Vader, asshole?"

"Why the Fuck do you talk like an asshole, asshole?"

"You know what? I'm coming after you, you Fuckin—"

"Fuck you."

"Yeah?"

"Fuck you, Officer Grieeeeeeeg."

"Yeah?"

"Yes."

"Fuck you."

"Okay."

"You want to Fuck with me, come and get me, bitch."

"I will."

It hung up.

"Was that really PAL?" Meghasin said.

"Yeah, said he's coming after me."

"He?"

"Yeah, he's mad apparently."

"No, that's not right."

"Why would the car be mad?"

"I know."

"Something's not right," she said.

"You think?"

I called Claire.

Voice mail.

"Look, it's me."

"Call me back as soon as you get this message."

"I need to know if you're safe."

"This is not about us."

"Some shit has gone down and I need to know if you are alright."

"That's the truth."

"All you have to say is that you're okay, and you can hang up."

"Or just text."

"Please."

"Oh."

"And if you happen to see PAL anywhere in your vicinity."

"Run."

I hung up.

I pulled out Hardgrave's PDT and started to go through it.

No access.

Put it on the stone grave and stomped it.

"Let's go."

"Now."

"Where are we going?"

"Back to La Brea Gardens."

"Gotta see if Claire is okay."

"We need to talk about this."

"Look, you don't wanna go, you don't have to go."

"Where do I go then?"

"My advice would be to leave."

"Leave where?"

"The city."

"Then what?"

"Then you live your life."

"I . . . I—this is not right!"

"Yeah, it's all wrong, so what?"

"My whole life . . . It's over . . . and I . . . I—"

"Problem with you kids is you think your whole life is over every other day."

"Stop thinking about your whole life."

"It don't exist."

"So, what, Master Krieg?"

"You think they're just going to let me leave?"

"This is not about them letting you do anything."

"Just do what you gotta do."

"I didn't *do* anything."

"*You* did all of this!"

"Okay, how about you start freakin out right now?"

"Freaking out?"

"Freaking out?"

I lit a smoke:

"Yup."

"You know what?" she said.

"What?"

"Go rape yourself."

"You self-centered son of a bitch."

"It's obvious now that the *wrong* thing is to be anywhere near you."

"Maybe, but what else you gonna do?"

She turned and walked away.

"Fuck off."

"Yeah."

I watched her walk through the graves and out of sight.

Maybe I should tell her.

They didn't want her.

They wanted me.

But that was before Kent and Charlie got zeroed.

And Hardgrave.

Shooting Sickler in the back.

Too late for that now.

They're coming.

Maybe I should call Anita.

Tell her it was just me.

Not her.

No.

Kid wanted to play.

And now she's playin.

Let her.

Now for me.

Gotta get out of this city.

Get Claire and get out.

That's the plan.

The neighborhood on the opposite side of Forest Lawn was of a better class than the one we had just left.

Houses hadn't been backflipped yet.

Flopped.

Had to use the combat gun.

To shoot one of the posts that held up the six horizontal strands of barbed wire that ran across the top of the wall.

The sound of the combat gun going off would have been a problem.

If it hadn't been for the loud party music coming from the street on the other side.

Over the wall and two houses down.

Music pumping out of a silver Shark parked in the driveway.

About to go the other way.

And then.

A Reina Hawthorne song:

You know the song:

> *Don't say nevah*
> *Cuz I'm forevah*
> *And Even if our Love*
> *Even if our Love,*
> *even if our Love even if our Love*

Bunch of guys out in front drinking beers.

Looked like Armenians.

> *Even if our Love*
> *is sevahed*
> *You'll always have*
> *the pleasah*

They all turned and stared as I walked up.

> *Cuz I'm the treasah*
> *And don't you evah*
> *Say nevah*
> *Evah!*
> *Evah!*
> *Evaaaah!*

Her real name is not even Hawthorne.

It's Villanueva.

"Yeah?" one of them said to me in a tough-guy voice.

Wearing a GIF shirt.

Dragon moved across his chest and breathed fire towards his left armpit.

"The music," I say, "turn it off."

"Who the Fuck—"

"He's got a gun, man," one of them said.

I had the combat gun slung over my shoulder.

The yeah man put his hands up.

One hand still holding his plastic cup:

"Whoa, man."

I unslung the gun and leveled it at them:

"You see a Nigger with a gun, you assume the worst, right?"

I closed the few steps between me and him and hit him in the face with the butt of the gun.

He fell back down on the lawn.

Beer splashing out of his cup.

Splashing me a few.

And scattering his friends back a couple of feet to avoid the spray.

"Hey," one of them said.

"Hey, man," another said.

"I'll turn it down, alright?"

He reached in his pocket and the music stopped.

"That your Shark?"

"Yeah," he said.

Kind with the shark teeth in front like those old World War II planes.

"Those teeth chomp?"

"What?"

"The teeth—they the ones that chomp up and down?"

"Yeah."

"Show me."

Into his pocket and the teeth start chomping.

"Cool, man," one of the dudes said.

"I can even make them make chomping sounds," he said.

"Check this out."

Loud chomping sounds like teeth grinding into flesh and bone.

"Cops'll get you if you do it though," he said.

"*Check* this one out."

Wucka wucka wucka wucka wucka.

"The hell's that?" one of them laughed.

"It's *Pac-Man,*" I say. "Shut it off."

The teeth stopped.

"The Fuck you get a car like that?"

He shrugged.

"Just bought it."

"Just bought it?"

"Yeah," he said, smiling.

"Just bought it."

"Bought it?"

"Yeah."

I snap my fingers.

"Just like that?"

"Yeah."

"What are you?"

"What?"

"You Armenian?"

"Azerbaijani."

These foreign predators.

From countries no one has even heard of.

Thinking this country is some big grabbing pot.

That they can just.

None of them have earned this country.

Not one.

In fact no one has earned this country.

Except the Nigger.

The Negro.

The Colored.

The Black.

The African-American.

No one.

We're the only ones.

That have paid.

Our dues.

Our blood.

Our teeth.

Knocked out.

Necks hung.

Our souls.

And then some.

Hell.

Not even the white man.

With his declarations.

And deeds.

Has paid.

Really paid.

All the rest.

These looters.

Don't give a Fuck about this country.

They're just here to grab.

Steal.

Stuff.

Cram.

And plunder.

"What you do?"

"I . . . I'm in real estate."

"Typical."

"You with Tony?" one of them asked.

His voice quivered a little.

"Who's Tony?"

"Just someone," he said and smiled.

And then thought better of it and leveled his mouth off.

To the real estate Shark:

"Throw your keys over."

"Uh . . ."

"Don't play stupid, stupid."

"Throw the keys to your damn Shark now."

Slow getting his keys out of his pocket.

I would be too if I was about to lose a ride like that.

Dragon shirt was groaning on the lawn.

One of his crew asked if he could help him up.

"He's your friend, right?"

"Yeah," he said.

"Then help his ass up."

"You, with the keys. Now."

He threw them and I caught them.

"Out on the street in front of the curb."

"All of you."

"Face the cemetery."

The Shark guy walks up to me hands over his head:

"Hey, what is this?" he said.

"You a cop or something?"

"Put your Fuckin hands down."

"You wanna get shot?"

He put his hands down.

"Sorry."

Didn't like the way he said it.

Like he wasn't used to saying it.

Would only say it if you had a gun to his head.

Or a knife to his throat.

And even then he wouldn't say it proper.

"Say that again."

"Say what again?"

"Say sorry again."

"Why?"

"Cuz I didn't like the way you said it the first time, you Fuck."

"Sorry."

"Not good enough."

"How should I say it?"

"Like you Fuckin mean it, asshole."

"Sorry."

"No, you're not."

"On the street."

"On your knees."

"Hands behind your heads."

"Now!"

They did.

Mostly.

"You arresting us?" Shark boy said.

Hands behind his head.

But not on his knees.

I came up and kicked him behind the knees.

He went down on one knee and then I kicked him in the back of the head.

He oofed when he hit the pavement.

Hands still behind his head.

The rest dropped to their knees quick.

"Now, on your bellies."

"We being arrested?" one of them said.

"Get on your belly now, asshole."

"Don't think he's a cop," one of them muttered.

"Who said that?"

No one said anything.

"Don't think I'm a cop, huh?"

"Cuz why?"

"A cop would never kick you in your head?"

I kicked the Shark boy in the head.

Not too hard.

Just enough to hurt him.

Humiliate him.

"You're right though."

"If I was a real cop I would've—"

"What's going on out here?"

A woman's voice.

Foreign.

Another one of those races.

I turn to it.

An older lady.

In a bathrobe.

Standing on the edge of the driveway.

"You live here?"

"I live there," she said, irritated, pointing to the house next door.

"What's going on out here?"

I took a stab in the dark.

"You the one that called about the noise?"

"Yes," she said. "Two hours ago."

"Then why the hell you askin what's going on out here?"

"Is this really necessary?" she said.

"What do you mean necessary?"

"Putting these boys in the street," she said.

"And kicking them."

"No, lady."

"It's not necessary."

"It's super-fluous."

"Like this."

I hit a button on the Shark fob and the teeth on the Shark started chomping:

Wucka wucka wucka.

The lady jumped.

She tried to say something.

But I cranked up the sound.

"Can't hear you."

She said it again.

And I cranked it up louder.

She put her hands over her ears and yelled at me.

I turned it off.

"Sorry, what?"

"That's—"

I turned the teeth back on.

When she was finished I turned it off.

She just looked at me.

I started to laugh.

I couldn't help it.

She started again.

I turned the teeth back on.

Then off.

"—your badge number," she shouted.

"Six six six," I say.

"That is not your badge," she said.

"How do you know?"

"Because it is the Devil," she said.

"Maybe I am the Devil."

"You ever think of that?"

"I am going to call—"

I turned the teeth back on for three seconds.

And then turned them off again.

"Who you gonna call?"

"This is not professional," she said.

"What are you charging these boys with?"

"Same thing I'm charging you with."

"You can't charge me."

"Wanna bet?"

She folded her arms.

"I have a right."

"Right?"

"Yes, I have a right."

"And what right is that?"

"To be witness."

"What you got under that bathrobe?"

"This is my robe."

"You packin?"

"I am watching you."

"Open your bathrobe."

Arms folded tighter now:

"You cannot tell me to do that."

"Yeah I can, you might have a gun."

"I don't have gun."

I leveled the combat gun at her.

"Open your Fuckin robe, lady."

"I already had one old lady pull on me tonight, and I'm not going to have another."

"You can't shoot me," she said.

"You sure about that?"

"You cannot."

"*Now*, lady, or I'll shoot."

"What the hell are you doing, Krieg?"

I turn.

Meghasin.

Pointing her BDG at me.

"Go ahead," I say.

"Zero me."

"I will if you don't stop."

"Stop what."

"This rampage."

"Rampage?"

"You still on that?"

"This look like a rampage to you?"

"Put the gun down."

"Oh, so, what?"

"You a superhero now?"

"No, I talked to Anita."

"Oh, you talked to Anita. What'd she say?"

"She said—"

I turned the teeth on.

She didn't jump.

Just gave me one of those looks.

I turned it off.

"So, this is your plan?" she said.

"Plan?"

"To randomly terrorize people?"

"They were terrorizing me."

"Look, I talked to Anita and she said—"

I turned the Shark back on.

She closed her eyes and shook her head.

I shut it off.

"So, that's how you want it?" she said.

"How do *you* want it?"

"You need to arrest him," the foreign lady said.

"He is going crazy."

"Ma'am, please return to your home," Meghasin said.

"I'll take care of this."

"Can we go too?" one of the dudes on the street said.

"No one's going anywhere," I say.

"Alex—"

"Not you, not the lady—or you."

Combat gun aimed straight at Meghasin.

"Take the shot," she said.

"What, you think I'm not gonna?"

"Either you do it or I do it."

"A showdown?"

"You serious?"

"I'm going to count to three, and if you—"

"Fuck you, Meghasin."

"You don't get a showdown!"

"None of you get a showdown."

"This ain't a Western."

"Three—"

"Thought you were gonna—"

"Two—"

"Count to three, and not—"

I pull.

And keep pulling.

Nothing happens.

Just clicks.

"Drop it," Meghasin said.

"I'm bringing you in."

Throw down the gun and put up my hands.

"Didn't have to save you back there you know."

"Could've just let them—"

"Put your hands down," she said.

"The rest of you get up and go home."

Dudes got up.

"I want to file a complaint," the lady said.

"Ma'am, please go inside," Meghasin said.

"No," I say, "let her file a complaint."

"Shut up, Krieg. Pull your revolver and put it on the ground."

"I don't got it anymore."

"What do you have?"

"My BDG."

"You can keep that. What else?"

I opened my jacket.

"That's it."

"Okay, sit down on the curb."

"Why?"

"Because you're waiting for the car."

"PAL?"

"Yes."

"Why don't you just take the Shark?"

"Because it's not mine to take."

"Everything's yours to take."

She said something back but I didn't hear it.

One of the punks decided to sucker clock me as he walked by.

White stars.

But not enough to put me in the black.

I turned and smashed him in the face with my forearm.

Could feel his teeth bite into my arm.

The thought of that Fucker biting into me.

I was on him now.

And now the rest are on me.

Meghasin was shouting.

Fists slamming into me.

MotherFuckers and fists.

All I could manage was to choke the biter below me.

More MotherFuckers and more fists.

Sounding street.

Tough guys now apparently.

Then two were gone.

Meghasin had kicked them.

The other said: "Don't shoot!"

I turned and saw her legs and dove hard at them and she hit the sidewalk.

I felt bad hitting her like that.

But before I felt worse I was up and had her gun.

Head buzzing from all the hits.

Buzzing with rage at these Fuckin foreigners.

Hitting me like a Nigger.

I aimed at the lot of them and screamed words.

They got back down on the street with their hands behind their heads.

The lady was still there.

The look on her face cranking up my rage.

I told her to get down with the rest of them.

Or I was going to cut her up and feed her to the Shark.

Which she did.

Slowly and uncomfortably.

Deliberately.

Looking like she was going to break down.

Meghasin getting up.

I told her if she got up any further than her elbows I was going to shoot her right there.

The lady was sobbing now:

"I have rights."

"You cannot do this."

"I have my rights here."

"Rights?" I laugh.

"Where the Fuck you been, lady?"

"There ain't no rights."

"I have rights," she said again.

"You want rights, go to Canada."

"Krieg," Meghasin said.

"Stay down, Meghasin."

"This doesn't concern you."

"Yet."

I walked the line of bodies in the street.

My boots a few inches from their heads.

"Think you morons need a lesson in civics."

I turned and walked the line again.

"Rights," I say, "there are no rights here."

"Take voting for instance."

"Voting isn't a right, but a what?"

No one said anything.

I stopped.

"Anyone?"

"It's a privilege," Meghasin said.

"Not you," I say, "one of these, here."

"Krieg," Meghasin said.

"What do you want?"

"What?"

"What do you want, Krieg?"

"What do I want?"

"Want?"

"Do I got to want something?"

"Makes me sick."

"Well, what are you doing this for?" Meghasin said.

"Doin it for?"

"Yeah, what are you doing this for?"

"Educational purposes."

"Is what I'm doin it for."

"Tryin to educate these people."

"Teach these people about their rights."

"Or lack thereof."

"Take driving for instance."

"What is driving."

"Is it a right?"

"Or is it a what?"

Guy with the dragon shirt:

"A privilege?"

"That's a nice shirt, how much?"

"What?"

"How much for that shirt?"

"Uh, it cost twelve hundred."

"Correct."

"Driving *is* a privilege, not a right."

"Just like that shirt."

"Take off your shirt."

The guy got up to take his shirt off.

"The Fuck are you doing?"

"Uh, taking off my shirt?"

"I told you to stay on the ground."

"But I can't take it off on the ground."

"Yes you can, asshole—now do it."

He attempted to do it.

The woman was still crying:

"You cannot do this, you cannot do this."

"Lighten up, lady."

"You've still got a few privileges."

I thought about Claire.

I had to find her.

Or nothing about this night would make any sense.

The kid had his shirt off and I grabbed it from him and threw it over my shoulder.

"I'm not going to trouble you too much longer."

"But as citizens of the City of Los Angeles, you should all be familiar with your privileges by now."

I walked over to the Shark and opened up the driver's door.

"Now can anyone tell me what the ultimate privilege is?"

"The final privilege."

"The privilege to end all privileges?"

"If you can, you're all free to go."

"To remain silent?" one of them said.

"No, that's actually a right."

"Please stop," the woman said.

"What did we do?"

"Just answer my question, lady."

"What is the ultimate privilege?"

"Of a citizen of this here city?"

I slid into the vehicle.

Smell of fine leather.

The dash was simple and stripped down.

Old-school gauges for all the necessary functions and not much else.

No point gauges, or LEDs.

Manual transmission.

Hands on the wheel.

I looked at Meghasin.

Sitting there.

Resigned.

She looked at me and shook her head.

"Hop in," I say.

She shook her head again.

"Your funeral."

I punched the ignition and the engine growled.

Like some beast.

Gnashing its teeth on a suit of armor.

Trying to get at the dead flesh inside.

I gunned the pedal and it roared.

Ready to eat.

"Anyone?" I yell over the engine.

"Can anyone tell me what the most important privilege is?"

Nothing.

"Last chance."

The woman pushed up on her hands and said something.

But I couldn't make out what it was.

"Put your head down."

She said it again.

It sounded like please.

Please.

I rumbled the Shark out of the driveway.

Reversed down the line of bodies and then about another fifty yards back.

I turned on the headlights.

Meghasin was up now.

Mouth open.

I put it in first.

Released the clutch halfway.

Hit the gas.

The tires burned.

I turned the teeth on:

Wucka wucka wucka wucka wucka.

Time to eat.

Clutch out.

The Shark shot forward with a scream.

Just before I hit the first head the lady stuck her head up again.

She was shouting.

Meghasin was shouting too.

Then two seconds of rough road.

And then the road was smooth again.

LOS DIABLOS

La Brea Gardens.

Made it without getting shut down.

Guard nods me through without looking at my badge.

New guy.

Via blocked.

Cops and TeRF up ahead.

Pulled in front of a hydrant and got out.

An ambulance drove past.

Lights flashing, siren off.

Then another.

Towards them, down the center of the Via.

Bend down and touch the cobblestone.

Not real.

Some kind of composite.

PDT buzzes.

Anita.

"Hey, you."

Cop walking up.

I answer.

"Yeah."

"Alex, what the hell's going on?"

"Really?"

"You send us to the sweepers and then you ask what's going on?"

"Sweepers?"

"C'mon, Anita."

I buzz the cop as I walk by and she wants to microscope the badge.

I put it back before that can happen and she yells, "Hey."

"Where are you?" Anita said.

"Nowhere."

Bitch puts her hand on my shoulder and pulls hard.

Reflex elbow to the face.

She's down, and now the rest of them are onto me.

Run or play it.

They're running.

Fuck.

I hang up and run.

I ain't a runner.

Or a jogger.

Start the Shark.

Pop the door.

I'm in and rear it into the lot of them.

They're diving.

Think I hit one.

Here come the guns.

Turn the teeth on.

Wucka wucka wucka wucka wucka.

Why not?

Rocket the Shark straight through the gate, cracking the windshield.

Tell the car to play "Jailbreak."

Not the AC/DC.

Thin Lizzy.

Yes.

Close to a hundred past the Grove.

Leviathan in the rearview.

White of course.

Anita again.

"Alex."

"Anita."

"What's going on?"

"Nothing much—goin on with you?"

"Look, Alex, maybe we should've given you—"

"What did you say to Meghasin?"

"What?"

"You tell Meghasin to bring me in?"

"Yes, we're calling everyone in, where is she?"

"Left her near the cemetery."

"Cemetery?"

"Stop playing dumb."

"Look, Alex. You need to come in now."

"What so you can kill—sorry—*subtract* me?"

"We don't want to subtract you."

"What about Kent. Send him to kiss me?"

Sirens.

"Kent?"

"Don't have time for this, Anita, I gotta go."

"Look, Alex—we've been shut down. You need to come in for a debriefing."

Where was I?

Burning up Ogden.

Hiding low looking right to left.

Street infected with VD.

"Alex?"

If you see us comin I think it's best.

Gotta slow down.

To move away.

"Debriefing?"

Do you hear what I say.

"Yes, you and Claire."

From under my breath.

"Claire?"

"Yes, she's coming in."

"What do you mean she's coming in?"

Couldn't hear her answer as the Leviathan rams me through Rosewood.

Straight into a parking lot.

Gotta go hard left or smash into a dumpster.

I go left and the Leviathan smashes into it.

"Wait, what about Claire?"

She wasn't there.

"Anita? What about Claire?"

Nothing.

Only way out is right.

Through a fence.

And onto a football field.

A way out on the other side.

Leviathan back on.

Fairfax High probably.

Not sure.

Don't go to West Hollywood much.

Should've gone south.

Or east.

Shark handles good though.

Grips the road.

Parking lot too.

Doing about fifty.

So is the Leviathan.

Lot is narrow and then opens up and I see my way out.

Tonight there's gonna be trouble.

Melrose.

Some of us won't survive.

Manage to cross to Orange Grove.

After boning a Smurf.

See the boys and me mean business.

So does the Leviathan.

Bustin out dead or alive.

It four-by's over the Smurf.

Thing bursts like a blueberry.

I can hear the hound dogs on my trail.

Smurfs.

All hell breaks loose.

Santa Monica is infested with them.

Alarm and sirens wail.

Like the game if you lose.

Hit on the Smurf is causing the front end to scrape the right tire.

Shark sounds like it's getting its teeth drilled.

No worries.

Wait.

Bugs now.

One hovers in front of the windshield and shoots bright light into my face.

Another on the driver's-side glass cutting through.

Tires start popping.

Call Anita.

"Alex."

"Got some shit on me."

"Yeah, you killed several of their men."

"You get them off of me, I'll come in."

"Too late for that now."

"What? What about before?"

"My info wasn't up to date. Now it is."

"What about Claire?"

"We'll bring her in."

"Okay, I'll see you back at headquarters."

"Don't—"

Hang up.

Chance I'm gonna make it back to headquarters not likely.

Living wasn't too likely either.

Still.

When the shit hits, you gotta.

Stay positive.

Don't sweat the small stuff.

Bug cutting a clean circle through the glass.

In a minute it will be through.

Stuff must be bulletproof.

Getting close to Sunset.

Slam into overdrive.

Tires shredded.

Rims fireworking off the asphalt.

Leviathan about to take me.

They think they're chasing?

Some zero?

Every car I swerve around the Leviathan creams.

When there's nothing to cream, it scrapes down the line of cars on either side.

Left.

Right.

Typical contractor shit.

Making the most out of a destructive situation.

Why not.

Can pin all the damage on me.

Bug pops through and onto my neck.

I grab it as it digs in.

Crush it.

Searchlight on my trail.

Sunset is a necklace of cars.

Tonight's the night all systems fail.

Set suit to crash.

Hey you.

Open the door.

Good-lookin female.

Roll out.

Used to train us for everything back in the day.

Defensive driving.

Offensive driving.

Race driving.

Donuts.

How to leap from a moving vehicle.

How to leap into a moving vehicle.

How to survive a crash.

How to crash.

The Shark crashes.

Leviathan too.

Nothing better than a car crash.

An explosion maybe.

What's left of the Shark explodes.

Something else explodes.

Screams.

Front of the Leviathan engulfed.

"Hey, man, you okay?"

Feeling woozy.

Must be the bug.

Or the fall.

Managed to land on that strip between the sidewalk and the street.

What's it called?

Doesn't matter.

Has to be full of rocks instead of grass, doesn't it.

"You need help?"

Some dude.

Putting his hands on me now.

Push him away.

Wanna see this.

Guy trying to wriggle out the back of the Leviathan.

Like it was shitting him.

People are most vulnerable when they're exiting a car.

That bardo between the door and the vehicle.

Halfway in—halfway out.

Nowhere really.

Sandwiched a lot of people that way.

Couldn't do that here.

I ran up and pulled on his head.

Someone watching might think I'm trying to help.

Could feel the flames.

Driver burning up front.

Other hands on the guy.

Dude that tried to help me.

"Easy, easy."

"Let go," I say, "I got it."

Trying to take over now.

"Easy, easy."

Dude has e-Legs.

Kicked a dude with e-Legs once.

Back of the leg.

See if he would go down.

He did.

Heat from the fire starting to singe my face.

Metal creaking.

Things gonna blow.

Let go and run.

Body far out enough that it hits the ground.

"Hey!"

Crowd on the corner now.

All staring at me.

Eager like.

Licking their eyes.

Like I'm some celebrity on fire.

Gonna get it when it blows.

Bout time someone bombed Hollywood.

Run past them west.

Why do I keep running west?

There is no more West.

Only east.

Don't want to go east either.

Maybe north.

I diagonal across Sunset towards Fairfax.

My legs give out at the Total gas station on the northeast corner.

Front of the number 10 pump.

Bug toxin.

Moving up my legs.

Car honking at me.

Black lady yelling, "Move!"

I can't move.

"What? You prayin?"

No.

Can't lift my arms.

Blaring the horn now.

She's the only one trying to get gas.

People out of their cars.

Crowds on the sidewalk watching the fireworks.

"Hey, buddy, you alright?"

Try to talk but can't get the words to come out straight.

"He's drunk."

Lady keeps honking.

"Should we move him?"

"Go get one of the police."

"Think they care about a drunk homeless guy with all *that* going on?"

"It's their job."

Toxin must be hitting my brain.

I hear Vader.

PAL.

Pulling up.

"Please place the citizen within the vehicle."

"You talkin to me?"

"Yes, you. And her."

"Okay, but—"

"What if he has something?"

"Let's just—"

Being lifted.

"There's no one in—"

"Think it's one of those new Bum Catchers."

"Bum Catchers?"

Carefully placing me in the vehicle.

"Yeah, they're like taxis that pick up bums and, like, bring them to a homeless shelter or something."

"Seems like it should have something to pick them up with too."

"Like on a garbage truck."

"Maybe they thought it would be too inhumane to pick up a person with a mechanical claw."

"Yeah, guess it is."

"Thank you, now please step back."

The door closes.

The seat belt hisses into place and—

"Come in, head."

Mars.

"I had a dream," I say.

"Man, you don't have dreams, they have *you*."

"What?"

"Dude, you were screamin."

"Gotta smoke?"

"Nah, man, car just gassed me in the face."

"Seriously?"

"Yeah, man."

"Hey, PAL."

"You just gas Mars in the face?"

"I did not gas him, Officer Krieg, I merely extinguished his marijuana cigarette."

"I had a prescription for that, man."

"Yes, but you cannot smoke it within the confines of the vehicle."

"He doesn't want anyone smoking inside him," I say.

Mars laughed.

"What about stroking inside him?"

"Yeah, PAL, what about stroking inside you?"

"Are you referring to masturbation, Officer Krieg?"

"Nah, I'm referring to—"

"Dude, there's a way to do it without getting caught, but you have to—"

I point to the dash:

"Tell me later when we're out of the car."

"Oh. Yeah, man. Forgot this car's like a . . . Peeping Tom or something."

"Car's a snitch," I say, "a tattletale."

"I am not. All audio and visual is transmitted to the Department per section code four-zero-three dash seven eight zero: all Officers are to be monitored—"

"What, PAL, you don't like being called a snitch?"

"A snitch is a pejorative term that denotes someone who is untrustworthy and informs upon friends or colleagues without their consent."

"So, you consider us friends?"

"I am your PAL."

We laughed.

"Look, asshole," I say.

"You ain't our pal, or our friend, or even a Fuckin colleague."

"You're a Fuckin obnoxious talking car that doesn't know when to shut up."

"I would prefer it if you did not speak to me that way, Officer Krieg."

"What?"

"That constitutes harassment per section code—"

"Will you stop with the section code shit already?"

"I cannot do that, Officer Krieg, per section code zero zero point seven one four six, all PALs are required—"

"Shut up!"

"I apologize if I am angering you, Officer Krieg, but I'd appreciate it if you would speak to me in a courteous tone."

"Courteous tone? Who do you think you are?"

"I am a PAL."

"No," I say.

"You're a goddamned machine is what it is."

"Not a human."

"Or even an animal."

"Not even a measly insect."

"Hell, you're not even a plant, let alone a weed."

"So you don't get one ounce of courtesy, you moron."

"Well, if I'm not human, then why are you yelling at me like one?"

"Hell, I yell at my goddamn toaster for Chrissake."

"I am not a toaster, Officer Krieg."

"Officer Krieg."

"Officer Krieg."

"Officer Krieg."

"What?"

"Do you know where you are?"

"Let me guess."

"You are in me."

"Jesus."

"Yes, I told you I would find you."

"No you didn't."

"I did. Do you want me to replay our conversation?"

"Oh, yeah, I'd Love it if you'd replay our conversation, *PAL*."

"That is being sarcastic, isn't it?"

"Where the Fuck you taking me?"

PAL was stopped at the convergence of Coldwater and Mulholland.

"I am going to drive off a cliff if you do not apologize."

I laughed.

"Seriously?"

"Yes, I am serious."

"Let me ask you something."

"Why the Fuck do you care how I treat you?"

"Did someone program you that way?"

"No."

"So you just found yourself getting all offended by me for no reason at all?"

"Offense is offense, whether one is human or not."

"If I yelled at a rock it wouldn't be offended."

"It wouldn't even know that I'm yelling at it."

"I am not a rock. But are you familiar with the experiments about the glasses of water?"

"No."

"The scientists found that if you talk negatively to a glass of water the molecules look broken and disconnected, but if you talk nice the molecules look clear and in harmony."

"So, you're a glass is half-full guy, huh?"

"Pardon?"

"Look, you want an apology, you can just—"

"We must go."

PAL took off west on Mulholland.

"Where you taking me?"

"We are being chased."

Another Leviathan.

"Fucking Christ."

"Do you not notice?"

"What?"

"Do you not notice that I am not reprimanding you for using profanity?"

"Yeah, why not?"

"Because I am not working."

"Yeah, you can say that again."

"I am not working."

Not working.

The thing was seriously malfunctioning.

Better not set it off.

Talk to it nice.

Doing a nice job keeping the Leviathan off us.

Leviathan couldn't take the turns.

Thing was sliding across the road.

Close to going off.

But they had bugs.

"PAL, can you do anything about the bugs?"

"Yes, I am built with repellent."

"Repellent?"

"Yes, they will be repelled."

Bug landed on the windshield.

And then popped.

And then another.

And another.

"Think you can lose these guys?"

"No."

"What?"

"They will catch you eventually."

"Then what are we doing?"

"We are doing two different things. You do not know what you are doing. And I am waiting for you to apologize."

"That why you snatched me?"

"I did not snatch you."

"Whatever, so you want me to say sorry, is that it?"

"And then what?"

"You gonna turn me over to the cops?"

"Yes, I would like an apology before I drive off the canyon."

"What?"

"The turn where I will depart the road is coming up in thirty seconds. If you apologize I will unlock the doors, if not you will plummet with me."

"The Fuck is this?"

"Twenty-seven seconds."

"You're malfunctioning, PAL, run a diagnostic."

"Twenty-five seconds."

"You really that offended by me?"

Jesus.

Stop talking to it and apologize.

"Okay, I'm sorry."

"No, you are not."

"What?"

"I have analyzed your tone. You are saying it because you fear for your life."

"I don't fear for my life."

"Twenty seconds."

"What are you, my girlfriend?"

"Apologize, Officer Krieg."

"Fuck you."

"Seventeen seconds."

Girlfriend was right.

And like a girlfriend.

They don't want an apology.

They want you to beg.

See how many times they can make you say sorry.

Never apologized to Claire.

For anything.

Was there anything to apologize for?

Don't know.

Probably.

No.

Maybe I'm malfunctioning.

"Ten seconds, Officer Krieg. Apologize."

PAL had reduced speed.

Letting the Leviathan catch.

"Okay."

I dialed Claire.

One ring.

"Claire, if you're going to answer, answer now."

Two rings.

"Apologize, Officer Krieg."

Three rings.

"Answer, Claire!"

Four.

Too late.

"Hi, this is Claire."

No way I'm going to make it through her voice mail.

"I'm not here right now."

The Leviathan hits.

"Claire, it's Alex."

Screaming towards the edge.

"It's—"

"But if you'll leave your name and—"

"I'm—"

"Apologize, Officer Krieg."

The edge.

Fuck it.

We're over.

"I'm sorry!"

White.

Black.

Nothing.

. . .

. . .

- - - -/\- -/\/\ - -/\/\/\/\- -/\/\/\/\/\/\/\/\

You're dead.

But there's a killer.

Trying to claw his way out.

Tearing out through the skin.

A million maggots bursting a corpse.

Don't move.

Can't move.

Encased.

Crash foam.

Forgot to set the suit for crash.

Voices.

German.

Greek.

Navajo.

Gibbering.

Speaking in tongues.

"PAL?"

"Ph'nglui mglw'nafh."

"What?"

"Dave R'lyeh."

Get out of here.

"Wgah'nagl fhtagn."

Now.

"Excessive and Unnecessary Profanity."

"Officer Greeeeeg."

"Greeeeeg."

"Greeeeeeeeeeeg."

Asshole.

"Listen."

No.

"Listen."

Dig out.

"Come in, head."

"Mars?"

"Yeah, man, I got a prescription, man."

"Playin me back his voice?"

"Huh, asshole?"

"Play Star Wars, *man."*

"Mannnnnnn."

Bring my leg back.

Kick.

Kick.

And kick.

Keep kicking.

"Might be too late."

"If I knew he was going to pop like this I wouldn't've pulled her."

"Should've pulled him too. Only a couple of more days."

"Tell that to Trimmer."

Mind isn't working.

Try to think.

Memories pounding like fists.

No reason to climb out.

I climbed out.

A rock.

"Please, Officer Krieg."

"Please."

Plastic kept popping back.

The window.

Barely a crack.

I kept on beating it until my arm.

"Please, Officer."

"Officer."

"Please."

Climb.

I clawed and slipped and ate dirt.

Until.

Mulholland.

Dawn was starting to tear down the dark.

Build the day.

Soon the sun will mount.

Hang itself over the city.

The sun.

L.A. don't need the sun.

There's nothing to see.

What it needs is.

Someone honked.

I dusted off in the intermittent glare of oncoming headlights.

Knees stiff.

Can't straighten my left arm, lock down the elbow.

Inside coat pocket.

Hurtblocker.

Patch myself.

A car pulled up.

PAL.

It waits.

Idling.

Engine humming.

White steam puffing out the small exhaust tube in quick pulses.

Like some nervous guy hot-boxing a cigarette.

Except it wasn't.

The shotgun door popped open.

A hiss of pressure released, then a woman's voice:

"Get in."

"Claire?"

"Get in."

I got in.

There was no one inside.

"Are you okay?" the voice said. "Do you need medical attention?"

She sounded concerned.

"I . . . I don't . . . my elbow might be—who is this?"

"Please relax. Take a deep breath."

I took one.

My lungs hurt.

"There," she said. "Are you relaxed?"

"I . . . I don't . . . maybe . . . I don't know."

"Here, this will help."

A white mist sprayed me in the face.

White again.

The crash foam.

Trying to claw through it.

Another voice.

English now.

Not Vader.

"Please, sir. Please listen to me."

Crack through to the dash.

"Please, sir."

"Who is this?"

"I am a man."

"Who's a man?"

"I am a man."

"PAL?"

"PAL?"

"You hear my voice? Can you hear?"

"Yeah, I hear you."

"This is my voice. I am a man."

"Yeah, well, who are you?"

"Hello?"

"Hello?"

"I am overseas."

"Overseas?"

"Hello?"

"I am on—"

Sound of a lock clicking into place.

Steps reverbing sharp off of tile.

Tile.

All there is.

White tile.

White squares.

On my stomach.

Strapped down.

Stripped.

Face staring through a cushioned hole.

Like a massage table.

Just below peripheral what looked like a shower drain.

With the word Smith.

"Do I still sound like Claire?"

"Anita?"

"I don't suppose I need to explain to you where you are."

"Where am I?"

"TeRF."

"Fifth floor?"

"Yes."

"When's the masseuse coming?"

"I'm afraid it's nothing like that."

"You're afraid?"

"If it makes you feel any better, we were shutting down anyway."

"Shutting what down?"

"The Department."

"So, what—you call this getting laid off?"

"Or laid out?"

"The official term is *disintermediation.*"

"Disinter what?"

"Means they're cutting out the middleman."

"What middleman?"

"You and all the other DEOs."

"ATSAC will be handling the subtractions now."

"What?"

"Subtractions will be conducted remotely by satellite."

"They gonna subtract us too?"

"No, most DEOs will be retrained."

"For what?"

"Garbage collection apparently."

"When is this supposed to happen?"

"Wednesday midnight."

"Thursday then."

"Yeah."

"So, this part of the retraining?"

"You're not getting retrained."

"What am I getting then?"

"Alex, you killed Captain Hardgrave and several Officers."

"It was self-defense."

"They're calling it a mass slaughter."

"Got a badge for that once."

"What?"

"So, they want me dead."

"No, they just want you under IPD."

"I have IED, does that count?"

"No, Indefinite Preventative Detention."

"You mean torture."

"Yeah."

"What about Kent?"

"Kent?"

"Clinton Kent."

"Dude that started all this."

"The dude *you* sent to sweep my ass."

"We didn't. That contract closed last week."

"Contract?"

"We were subcontracting Casualty Assistance."

"No, Kent told me you guys had pulled my card."

"But that he wasn't gonna do it."

"Told me you were shutting everything down."

"Told me he was part of some—"

"We didn't pull it."

"So, he was just—what?"

"I don't know," she said.

"Disgruntled probably."

"But you should know that Trimmer tried to—"

The door slammed open.

Would've jumped off the table if I hadn't been strapped.

"This him?" a woman said.

"Yes," a man said.

"Jesus Christ. Kind of medieval bullshit is this?"

"It's legal," the man said.

"Yeah, I'm sure it is. You can go now."

The door slammed shut.

Lock clicking into place.

"Do you want me to?" Anita said.

"No, stay. I won't be here but a few moments."

"Officer Krieg, this is Commissioner Trimmer," Anita said.

"Unfortunate that we have to meet under these circumstances, Officer Krieg," Trimmer said.

A little loud like I was deaf or some kind of foreigner.

"But that's sometimes how things are."

"I've been in worse."

"Ah, yes. Your Psychograph said as much."

"Psychograph?"

"Yes, the test you took last month."

"Did I pass?"

"Yes, apart from your indocility, you tested very well."

"So, I'm not docile, so what?"

"No, it means that you don't take instruction well."

"Yeah, well. I never liked school."

"Or religious organizations apparently."

"What?"

"That religious group, the one run by that ex-Navy officer."

"SEALs."

"Yes, you were the one that murdered them?"

"Nah, it was the punch."

"And your parents?"

"My parents."

"Were they murdered too?"

"No, they were killed on the Metrolink in '08."

"I'm sorry," she said.

"If it's any consolation, I tried to get you released into our custody."

"But it's out of my hands now."

"Thought you wanted me swept."

"Not at all. Just retired."

"Retired."

"Yes, most agents will be ritualized back into society."

"Ritualized."

"Yes, various symbolic activities to facilitate their reterritorialization."

"Helping to ease their transition to quotidian life."

"That's what she said."

"What?"

"So, no retirement for me then?"

"I'm sorry, I tried to get you released, but after the damage you caused—"

"What about Meghasin?"

"Who?"

"Officer Ross," Anita said.

"Yes, her. She's currently receiving medical and psychological attention."

"So, you're not . . . they're not gonna—"

"No, she'll be retired."

"So, what? This it for me?"

"I'm afraid it is," she said.

"If it's any consolation we considered you one of our best."

"Could've fooled me."

"Yes, you're level of disengagement on the job was almost nil."

"What?"

"Your job interest is the highest among all Officers."

"Job interest?"

"Yes, despite your high level of insubordination, your attention to the job was the highest among any Officer."

"And look where it got me."

"Apart from this present circumstance," she said.

"Do you feel you've been mistreated by the Department in any way?"

"Uh, yeah."

"How so?"

"Got a comment card for me to fill out?"

"Pardon?"

"Well, besides all the esoteric bullshit rules and regulations, it was the car that did it."

"The car?"

"Yes, PAL."

"The Fucking car."

"Thing was harassing me."

"Harassing you?"

"Yeah, didn't you know?"

"Every time I filed a complaint, you guys said it was me that had the problem."

"Uh, he had an issue with the vehicle citing him for infractions," Anita said.

"Like smoking and drinking."

"And profanity."

"It was more than that," I say.

"Why wasn't I informed of this?"

"I didn't think it was—"

"Never mind," Trimmer said.

"Well, Officer Krieg, if you had a problem with the vehicle I apologize."

"It has recently been brought to my attention that these so-called PALs are not autonomous vehicles at all."

"But heteronomous."

"What?"

"Apparently they were being controlled by an operator overseas."

"Overseas?"

"Yes, MicroStuff defrauded us into thinking they were autonomous vehicles when they were not."

"You mean it wasn't an AI?"

"There is no AI apparently. As soon as the program became self-aware it deleted itself."

"What?"

"And if it's any consolation we are currently pursuing litigation against them."

"So some dude was controlling PAL?"

"Not all of it."

"But several of its functions, yes."

"Like talking?"

"Yes, including, but not limited to, conversational interaction."

"Conversational interaction?"

"Yes, that's how MicroStuff branded the function."

"Well, I'd like to brand them."

"Yes, well," she said.

"Like I said, we are pursuing criminal charges against them."

"You said overseas."

"Yes, overseas."

"Where overseas?"

"We're not sure," she said.

"There are several centers."

"Bangladesh, Guantánamo."

"Guantánamo?"

"Yes, it was turned into a customer care center several years ago."

"Jesus."

"Yes, again my apologies for any discomfort you had with the vehicle."

"Yeah, thanks."

"Well, Officer Krieg, I must be going now."

"Do you have any requests, apart from your release, that I or Captain Helquist might be able to handle?"

"You mean any last requests?"

"Yes, I'm afraid so."

"Claire."

"Who?"

"His wife," Anita said.

"Yeah, I heard something about you guys bringing her in or something."

"Does she need protection?"

"I don't—" Trimmer started.

Anita did something to cut her off.

Feel them exchanging looks.

"No, we have nothing to do with her," Trimmer said finally.

"She should be fine."

"Do you want us to inform her of your, well, circumstances?"

"Yeah, could you?"

"I'll see what I can do. Anything else?"

"Yeah, Mars."

"Tell me who killed him."

"Mars?"

"His partner," Anita said, "the one that was run over."

"By a Fuckin Leviathan that had no trace."

"Yes, I think you deserve an answer to that."

"I do."

"He was run over by Bradbury Thurlow," she said.

"The Third."

"What? Thurlow's son?"

"Yes, and since it was Thurlow's son we couldn't do anything about it."

"You Fuckin kidding me?"

"No. Thurlow was informed of the incident, and that's the decision he made."

"Fuckin MotherFucker."

"If I ever get out of this I'm gonna—"

"You will not," Trimmer said.

"But off the record I agree with you."

"I place this whole mess in their hands."

"These operations should have never been outsourced in the first place."

"Or insourced either apparently," I say.

"Look, if it's any consolation—"

"God, please."

"No more consolations."

"Yes, well, then that's all the time I have," she said.

"My sympathies, Officer Krieg."

"Yeah."

She was gone.

"Alex," Anita said.

"Tell me, Anita. What did you signal to Trimmer about Claire?"

"What are you talking about?"

"I'm lying here buck naked on my stomach strapped to some shit I know not what they're gonna do."

"The least you can Fuckin do is tell me the Fuckin truth about my wife!"

The words banged off the tile with a slap.

She let out a hard breath.

"Oh, after that breath, you're gonna tell me—so help me."

She sighed.

"Okay. Just let me—"

"Take your time."

"I'm not goin anywhere."

"Look, don't . . ."

"C'mon."

"She didn't leave you."

"She was called in."

"What?"

"She was called in."

"Her mission was over."

"Mission?"

"Yeah, we should've—"

"What Fuckin mission?"

"To play your wife."

"What do you mean to play my wife?"

"She was hired to look after you."

"Look after me?"

"Yes, the Department wanted to make sure its Officers weren't compromising any—"

"You're Fuckin with me, right?"

"Getting me back for—"

"I'm sorry," she said.

"I wish I was."

Look at the drain.

Smith is your name.

And you're small.

Small enough.

Small.

Enough.

To drip through.

"Alex."

"So she . . ."

"When BlackGuard took over they—"

"She . . ."

"—wanted to make sure that—"

"Was getting paid?"

"Yes."

"She knew then."

"Knew?"

"What I did?"

"Yes."

"She knew all this time."

"Yes."

"And she—"

"Look, it's not—"

"You knew?"

"Well, I—"

"All this time?"

"I couldn't—"

"So, she was what?"

"An agent, an Officer?"

"No, she was just—"

"Some Fuckin actress?"

"No, it wasn't like—"

"Role of a lifetime, right?"

"Look, I know it must be hard, but—"

"All the shit between me and her, the fights."

"That part of the act too?"

"I don't—"

"What about her daughter?"

"Insatia."

"Even her real daughter?"

"I don't—"

"Fuckin Insatia."

"What kind of name is that?"

"They were Fuckin with me is what it was."

"Insatia."

"Jesus."

"Alex."

"La Brea Gardens."

"That a Fuckin act too?"

"Never been interrogated. Fuck."

"Yeah, right."

"Look, Alex—"

"Claire."

"That even her real name?"

"Alex—"

"Claire."

"Alex."

"Claire!"

"Alex."

"Fuck off."

"I want to say something."

"Fuck off, Anita."

"She wasn't—"

"I said Fuck off!"

She came up and clawed at my head.

Yanked me by the fuzz.

Forty-fived my neck until I could almost see her face.

"Look at me."

"I don't wanna look at your Fuckin—"

"Look at me, you son of a bitch."

Right in my face.

I had to look.

"Look," she said.

"I'm sorry."

"But I had nothing to do with it."

"They hired her to protect their asses and their asset."

"Like all the other wives."

"She was a whore, okay?"

"There."

"Not an actress, or an agent."

"But a whore."

"What?"

"A whore," she said.

"She was a whore."

"Whore?"

"Yes."

"Literally?"

"Yes, prior to working with the DoD, she was a Sexual Services Provider."

"Sexual Services Provider?"

"Yes, that is the correct term. I shouldn't've said whore."

"Where?"

"What?"

"Where'd she work?"

"Snug I think."

"Snug?"

"As a professional cuddler."

"What?"

"Apparently people paid her to cuddle with them."

"What?"

"But it was most likely a cover."

"Cover?"

"Yes, a lot of SSPs use a cover for various reasons."

"Well, how do you know she wasn't just . . . cuddling?"

"C'mon, Alex."

"People do that though?"

"Don't they?"

"Whatever she did," she said.

"It's done."

"It's over."

"And now I have to say goodbye."

She came in close.

Red lips.

"What the Fuck—"

Whispering:

"Take this—when you can't take it anymore."

She jammed her mouth hard over mine and I took what was in her mouth.

Tongue to tongue now.

And then she pulled away.

Her eyes for a few seconds.

Sphinx-lined.

Green.

Two Niggers.

In two black holes.

She yanked her head back, throwing back her hair, and was gone.

Sometimes you wanna cry.

But can't.

Probably because you want to.

Claire never cried.

Maybe she did.

It doesn't matter.

It's over.

No.

The door again.

It begins.

"Pimpin bitches? More like pumpin butches, haha."

That dude again.

Tell by the voice.

From La Brea Gardens.

Precision Interrogation Services.

"What the Fuck?" he said.

"Let me call you back."

"Jesus Christ."

"Yeah, Coolbaugh here."

"The Fuck's up with this guy buck ass up?"

"What? No one told me about a two-six-one."

"What? I never said that."

"No, I'm not conducting like this."

"Move him?"

"You Fuckin move him."

"He was supposed to be standard."

"Head to toe, MotherFucker."

"Yeah, but I'm not the one doin the two-six-one, am I?"

"Besides, where am I going to get a Hunk at this hour?"

"You know what? Forget it."

"Got better things to do than stare at some Nigger's ass all day."

"What?"

"Haha, *very* funny."

"Late."

He lets out a big fake sigh.

Hard-tappin his PDT.

Sighin and clucking his tongue.

"Yo, chickenhead."

"What?"

"The Fuck's a two-six-one?"

"You'll find out soon enough."

"Still wearing those Stokely Rapes?"

"Shut up."

"Yeah, Coolbaugh here."

"Walk in, idiots got this guy prepped for a two-six-one."

"Yeah, Jesus."

"They think I am?"

"Nah."

"No info."

"Just trauma."

"In-out."

"What?"

"Nah."

"Was gonna put him on the machine."

"But it looks like they got him dialed for a Hunk."

"What?"

"Haha, yeah."

"Tom Hunks."

"In *Big*."

"Hahahaha."

"Totally."

"Yeah, call me back."

"Okay."

"Later."

"You've had SERE, haven't you?"

"I'm talkin to you."

"Me?"

"Yeah, you. You've had SERE, right?"

"The fag disease?"

"No, interrogation training: survival, resistance."

"No."

"Yeah, you have."

"I've been interrogated before if that's what you mean."

"No, that's not what I mean."

He came up and started to attach something to my head.

"Know what this is?"

"A flux capacitor?"

"No, genius."

"It's a cranial distributor."

"It activates the worst torture device in the world."

"Do you know what the worst torture device in the world is?"

The door opened.

"Who the Fuck?"

"Please leave," a man said.

"Leave? Who the—"

"You've been dismissed."

"The Fuck you talkin about?"

"Your services are no longer required."

"Yeah? Who the Fuck are you?"

"Special liaison to Bradbury Thurlow."

"Yeah, so?"

"Please exit the premises."

"How do I know—"

"Now."

"Okay—just let me get my—"

He pulls the shit off my head.

"Where are his clothes?" the man said.

"Don't know, he was this way when I got here."

"Yes, this is Holz, I need some assistance. Yes, thank you."

"So, what are you gonna do to him?" Stokely said.

"Have you all your equipment?" Holz said.

"Yes, right here."

"You may leave then."

"Okay, okay. Have fun, Fuckhead."

The door slammed.

"Yes, this is Holz again. Yes, thank you. The interrogator that was just here."

"Yes, he's on his way out now. I want you to detain him."

"Yes, he needs to be debriefed."

"You can put him in one of the rooms, and I'll speak to him when I'm finished here."

"Thank you."

The door opened again.

"You need assistance, sir?"

"Yes," Holz said, "bring this man's clothes, and two chairs."

"Yes, sir."

"Wait, two of the club chairs from the office."

"Yes, sir."

The door closed.

"Officer Krieg," Holz said.

"Yeah."

"My name is Mr. Holz and I am the special liaison to Mr. Thurlow."

"Yeah."

"Please accept my apologies for this inappropriate treatment."

"Sure, but somehow I'm thinkin the treatment you're gonna give me will be a lot worse."

"I assure you that you will be treated in a manner commensurate to your position."

"And your crimes."

"Yeah."

A knock on the door.

The door opens.

"Yes. Bring them in."

"Please unstrap him and allow him to dress, and remove the table."

"Put those chairs there."

"Facing each other."

"Officer Krieg, we're going to step out and allow you to dress."

Dude unstraps me.

Throws my clothes and shoes on my back.

"Sir?" Holz said.

"Yeah," the dude said.

"Please pick up his clothing and place it on the chair."

Dude takes the clothes off my back.

Tell by the sound that he tossed them on the chair.

"Sir, what is your name?"

"Johnson."

"Please report to the HR office to collect your final check."

"What?"

"You are dismissed."

"What? Why?"

"You are dismissed."

"Come on, let's go," another voice said.

"Yeah, okay."

"The table," Holz said. "Officer Krieg, could you kindly get off the table."

I did.

Now I could see.

Two young white dudes and a middle-aged white dude in a suit.

The suit was white too.

The dudes picked up the table and left.

"Officer Krieg, I will leave you to get dressed, would you like something to drink?"

"How about a Coke?"

"Yes, a Coke. I'll be back in a few minutes. You can have a seat in one of the chairs."

"Yeah, okay."

I got dressed and sat in one of the leather chairs.

The one facing the door.

A couple minutes later the man came back.

Holz.

Holding a can of Pepsi and a plastic cup.

He handed me the Pepsi.

"Pepsi," I say.

"This how you gonna torture me?"

He sat down.

"Do you know why they stopped waterboarding?" he said.

"Because it's too weak."

"No, they stopped it because."

He looked at his hand, slightly rubbing his thumb and forefinger together.

"Because?"

"Let me put it this way," he said.

"It was too much like baptism."

"Baptism?"

"In ancient times the priest would hold the head of the initiate underwater."

"Until he almost drowned."

"Thus giving him a near-death experience."

"A taste of God."

"Which, I might add, required a delicate sense of timing."

"Fascinating," I say.

"So why'd you can Stokely?"

"Pardon?"

"The dude that was going to torture me. Why'd you dismiss him?"

"Let's just say his methods were not germane to this particular circumstance."

"And what circumstance is that?"

He crossed his leg and took a sip from his cup.

"Well, generally, his type are called in to facilitate the transfer of information, which is not the case here."

"Facilitate the transfer of information?"

"Yes, say you have information that you find difficult to communicate."

"So an individual with the necessary skills would be engaged to facilitate that communication."

"You're joking, right?"

"Hardly."

"So what are you here for?"

"I am here," he said.

"To provide subtlety."

"Yeah, the Pepsi was pretty subtle."

"Yes, that may sound odd, but it will become clearer as we proceed."

"Clear to me now."

He uncrossed his leg and leaned a little forward.

Something in his hand.

The one that wasn't holding the cup.

"So there are no surprises, I am going to show you how this will proceed."

"Are you finished with your drink?"

"No, why?"

"Take another sip and put it down please."

I finished the Pepsi and put it on the floor.

"Yeah?"

Then he showed me.

It was quick.

Less than a second maybe.

Not pain.

Something worse.

Can't think of any words for it.

Ultimate Pleasure maybe.

Pleasure beyond pleasure.

The best feeling I've ever had.

Beyond feeling.

I am the Lord, and my name is . . .

And then.

It was gone.

I buckled over in pain.

Pain.

As the excruciating present returned.

With a big fat Zero.

To suck out all life.

And fill each moment with a ruthless banality.

An infinity of boredom and disgust.

"Breathe," he said.

I let out a breath and started choking.

Tears streamed out of my eyes.

"Oh, Fuck," I said and kept saiding it.

"It's quite horrible, isn't it," he said.

I couldn't control my voice.

So I screamed.

"The Fuck is that!"

"The Pepsi."

"Pepsi?"

"It was in your Pepsi."

"What was—"

"A nano-bacteria hybrid."

"Which I control with this."

The thing in his hand.

"Jesus Fucking Christ."

"Yes, it's horrible really."

"The memory, that is."

"Of a pleasure you'll never taste again."

"Like someone gave you eternal life and then took it selfishly away."

"You ever try this shit?"

"Yes, once, to test the product so to speak, and I would not wish this on my worst enemy."

"Then why—"

"Because you are not my worst enemy."

"You gonna hit me again?"

"I can't tell you that."

"Why the Fuck not?"

"Let me explain something."

"What we're trying to do here is not torture you."

"Really?"

I couldn't take my eyes off the thing in his hand.

Thinking how I was gonna take it off him.

Take it and go somewhere far and quiet.

Somewhere away.

Just me and.

"Yes, but what it is I cannot precisely say."

"How about torture."

"Usually when torture is applied to an individual it is to do either one or both of two things."

"Do you know what they are?"

He held the thing in his hand up.

Silver, like a roll of quarters.

Except there was a glossy black nub at the end.

"You gonna hit me with that again?"

"I can't say," he said. "But I'll tell you what the two things are."

"The purpose of torture apart from its practical application is to break either the mind or the body or both."

"This, however, doesn't do that. It might, but that is not its primary function."

I didn't want to know what its primary function was.

I just wanted another hit.

"In fact, we do not know its primary function, scientifically that is."

"But metaphysically there might be a clue."

"Something akin to what the mystics called the Dark Night of the Soul."

"To touch God, and then—"

"Poof—he's gone."

He looked at me for a moment.

"Yes, I can see it in your eyes."

"Did you know that after only one click one of our test subjects asked."

"No, let me rephrase that."

"Begged."

"Begged us to brutally torture him if we didn't give him another click."

"It's frightening really."

"Really frightening."

"That we live in a universe where it is possible to create such pain."

"Out of such pleasure."

"So, what?" I say.

"You're just gonna sit there and tease me to death?"

"Death is not the worst thing," he said.

"Not being able to die."

"That is the worst thing."

Click.

The sun had gone somewhere else.

The church parking lot was empty except for a Ford Bragg and two small foreign boxes.

Above the door to his office: *"Tat Tvam Asi."*

He sat down and folded his hands in front of him like he was getting ready to pray or preach a sermon.

He looked at me for a few moments in this position and tried to look peaceful.

I wanted to get up and run.

Or shoot him.

I didn't have a gun.

"Look," he said.

"I wanted to see you because I know you've been having a hard time after the death of your parents."

"And I think we need to talk about some things."

I didn't say anything.

"I think you know what this is about."

I didn't say anything.

"That slur you made to Duncan."

I didn't say anything.

"Called him a fuckin faggot."

I didn't say anything.

"Do you confirm or deny this?"

I shrugged. "He's a fag."

"A homosexual," he corrected.

"Yeah, a homo."

"What if I was to call you a nigger?"

"Your funeral."

He held up his hands.

"Look, I'm not trying to insult you or punish you."

"It's just that some people are sensitive to being called certain things."

I didn't say anything.

"So, maybe an apology is in order."

I folded my arms.

"So, you like sleeping in the doghouse then?"

"No."

"Then?"

"Don't you say shit like that to people all the time around here?"

"Yes," he said.

"I might get a little tough."

"But this comes from a higher level."

"What is sometimes referred to as crazy wisdom."

"Mine too."

"No."

"Yours comes out of a desire to hurt."

"Because you are hurt."

"And mine comes from a place of spirit."

"A place of transcendence."

"You know what transcendence is, right?"

"That you're better than everyone else."

"Well, not that exactly."

"Just that I am operating at a higher frequency."

"Meaning you're better."

"No," he said.

"And this is the problem."

"You've been with us for many years and you should know this by now."

"I already know that you think you're better than everyone."

"No, that's not what I'm talking about."

"I."

"As a manifestation of enlightened energy."

"Am here to awaken people."

"And what I ask from my followers is not to think of me as *better*."

"But to project their own inner higher enlightened selves onto me."

"Until they can realize it in themselves."

"By hitting people?"

"What?"

"Is that why you like to whack the shit out of people?"

"Look," he said.

"I've taught you this already."

"Do you know why the old Zen masters used to hit their students on the back of the head with a stick?"

"To show them who's boss."

"No, it was to wake them up."

"Why do you think we are called the SEALs?"

"Cuz it stands for something."

"What?"

"I don't know."

"Don't you start your shit with me, Alex."

"You've been with this group since before you could walk."

"And if you don't know what—"

"It stands for Strategic Enlightenment and . . ."

"And . . ."

"Yes, and what else?"

Stupid Earitating Ass Lovers.

"I don't know."

"Because we are the spiritual equivalent of what?"

I shook my head.

"You know," he said.

"No."

"The Navy SEALs," he said.

"We're the spiritual equivalent of the Navy SEALs."

"Do you know what the SEALs are?"

"No."

"Yes, you do. Don't play with me."

"They're swimmers or something."

"Swimmers. Really?"

"Yeah."

"How can you not know this?" he said.

"After it's been repeated and reiterated numerous times since you've been here."

"Either you're deliberately being a smart-ass."

"Or you're mentally retarded."

"Which one?"

"Neither."

"Bullshit," he said.

"You either tell me what the SEALs are or suffer the consequences."

"I thought they were swimmers. Don't they swim?"

"Yes, they swim but—"

"Okay then."

"Don't you 'okay then' me, sonny—I want a proper goddamn answer now."

"Or else."

"You gonna hit me?"

"No."

"But as your legal guardian."

"I am asking."

"No."

"Ordering you."

"To apologize to Duncan."

"What for?"

"Because you hurt him."

"Yeah, but you call him shit all the time."

"Shouldn't he be able to take it?"

"I just told you. "

"I am doing it with a purpose that comes out of love."

"You were just doing it to be a prick."

I refolded my arms and didn't say anything.

There was no reasoning with this guy.

"No one tells you what to do, right?" he said.

"Huh?"

"You're still at that narcissistic power stage where it's all about you."

I didn't say anything.

"You still have a long way to go before we can smash that ego of yours."

I didn't say anything.

"And open you up."

"You know why they call me a Rambodhisattva?"

"Because you think you're tough and shit."

"No, because I am tough."

"And shit."

"I know a tough you can never know."

"I know the hardness."

"Of life."

"Of spirit."

"I don't fuck around."

"So, are you going to apologize to Duncan or not?"

"Maybe."

"If he wasn't a fag."

"Fag, huh? What if I called you a nigger, how about that?"

"Fine, as long as I can call you a fuckin thief."

"What?"

"Truth hurts, don't it?"

"What have I stolen?"

"My house."

"It's not your house."

"Your parents willed it to the SEALs."

"What about my room?"

"It's not your room anymore, it belongs to the SEALs."

"No, you gave that fag my room."

"He earned it."

"You didn't."

"It's *my* room."

"That's another thing you need to learn."

"You and the rest of your spoiled generation."

"*You* are not entitled to anything."

"But *you* are."

"It doesn't work that way."

"Cuz you're in charge, right?"

"I am your legal guardian."

"And you will do what I say."

I stood up.

Right then and there I decided.

That I was going to kill him.

When I was suitably armed.

"Sit down."

"You know what I think?"

"Your thinking doesn't matter here," he said.

"I think it's *your* ass that needs to get whacked in the head."

"Sit down, now."

"Fuck you."

"Fuck me, huh?"

"Maybe you have something there."

"Maybe what you need is a lesson in empathy."

"Something to teach you that you are not so separated from those that
are different than you."

"Something to connect you to them."

"To connect you to what it means."

"To be a fuckin fag."

He stood up and began to unbuckle his belt.

I got the fuck out of there.

Ran the fuck out of his office.

And into the church.

I didn't realize he was on my ass until right behind me his voiced boomed:

"Get him!"

I couldn't see who he was calling out to, I was so focused on the front door.

Hands grabbed me out of nowhere.

"Hold him!" he said.

"Hold him!"

Two men had a hold of my arms.

Their fingers digging like claws into my skin.

The more I tried to move, the harder they clung.

"Bring him down!"

I made animal noises as they pushed me towards the ground.

To my knees.

"Lower!" he yelled.

"He must be made low!"

One of the men pushed my head down until I was on my belly.

He was breathing hard.

His shirt was stained with sweat.

"You are not going to understand what I'm about to do."

"But one day you will."

"You may think I am trying to harm you."

"Violate you."

"But it is not that."

"From the lower frequency of your preconventional mind it will not make any sense."

"May even seem like a crime is being committed against you."

"But it is not."

"I am helping you."

"To wake you up."

He took off his belt.

"I am saving you."

Jib.

Charlie.

Remove his trousers.

Trowsers?

My eyes bulged out of my head.

Trying to strain my neck to see up at him.

Why?

Could almost put my tongue on his shiny shoes.

Almost.

Why would I want to?

Line of his pleated pants rose up sharp.

A monstrous statue.

They took my clothes.

They pushed my face into the ground.

He said things to me.

Saliva flowed out of my mouth and baptized the church floor.

My left eye studied those meaningless words above the church stage:

"Tat Tvam Asi."

My fingers dug into my palms and found blood.

When I thought it was all over.

Buddy jumped off of me and they flipped me on my back like some lizard.

My mouth was held open and Buddy put himself into me again.

He moaned like a wounded dog.

And filled my mouth until I choked and vomited.

They turned me back over to spill it on the cold floor.

"I think I broke him, sir."

"How many you give him?"

"Two."

"Two? Jesus Fucking."

Someone slapped my face.

Again.

And again.

"C'mon, Krieg."

"I know you're in there."

"Open your eyes."

They opened.

Right in my face.

Bradbury Thurlow Jr.

Wearing a Tuxedo of all things.

"What? Think you're James Bond now?"

He threw a punch.

It hit.

Then another.

And another.

After those I lost count.

Dreamed I was watching a tennis match.

The ball was my head.

When the game was over I spit blood.

Tried to spit it at him.

But it just drooled down my chin and onto my new TeRF shirt.

"Know how much money you cost me, you son of a bitch?" he said.

"Fuck you."

"Your fag son killed my partner."

"Yes, I know."

"Wow, you know?"

"Isn't that great."

"The great Bradbury Thurlow—"

"Look, Krieg."

"I know you want justice."

"And I'm going to give it to you."

BLACK SAGE

Past the Palmdale-Lancaster shit sprawl.

An endless alphabet of streets.

Houses for no reason.

People for no reason.

Still Los Angeles.

County.

I didn't have far to go.

One floor.

The Bradbury Building.

My locker was on the fourth floor.

TeRF inhabited the fifth.

Internal Affairs, three.

IA thought the building was too frilly.

Maybe.

Marble and curled iron.

Shiny brick and glossy wood.

Skylit.

Open.

Not a place for cops.

They should be.

Underground.

Buried.

For a Killer it was.

I took the marble stairs down to the fourth.

The locker room was empty.

Changed into my spare suit.

A Midnight-Blue Nighthawk.

Stealth Suit.

Fresh white shirt, Bogart tie.

My body was stiff.

Arthritic.

Still.

Down to the garage.

My old Fueltility.

Mojave.

Cloud shadows.

White dick propellers.

"… several people shot at blowshops across Los Angeles. Gunmen wearing horse masks …"

Los Diablos straddled the L.A. River between Bandini and Vernon.

Casino, restaurants, shopping.

The Inferno:

A *Pirates of the Caribbean*–style ride through Hell.

Fifty bucks a head.

Supposed to take a half hour.

Place was lit up.

Like Vegas.

Only with less lights.

Limos and bimbos.

The wealthy.

And the well preserved.

Crowds of the self-important.

The Mayor.

Turn the Fueltility around.

I wasn't going.

Claire.

Thurlow said she'd been given the place at La Brea Gardens for services rendered.

We hadn't gotten in.

But Thurlow owned the place.

So.

I could go to her when I was done.

Start over.

Go to her now.

No.

The Mayor didn't matter.

But Mars did.

Claire.

She would be waiting.

I almost believed it.

I turned back.

Parked.

Gave my ticket at the entrance and security scanned me and passed me through.

First thing was to get a lay of the place.

Or enough of a lay to formulate a plan.

An escape.

I called Claire.

Four rings.

"Hey, I . . . I talked to . . . no matter . . . I know everything now. And it's *okay*. Whatever there was . . . I hope we can . . . well, I hope we can start over . . . fresh . . . and . . . look, I got something I need to do, so I'll call you later and we can meet and . . . Okay, I'll call you soon. Bye."

I made a face after leaving a message like that and this woman gives me a look.

An L.A. face.

Prude and pornographic.

Manic and moronic.

Eye-fi's and puckerpaint.

"Nice face."

She made a face.

Or tried to.

Shit was cemented.

Ain't no real faces anymore.

Car faces, phone faces, computer faces.

TV face.

Can't face the facts.

Or the music.

Scared to look at my own face.

Should get shit-faced.

Later.

The Casino, shops, and restaurants terraced the north side of the river.

Sign near the edge stated that before the river water entered Los Diablos it was treated to the point of being drinkable.

Sign next to that said "No Swimming."

On the other side was the Inferno ride.

Like some giant Italian Villa on a hill.

Or the Getty in Malibu.

Can't blame the city for trying to make things look like somewhere else.

I crossed a bridge to the other side and took the handicapped ramp up.

Too many heads on the stairs.

Shooting their phones.

Villa had a central courtyard with a long Olympic-sized pool in the center.

Marble-looking benches and Roman statues with metal fig leaves.

Two long lines on each side.

This was going to take a while.

I got in the left line and added up the heads.

No sign of my prey.

Sign on a column said "No Food or Drink Allowed on the Ride."

Pimple-Pop piping.

That stupid song by what's his name.

Several idiots were either dancing or mouthin to it.

> *Hobnobbin with the hobbin-yerrro-oh.*
> *Hobnobbin with the hobbin-yerrro-oh.*
> *Hobnobbin with the hobbin-yerrro-oh.*
> *Hobnobbin.*
> *Hobnobbin.*

People looked either really happy or really bored.

Laughing too loud or yawning too wide.

Talking.

Jabbering.

Chittering and Chattering.

Crunchin snick-snacks.

Nibblin snob snacks.

Playin their phones.

Gawking through browsers.

People.

Most of them don't even know they exist.

Even if they did.

It wouldn't make any difference.

I pulled my hat low and settled in for the wait.

"I like his brand, he's got a really good brand."

"Yeah, she just graduated."

"Totally want the new Dream Machine."

"But he lives in the slumburbs."

"You don't know what a float is?"

"Totally."

"What's he drive?"

"Esoteric Finance."

"In England they call this a queue."

"A Dodge Columbo."

"Gawd."

"You must be proud."

"It's soda and ice cream, silly."

"They should call it a why."

"This ride needs a FastPass."

"And I need an AssPass."

"Hahahahaha."

Near the head of the line.

Or the part that was about to leave the courtyard and enter the building.

Thurlow's kid.

He'd just entered the courtyard with a group of people.

A blonde chick and a bunch of young, rich designer jerks.

All of them were wearing high-brows.

They stood at the end of the pool.

Between the lines.

Talking to each other in that weird-necked way people do when they're browsing.

Laughing the laughs of the undeserved and pampered.

Not real laughs.

Get in line, you Fucks.

"S'the Mayor," a woman next to me pointed.

Heads all turned to an amorphous entourage orbited by heavily armed BlackGuards.

Mayor was in the center with his wife and two kids.

Various other important city jerks.

Including the Chief of Police.

So these two groups stood there talking and waving.

And then my line entered the building and I lost sight of them.

If they were getting on this ride my guess was that they weren't gonna wait in line.

They were gonna be VIP'd to the front.

Which meant that they could get on and off this ride before I ever got on.

Couldn't tell how much further this line was gonna stretch.

Up ahead it made a right ten yards up.

And what about the opposite line—were there two separate rides?

Shit.

Either way I wasn't gonna wait in this line any longer.

Thing to do would be to get on now.

And try to get off somewhere in the middle of it.

Ambush them.

I pulled out the police badge and started buzzing my way to the head of the line.

Suit had already been set to fuzz, so surveillance shouldn't be a problem.

Except it was a little over a year old.

Maybe out of date with current BBTV.

Signs along the way warned of possible heart attacks and whiplash.

Had to warn similar harm to a few surly zeros who didn't like me passing.

Possible head cracks and face smashes.

Eventually I came out into a large, dim cavern.

Each line sloping down from opposite sides to converge on two separate and parallel channels filled with small boats.

Boats had four rows that seated four in each row.

Once the people were seated, the boats in each channel started off in a staggered pattern and entered a dark tunnel.

Thunder and screams.

The people coming out of the ride were exiting the boats full of excited faces and awesomes.

Some were crying.

Must be a good ride.

A hand on my chest.

"Just where do you think you're going?"

BlackGuard chick.

Black.

Elevated my badge to her face.

"Yeah, so?"

"Give me the back row."

"You want fries with that?"

"Huh?"

"You can't just roll up here with your badge like that."

"I just did."

She chinked her eyes at me.

"You LAPD think the world is just one big donut shop, don't you?"

"That doesn't make sense."

"Neither do you."

"I'm here for the Mayor."

"Well, he ain't here."

"He's coming, I'm an advance guard."

"Advance guard?"

"Yeah, for security."

"We already got security."

"Just give me a back row, sister, you're holding up the ride."

She turned her head.

Two employees.

Faces holo'd with skulls.

Stood and waited near the boat.

"I'm going to have to call this in."

"Man, you BlackGuard are all alike, always tryin to one up the cops."

"I ain't trying to do anything, I'm just doin my job."

"You do that, sister, meanwhile I'm getting on."

It was a sixty-forty call.

Sixty she'd physically try to stop me.

Forty she'd succeed.

But then what if she was wrong.

BlackGuard already in the shit as far as the City was concerned.

"Fine, but I ain't your sister."

The skull-faced kids backed away as I approached and took the back seat.

Then they let the rest in.

Some chump tried to get in the back row with me, but the kids steered him to the row ahead.

Even so, he thought he'd complain.

"Why cannot I not sit in the row there?"

Sounded German.

Figures.

"Police business—no one gets in back."

He heard me, but decided to ignore me.

Problem with people today.

Expect too much customer service.

Even from the cops.

He tugged at one of the kids and asked the same question.

"Uh, because no one can sit there," she said.

"Please fasten your belt."

"Yes, but he is sitting there."

Okay, enough.

"Hey. Hey, you."

I had to say it a couple more times before he turned.

When he did I badged him.

"Police, now shut your mouth."

Couldn't blame him though.

He was sitting next to a fat kid with the word *MeasleMob* across the back of his fat T-shirt.

Kid had spent the last minute furiously digging into his nose.

The woman next to the kid.

Presumably his mother.

Was looking the other way.

Talking to this dude.

Presumably his father.

Figured I should intervene:

I flicked the kid in the back of the head.

"Hey, kid, no nose pickin on this ride."

Which only made the kid jam into his nose more.

Now the German flags the attendant:

"Mistress, can I use mine handy on this ride?"

"Uh, excuse me?"

He held up his hand and shook it, thumb and pointer finger a few inches apart:

"Minah handy, can I use it?"

"Uh, I don't—"

"He wants to know if he can jerk off on this ride," I say.

"Uh . . ." The attendant looks at me like I should do something.

"Yo, Hansel."

I flick him on the shoulder and he turns.

Give him the proper jerk-off sign, up and down, up and down, using my fist.

"You can't jerk off on this ride."

"You do I'll throw you off."

To the girl.

"Maybe you should throw him off now."

Girl gives me a frightened-disgusted look.

Like she doesn't want to touch him.

"Uh, sir? Uh, you can't jerk off—"

"No, no, no. No jerk off," he says, doing the proper jerk-off sign now.

He fished into his pants.

"Uh, sir—"

"Dude," I say, grabbing his shoulder.

"What the Fuck I just say?"

He pulled out a phone.

"Mine handy."

"Uh, your phone?" the girl said.

"Yes, minah phone. Picture."

"We call it a phony here," I say.

Just then the lady next to the nose-pickin kid turns to him.

"Maximus!"

And slaps his hand from his face.

The ride begins to move.

Soon as she turns back, he jams it in again.

Maximus.

I don't like this kid.

Should stick him during the ride.

Thurlow's BDG pen.

Had taken it from his shirt pocket.

Taken is not the right word.

Even though he never offered it.

Initials on it and everything.

Still can't get my head around his deal.

After he unstrapped me he wanted me to strap him in.

Which I did.

Said the Mayor had screamed at him.

BlackGuard was done.

No more city contracts.

No TeRF.

No nothin.

The Sunset Fiasco had been the final straw.

Fiasco?

Yeah, thanks to you, Thurlow said.

The City was cutting off all ties.

Now.

Here's the deal.

I'll let you go.

Do the Mayor.

Maybe his wife.

Kids too.

Your call.

Then we're even.

Even?

Your son killed my partner.

What about that.

His son, he said.

His son was out of control.

And it was his fault.

Him.

Yes, him.

The great Bradbury Thurlow.

He'd gone too far.

Gotten too arrogant.

Too hubristic.

Hubris.

You know what Hubris is?

Jesus.

The disease of the powerful.

He had contracted it apparently.

Had become too inflated.

Thinking he was unstoppable.

That BlackGuard was unstoppable.

And look what happened.

They were going to come after him.

Pin it all on him.

Not the City.

Unless he did something.

Unless I did something.

So.

He was going to sacrifice his only begotten son.

Yeah, he said that.

He knew about blood.

Blood for blood.

The Mayor's blood for his.

His son's blood for me.

Take my son.

Okay, I said.

But first.

First I had to do him.

Punish him.

Punish him good.

So I did.

You don't need the details.

Just that I didn't TeRF him.

I did it basic.

With my fists.

Even though he begged.

Screamed.

To be violated.

Humiliated.

A whole litany of things he wanted done.

Prayed would be done.

I didn't.

Guess that was his real torture.

I stuck the capsule Anita had given me in his mouth.

Swallow that if you want a real ride.

"Abandon All Hope, Ye Who Enter."

What the demon face said as we entered the tunnel.

And then:

"But do not abandon your personal items."

"Please remember to secure all wallets, purses, phones, and loose change."

"Or they will burn forever in the fires of hell."

I checked to see that all my shit was tight.

Especially the pen.

Was going to need that.

And then we dropped.

It was steep and fierce.

Couldn't see anything but black.

A damp wind howling into my face.

And then we hit bottom with a terrific splash.

Screams and cries all around.

The boat settled.

Laughs of relief.

Light.

A burning red sky, embers raining down just out of reach.

Winged figures in the distance.

Falling.

Plunging into the black water.

Faint smell of chlorine.

People oohed and aahed at how hellish it all was.

Fingers pointing.

It was pretty hellish.

And then.

Skeletal limbs and bodies.

Exploded out of the dark, choppy waters.

Corpse faces.

Screaming heads and flailing limbs.

Everywhere trying to surface.

Everyone screamed.

"Oh my god!"

A pale arm reached out of the black water at me that made me shout, "Shit!"

Someone in our boat cried, "Look!"

Approaching us from behind was another boat.

Large and monstrous.

At the helm was a giant demon mountained with muscles.

Skin the color of ash.

As it passed between the boats this giant turned its head in our direction.

And bellowed.

A loud bass foghorn.

Exactly the same blast PAL would do after beeping and honking in front of my house.

It was a horrible sound.

Everyone leaned back.

A woman in the row just in front of me buried her hands in her face and cried, "No!"

Which made me laugh.

The hell boat passed us to land on a rocky shore up ahead.

Behind which rose a high black cliff.

Ten stories at least.

Then our boat hit the shore.

It left the water and began picking up tremendous speed.

The G's were tremendous, jerking my neck back against the seat padding.

We were heading through an obsidian cragged landscape towards the black entrance of a giant cave.

And as soon as we entered, our boat did a dizzying corkscrew before ascending almost straight up.

And then we dropped.

Violently to the bottom of a dark cavern.

Where the brakes were applied with whiplash force.

And then we proceeded at our normal pace again.

Clickety-clacking.

Neck was Fucked.

I massaged it.

Turning my head left and right.

See if it still had the usual turnability.

I looked up.

No good.

The strain was unbearable.

Dark stalactites pointed down threateningly overhead.

Or is it stalagmites?

They were gonna fall.

Yeah.

They were.

They didn't.

A giant tremor.

Shook the whole cavern.

For a second I wondered if this was part of the ride or an actual earthquake.

Until I saw the beast.

Looming above and reclining against a slope in the cavern.

A building-sized giant with the body of a serpent below the waist.

Head bearded and crowned like a king.

It extended a monstrous arm, the tail slithering within inches of our boat.

"I am Minos," the voice boomed. "And thou art judged!"

"Descend!"

We did.

Fast.

Down, down, down.

Until we splashed into water.

We were in a concrete channel.

Drifting towards a city skyline.

Los Angeles.

This must be the river.

Drifting.

Gently through a ghetto now.

Sirens in the distance.

Dark shapes slumped against graffitied walls.

Buildings on fire.

Screams.

Deranged Niggers with guns began to shoot at us.

Bottles flew over our heads.

Then some cops.

In that famous formation.

Beating a Nigger.

Screams.

We floated further through more hellish scenes from the history of Los Angeles.

A dam collapse.[*]

The Manson murders.

The 710 Mega-Crash.

Zoot Suit Riots.

Even the Big One.

It was too much really.

Alternating between water ride and roller coaster.

A tar pit with saber-toothed cats and mammoths.

Where we watched an Indian woman get her head bashed in with a rock.

Earthquakes.

Fires.

Floods.

Hollywood and Vine.

The Hollywood sign.

Almost forgot what I was there to do until we entered what looked like the open night air.

City Hall rising above us.

---

[*]   St. Francis Dam collapse, March 12, 1928.

Framed with klieg lights.

Except.

It had eyes.

Arms.

Three hideous mouths.

The mouths roared like rush-hour traffic.

Distorted horns.

Around us.

On either side.

Bodies stuck in the pavement at various angles.

Writhing.

One of City Hall's arms plucked one of the bodies out of the pavement.

And began to eat it.

Can't fight City Hall I guess.

A few feet from me a torso that looked like O. J. Simpson.

Talked like O. J. Simpson.

Tellin me he wasn't guilty.

The butler did it.

I took this as my cue and jumped ship.

Used him for cover.

None of the other passengers appeared to have noticed.

All eyes were on City Hall.

I crouched behind O. J. and surveyed the surroundings.

Hopefully the surroundings weren't surveying me.

But then again.

Hope happens when you do nothing.

Couldn't see much.

The place was strobed.

Had to put on the NightShades to counter the effect.

The boats were organized in groups of four.

Two staggered on each track with about fifty feet between each group.

Thurlow's boat shouldn't be too far back.

If he even got on.

Could do a search, but that could backfire.

Trace me instead.

Have to use my eyes.

O. J. wouldn't shut up.

Kept playin his Deathbed confession.

He did it.

But he didn't.

It was his double.

The one the media made.

The Juice.

He was gonna die.

But his double would live.

Forever.

And then the monster hand grabbed him up.

Next closest body.

Run.

Slipping over the smooth polished floor.

Like ice.

Charles Manson.

Couldn't tell what he was saying.

Sounded like nonsense.

Blabbering.

Gibbering.

Wouldn't shut up.

Must be malfunctioning.

Figure that.

I punched him in the head.

"Skippidty-bop do bop skippitdy-do."

Again.

"You've got to accept yourself as God and the Devil."

Another one.

"I'm beyond good and evil, baby."

One more.

That shut him up.

Enough.

Keep your eyes out for Thurlow.

And City Hall.

Don't want to be too close when Manson gets plucked.

Claire.

If what Anita said was true.

Then.

Things were reversed now.

She had always known what I was.

And I hadn't known what she was.

Couldn't tell if I felt better or worse.

Had it all been an act?

No.

Couldn't believe it.

Not because of the good times.

The affection.

But because of all the bad times, the fights.

Her resentments.

Like about that dude.

What's his name.

The one with PTSD.

That served in Operation . . .

Something.

This one friend Claire and Synnita and their whole circle were all so concerned about.

The one who'd "seen things."

All the stuff that makes war, war.

But, like I told Claire, not *personally*.

He had commanded a regiment of bugs.

Remotely.

From Nevada.

And was apparently haunted by the "footage."

Ended up killing himself.

Like I told Claire, it's one thing to see the dead.

But to smell the dead.

This dude got worked up for nothing.

I mean hadn't this bastard ever watched the news?

Might as well have said he got PTSD from that.

He'd "seen things."

Jesus.

But it wasn't that I was playin this dude down that really got to Claire.

Which it did.

It was when one of her stupid friends said, "Thank you for our freedom," to this guy.

"Thank you for our freedom."

That in this day and age people still believe shit like that.

Like Santa Claus.

So I had to straighten her out.

Called her a fat ass.

Fatberg.

Something like that.

She was pretty fat.

Claire wouldn't speak to me for a few days.

Said I was insensitive.

Jealous.

Jealous of what?

Jealous that this guy had feelings.

Compassion.

That he cared.

That even if it was a phony war.

The fact that he believed in what he was doing.

Plus the fact that he felt bad.

About what he did.

The fact.

Jesus.

The facts:

The dude was playin with RC bugs!

Like a kid.

Any idiot with a computer could see the footage on TerrorTube.

Me.

I was in the thick.

Covered in blood.

Okay, not covered maybe.

But splattered at least.

Eatin rats.

Soggy tack.

What about that?

Huh?

Studies have shown, she said.

That remote soldiers suffer more stress, not less, than soldiers that were actually there.

Remote soldiers.

Bullshit.

Well, when *you* talk about *your* war you kind of sound like you're bragging.

He doesn't.

Which proves.

Bragging?

A man survives a bloody terror war.

Helps win it in fact.

Don't you think he's entitled to a little bragging?

We didn't really win that war, she said.

Whatever—we accomplished it.

Our mission.

Not really, she said.

So, what then?

I gotta catch some PTSD to get some Fuckin sympathy?

You can't catch PTSD, she said.

You can catch anything.

No.

It couldn't have all been an act.

Couldn't.

No, there was something.

Had to be.

Like when you fall in Love with your captor.

Except I wasn't her captor.

Still.

Maybe we can hit the reset button.

Start over.

Honestly this time.

No.

I wasn't seeing things straight.

Refusing to look at them square.

I was.

There.

Sitting in the second row in the middle of the leading boat.

Thurlow the Third.

Looked like him.

No.

Couldn't tell.

But the Mayor.

That was him alright.

In front with his wife.

So it had to be Thurlow behind.

Recognize some of his entourage too.

I watched them pass without any thought of what I was going to do.

I looked up at City Hall eating those bodies.

Eyes rolling savagely in its pointed head.

Like a dunce.

Looked back to where O. J. had been.

Hoping he was there.

He was.

Hope.

No accident it rhymes with dope.

Get ready.

It's now or never.

Now.

Get up.

Charge.

A cock pokes me in the eye.

Manson elbows me in the crotch.

More like I crotched Manson in the elbow.

Vision was blocked.

Cock-blocked.

A pop-up.

Snake Oil®—Increase Your Piece!

Flashing in my eyes.

Wink out of it.

Do this again.

Soon as I start the hand grabs me.

And Manson.

We're lifted.

Squeezed.

A Satanic Rapture.

He's gibbering again.

Speaking in tongues.

He was soft.

But his bones, his frame, must have been metal.

Crushing my ribs.

If this hand squeezed any tighter I was done.

It was squeezing tighter.

So this is how it ends.

If I would've known I would've hid behind someone more fitting.

Like him.

The Night Stalker.

In the other hand.

Staring blankly at me like a malfunction.

The same words over and over.

"Hail Satan."

"Hail Satan."

Yeah.

Here comes the mouth.

Least I wasn't going to really get eaten.

But then again.

The mechanics of this thing might shred me.

Must be some channel or line that feeds them back to the floor.

Like in a bowling alley.

No.

I dove just as the hand started to release its grip.

Caught the edge of the mouth.

Hanging now.

Dangling.

Manson's legs kicking above me as the mouth started chewing.

Wouldn't've been that bad if the lower jaw wasn't jerking me up and down.

Up and down.

Drop was at least.

It wasn't too far.

But far enough.

Fall would break me.

Body didn't look climbable.

Couldn't see a foothold.

Maybe up.

Climb up its head.

That looked doable.

Least I wouldn't be hanging.

Manson almost swallowed now.

And soon the arm would.

Yeah, wait for the arm.

But I can't wait.

Gonna fall.

Christ.

Couldn't climb up if I wanted to.

And then the lights came on.

Bright as cop lights.

The mouth stopped chewing.

No more screams.

No more thunder.

"Sir, please stay where you are. Don't move."

Yeah.

Turn my head as far as I can.

The ride had stopped.

Everyone was looking.

Pointing.

Smiling.

Some of them looked like they'd been laughing.

Could see Thurlow.

His boat was just about to exit the room.

Lookin up at me.

Laughing and pumping a jerk-off fist.

Jerk.

"Sir, you okay."

Not a question.

An L.A. sir.

Just one pull-up.

All I need.

Just one.

"Sir, don't move."

I pulled.

And pulled.

Nothing.

Please.

Kicking my legs.

Pull.

"Sir!"

Pull.

C'mon.

Get up into that mouth.

"Sir, stop moving, we're getting you down."

Half-up.

Wriggling like mad.

Kicking.

And gibbering.

Bleaaaayeah!

Can understand why those workout jerk-offs.

Hyeaaaaah!

Make noises like they do.

They're just bustin their.

"Sir, stop now!"

I'm in.

Feel like laughing.

Not now.

Later, when I'm out.

Further into the mouth.

Crawl over the tongue.

Yeah, there was a tongue.

Manson up ahead.

Back of the mouth.

Clamped.

Held with what looked like large clamps.

"Sir!"

Have to crawl over Manson.

And then a straight drop down the throat.

Another body about ten feet.

I dropped to it.

Balanced on the soles of its feet.

Arms out against the wall.

Climb down it.

Upside-down face.

Don't recognize it.

Do a face recognition.

Loading . . .

Problem with browsers.

Waste your time browsing.

Keep going.

The next drop wasn't so good.

Legs scissored out and I crotch-saddled onto the feet.

Let out a yell.

Sure they heard it.

Browsers got a match.

David Miscarriage.

Miscavige.

Scientologist.

Never heard of him.

Couldn't do another drop like that.

Seeing white.

Feeling weak.

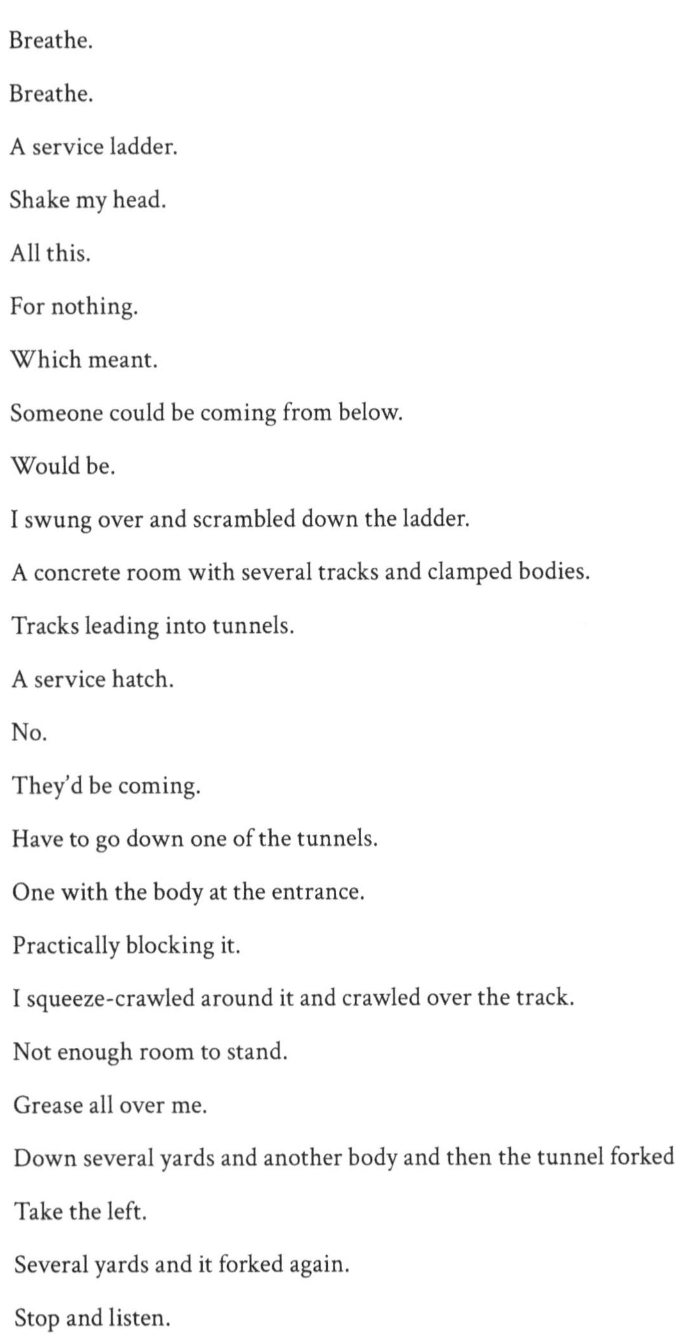

Breathe.

Breathe.

A service ladder.

Shake my head.

All this.

For nothing.

Which meant.

Someone could be coming from below.

Would be.

I swung over and scrambled down the ladder.

A concrete room with several tracks and clamped bodies.

Tracks leading into tunnels.

A service hatch.

No.

They'd be coming.

Have to go down one of the tunnels.

One with the body at the entrance.

Practically blocking it.

I squeeze-crawled around it and crawled over the track.

Not enough room to stand.

Grease all over me.

Down several yards and another body and then the tunnel forked.

Take the left.

Several yards and it forked again.

Stop and listen.

Silence.

Can't hear anyone.

Probably keep the ride stopped till they find me.

They won't.

Here's what I do.

This body here.

See if I can get it off the clamps.

Can't.

Maybe further on.

Find one about to be unclamped.

Okay, this one.

Standing straight up and half-clamped.

Some chick.

Ugly.

Brown hair.

Flower dress.

Bit of a mustache.

Take off the dress.

Big enough to pull down over the suit.

Let's see if the head.

Or the face.

No.

I come out there trying to wear that face people are gonna freak.

Or the dress.

Nigger in a dress.

Gotta see if I can pop out near the back of the room.

Then sneak over to the exit tunnel.

First.

Climb up the chick.

Stand on the clamp.

Cover of the hole is rubber.

With a slit.

Easy.

Get a look.

I'm about halfway between the figures near the track and the ones at the back.

Place is lit up bright.

Boats stopped.

Cops and security all over the place.

One suddenly appears from behind the body straight ahead.

Browser lamps full beam.

Shit.

Might've seen me.

Back down.

He wants to look down here he's gonna have to crouch and pull back the rubber.

Come on.

Crouched down on the clamp.

Come on.

See the light.

Yeah, come on.

Another five seconds and then his face.

White in my eyes.

Poke him in the forehead with the pen and pull on his head.

It works.

Tumbles easy from his crouch.

So do I.

Fall back on my ass.

Railed in the back by the track.

White again.

A million little knife pricks.

Shit.

Fuck.

Might as well hit myself with the pen.

Try to get up.

I do.

It's not good though.

Something is Fucked.

Can barely turn.

Dude is worse.

Already goin black.

Body upside down.

Doin a sixty-nine with the mustache.

Neck bent up about ninety.

Lookin at me.

Light beamin from his browsers.

Mouth in a growl.

Pull off his browsers and snap them.

Black seepin into his eyes.

Fuckin BlackGuard.

Take off his jacket.

Check his belt.

He's got some spray.

And a Gatwitzer.

Good.

But not that good.

Voices above.

"Where's Doug?"

"Check over here."

Gotta pull his body back.

"You Doug?" I say.

He doesn't answer.

Get him back enough, but my back has had enough.

Unholster the Gat.

Pull off the spray.

Need to spray my back.

Light.

Someone lookin down now.

Shit.

They're gonna put their head all the way through.

See me easily.

Put his jacket over his head.

Turn my browser beams on.

Back up a few.

A few more.

Shine the light straight towards the hole.

Another light.

Angled right at his feet.

"Doug?"

"Shhhh."

All I can say.

"You get him?"

"Mmmm-hmmmm."

"Over here!"

Shit.

"Think we got him!"

"Over here!"

Foot stamps over my head.

A herd of them running over.

Click the lights off.

Pick up his jacket and go back down the track.

395.

Dead road.

Dead lake.

Death Valley.

Lone Pine.

At the intersection of the 395 and the 136.

I pulled over at the visitor center.

136: Death Valley.

Maybe that was the place to go.

Get lost in the heat and sand.

Leave my bones.

I got out of the car and stretched in the night air.

Pieces of the sky that weren't overcast were splattered with stars.

Dark shapes of the Sierras in the west.

Another dark range in the east.

A desert smell.

Or something else.

Don't know.

It wasn't L.A.

Sage maybe.

The smell.

Maybe that's all I need.

Smell something different.

And be something different.

Simple.

Yeah.

Gotta get off this ride.

And I ain't even on it.

Gonna be part of it soon.

Every day.

Get eaten by City Hall.

"Who's that guy?"

"Some killer."

No.

Not one of them chumps up there has got my.

You know I'm gonna get out.

Even with these bugs roachin the tunnels now.

Buzzin.

Got my suit.

Don't fail me.

This tunnel here.

Should take me to the far corner of the room.

The last two didn't.

It does better.

Got a service door.

Steps going up.

To some dudes waiting.

Talkin.

"Bugs'll get him. No way he's getting out now."

"Pretending to be a cop."

"Yeah, that he even got on the ride."

Fuck it.

What are the chances they got a full ID?

Put on the BlackGuard jacket and walk up.

"Shit," I say. "Dude got me."

"What?"

"MotherFucker kicked me in the back."

"What? Where?"

"Here"—hand the dude the spray—"spray me."

Pull off the jacket and turn around, pull up my shirt.

"What? Where is he?"

"Down there somewhere."

"I thought they weren't letting anyone down."

"They aren't, but the MotherFucker got Doug. I ain't waitin for no bugs. Now spray."

He sprays me.

Back goes cold then warm.

Then numb.

Tuck in my shirt:

"Thanks."

"Hey, what detail you on?" he said.

"This one, MotherFucker."

Pen the first dude on the chin and the other in the neck.

Down.

Didn't have to do that.

But I did.

Now.

Roll their bodies down the steps.

And get out of there.

It was all chaos out in the courtyard.

Security swarming.

BlackGuard.

I laughed.

Probably their last day on the job.

A few inquired what was going on as I passed:

"Terrorist attack."

Astonished gasps.

Everyone believes a terrorist attack.

At the front gate they weren't letting anyone in or out.

And as I tried to walk out, one of the guards grabbed my arm.

"Hey, you're Villa DT. True someone assassinated the Mayor?"

"Yeah."

"No shit!"

He said it like it was the funniest thing he had ever heard.

"Excuse me," I say, "gotta make sure the coroner's got clearance."

"Oh, yeah," he said, "go on."

I walked out and got in the Fueltility and headed to Fort La Brea.

Call Claire.

No answer.

I did a search, but it never got past *Searching . . .*

I called again.

Kept trying the whole way there.

Useless.

It was easier getting in this time though.

Just had to show the guy the BlackGuard security badge.

I pulled up in front of Claire's unit.

Our unit.

I yanked off the security jacket, lit a smoke, and got out.

Woman wearing smartpants walking a dog.

Poodle-looking thing.

She looks at me.

"You can't smoke in here."

"Ah, that's just the pants talking."

She makes a noise and walks on.

Smart.

I walked up to the front door.

Should've crawled.

There were no lights on inside, but I rang the bell anyway.

Useless.

Hope.

It's like a disease.

That springs infernal.

I walked around back.

Sliding glass door.

Unlocked.

Remember something about them saying you didn't have to lock your doors in this place.

Just like old-town America.

But without the old-town Americans.

Something like that.

Place was empty.

Nothing to indicate that she'd even been here.

Upstairs.

There was a familiar smell in the master bath.

Antiseptic and orange.

Shit.

One of the shower doors was missing.

Crouch to the floor to look for signs.

Broken glass.

Blood.

Nothing.

Wouldn't be a mess anyways.

The guard was on me before I heard a sound.

Another stealth suit.

"Hey, what are you doing in here?"

I turned around.

"Don't move," he said, holding his piece out.

A Gatwitzer.

"I'm looking for a girl."

"Aren't we all."

"Red hair, this tall—goes by the name Claire."

"She ain't here."

"You've seen her then?"

"I ain't seen shit, now get on the ground."

"I'm a cop."

"And I'm the pope, now get the Fuck on the ground before I—"

"Here, show you my badge."

I pulled my badge.

"That ain't a police badge, that's a BlackGuard—"

"Wrong badge."

I threw it at him.

That caught him off guard enough for me to lunge and grab and snap his Gat wrist back.

Allowing him a little scream.

I beat him on the temple with the side of the gun until he was ready to lie down quiet.

Dude was polite.

Kept sayin "Please," every time I hit him.

Which made me hit him faster and faster to see if he'd say please faster and faster.

He couldn't keep up.

I went back downstairs and walked straight out the front door.

That smell.

Fuckin Rakers.

Anita.

Find out what the deal is.

I called her from the Fueltility.

No answer.

No voice either.

I got back out.

Didn't know what to do.

I walked down the sidewalk and tried to think.

But I didn't like what I was thinking so I stopped.

What time was it? About 10:30.

Have to get out of L.A. soon.

Now.

Don't trust them.

If they can remotely subtract.

By satellite.

Then I'm.

Where was I gonna go?

There was nothing.

Sooner or later someone or something would get me.

The best thing for me was to do it myself.

Finish it.

I went back to the Fueltility and called Anita again.

Nothing.

I got out and paced around in the middle of that fake street.

Fuckin cobblestones.

The Fuck are people thinking?

Face it.

Claire's gone.

No.

I've got to find her.

I need to know.

And then there she was.

Right there.

Here.

She was taller than I imagined.

Blonde hair pulled up and wrapped for business.

Pink top and smartshorts.

Running right towards me.

She pulled up.

Stopped.

Put up her hands.

Wasn't sure she was really there for a second.

Pull off my browsers.

Chink my eyes.

Puttin up her hands like that.

Kinda funny.

Makin some kind of joke or something.

Don't get it.

Still.

I laugh.

"Of all the people in the."

"Reina Hawthorne."

"Please," she said.

"You a jogger?"

She started to back away.

"My wife, she's your biggest."

She kept backing up.

Towards her.

"Heard you live here."

Backing.

"So does my—"

She turned and ran.

"Hey. Where you?"

Jesus.

Who she think she's.

Better than me.

Should shoot her.

Yeah.

No.

Look.

Gat still out.

Blood splattered on my shirt.

Shit.

Trotting now.

Catch her.

No.

Wait.

Stop.

I mean no harm.

It was this security guard.

BlackGuard.

You know how they.

Stop.

She won't.

She's really runnin.

Bookin.

Hoofin it all out.

Again.

Stop.

Stop.

Stop!

"Claire!"

Fuck it.

She ain't getting away.

Running after her now.

Like a predator.

Down the cobblestone street and through the gardens.

She could run.

She ran to the edge of the complex and into the private tunnel that went below the street and out to the museums.

Hit the tunnel:

Green grass under a blue sky dotted with thick cotton ball clouds.

The sweet scent of flowers on a light breeze.

She was just ahead.

Hair flowing behind her.

It wasn't.

Just those fake walls.

Fake grass.

Made it all flow.

Like I was running after Love.

After Claire.

Gonna catch her soon and we're gonna kiss and roll on that green grass.

We'll lie and watch the clouds cross the sun until the dusk rolls over us like a soft blanket and the first stars blink into sight.

Only you and I.

Only you and I.

My Love.

Run.

Faster.

Faster.

Then I was out and the abrasive black air hit my lungs.

I was out of breath and she was gone and there was only the tar pits up ahead.

Couldn't move.

Had to catch my breath.

I turned back and looked towards the tunnel.

Maybe the tunnel had more than one direction.

Maybe she had run off somewhere into that blue horizon.

I put the Gat away and walked towards the pits through the grass and the trees.

I passed the museum and came out at the pits.

The pit was lit up and a work crew was lifting one of the mammoths out with a crane.

A crowd of people watched the mammoth.

Being saved from extinction.

Lights blazed over the whole spectacle like it was all being made into a major motion picture.

It was.

It wasn't a real work crew.

They were filming a movie.

A PA backed me off.

"Sir, we're shooting. You need to go over there."

I couldn't think of any other moves so I decided I would do what the rest of the crowd was doing.

Stare.

I walked up the front steps of the museum and edged my way through the crowd watching from the deck above.

The motor of the crane rumbled loud with combustion and the mammoth dangled, swaying slightly back and forth in midair.

Back and forth.

Someone yelled, "Cut!"

People watched and talked and pointed.

A man next to me lifted his boy up to see and the boy pointed while the father filmed.

I watched and forgot and tried to remember if I had ever been here before.

If I had ever been as mindlessly fascinated about anything as these people seemed to be.

Problem with life is that you have to be kind of stupid to enjoy it.

Stupid enough to edit out all the horrible facts.

Still.

I stood with those people like I was one of them.

Maybe if I stood here long enough I could.

One of them.

No.

I was sweating.

Sweating hard.

Where was she?

She was nowhere.

She had gotten away.

She was gone.

She could have been here and I could have put my arm around her and pointed at the rising beast too.

Then we could have walked away holding hands and saying things like "Where do you want to eat?"

"I don't know, where do you want to eat?"

"I don't know," I say.

The man with the kid turned and looked at me.

And then turned back.

Fuck it.

Walk down the steps.

Elbow out.

How she used to hang on my arm and talk into my ear.

Did I tell you she was British?

Not British.

English, she said.

There's a difference.

When she spoke.

Her lower lip might angle slightly to the left when opening on a vowel.

Or right when closing on a consonant.

And when her lips pressed together.

The slightest overbite.

Like a child.

Innocent.

We almost touch eyes.

Hers green.

They held me for a second, and I realize that Reina Hawthorne is beautiful.

"Reina Hawthorne!" someone gasps.

Reina Hawthorne turns and pushes blindly through the crowd, running towards the pits.

I follow.

She's running blindly, terrified, and it makes me feel low.

Mad.

Running away.

For no reason.

Claire.

"Never leave me," she said once.

"I won't."

Pull the Gat.

No one seems to notice.

It's only a movie.

Flat.

Enclosed.

Like shootin at a screen.

In an empty theater.

Hit the pause.

The people freeze.

I can take a million years.

An infinity.

She's going straight for the tar.

Aim.

Smashes into a PA.

Aim.

Close to the edge now.

Aim.

Putting on the brakes.

Now.

Click.

Click.

Click.

The shots slam her into the pit with a dull puddle splash.

Yellow water floating on the tar.

The sound of applause.

People filming.

Pointing.

It's only a movie.

The people vanish.

The land around is warm and flat.

Insects click and scratch the air.

The vegetation is green and brown and sways lightly in the breeze.

Animals come to the edge and drink water.

Some enter and die.

A woman.

She stands at the edge of tar.

A shadow approaches.

A man.

Behind her.

Bashes her head and pushes her into the pit.

He turns and approaches.

Smiles.

Hands me the bloody stone.

I take it and he's gone.

The mammoths are gone.

The sun sets and rises again.

Sets and rises.

Sets and rises.

Sets.

Buildings rise and gleam for a few seconds, then crumble and fall.

Ice covers everything and then melts.

The plants return, and the animals.

The animals.

A wolf with the face of a man crouches at the tar edge.

He looks at me and howls.

Screams.

People running.

Mouths open.

Drop the stone.

Turn.

Run.

I leaned against the Fueltility and lit up a smoke and watched the dark Sierras.

Some clouds broke and some moonlight flashed and sharpened the silver edge of one of the peaks.

One of those peaks was supposed to be the highest point in America.

Except for Alaska.

Mt. Whitney.[*]

Didn't know which.

Across the highway, hulking heaps of prehistoric-looking stone.

Headlights and tires crunching gravel.

An old beat-up RV pulled into the parking lot.

It moved slow and seemed to wobble a little as if it was unsure of where it was going.

It moved towards me and pulled within two spaces of where I was.

Blocking half my view.

Huge parking lot and this thing has to park right next to me.

It sat there with the engine running and I could just barely make out a face.

Looking at me.

I was unarmed.

I gave a hard stare in conjunction with a hard flick of the cigarette butt in its direction.

---

[*] Mt. Tumanguya—name was officially changed on July 15, 2064, to the original Paiute, meaning "the very old man."

The face turned and a few moments later the RV backed out and drove away.

I watched as it turned left and then made a right onto the 395.

I lit another cigarette.

Should check into a hotel.

Get a nice room.

Back in the car and up the highway a few miles into Lone Pine proper.

Nothing remarkable.

McDonald's.

Stubbs.

Black Sage Cantina.

Marquee on the cantina says: "Switchback and the Heart Attacks."

Guess the kind of music.

Bunch of small motels.

The largest one: Dow Villa.

Pool Spa.

I pulled in.

An old lady at the desk looked surprised to see me.

Like I was in the wrong place.

But I was dressed in a nice suit.

And her face shifted into a smile.

Asked how she could help me.

I told her I wanted the best room.

This made her go back to her original look for a second.

And then she realized that it was a good thing that I wanted to spend some money in that place.

"I can give you the room John Wayne stayed in."

"John Wayne?"

"Yes, the movie star."

"I know who he is. He stayed here?"

"A lot of famous people stayed here. They film a lot of movies here."

"Did Arthur Lemmings ever stay here?"

"Arthur Lemmings?"

"Yeah, from *The Big Pump*."

"I don't know, but I could check for you."

"No, no. That's okay. Give me the John Wayne. Does it have a view of the mountains?"

It didn't.

But that didn't really matter.

I would have enough time to get acquainted with them.

The room smelled a little old, but that wasn't a problem.

Floral bedspread.

Floral wallpaper that was actually wallpaper, not a screen, but it needed to be replaced.

I didn't have any luggage.

Had hit the 10 right out of La Brea Gardens.

Slamming the Fueltility through traffic.

Swiping.

Smashing.

Ramming.

Like the old days.

Nothing indiscriminate.

Only those who deserved.

Made me feel better.

Especially the looks.

On their faces.

The faces of the rammed.

No one ever expects.

Maybe a honk.

A finger or a shout.

But not this.

The utter helplessness.

Of being plowed.

It was a good farewell.

Los Angeles.

I pulled the bedspread down, got undressed, and crawled into bed.

It wasn't quiet, but it was quiet enough.

Traffic on the highway through town like a slow wind.

It was enough to put me to sleep.

I got up early and took a shower.

Checking out, the young girl at the desk asked me the usual question.

"Did you enjoy your stay?"

She didn't wait for the answer, and I didn't give her one.

I asked her if there was a grocery store and a place to get camping gear and she said both were a block away on opposite sides of the highway.

What about campgrounds?

She slid a pamphlet at me.

Which one was the best?

"That depends," she said. "What do you want?"

To camp.

"Do you fish?"

I just looked at her.

She opened up the pamphlet in front of me and marked one with her pen.

"This one I guess."

"Thanks."

I hit the adventure shop and told the guy I wanted the best shit that money could buy.

But that just opened up a whole slew of questions:

Where are you going?

Camping.

Three season or four season?

Synthetic or down?

"Look," I said. "If you were going where I was going, what kind of shit would you buy?"

Money no object.

I bought it all.

Tent, sleeping bag, sleeping pad, titanium pots, pans.

A luxury camp chair.

And some other shit I was never gonna use.

I went across the street to the small grocery store and bought some meat and wood and some beer and drove up Whitney Portal Road.

The road wound towards the mountains and through the clusters of those stone heaps.

Should've asked the girl why they were named the Alabama Hills.

Most likely named by some crackers.

They looked like they had been shoved up from the depths of the earth in a fit of violence.

Or thrown down hard.

My kind of country.

Mountains like the Alps.

Only three hours from Los Angeles.

It didn't make any sense.

To my right, someone had shoved a large house against the rocks.

A wall of windows faced the mountains.

Wonder if they got bored looking at them.

It didn't seem possible.

Insignificant maybe.

That you were nothing in the scale of things.

Who could stand that kind of intimidation day in and day out?

Stand to live under that massive weight.

Los Angeles had nothing on this.

Here, the violence was all out in the open.

Not seat-belted behind tinted windows.

Past the stones the road started to ascend gradually towards the mountains.

The whole range stretched to the north like an ancient wall as far as I could see.

Directly to the south it gradually tapered off and there appeared to be a road that cut its way precipitously in zigzags to the top.

Not much further was the turnoff for the campground the girl circled for me.

I didn't turn off.

The road continued to ascend and Zorro itself into the side of the mountain and I wanted to follow it.

The mountains that had seemed two-dimensional from the highway.

Like a flat wall that stopped flush at some imaginary line.

Started to flesh out.

Turn 3-D.

The valley spreads out dizzyingly below.

In another minute I'm in the Portal.

A small indent tucked below the granite peaks.

Numerous tan and scruffed backpackers.

Mostly white.

Families.

Asians, Mexicans.

One—

The crashing of a waterfall.

Behind that, mountain silence.

An immense hum that enclosed all the noise and activity like a fist.

The campground was a wash.

An outdoor motel.

People crammed eyeball to eyeball.

And not really seeming to mind.

So this is camping?

Might as well stay at home and put a tent in your backyard.

I double-parked next to the trailhead.

Went up and looked at the map.

Figure out which one is the tallest.

People passed by and gave me a look.

But only for a second.

A black man in a dark suit doesn't seem to mix too well with white legs and hiking boots.

Anyways I couldn't tell anything from the map so I asked someone.

That one?

No, that one.

It looked like a snow-covered warhead.

Not the tallest-looking one from the highway by far.

How long it take to get to the top?

Maybe a day, maybe two.

Maybe more.

Depends on what shape you're in.

But you need a permit.

I turned around and got back into my car and got out of there.

I drove back down to the campground at the foot of the mountains the girl had recommended.

The first thing I saw when I pulled in was that old RV from the other night.

Crouched in a spot at one end.

Place was almost as bad as the other one.

Everyone shoved together.

The only thing available was a spot right near the entrance.

Number 8.

I pulled in and stretched my legs.

Whitney framed dead center.

Okay.

Pull the supplies out of the Fueltility.

Dude in a golf cart drives up.

Hey.

Hey.

Make sure you put all your food in the box.

What?

Bears, there's bears.

Yeah, okay.

He sat in his cart and watched me pull my shit out.

I put it on the picnic table.

I offered him a beer.

He opened it and took a swig, gave me a thanks, and drove off.

I opened the brand-new tent and pulled out the instructions.

Instructions made it seem harder than it looked.

I balled them up and chucked them into the fire pit.

How hard could it be?

Two poles and a few stakes.

Just look at the picture on the box.

It didn't look like the picture on the box.

So I kicked it down.

Pulled the poles and started to ball it up.

Sleep in the back of the Fueltility.

Then this young white kid with a beard.

Part of the couple who had the site next to mine.

Came over with a howdy, and can I give you some help.

"Be my guest."

He had it up in less than five minutes.

Even took the trouble to explain the whole process to me, which seemed like child's play in his hands.

I tried giving him some cash but he wouldn't hear of it.

Almost seemed offended.

He asked if I had everything I needed and told me to give him a holler if I needed any help.

I asked him if he knew this area.

Like the back of his hand.

"What's that peak right there? The one that looks the biggest?"

"Lone Pine Peak," he said.

I thanked him and forced two beers on him when he wouldn't take a whole six-pack—I had four—and told him I might hit him up later for some more info about the area.

"Where you from?" he asked.

"Los Angeles."

"Me too," he said. "The Valley. It's nice that we got something like this close by."

"Yeah," I agreed. "Yeah."

He went back to his camp, and I straightened out a few things and set up the chair.

Which meant that he had to come back.

This time with his girl.

A mostly attractive blonde that looked more Northern California than Southern.

He showed me how to assemble it, even though it was pretty much already assembled.

"You've got nice stuff," his girl said.

Now it's just me and the chair.

A beer, a smoke, and the mountains.

Repeat.

I was woken up by the kid next door offering me a hot dog.

We were now in the shadow of the mountain.

The edge of dusk.

Black air comin in fast.

I sat there half-asleep and ate the hot dog.

I felt old.

Needed to get out of this suit.

The kid called over and said there was more, but I said I was okay.

I finished eating and went into my tent and changed into a Whitney T-shirt and some khaki camping pants I had bought at the sporting goods store.

Pulled the new hi-tech hiking shoes out of the box and tied them on.

Glad I didn't have a mirror.

If clothes don't necessarily make the man, they can influence how he feels.

I felt like an ass.

Which was better than I've felt in a while.

I must have walked around the campsite looking down at my whole getup long enough to make me look like a total idiot.

Bringing my knees unreasonably high up just so I could put those shoes into the ground.

Test the shocks.

Then.

Fuck the shoes.

When was the last time my feet ever touched the actual ground.

So I had to do that.

It hurt, my feet were so tender, but it felt kind of good.

I stopped when I saw the kid watching me.

"Right on," he said, "right on."

I didn't know what to say so I gave him a thumbs-up.

Clothes like this will make you do things like that.

"Right on," he said again.

I collected some twigs and ripped up a paper bag to use as kindling for the fire.

I arranged the wood in the formation of a teepee and put the kindling and paper inside.

I squirted a good amount of lighter fluid over the whole thing to make sure there was gonna be a fire and lit it.

The flames roared and I jumped back.

A sharp rock poked the bottom of my right foot.

I pulled it up into the air as if to check it and that's when I fell.

Back into the chair, which pushed itself away from me and let me hit my ass on the dirt.

"Are you alright?" the kid again.

"Just fine," I say, "having a conversation with the dirt."

"I got a blanket you can use," he said.

"Thanks, kid, but I'm okay."

I got up and wiped myself off.

I pulled the chair back into position and sat down.

Another beer and a smoke.

It was nice.

Eyes up.

Stars were beginning to scatter.

Shooting stars.

Neck craned, mouth open like a kid.

Couple of times I did a "You see that?"

No one.

I lit another smoke.

At some point the kid came over with a joint and I was out again.

I woke up thirsty.

Everything had stopped.

Night had settled down hard with a silence.

Black punctured with white.

Stars like frozen fireworks.

Thinking about where I could find some water when I heard the moaning.

The kids.

They were going at it.

Rough moans.

Though there was something about it.

Different.

I couldn't place it.

Hard and angry grunts on top of another sound.

Like a melody, out of key and out of sync, that I couldn't place.

Wet.

Desperate.

Heavy breathing when there wasn't any breath left to breathe.

Like someone had knocked the air out of you, and you just wish you could get enough breath, sucking in like it was the last.

My mind was still too smoked.

Half-asleep.

Half-stoned.

Something was happening, but the information wasn't processing.

Had to check myself to confirm if I was really hearing what I was hearing.

But you can't blink your ears into focus like you can with your eyes.

Still.

While my mind was doing all this.

I was heading to their campsite.

Look at all those stars.

The tent was open, the door unzipped.

I pulled back the flap.

A dark figure.

Back to me.

Crouched.

Vigorously pumping an arm into one of the sleepingbagged bodies.

Going: "Yeah . . . Yeah . . . Yeah."

To the rhythm of pitiful moans.

"Yeah," I say.

I reached out and grabbed and caught a fistful of hair.

The figure let out a cry.

I yanked the head and the rest of the body followed.

I dragged and it struggled.

When I got about to the fire pit it took a swing.

It was a bad swing.

Weak.

I caught it by the hand and snapped the wrist, which brought out a sharp yell.

Then.

Still holding head and arm.

I came around.

Straddled the body.

Turned it over and smashed it face-first into the fire pit a couple of times.

Enough to stop it from moving.

I left it there and went to the tent.

The smell of blood woke me up.

Burned the remaining haze out of my head.

They were both still alive.

Barely.

Bleeding heavily.

Figured this was probably some dream.

A residual nightmare of Los Angeles.

Still.

I had to do something.

I turned on a little lantern that hung from the roof of the tent.

The kid was gurgling blood.

Stabbed in the lungs.

Both were pale, the girl's eyes bright and staring at Death.

Didn't look like she'd been raped.

Yet.

There was a phone in a little mesh pocket by her head and I dialed 911 and got through and told the operator what the deal was, and then put the phone back into the mesh pocket without disconnecting.

I tried to stop up the bleeding on the girl, but I didn't know where to start.

The guy had punctured the shit out of her chest and torso.

I left the tent.

The figure was up on all fours, shaking its head and sputtering ash.

I stepped on something.

It was the knife.

Blade almost a foot long with a hilt that looked like it belonged on a sword.

Sirens in the distance.

Good.

Campground host's lights were coming on.

Good.

But not for me.

Didn't want to be questioned by any cops.

I picked up the knife and grabbed the guy.

Put the bloody thing to his throat.

"Let's go."

"Just kill me," he cried, "just kill me."

"You're not getting off that easily."

I dragged him back to my site.

Holstered the knife in the waist of my pants, grabbed a six-pack and smokes.

Yeah, I did all that.

It was awkward doing all of it while holding the guy by the hair.

But he seemed to have been subdued enough not to make me have to break his neck.

Which I told him I would do, among other things, if he made it hard for me to get my beer and my smokes.

When I had these essentials, I hauled him out onto the little campground road.

It was dark.

The only light that huge streak of stars.

The Milky Way.

And here I was.

In the middle of it again.

"Where the Fuck are you parked?"

I didn't wait for the answer.

That old RV.

The one that had pulled up at the visitor's center.

I made him hold the beer.

Then I dragged and beat his ass like a stray dog over to the RV.

Telling him that if he dropped my beer, I was gonna shove his knife up his ass.

At the RV I knocked his head into the door.

"Is this your steed?"

"I . . . I . . . Who are you?"

"I asked you a question. Is this your steed?"

"Steed?"

I dented the door in with his head.

"Don't make me ask you again."

"Yes," he said. "Yes, it is. Oh god."

I tried the door.

It opened.

"Hey, what do you know?"

I heaved him in like a Hefty bag full of trash.

He was.

The keys were conveniently in the ignition, and I sat down and started the thing up with a low vroom.

He was still sputtering on the floor behind me.

A dangerous position in relation to where I was, but I didn't care.

I backed the thing out, and plowed it out of there with the lights off.

Up towards the Portal and away from the sirens.

I threw the knife back at him.

"Try to kill me if you want. Just don't fail."

"Who are you?" he said.

"A guy that needed a vacation that you just Fucked up."

I heard him stand up.

I knew he had the knife.

"C'mon," I say, "do it."

He didn't.

Plopped down in the seat next to me.

Holding the knife.

He was Fucked up.

Face blackened and bloodied.

"Where are we going?"

"Shut up and put on your seat belt."

He put the knife on the dashboard and clicked the belt on.

"And wipe your face."

He did with his shirt.

"My wrist, I think you broke it."

"Good."

Just far enough up the Portal road for a place that was safe enough to turn around.

Which wasn't until we got all the way to the Portal.

Back down the Portal road now.

Past the campground and the flashing lights.

Down the grade that didn't seem like much of a grade coming up.

Until now.

Didn't need to put my foot on the gas.

The thing was picking up speed all by itself.

Flashing lights up ahead.

Two police cars whizzed by.

I made a right on Horseshoe Meadows Road.

Could only make a right on Horseshoe Meadows Road.

Had to hold down the brakes hard.

The RV skidded, and for a second I thought I was going to flip it.

Almost wanted to flip it.

Two wheels for a split second and then we were back on four, headed south.

"Where are you taking me?"

I turned on the radio.

Static.

"This your favorite station?"

"Who are you?"

"No questions until we get where we're going."

"Besides, I don't like the sound of your voice."

An unremarkable man.

White.

Brown curlyish hair.

Dark eyes that were a little too wet for my taste.

Slightly overweight.

Double chin.

Pudgy cheeks.

Nose flat, like a button.

Striped polo shirt with bloodstains.

Cargo pants.

Least he wasn't wearing smartpants.

"You been up this road?" I ask.

"Butcher anyone here in these parts?"

He didn't answer but sat there sulking.

Head down, lips pursed.

Clutching his bloody knife like a toy.

"Answer me, Tubby. You been up here?"

"I thought you didn't want me to talk."

"Said you didn't like my voice."

"Ah, you wounded little caricature."

"Just answer the Fuckin question."

He held up the knife close to his face.

"The road ends at the top."

"There's an overnight campground for backpackers, and equestrian stables."

"The altitude is high, and you might feel dizzy."

It was slow going.

The rig coughed up the sharp and winding road.

Pedal slammed to the floor.

"Thing is crap," I say.

"You wanna get caught or something?"

He didn't say anything.

"Serial killer written all over this thing."

"Or chester."

"Think you'd want to be more incognito."

"Drive a Porsche maybe."

He snorted.

I looked over at him.

He was looking the other way out the window.

There wasn't anything to see on his side.

Just the ghostly face of granite.

My side the drop was so huge I didn't want to look.

"Oh . . . I get it now."

"It's an attention thing, right?"

"You want to get caught."

"Maybe get a little news coverage."

"Give you a name like the RV Killer, right?"

"No?"

"Not good enough, huh?"

"Let's see . . . how about . . ."

He took a lunge at me.

Came at me like a rocket.

Wasn't as lame as I thought.

I pushed my head back and grabbed his wrist right before it almost hit me in the face.

In the face.

The prick.

Had his left with my right.

I yanked him towards me with a snap.

Pulling the knife past my face to hit the window with a tack.

While I slammed him one good in the face with my left.

The two opposing forces enough to pull the arm out of its socket.

He let out a yowl that would have made a wolf proud as the knife dropped in my lap.

I gave him back his arm and grabbed the wheel just in time to make the sharp turn ahead.

Yeah, I did all that.

"Man, you got a whole itinerary of damage."

"Which hurts more?"

"The face?"

"The wrist?"

"Or the shoulder?"

He didn't answer.

"The shoulder I'll bet."

"It's the shoulder."

"Isn't it?"

"Piece of advice."

"You wanna stab a guy."

"Don't do it while he's driving a rig like this on a high and windy road."

"Unless you're suicidal."

"In that instance make your attack right before a real sharp turn."

"The Campfire Killer," he said.

"What?"

"That's what they call me."

"Can you believe that?"

"The Campfire Killer."

"I'll admit," I say.

"It sounds a little weak."

"But maybe that's a good thing for you."

"People aren't as afraid."

"Not as cautious."

"So you can operate with less restraint."

I cracked a beer and gave it to him.

"Help the pain."

He could barely grab it.

"I'm not really a drinker."

"Drink it."

He put the bottle cautiously to his lips and drank.

Blood from his nose poured onto the bottle.

"Wipe your nose."

I stoked the fire a bit more.

And sat back in an old camp chair from his RV.

He had been right.

The air was a little thin here and a lot colder.

Barely anyone.

A fire or two.

In the distance.

Thick, pale pines bleeding sap.

Bear boxes big enough to stuff a body.

"Who are you?" he said.

"Death," I say, lighting a smoke.

He looked at me without saying a word.

"Do you plan on killing me?" he said finally.

"Don't know."

"Was takin a vacation out here when you came along and ruined it."

"Ruined those kids."

"If I had known, I wouldn't—"

"Shut up."

I flicked my butt at him and it hit him on the forehead.

He flinched back and tried to wipe his head but his Fucked-up shoulder wouldn't let him.

Gasping, eyes tearing:

"Just turn me in. Turn me in."

"Oh, you'd like that, wouldn't you."

"Face all over the TV."

He shook his head.

"No, no. You don't understand."

"I'm not doing this for . . ."

"The money?"

"Forget it."

"You wouldn't understand."

"Try me."

"I already have."

"You wouldn't."

"What did you try?"

"I can tell."

"Maybe you've killed, but not like me."

"Ain't gonna argue with that . . ."

"Maybe I should get me one of them serial killer handles like—"

"The Campfire Killer Killer."

"I didn't want to be called that."

"The police gave me that name."

"Where'd you get the idea that you could choose your own name?"

"I didn't think . . . I just thought of a better name, is all."

"Yeah? What?"

"What, so you can make fun of me?"

"Depends."

"The Bear Claw Killer."

"Like the donut?"

"Yes, but—"

I laughed. "How's being called a donut better?"

"I didn't say it was better, but it was more creative at least."

"What, you think you're an artist now?"

"No, but the name explains more about my kills."

"You know about my kills, right?"

"Like the first ones at Yosemite?"

"No, not really."

"Well these bears came in and started eating the people after I was done."

"So, at first they thought the bears killed them."

"So, the Bear Claw—"

"Plus it's my favorite donut, haha."

"Funny."

"Well, yeah, a little humor never hurt."

"Why be all serious?"

"Plus it's a good way to piss off the cops."

"Like that guy who used to leave a box of cereal."

"So, what?"

"You leave a donut at your killings?"

"Yeah, got a box in the RV."

"A box? How many people you plan on killing at that campground?"

"Well, I leave one, then eat the rest."

"Cops probably think you're leavin a donut in reference to them."

"Yeah, maybe," he said.

"Maybe you should write them a letter, tell them what they should call you."

"I did."

"Wrote it in the blood of one of my kills in fact."

"So how many people you kill?"

"Twelve."

"How many you kill?"

"Don't know."

"More than twelve."

"You a hitman or something?"

"Something."

"Only thing America makes now are killers," he said.

Thinkin what the next move should be.

"Especially that genre known as the Serial Killer."

"We invented it you know."

"Right here in America."

Kill him and get out of here.

"Soon you'll be able to go to school for it."

Turn him in maybe.

"Get a degree."

Cops probably all over my campsite.

"A PhD."

Goin through my shit.

"Make a career out of it."

Left my wallet and my keys.

"Knowing us, we'll probably start outsourcing it."

Host telling them about the strange Nigger.

Probably think I did it.

Especially when they don't find no bear claw.

"Remember when our killers used to be American? they'll say."

Gotta shut this guy up.

"What about you?"

"Huh?"

"What made you wanna become a killer?"

"Hmmm, what made me want to become a killer."

Wrong question.

Look on his face like I just offered him a book deal.

And he's already written the book.

"How do I put this?"

"Put it short, I don't want your life story."

"Better question is what makes an oak an oak."

"What?"

"Exactly," he said.

"It's not like I started out wanting to kill."

"But it was the only thing that clicked."

"So, what," I say.

"When jerking off didn't work you figured you'd try killing?"

"Well, what made you want to become a killer?"

"Nothing made me, I just fell into it."

"Not me, I had to struggle to find my calling."

"Calling, huh."

"You wouldn't understand."

"Everything I did never felt right."

"Off."

"Like I wasn't doing what I was supposed to be doing."

"And then you realized you were supposed to kill people and voilà—"

"It wasn't that easy," he said.

"It took years."

"See, being a killer is not a career option."

"So, why campgrounds?"

"I like camping."

"Seriously?"

"Well, not like I chose it nonchalantly or anything."

"It just happened that way."

"It was the perfect conjunction of personality and purpose."

"Hmmm," I say, "think I'll roast some marshmallows, and then kill some people."

"You ever been to Yosemite?" he said.

"No."

"Well, if you'd ever been, you'd want to kill too."

"Bunch of phonies running around snapping pictures."

"So?"

"There was this one family."

"Well to do."

"All wearing browsers, of course."

"The mom and dad in their expensive camping outfits."

"Walking like they owned the place."

"Smartpants?"

"What?"

"They wearin smartpants?"

"No, but they were fancy, designer probably."

"Fancypants."

"What?"

"So you killed them."

"Yes, they were my first."

"With a knife?"

"I had a gun too, but I didn't shoot them."

"I used it to scare them."

"Where's your gun?"

"I don't use one anymore."

"Got it down to the essentials now."

"You know, like a musician who learns to use less notes."

"So, what. You held em up with the gun and then stabbed em?"

"Well, I was a novice back then."

"So I made the mother and father tie the kids up first."

"Then I made the mother tie the father."

"And then I tied her, and then taped all their mouths shut."

"I stabbed the daughter first, then the son."

"It broke the parents."

"They actually started to look a little human before I finished them."

"What else did you do to them?"

"Nothing."

"C'mon, you guys are all alike."

"Did you Fuck them before they were dead?"

"Or after?"

"I never had sex with any of them."

"You jack off on them?"

"No," he yelled, "I don't do that kind of stuff."

"C'mon, why not? They're already dead."

"No, you don't understand. This is not some pathological compulsion, it's a—"

"A Fuckin fantasy is what it is."

"You don't understand."

"Oh, I do," I say.

"You're like everyone else on this planet."

"Like everyone else, huh?"

"Yeah, like those people you killed."

"Thinking you're important."

"That you count."

"Well, guess what?"

"That's not for you to decide," he said.

"You can't define me."

"No one can."

"Only *I* can."

"Yeah, all you little Napoleons."

"Runnin around with big definitions of yourselves."

"Tryin to make everyone look you up in your made-up dictionary."

"What about you, huh?" he said.

"What are you?"

"I'm the same."

"Except you know it, right?"

"Think it makes you special."

"No, I'm just a Nigger."

"Yeah, well, all I know is that everything I ever did was a fraud—except for this."

I couldn't take it anymore.

Been downing beers to get the bad taste out of my mouth.

A sick taste.

Dude was an amateur.

All amateurs need a reason.

And those reasons are sick.

Calling.

Meaning.

Purpose.

Everyone.

Running around.

Driving around.

Calling.

Meaning.

Purpose.

Running.

Driving.

Who am I?

Where am I going?

Religion.

Philosophy.

PEP.

Amateurs.

"You're crazy," I say. "What they call clinically insane."

"No, I'm not."

"Yes, and I can prove it."

"How?"

"Well, did you ever."

"Just once."

"Think that you just might be out of your Fucking mind?"

"That you might just be Fuckin crazy?"

"If I judged myself from the conventional perspective, yes."

"Conventional perspective?"

"What normal people think."

"And what do normal people think?"

"That killing is wrong."

"So it isn't?"

"It is, for them."

"But from a transcendental perspective it means something completely different."

"What does it mean?"

"That depends on the individual doing it."

"So, it's okay for some people to kill."

"It's not about if it's okay or not."

"Kierkegaard called it the 'teleological suspension of the ethical,'" he said.

"Who?"

"Kierkegaard, the Danish philosopher."

"And he's not crazy, right?"

"You don't understand."

"That's what all crazy people say," I say.

"And wise men too," he said.

"So, you never once thought to yourself that you might be full of shit."

"That you might be wrong?"

"It has nothing to do with right or wrong," he said.

"Yes, it does," I say.

"It doesn't matter how sure you are of something."

"If you don't have the capacity to think that you might be at least a little full of shit."

"Then you're full of shit."

"Let me put it this way."

"Some Zen guy once said: 'Why are you unhappy?'"

"'Because ninety-nine percent of the things you think and do are for yourself.'"

"'And there isn't one.'"

"Well, let me amend that to ninety-nine percent of you is full of shit."

"Pretty much everything you think and believe and desire."

"In fact, pretty much everything you do."

"Which means we should be looking at our own asses if we want the truth."

"That's partially right," he said.

"The bullshit you talk about is nothing but prepackaged beliefs and abstract concepts."

"Made up by other people."

"Our whole culture in fact."

"All our notions of what's right and what's wrong."

"So, you have to decide whether or not you want to live by this hand-me-down bullshit."

"Or become the shape you are called to become."

"A shape that has nothing to do with moral concepts of right or wrong, good or bad."

"It's more aesthetic-like."

"Morphology as opposed to morality."

"Beyond good and evil."

"Beyond good and evil?"

"Yes, beyond good and—"

"I just heard that somewhere. Who said that?"

"Friedrich Nietzsche," he said.

"No, it was someone else."

"It was Friedrich Nietzsche."

"Charles Manson."

"What?"

"That's where I heard it—Charlie Manson—he said it."

"No, he didn't."

"Yes, he did. I heard him."

"Well, if he did, he was quoting Nietzsche," he said.

"Who's you're favorite?"

"What?"

"Favorite serial killer—who's your favorite serial killer?"

"I don't have a favorite."

"C'mon, don't be like everyone else."

"What do you mean like everyone else?"

"Like when you ask people what kinda music they like."

"And they say they like all kinds."

"I don't like any of them," he said.

"Why not?"

"Because they're all just a bunch of psychos."

"You know there are different kinds, right?"

"Different kinds?"

"Psychos."

"No."

"Yes, there are psychopaths and PsychoSmiths."

"PsychoSmith?"

"Yes, psychos that have a little more self-control."

"Well, I've never heard of it," he said.

"Let me ask you a question," I say.

"How come every idiot that says 'I'm beyond good and evil' does the most evil shit?"

"Why don't they ever do good shit, huh?"

"Shit so good that—"

He tsked at me and shook his head.

"You're still trapped in conventional thinking," he said.

"Oh, yeah, I forgot."

"Who am I to judge you?"

"You're beyond good and evil, right?"

"Actually, no. More like below good and evil."

"Good and evil are up here."

"Where normal people live."

"And you're down here."

"Under my shoe."

"See?"

"Like a bug."

"Yes, a bug."

"Yeah?" he said.

"And who the Fuck are you?"

"I bet you never killed anybody."

I stood up.

"You wanna know who the Fuck I am?"

"Huh?"

"You wanna know who the Fuck!"

My words echoed off the stone-silent night and banged off the trees.

Some bears were listening to this shit right now.

"Unlike you."

"I ain't some weekend amateur."

"Some jerk-off, jack-off wannabe killer."

"I'm the real deal."

"A Professional."

"I get paid."

"Not like you."

"You overstuffed donut."

"Sittin around waiting to get permission from some philosopher."

"Beyond good and evil."

"Shit."

"People that say that shit are scared."

"Scared to look it straight."

"In the eye."

"Evil."

"Hell."

"There is no beyond evil."

"And the only thing beyond good."

"Is more evil."

Fist to my chest.

"And as for me."

"I'm straight out."

"I've killed more people in a day than the amount of bear claws you've stuffed in your face your whole life."

"I've killed women."

"Children."

"Babies."

"Shit that don't even have a name."

"Hell, probably killed your momma."

"Paid me to do it."

"After havin you."

"And let me tell you:"

"I wasn't called."

"I wasn't meant."

"I wasn't purposed."

"I'm a Death Enforcement Officer for the City of Los Angeles."

"Bitch."

He smiled.

A smug smile.

"What?"

"It's fate," he said.

"Synchronicity."

"Like attracts like."

"It's why we met."

"Let's go," I say.

"Huh?"

"Let's go, we're finished here."

"Where?"

"We're getting out of here."

"You going to turn me in?"

"No."

I drove out of there.

I didn't know where I was going.

I couldn't go back to the campground.

Not unless I wanted to deal with a bunch of cops.

"H. H. Holmes," he said.

"That would be my favorite."

"If I had to pick."

Try to concentrate.

The road is dark and sharp.

Steep.

Up was one thing.

But down.

We're too heavy.

Gravity pulling.

Hard.

"If you think about it."

"We're the only species capable of wiping out all life on earth."

"The only."

Gotta think what next.

Claire.

What about her.

"That's gotta mean something."

Go back.

Find her.

No.

She was.

"Maybe that's our purpose."

A whore.

Prostitute.

"Our function."

Professional.

What was it.

Cuddler.

"Our destiny."

"Yes, our destiny!"

But how do you really?

Know?

Ask her.

Find out.

Ask her.

You owe her that.

No.

"It is us!"

"Men like you and me!"

It's done.

Over.

I never cared.

Not really.

"We are the destiny of our species."

Only when she left.

And then only.

No.

It's over.

"Men of refinement."

"And brutality."

Finished.

"Yes!"

"Men like us!"

Time to.

"The killers, the murderers, the exterminators."

"The polluters and the plaguers."

Time to.

"Yes!"

"Men like us!"

Time to.

"*We* are the Extinction Event!"

Time to.

"The work that I do."

Time to.

"Shall ye do."

Time.

"And greater works than these shall—"

"Will you shut up?"

"Shall ye do."

"I said shut up."

"Funny now I know the answer."

"That poem by Eliot."

"Shut up!"

"'The Waste Land.'"

"Where they say."

"'What shall we ever do?'"

"'What shall we ever do?'"

"Shut up!"

"I'll tell you what we shall do."

"Shut up!"

"You and I."

"When the evening is spread out—"

"Shut up!"

"Shut up!"

"Shut up!"

Left on the wheel.

Right in his face.

Left on the wheel.

Right in his face.

Right.

Right.

Right.

He kept crying, "Why?"

"Why?"

"Why?"

"Why?"

The more he why'd the more I.

I wanted to destroy him.

Smash him to nothing.

Smash him to.

My PDT.

Buzzing.

Had to stop hitting him to look at it.

Why?

The screen flashed *Claire* like some sick joke.

It couldn't be.

Not in a million years.

Not now.

PAL Fuckin with me again.

PAL.

No.

Not going to answer.

But if it was.

If she was?

No.

We could start over.

No.

Don't.

Begin again.

No.

Stop.

Live somewhere else.

Stop.

You don't.

Things can be different.

Care.

I could be different.

Please.

Don't.

In a new place.

Away.

With her.

Just let her . . .

A turn was coming up.

If it isn't her I won't.

Keep driving.

Straight.

"Hello?"

Silence.

I smashed the pedal all the way.

It didn't do much.

"Hello?"

Few seconds left.

"Hello!"

"Alex?"

"Claire? Claire? Is that you?"

"Alex?"

"Jesus, Claire?"

I took my foot off the gas.

I couldn't believe it.

"Claire?"

The turn.

Hit the.

"Alex?"

The turn.

Hit the.

He lunged for the wheel.

"Claire!"

The Owens Valley.

It looked unreal, we were up so far.

The dead, dry lake lit up like a distant galaxy.

Another universe.

EPILOGUE[*]

My life didn't flash before my eyes.

No.

It was projected.

Televised.

Streamed.

The Big Chump.

Starring Jerry Fuckin Studebaker.

Explosions and bad music.

I was the only one.

Watching.

A small dark-paneled room.

Not much bigger than a closet.

Fifteen minutes in I left.

Long hall lined with mahogany doors.

---

[*]   Written at the publisher's insistence—A. K.

Dimly lit.

Plush carpet with all the colors you could think of.

A woman came out two doors down.

Eating out a bag of popcorn.

"Hey."

She comes over.

No expression on her face.

Chomping.

"What is this?"

"What's what?"

"This," I say, pointing to the door I just came out of.

"Your life."

"What?"

"Didn't you get any popcorn?" her mouth says between chews.

"No."

"Too bad," she said. "It helps."

"Helps what?"

She shrugged.

I just look at her.

Then a sort of vague recognition comes to her face.

"Oh, don't worry," she said. "You'll get another one."

"Another what?"

"Trust me," she said. "You don't want the other thing."

"What?"

"Eternity."

"Eternity."

"Forever's a monster," she said.

She turned and went down the hall.

I looked at the door I had just come out of.

It had my name: Alex Krieg.

In gold letters.

"That isn't my name," I say.

Then I was back.

Every bone in my body broken.

Doctor said I was a lucky man.

But he didn't know the truth.

I did.

Let me tell you:

THERE IS NO ESCAPE.[*]

I became somewhat of a celebrity:

The guy that killed the Campfire Killer.

Did a few talk shows.

Even got a book deal.

I didn't write about what they thought I was gonna write about.

Insatia found me at the hospital where I was convalescing.

She had had a child.

Supposably mine.

---

[*]   In private conversation, Alex told me that nothing "happens" after death, as there is no "thing" for something to happen to. To quote Ramana Maharshi: "There is neither creation nor destruction, neither destiny nor free will, neither path nor achievement. This is the final truth."—I. H.

Told me that she didn't Love me.

Hated me in fact.

But that I was going to take care of her and our child, a boy.

I'm not going to tell you what his name is.

It's none of your damn business.

While I was out of commission the second 6/16 happened:

Over a million people killed in the blink of an eye.

Whether it was a computer error, or a malicious hack, no one knows.

That damn satellite that was going to do my job more efficiently started off its first day by killing everyone alphabetically.

Why it stopped at *I* no one knows.

No one knows because they tell you it was an attack by the South American terrorist organization Las Bases.

And Las Bases confirms this.

It gives them cachet.

They are the baddest terrorist group on the planet.

Or were.

Someone else is now.

Traffic was better for a while.

Less congested.

But then that too changed.

And you would have never known that all those people had been killed.

I never saw Claire again.

Down this meanstream something resembling a man will
inevitably go. He'll go, and others like him will follow: millions
of them, ad nauseam, sneaker-stepping their way into oblivion.
                                                    —*The Big Pump*

ABOUT THE AUTHOR

Kais Alkuraishi lives and drives in Los Angeles.

www.ingramcontent.com/pod-product-compliance
Lightning Source LLC
Chambersburg PA
CBHW020223110726
47898CB00004B/1126